THE
EASTERN
DOOR

THE EASTERN DOOR

BY

DAVID MORE

Fireship Press
www.FireshipPress.com

ISBN-13:978-1-61179-279-9: Paperback
ISBN 978-1-61179-280-5: ebook

BISAC Subject Headings:

FIC014000FICTION / Historical
FIC027050FICTION / Romance / Historical
FIC002000FICTION / Action & Adventure
FIC059000FICTION / Native American / Aboriginal

Cover Work: Christine Horner

Address all correspondence to:
Fireship Press, LLC
P.O. Box 68412
Tucson, AZ 85737
Or visit our website at:
www.FireshipPress.com

DEDICATION

To Donna and Claire

REVIEWS

What reviewers say about *The Eastern Door*, winner of the Independent Publisher Silver and Bronze Awards for regional and historical fiction in 2007:

"His action scenes—both military and those of a more passionate nature— are gripping." –Kitchener, *Waterloo Record*

".... a ripping good read." – *Queen's University Alumni Review*

"...an entrancing read that will linger in your memory." – former Dean of Fine Arts, York University

"... one to savor and enjoy." – *Main Street* (Lachute, Quebec)

"...solid and thrilling...excellent dialogue...respect for the history...a rewarding read." –Historical Novel Society

"We all LOVED your book!" –Manager, Johnson Hall State Historic Site

LIST OF CONTENTS

FOREWORD

It was my wife who said, "Why don't you write a book?" Probably because she didn't want me starting to build another boat. That was more than twelve years ago now. I had an idea of the story I wanted to tell, and, being a history buff, I wanted to begin at the beginning. In this case that ended up being Ireland in 1728, but the core events of *The Eastern Door* take place in the 1740s and 1750s, along the Mohawk River valley in what is today upstate New York. This is an obscure part of history for most people, myself included, and I now know why they don't—or perhaps can't—really teach us much about it in school: it was a very complex time.

But the more I delved into this era and place the more fascinated I became, and the more important I sensed it was, since so many of the elements still moving our world today were swirling about in there, hidden and disguised and gestating, but there nonetheless. It was the larger-than-life characters I found in the histories who inspired me to tell the stories. Many of them are nearly forgotten today. *The Eastern Door* is fiction, not history, but if you, the reader, find these pages resonating with history's songs, then I have honored the singers, as I intended.

Of course, although it is critically important to respect the facts, novelists sometimes have to simplify, twist, compress and expand history—there's a story to tell, after all—and I'm as necessarily guilty of that as anyone. I even made a few things up, where I felt they wouldn't stretch the realms of plausibility too far. For instance, although Handel conducted the world premiere of *Messiah* in Dublin shortly after our hero left Ireland, *Alcina* was not actually performed there in the 1730s. Well, it is a novel! I hope you have fun with it.

There are more great stories to be told of these people, both fictional and historical; so far I have written *The Lily and the Rose* and *Liberty's Children*. Please visit my website at: www.davidmore.ca, or www.wrytrguy.com, where you will be able to sample some of my other writing. You can Email me with your comments at: dmore1@cogeco.ca. I write an occasional blog at www.wrytrguy.blogspot.com

Acknowledgements

I need to thank many people, in no particular order:

• Steve Lukits, who as former editor-in-chief of The Kingston Whig-Standard shepherded me through some basics of the craft of writing and published a number of my pieces.

• M.G. Vassanji, whom I was fortunate to have as my mentor at the Humber School for Writers.

• My friend Ken Cuthbertson, author of the biographies Nobody Said Not to Go and Inside, and editor of the Queen's Alumni Review. Ken was a very generous source to me of encouragement, correction, and advice, including a referral to Cathy Perkins, my copy-editor extraordinaire, and he courageously put his own writing reputation at risk to give me a cover endorsement.

• Christie Golden, who guided me through the Writer's Digest Novel Writing Workshop, and tactfully helped me with the first draft of *The Eastern Door*.

• Brian Henry, whose workshops were a great stimulation.

• My friend and colleague Lloyd Kennedy, on whose imaging software skills I leaned heavily to help produce the cover graphic and inside maps of the original editions. Lloyd was struck down by cancer at an atrociously young age.

• My wife Donna and daughter Claire, whose support was, of course, fundamental. They let me dive into *The Eastern Door* for hours at a time, often with chores undone and homework help overdue.

• My sister, my good and loyal friends, and my extended family, all of whom steadfastly resisted laughing out loud when I told them I was writing a novel and who, twelve years later, still seem as excited about it as I am.

• My father, my mother and my brother, who died before this project was completed but continue in memory to teach me about life and love.

• Lindy Mechefske, photographer, who provided the author's photo.

• My editors and the graphic designer at Fireship Press, whose skillful kindness has been amazing.

David More
October 23, 2013

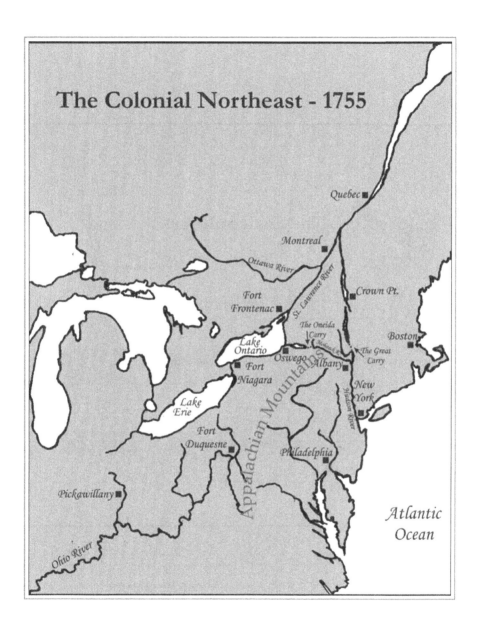

The Colonial Northeast - 1755

Quebec

Montreal

Ottawa River

St. Lawrence River

Crown Pt.

Fort
Frontenac

The Oneida
Carry

Lake
Ontario

Oswego

Albany

Boston

The Great
Carry

Fort
Niagara

New
York

Lake
Erie

Appalachian Mountains

Hudson River

Fort
Duquesne

Philadelphia

Pickawillany

Atlantic
Ocean

Ohio River

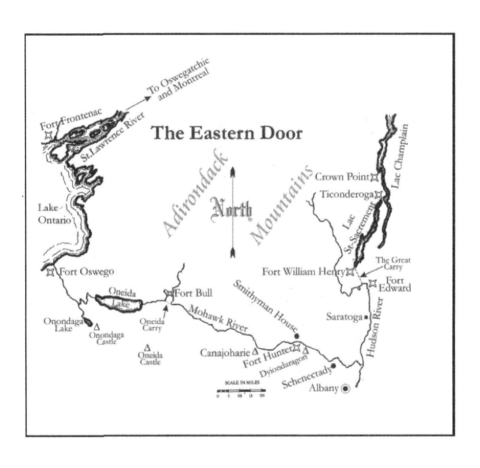

Only to the white man was nature a "wilderness" and only to him was the land "infested" with "wild" animals and "savage" people. To us it was tame. Earth was bountiful and we were surrounded by the blessings of the Great Mystery.

—Luther Standing Bear, Chief of the Oglala Sioux

PROLOGUE

The Great Carrying Place, Province of New York, August 1755

Major-General Billy Smithyman finished his ten-mile ride north from Fort Edward with a brief, joyous, hell-for-leather gallop. He weaved recklessly around the raw stumps in the newly cut roadway and even pushed his bay gelding, Kublai, to jump a few of them, where the sawyers had not yet tidied up the axe men's work. It was a cloudless, late summer day and he had finally found another big horse without fear. Kublai reminded him of his beloved stallion, The Colonel, which he had left behind in Ireland so long ago.

He saw the cluster of men and oxen teams a half-mile ahead, tiny figures against the tall forest, and then a tree fell, and he eased Kublai slowly to a walk. When he halted, just short of the end of the road, he sat for several minutes watching the activity.

Bright felling blades flashed up and down, chunking deeply into the soft wood. The axe sounds were muted—the forest released no echoes—but a sweet, pure fragrance filled the air from the sap and from the crushed evergreen needles. A tree crashed down every few minutes. He could feel the ground shake, even from his saddle.

The sweating fallers were putting their backs into it, working two to a tree, ejecting chips the size of pies with every swing. They were civilians from the Massachusetts Bay colony, hired by the British Army—Billy Smithyman's army —to hew a wilderness road through a section of His Majesty George II's Province of New York, 200 miles north of New York City. Billy's impatient expeditionary force of 3,000 colonial soldiers crowded their heels. They were at war with France and her aboriginal allies.

His closest friend, Lieutenant Richard FitzHugh, walked over to meet him from within the forest shade and sketched a quick salute, grinning. A corporal also jogged over to take the reins of his horse. Billy returned both their smiles and the salutes.

He jumped down and pulled a silver flask from the pocket of his bright red uniform coat.

"I had to get away from the preachers at Fort Edward somehow, Richard, so I decided to come up here and see our new road for myself." He took a long swig and handed the flask to his friend, who did the same.

It was the summer of 1755. France and England would not officially declare the Seven Years' War for many more months, but one year before and several hundred miles southwest across the rugged Allegheny Mountains, an obscure major of the Virginia Provincial Regiment named George Washington had surprised and attacked a small French patrol in the Ohio River wilderness.

The French commander was killed in the ambush. Then the French commander's enraged brother Coulon de Villiers defeated Washington's little force, forcing them to retreat back across the mountains to Virginia. The French accused Washington of murder, but the accusation was a charade; everyone knew it was normal for France and England to be at war.

Since then, although war did not yet officially exist, hundreds more had died, armies were mobilizing and naval engagements were being fought on the Atlantic.

The axe men were anxious to finish the road and leave with their pay, because notoriously bloodthirsty raiders based at a French stone fort only 70 miles north infested this particular stretch of forest. Fort Saint Frédéric guarded the narrows of Lac Champlain, at a place the English called Crown Point. The French preferred to call it Pointe à la Chevelure—Scalp Point. Destruction of the fort at Crown Point was the objective of the army.

The joyful galloper, Major-General Billy Smithyman, commanded the Crown Point expedition. He was a very tall transplanted Anglo-Irishman, a successful fur trader and important landowner, and a member of the Governor's Executive Council of New York. He was not a trained soldier. He insisted that his tenants, customers and friends call him Billy, but to the rest of the world he was Smithyman, and to some the name was an epithet. He also proudly bore a Mohawk name, Io'tonhwahere, Beaver Dam.

Richard said, "I have some decent bread and cheeses, Billy, that came up on yesterday's wagon."

Billy shook his head. "I can't stay. God knows what the schemers at Fort Edward might get up to while I'm gone." He had another drink of the rum and offered it to Richard, who refused.

"I have some brandy of my own, Billy." He nodded down the road. "How bad is it?"

Billy shrugged. "It's still the same—3,000 militiamen without enough training, from six different colonies, each with their own commander, plus 200 Iroquois from six different nations, although they are mostly Mohawks. It's bedlam, really. I had to get out of it for awhile." He smiled broadly at Richard. "What's the sharp end like, up here?"

FitzHugh grimaced. "It's still quiet. Our boys are fine, but the New Englanders aren't happy and they don't hesitate to show it."

Billy had first-rate organizational talents, and the Mohawks trusted him. During the last war, these qualifications had convinced New York's Governor to appoint him Colonel of the Albany County militia. This included every able-bodied man in the county—the thousands of square miles of sparsely settled frontier to the north and west of the old Dutch fur trading town of Albany. The Governor also appointed him Commander of the British Crown's Indian allies —mainly the six Iroquois League nations: Seneca, Onondaga, Oneida, Tuscarora, Cayuga, Mohawk.

All North American military operations of the time required Indian support to be successful. General Braddock, newly arrived British Army Commander in North America, had decided the previous spring that Billy was the logical person to command the Crown Point attack.

Braddock had taken most of the regular army axe men with him to cut another road west across the Appalachians from the headwaters of the Potomac River, leading two Irish regiments of red-coated British infantry. This forced Billy to hire civilian help at extortionate rates from wherever he could, because he urgently needed a road to transport his few pieces of artillery.

Now more than a thousand scalped corpses, along with General Braddock himself, rotted in the forest near the forks of the Ohio River a few miles short of their objective, Fort Duquesne, and only a few dozen miles from where Washington's skirmish had started the war.

The anxiety of the loggers and much of Billy's army had an extra edge to it, because there were no women. Women were traditionally the unrecorded part of every army, easing the hardships of campaigning by cooking, sewing, peddling, whoring and loving. Occasionally they even participated in battle.

The New England contingent of Billy's motley army was the largest, and its puritanical officers had persuaded him to send the women away. However, the civilian loggers and many of the soldiers, including the Massachusetts Bay colony levies, missed them.

The axe men were cutting a road 12 feet wide and 15 miles long through a dense pine forest. Many of the ancient trees were over 100 feet tall and three feet in diameter, and the narrow avenue they were clearing remained in shadow, except for a few hours around noon. It was the end of August. Soldiers and civilians slapped and cursed at deerflies and looked fearfully over their shoulders for hostile Indians, but it was impossible to see more than a few dozen yards into the dark tangle of ancient trees.

Billy tucked his flask back into a pocket. He wiped some sweat from his forehead with his sleeve and put his black felt cocked hat with its gold lace back on.

"I'll be heading back, then. Are you coming to the conference tonight? Usual nonsense, I expect."

"Perhaps. If there's nothing important I'd just as soon stay here." Richard smiled a lop-sided smile, "But then again, your food's too good, Billy."

Billy mounted up, smiling. "Eat well when you can, my friend."

Richard waved once as Billy cantered back down the narrow, stump-filled road, then walked to where his men watched over the loggers.

They all relished nothing better than to let sunlight into the forest, dreaming of a day when it would all be farmland. Even after a century of sporadic warfare against the French, the Spanish and the native peoples, the million-and-a-half colonists of British North America remained tightly hemmed in against the Atlantic Ocean. French colonies and forts confined them on the north; the difficult ridges of the Appalachians blocked them from the west, and to the south lay the Spanish colony in Florida.

The forest that they lusted to destroy was nowhere less than a thousand miles wide, from the Atlantic coast to the western plains. If a fur trader wandered north along the ancient trails from the sandy tip of Florida until he reached the skinny black spruces fringing the continent's Arctic tonsure, and then turned west, by the time he finally soaked his aching feet in the Pacific Ocean he might have traveled 6,000 miles without ever having left the shelter of the trees.

Dozens of indigenous nations called this continental forest their home. For five generations, fur trade competition had fueled near-genocidal ferocity among Europeans and natives alike and they had suffered and executed wars of sudden and startling brutality.

In the present war, it was clear that the stakes were no longer simple possession of the forest itself. Europeans now knew that to the west lay a vast continent, almost unexplored, except by the restless French.

After two centuries of European contact, most of the surviving eastern woodland Indian nations had allied themselves with France. The French seemed much less interested than the English in the possession and destruction of their home lands.

The main British ally was the powerful six-nation Iroquois League whose

4

members called themselves the People of the Longhouse. Their homeland lay just south of Lake Ontario and Lake Erie. This Confederacy remained close to the British largely because their easternmost nation, the Mohawks, maintained a deep and affectionate friendship with Billy Smithyman.

In that vast green domain, few places were more important to either side than the stretch of forest the New England axe men were hastily clearing. English colonists called it the Great Carrying Place. From its southern end, Hudson's broad river carried sloops filled with pelts and food south to New York City. From the other end of the Carry, bark canoes and wooden bateaux filled with fur trade goods floated north to Montréal along deep, narrow lakes filling clefts between the mountains. Between these two headwaters, traders and soldiers walked across the height of land for fifteen miles, carrying their goods, transport and arms. Now Billy's army was cutting a wagon road across it.

The French stone fort at Crown Point and its garrison controlled the route north. Major-General Billy Smithyman's jury-rigged army was the only thing that stood between a French army and New York, for no serious English fortifications existed between Montreal and New York City.

Richard FitzHugh did another circuit among the axe men, exerting all of his considerable Irish charm and humor, trying to reassure them that Billy's Mohawk scouts and his West Albanian Volunteers would protect them from massacre and see them home to Boston.

The Volunteers were a unit of half-trained, part-time soldiers from Richard's community in the Mohawk River Valley, 50 map miles west. They were his homesteading friends and neighbors, members of the Albany County militia in peacetime. They wore the long navy blue wool coats, buff waistcoats and breeches, and black, white-trimmed cocked hats of the New York Provincial Regiments.

When the army marched, the Volunteers had demanded and been given the honor of defending the civilian loggers at the head of the column, the most dangerous place—the one most likely to be cut off and surrounded in an ambush—largely because Billy was a Mohawk valley man himself.

The troops enjoyed watching the axe men at work. When a tree fell, they set their muskets down and ran to help the loggers limb the tree, hitch up the oxen, and drag it to the side of the road. They were relaxed, laughing and joking, making bets on when the next tree would fall. They trusted Billy, and the Indian warriors Billy had sent out, to provide warning of impending attacks. The nervous New Englanders amused them.

Richard's men knew that Mohawk warriors, not white armies, had saved them from fire and murder at the hands of the French and their Indian allies throughout the last war. Richard knew many of the warriors by name, because he and his neighbors had settled peacefully in Mohawk country over the past 15 years.

Billy was the same age as Richard, 39, and had been an Indian trader in the Mohawk River valley for 18 years. His wife, Laura Silverbirch, beautiful and fierce, was the youngest niece of the ancient Mohawk war chief, Emperor Marten. Billy had obtained his huge estate from the Mohawks; it was one of a very few land deals with white settlers that the Mohawks never doubted was perfectly fair. Unlike most of the land-hungry British, Billy did not sell rum until the business was over.

The army column crept forward, tree-by-tree. The loggers did not respond well to Richard's attempts to jolly them along. They had no faith in Billy or his Mohawk allies. Having done what he could to bolster civilian morale, Richard ordered the Volunteers to perform some musket drill. *Perhaps that will make the loggers think we are serious soldiers.* He reminded his sergeant to keep them quiet. "Mind you, Watts, there's to be no live firing, or Billy will banish you to Boston." The sergeant, who had been complaining again about the absence of women, grinned and saluted before leaving.

Richard took his writing case out of a saddlebag and sat in his camp chair beside an oozing stump. He added to the pencil sketch of the scene he had begun the day before. The army was moving about five miles a day. *A day to go, then, until we get to the edge of Lac St-Sacrement and regroup.*

The oppressive anxiety about being ambushed in the forest had wound an otherwise tedious march into extreme tension. Tempers flared easily, and Richard had to take care that fights between the other New Englanders and his New Yorkers did not get out of hand. Fortunately, none of the Mohawk scouts had reported seeing anything so far. In spite of his confident air, Richard himself had grave fears for the future.

Three weeks ago Billy's force had been assembled outside of Albany, now 50 miles behind them to the south. Richard had been in the midst of a sweet daydream about his wife, Eva. In it, they were lying naked in the cool stream above the millpond, sipping lime rum punch. Distant shouting had interrupted his reverie, and he had risen from his folding chair and emerged into the bright sun outside his tent, blinking and sweating and buttoning his wool officer's coat.

It had been appallingly humid, the hottest July in years. The raised voices belonged to contractors in the weekly supply wagon train from Albany to Schenectady. One wagon had broken down, blocking passage for others, while the head of the column slowly moved on, disappearing west into its own dust cloud. It was dangerous to be separated from the army escort, and so the wagoners were upset.

The camp in front of him consisted of hundreds of triangular white British army tents, pegged out in neat rows. Scattered among them were the taller, bell-shaped tents of the officers. The tent nearest to Richard belonged to Billy Smithyman. By July, Albany's tent suburbs had existed for 12 weeks, slowly growing as levies from the other colonies arrived and Billy gathered supplies.

Squads of soldiers drilled here and there. Some were in colorful uniforms, some in homespun clothes. They came from New Hampshire, Connecticut, Massachusetts, New Jersey, Rhode Island and New York. Barked commands mingled with the sounds of carpentry. The army was hastily building flat-bottomed bateaux, for after it had cut its way across The Great Carry, the road to the French fort at Crown Point lay entirely on water.

He watched several desperate wagoners gather to push the broken wagon off the road. *I'll see an expense claim in by morning*, he thought. The wagons and their drivers, like the loggers, did not belong to the army. Albany's civilian contractors were notorious for taking advantage of the army's need. In the last war there had never been enough wagons, bateaux or food, either.

Richard ducked back inside his tent to finish scratching out a memorandum to Artillery Major Bolton, regarding the transport of the precious siege guns. Bolton was the only regular army officer in the Crown Point expedition, and the ancient cannons they were dragging were the only hope that Billy's amateur army could penetrate the thick stone walls of Fort St-Frédéric. Richard dated the note, July 18, 1755, signed it and returned his quill into the inkpot with such force that it revolved precariously several times, threatening to splatter his letter. He leaned back in his canvas chair with a sigh.

He still wondered whether the absence of professional officers and soldiers was a backhanded compliment to Billy, or a calculated plot to embarrass and destroy him. He had powerful enemies in the province, including one who had followed them from Ireland.

Everyone had tied up their tent skirts, but there was no relief in the still afternoon air. The citizens of Albany had denuded the surrounding hills of trees years before. This summer, the army's horses, cattle, pigs and sheep had stripped them of grass as well, and a fine coat of pale brown dust covered everything. Outside, under an awning, Richard's Warrant Officer Simmons was screening the General's callers.

Richard heard footsteps approaching and a murmured conversation. Then, Simmons' voice had bleated, "Lieutenant FitzHugh, Sir. There is a man here to see General Smithyman." His voice was even more dry and squeaky than chalk on slate.

Richard sighed in exasperation. *Jesus, Mary and Joseph, would the day never end?* Warrant Officer Simmons' tone, Richard reflected, probably meant that he saw a ruffian or a native outside and was therefore extremely dubious whether the Lieutenant ought to bother the General.

Since Braddock had also appointed Billy Superintendent of Indian Affairs for the Northern Colonies, tens of thousands of native-appearing individuals had a perfect right to see him and were, in fact, most welcome. Billy was notorious for taking great pleasure in the honor of having been named a Mohawk brother and warrior. Simmons, though, was from London. Like most of the army, he disliked natives. He also disliked frontiersmen. Richard had often thought that Simmons would faint if he ever saw Billy dance the war dance at Dyiondarogon.

Perhaps this was one of the scouts returning from Crown Point, with news of the French. He had called out, "Send him in here, Simmons, if you please. And get us another lemonade, will you?"

A stout, hairy figure had come in through the door of the tent, and Richard recognized Henry Chilton, a trader and sometime Indian diplomat like Billy. A prickle of apprehension had tightened the skin on the back of his hands and raised the hair on Richard's neck. Had not Chilton gone back west with Washington, under General Braddock's personal command? What was the man doing here then?

Richard had stood and offered his hand, knowing that Chilton must be bringing important news. The man was sweating, flushed, and appeared not to have eaten for days. *And that was blood, crusted all over Chilton's buckskins! By the Blessed Virgin!*

It still seemed like a nightmare. Remembering the scene with agonizing clarity, Richard looked across the road the axe men were building, at the darkness beneath the trees so close beyond, and then crossed himself surreptitiously. Catholics were barely tolerated anywhere under the English flag.

He had come around his desk and gently turned Chilton around, saying, "Sure, and it is good to see you, Henry. I know Billy will see you immediately. Come with me, then, and we will get some food and drink into ye while we're talkin'. The Lord love ye, Henry, but ye look like hell."

On the way to Billy's tent, Richard had directed Simmons to bring food and rum, "Quickly, man, quickly, now." The Union Flag hung limp on its staff beside Billy's office. A red-coated sentry straightened to rigid attention outside the tent door. Richard called out as they approached, "Billy, Henry Chilton is here to see you."

Billy met them at the door and his welcoming smile changed to concern at Henry's appearance. He gave a nod to Richard and they went inside.

Filling himself with a thick slice of hot smoked beef and washing that down with a mug of rum, Chilton had looked expressionlessly at Richard and Billy. Finally he had cleared his throat and said, "The Frogs and their Indians— Ottawas, Potawatamies and Ojibwas, mostly—slaughtered Braddock and his army at the forks of the Ohio, nine, mebbe ten days ago." He reached inside his leather pouch and handed sealed papers to Billy. "I came directly here as quick as I could, after Washington let me go." Billy and Richard gaped at him. Chilton tore another large piece away from the slice of beef. With his mouth full, he looked down and plucked at his stained jacket and fringed buckskin pants. "That's from one o' the poor fools right there," he mumbled from underneath his huge red moustache. "He turned to run like the rest of the red-coated cowards and got a ball plumb through his neck before he fell on me."

Chilton had appeared to think for a moment, then said, with a flat intonation, "Six officers left alive, out of a hundred and fifty. A full thousand o' the 44th and 48th regiment lobsterbacks were killed and scalped, from fifteen hundred. The Frogs got the artillery, the supply wagons, £25,000 of army pay, an' all Braddock's papers and plans. An' there were only a few hundred of them."

Billy had turned to Richard. "They will take the campaign plans to the French Governor in Canada, and he will soon know all about us, must know about us already if it has been nine days. Get Marten, Richard. He must hear about this. We'll have to send more scouts out. Call all the other senior officers together as well, please, for an immediate conference." Richard had risen at once, but Billy had said, quietly, "Remain a moment more," and Richard had sat down again. Billy turned back to Chilton. "Who knows of this?"

"I carried some of the first expresses back across the mountains, myself. But others were sent as well, and the official news will be public in another day or two, I expect. Colonel Washington, who was second in command, is bringing out what's left of the lobsters with his Virginians. At least Braddock and his officers and the colonial bluecoats stood up alright."

"Didn't Braddock put any scouts out? I sent wampum belts off to Tanacharison, the Ohio Half-King, just for that reason."

Chilton had nodded, then tilted up the mug and drank deeply with his eyes closed, the rum running out both sides of his mouth. He shuddered and gulped, then spat in disgust.

"Braddock was brave enough, oh yes, he was for a fact. But he nearly got every man jack of us killed, the ignorant bastard. First, your Six Nation Iroquois wouldn't stay, because they heard that Cherokees and Catawbas were coming with Braddock from the Carolinas, an' as you know, Billy, they're mortal enemies."

Billy shut his eyes and nodded. "Go on, Henry."

"Then, after the Iroquois left, we hear the Cherokee and Catawba weren't a-goin' to come up after all, because South Carolina didn't want Virginia getting any influence over them. Then, Braddock wouldn't listen to the advice of the Half-King's Seneca warriors, them few that did stay. Instead, he called them all dirty savages, for scalping one of the Shawnee they shot along the way. Oh yes, I forgot, Braddock started out by ordering me to send the Indian women and children back to Fort Cumberland, an' naturally some of the men went back with 'em, as well.

"An' then our nervous Nellie night pickets accidentally shot the son of one of the chiefs who stayed, but Braddock was smart enough to give them lots of gifts, and so seven stayed with us'n, not counting the Half-King. An' so finally, Braddock was leadin' us agin' Fort Duquesne, an army of two thousand and more cutting a road through the forest, with the grand total of eight Indian scouts around who knew anythin' about the Ohio Valley."

He had lifted his head and gazed at Richard and Billy, who were speechless with horror. "An' even at that we did discover the Frenchmen's force and warned Braddock that they were in the trees and we put a couple of solid volleys at them. Who would 'a thought that after that, two whole redcoat regiments would panic like children, screaming and crying for mother and shooting in the air? Shooting each other!

"Who'd 'a believed that a Gen'ral, of the Gawd-damned Royal Coldstream Guards, no less, would have to be buried like a dead dog in an unmarked hole in the middle of a wagon road? Georgie Washington ordered the rest of us to march over Braddock's grave, so's the French Indians couldn't find him and scalp him."

Chilton's face had then changed and he had spoken in a low, hoarse voice. "An' then that fool Dingwall burned all the cached supplies and retreated all the way east to Philadelphia, leavin' the way open behind him. So now all the back country is lost to the French, and all my goods with it."

He said, bitterly, "The Shawnee an' most of the Miamis and the rest of the western nations have turned, and they're driving the settlers in all the way to Philadelphia; for didn't Braddock and his axe men build a lovely road for them through the mountains? I'm ruined, finished. The Philly merchants staked me to ten thousand pounds of trade goods, an' the godforsaken forest got it all."

Richard had clapped Chilton on the shoulder as he'd gotten up and headed out to find the war chiefs and officers. Even then, he'd felt that his words rang a hollow. "It'll work out, Henry; Billy will set things right, if anyone can."

Richard returned to the dismal present when the New Englanders dropped another forest giant, accompanied by triumphant cries from the winning gamblers. The trunk thundered down and the top lashed the ground a hundred feet away from him.

Holy Mother of God, he thought, *Braddock was a real British General, and he led a real army, a regular army, only to be slaughtered out there in the forest like hogs in a pen, by a bunch of Frenchmen and Indians armed with only muskets. What is the likes of my ragtag scrabble of provincial militia going to be able to do, then, against a great bloody stone French fortress with twenty great cannon? Even our Mohawks don't like the cannons.* He was glad he didn't have to explain it to Eva.

I don't much fancy the cannons neither, us marching nice and slow and orderly in full view of them, me waving a nice bright sword, right up to those 18-foot high walls, and then climbing the walls with nice little ladders, while the cannons knock us into bloody, twitching heaps. And that's not all, no! Jesus, Mary and Joseph, then we have to fight our way into the 60-foot stone tower inside the walls, where the dear French have put all their lovely cannons!

Richard felt suddenly chilled, in spite of the high summer heat and his wool uniform coat. He remembered the last war, eight years ago. Leading a patrol down the river to investigate the sound of some shots fired, he had found a seven-year-old child. The boy had been scalped and his family killed, and there he was, standing perfectly still except for shaking like a leaf, bleeding and naked, in a blood-drenched creek; crying among their mutilated bodies, while his home smoked beside him. The boy had lived another week. A nasty vision of himself as a bloody, hairless corpse came to mind once again, and he shook it off.

Thank the Dear Lord that the Six Nations are still with us. I thought they would surely change their minds when they heard about Braddock's disaster, but Billy seems to have charmed them again. He heard orders shouted, and realized that the army was making camp. He waved at Sergeant Watts to begin setting up the tents. *It will be full uniform for the evening officers' conference again in spite of the heat. The New Englanders make much of such appearances, although most of 'em have no more experience soldiering than Billy and me, an' less brains.*

When his tent was ready, and his men were gathering around the cooking fires, he went inside. It was furnished with a campaign trunk, a folding writing table and a folding camp bed. He opened the trunk and with a touch of vanity pulled out a mirror and made sure his dark blue coat, with its silver officer's trim, pewter buttons and scarlet lapels and cuffs, was straight and clean.

Richard was a handsome man, of medium height with dark brown eyes and long dark brown hair, which was at present powdered white and neatly tied back. An incipient smile always seemed to glimmer in his eyes and on his mouth.

The silver officer's gorget hanging from its chain on his chest gleamed. He adjusted his hat. Sporting its own silver edging and a black silk cockade, it was another physical reminder to Richard that, thanks to Billy, he had risen above what seemed his permanent lot in life—the son of an impoverished but pedigreed Catholic Irish tenant farmer—in a world owned by the protestant English.

But it's never over, is it? As if this new war was not enough, that bastard Stoatfester is still trying to get his revenge. Richard swore a blasphemous mental oath. *We should have killed him when we had the chance, back in Dublin.*

He slapped dust from his white waistcoat and tan linen breeches and gave a cursory wipe to his black boots. He put the mirror back in the trunk and dug out a pewter flask. He shook it, pulled the cork and drank a large swallow. *At least Eva and the boys are safe in Billy's stockade.*

He sat, awaiting the time to ride down the new road to the officers' meeting in Fort Edward, whose broad earth-filled wood ramparts were rising as the main force of the army readied itself for the march north to Crown Point. And he thought, not for the first time, of the irony of being an Irish Catholic officer in the English army. Some of his relatives, he knew, were plotting once again to get French help to drive the English out of Ireland. He sent up his usual perfunctory prayer that his ancestors would forgive him. He lifted the flask again and drained it, then wiped his mouth. A small smile twitched his lips.

He saw motion out of the corner of his eye and he turned his head, ready with a mild reprimand. Sergeant Watts knew better than to enter without permission.

But it was not Sergeant Watts. A grotesquely painted warrior pushed silently into the tent, exuding menace, carrying a monstrous, carved club and a musket. Richard started to his feet and reached reflexively for his pistol, his heart hammering, knowing that it was already too late.

Then he recognized one of his Mohawk allies and grinned, a little shamefaced.

He said, "Jesus, Mary and Joseph, Beancutter, someone will kill you by accident if you creep about like that!"

His visitor laughed at him, and said, "Richard, my nervous brother, your white sentries are blind and deaf, and your scalp would already be in my belt if I were Abenaki. But I bring news of the French. They have sent an army south from Montreal in bateaux. Whitecoat soldiers with many northerners—Ojibwa and Ottawas—and Canadians. Even some of our cousins come with them from Kahnewake this time. They left for Crown Point last week, coming up Lake Champlain."

Richard's guts clenched. Boats were much faster than runners were. The enemy was coming, and already knew their plans. *I don't much fancy riding back here after dark from Fort Edward tonight.*

I grant this food will be somewhat dear, and therefore very proper for Landlords, who, as they have already devoured most of the Parents seem to have the best title to the Children.

—Jonathan Swift,
"A Modest Proposal for Preventing the Children of Ireland from Being a Burden to Their Parents or Country"

CHAPTER 1
Leinster, Ireland, May 1728

"Don't spit when you say my father's name, Stoatfester!"

At the crest of the hill, the rutted cart track from DeClare to Áthbladhma widened for several yards, making a lay-by in the woods where weary oxen and humans could rest without blocking the way. In it, two youths stood, eyes locked, smiling grimly, tensed to fight. Mud steamed around their feet. It was the first hot morning in nine months.

The bigger boy was tall, blond, sixteen-year-old Edward Stoatfester, the son of the local English Factor, agent for a Londoner who owned most of the local farms and pastures. He slid the square toes of his heavy, silver-buckled shoes apart in the muck to get a better purchase. He sneered at the boy facing him, Richard FitzHugh, and cocked his fists.

"And just what do you propose to be doing about it, then, FitzHugh? If your family's so blessed noble, explain to me again why you're so bloody poor, me Irish prince."

Richard held his ground just out of reach. His bare feet were sunk ankle-deep in the road and he held his skinny body braced to dodge any blow. He tossed his dark brown hair and raised his chin. He was a year younger than his antagonist.

"I don't have to explain my family to any bloodsucking, absentee landlord's servant," he said.

"Servant, is it?" Stoatfester laughed harshly. He edged nearer, his voice growing louder. "And if I'm the servant, then why be your da giving my da his shed full of fodder, and why be you dressed in such rags? Why be that, me prince?"

Richard's rage and ears grew hotter at the unanswerable truth of it. *The English dog.* But he still remembered his grandfather's words. *If you are to win when your enemy is bigger, you must be able to strike at your choosing, not at his.*

"This was our land, granted to us by Henry II himself," he shot back, "and none of your English lying tricks or the pack o' traitors and lackeys in Dublin Castle can change that."

Stoatfester spat, again. "The way I make it, FitzHugh, your families came over here and couldn't actually beat the natural Irish, so you joined them and betrayed your masters in England. I wouldn'a be putting on such great airs about it."

Richard knew Stoatfester was goading him into his third losing fight this spring, but was unable to help himself. *Jesus, Mary and Joseph, at least let me bloody his nose for once, before he knocks me down!* He wished, for the hundredth time, that he had paid more attention to his grandfather's interminable tales about their ancient ancestors. Now, it was too late.

"The rightful King of England is a Stuart," he hissed, half-remembering whispered conversations among his elders, "who is from the Isles, not some Hanoverian foreigners named George who can't even speak English."

"You ought to know by now, me treasonous Irish prince," came Stoatfester's mocking response, "that it's the Parliament of England which decides who its king will be, and it's not about to be a Papist, idol-worshipping Scotchman ever again."

A generation before, the English Parliament had invited Protestant Dutchman King William of Orange to depose their King, Catholic James Stuart II. He had done so at the Battle of the Boyne, north of Dublin. The victors were determined to bury Jacobite Stuart ambitions forever. They had disarmed Catholics, seized their lands, and erased their rights. The new masters of Ireland had then moved back to fashionable London, spending money extracted from their new estates on such extravagances as hats made from beaver fur, imported from the savage, exotic wilderness of America.

Richard hurled back his defiance, "England was ta'en by Rome and abandoned, and then the Saxons raped her, and the Danes and Normans too. Eire was conquered by none, ye lick-spittle, until you and your fathers came to trample us under the weight of your uncountable numbers of bastards."

The bushes behind Edward rustled and parted, revealing a freckled face topped by an unruly bush of sandy hair. Richard recognized the English magistrate's son, Billy Smithyman, to whom he had never spoken.

Startled, Stoatfester glanced back. Richard saw his opportunity. He kicked the blond boy's crotch with all his strength, crushing the soft flesh there against the bone. Gasping, keening, eyes bulging, Stoatfester curled up in the swampy ruts. Exultant, the young victor stood over him a moment, before speaking to the astounded newcomer.

"Smithyman, the next time he spits when he says the name FitzHugh, you might remind him to have a care. His betters might be watching."

Richard turned and ran lightly into the silent, ancient forest remnant. It had clung to the gently rounded hilltop through the ages, somehow holy, somehow protected from all-devouring axe, saw and fire. A moist carpet of leaves on the forest floor absorbed almost every sound.

His brows knitted as he ran, and his heart clenched, not from fear of pursuit, but from apprehension about what the Factor would do if his son told him of the fight, as the dog was almost certain to do.

His father had already as good as emptied the haymow to pay the rent. Only a few of their gaunt cattle remained. They stood shakily in knee-deep, hoof-rotting slime, awaiting sunny pasturage on the hills. Their shaggy hides were matted with filth and their long-horned heads were bowed. Sweating, he cursed the English as he ran.

It had been a cruel long time since autumn. Richard had lost his grandfather at Easter, pneumonia finally silencing his ever-shallower gasps for air. Two weeks ago, his baby brother had quietly followed.

Today, the hot morning had arrived like an oven door falling open, as if the weeks of missing sunlight were now to be packed into one exceptional day. The sudden warmth should have cheered everyone's soul, but many, like Richard's mother, Siobhan, felt only a dull resentment at the length of the wait.

She had stared out, unsmiling, at the brilliantly lit vista of the Sleive Bloom hills for a long time that morning, arms crossed. She looked down five hundred feet at flat farmlands and bogs stretching a hundred miles northeast to legendary Tara, where the ancient Celtic Kings had ruled, and east the same distance to the great Irish port of Dublin. She could just see the dark shapes of the Wicklow Mountains south of Dublin in the haze.

Tossing her lank hair back from her face, she turned back into the gloom of their home, a windowless and chimneyless hut, filled with an eye-stinging murk from the peat fire. She muttered, to no one in particular, "It's a nice thing, surely, but t'would have been fairer sooner."

A cold spring, smelling of death, had followed a hungry winter. An incessant, moaning wind shredded thick layers of wolf-colored clouds like rotted linen. Drenched fields dissolved into bogs. Bogs sank into black, ice-water ponds.

Irish babies and grandparents alike shivered, coughed, and died. Richard had watched his anxious mother add another heavy layer of damp homespun around her feverish youngest child. And he knew that the FitzHughs were lucky. At least they still lived on what had been their land, ship provisioners at

Cork still bought their beef—when they had some to sell—and they still ate.

But Irish sheep brought better revenues to London than did pedigreed peasant cattle, in spite of the tariff protecting English wool. Herds of sheep had displaced the O'Rourkes and the MacCarthys and many others. They now starved in country ditches and Dublin slums. The FitzHughs might be next, if their London landlord wanted better returns and directed Factor Stoatfester to produce them.

Richard had heard stories of hamlets left without enough living inhabitants to bury their dead. He had seen dogs eating corpses along the road that winter. Entire villages had simply given up, emptying themselves like sacks of soup bones into London's steaming cauldron, where even half the customary City laborer's wage was a princely sum, beyond all greed. But cheap Irish laborers were not welcomed by London slum-dwellers either.

As he ran, he glimpsed a sudden motion to his right, followed immediately by a sharp blow on his left shin. His legs tangled and he fell headlong. As he scrambled to his feet and looked back for the cause of his tumble, he heard smothered giggles, and recognized Eva O'Connor.

"Oh, it's just you, you silly girl," he gasped, brushing rotting leaves and mud from his face and shirt as best he could, and rubbing his shin.

"Just me!" She shrieked with laughter, waving the oak staff she had expertly inserted between his legs as he ran. "Even when you bow down to me you still can't be polite, can you, Richard FitzHugh?"

Fourteen years old, Eva was a year younger than Richard, the middle daughter of neighbors who were also clinging desperately to their bare subsistence from land that was no longer theirs.

He struggled to get his breath back. "Be quiet, can't you, Eva? Stoatfester is after me and he'll hear you if you can't button your lip."

She quieted immediately, but peered at him with her pale green eyes, her head tilted to the side like an inquisitive, auburn-feathered bird.

"Ye don't have the look of fightin' with him; ye aren't bleeding from head to foot like at Easter." She dropped the staff and stifled another giggle behind both hands.

He grinned back at her, his composure and his breath returning. He liked Eva O'Connor. She was all right, for a girl.

"No, he didn't lay a hand on me this time, and he won't be a-wooing Elizabeth Merner, not for a day or two at least."

Eva raised her eyebrow. "And how do you think your da will pay for your heroics, then, my fine hero?"

He frowned. "I don't know, but I'm rightly tired of Mr. Edward Stoatfester, the Factor's son, pretending to be God around here, I am."

"The son of God, actually, I'd say."

He looked sharply at her, unsure of her blasphemous words.

"That's an evil thing to say, Eva. You ought to watch your tongue or the priest will make sure you do."

She tossed her hair. "Fie on the priest, he's had his manly eye on me for months now, married to the Virgin or not."

He was shocked. "How can you say that?"

She looked him in the eye. "Don't be a fool, FitzHugh. All the girls have seen he's scheming how to catch me." She giggled, and jigged a step. "But he'll find I'm a fish a little too quick for his spear, I am."

He shook his head at her. "I hope for your sake that you're wrong about him, Eva. The priest ought not to be thinking of such things, and neither should you."

Green eyes blinked slowly at him. "And what about you?"

Suddenly speechless, he blushed. Eva's direct question triggered a conscious wave of feelings about her that he had never quite acknowledged to himself before. In seconds, his awareness of her changed, forever. He felt himself grow hard between his legs, and then harder. Their eyes locked for a long moment.

Then she dipped her head and long, auburn curls hid her eyes as she picked up the oak staff that had tripped him.

She turned and without looking back murmured, "Good day to ye, Richard FitzHugh."

Mesmerized, his heart pounding, he watched the suddenly fascinating sway of her hips below her slender back until she was lost from view. He breathed out a long, long sigh, and then resumed his run, along paths known only to a few.

*****

Weeks later, the expected hammer of doom had not fallen on his household. It was clear that by some miracle the Factor remained ignorant of his son's humbling on the hilltop. Other things had clarified themselves at the same time. Spring had finally arrived, followed by a cool, wet summer. Richard had called on Eva at home, causing an exchange of knowing looks in both families.

"Stoatfester is planning something for me, do you think?" Richard murmured aloud. "Else he'd have told his da about me kicking him." He and Eva were enjoying one of the rare flawless days. They were invisible to anyone, except from directly overhead. He lay stretched on his back, hands under his head, in a small meadow covered with thousands of fragrant flowers, staring at the tiny speck of a golden eagle, wheeling high up in the unmarked blue.

An answering murmur came from beside him. Eva was lying on her stomach with her chin in her hands, waving her bare calves and wiggling her toes in the air's caressing warmth. Her threadbare, bleached linen gown and blue linsey-wolsey petticoat were speckled liberally with bits of meadow. To get a view, she had parted and flattened a bit of the yard-high forest of yarrow, ox-eyed daisies and buttercups that palisaded their privacy. She nudged Richard and pointed to where a small figure wearing a white shirt was slogging along dark furrows in the valley.

"You might talk to that Billy Smithyman, then, and see what the weather's like. The Smithymans are freehold farmers, not beholden to any great thieves in England, and they are living here, not whipping us Irish to death from London. From what I've heard, Billy's not great friends with the Factor's son, neither, for all that the English have got to be polite to each other. My sister's a maid at Smithyman's and, from what she tells me, I've a small feeling that he'd be one you could trust, an' the Stoatfester might be a-boasting to him about his plans."

Richard scowled as he rolled over to face her. "Do you seriously think one Englishman would ever take up against another for the likes of us, Eva? His father's the magistrate!"

"Why not?" She shrugged, "My mother says his father's as fair as we Irish have seen in a generation. Surely, and you know, too, he's not orderin' whippings for every minor forgetfulness, like some others. Stranger things have happened, y' know," she said, adding a singsong Gaelic phrase that Richard could not follow.

"And what were you saying, then, ye sprite?"

She smiled enigmatically at him. "Oh, I was just talking to one of the faeries, out there in Tir Nan Óg now, wasn't I, Richard FitzHugh?"

Suddenly, she sat up, clapped her hands and pointed as several large black birds with bright red beaks and feet flapped low overhead. "Oh, look, Richard, there's a chough, two, no, three! Imagine, choughs this far away from Mayo!"

CHAPTER 2
Smithyman Farm, Leinster, Ireland, 1728

The next morning, fog and drizzle again draped the land in clammy gauze. Damp fields quickly became too muddy to work, and Richard put on his cleanest clothes and his only shoes and set off across the valley to the Smithyman farm.

Nerving himself for what he expected would be a chilly reception, for the Catholic Irish were generally regarded as hardly more human than slaves, he strode boldly up to the heavy wooden door, set square in the middle of the large stone farmhouse, and knocked loudly. After Eva had suggested the visit, he had talked himself into it. *You have nothing to be ashamed of.*

Eight centuries, sixteen hundred lifetimes spent stubbornly defending Erin. First, the ancient Gaelic Celts against the Vikings and their longboats, then Gaels and Norsemen united against armored Norman knights, then their triply mingled descendants against the efficient, implacable English.

Richard's ancestor Geoffrey FitzHugh had been an officer in William of Normandy's conquering army. Only a hundred years after the Battle of Hastings, many of those Earls were already restless under the centralizing eye of England's throne, even in their castles in wild, remote Wales, where they had gone to live their lives, free of any authority but themselves.

Strongbow, Earl of Strigoil, had led his friends, including several FitzHughs, across the Irish Sea to carve out new fiefdoms far from the King of England's interference, accepting an invitation from one of the ever-feuding Celtic Irish Kings to help retrieve his wife and his throne.

Richard remembered the story vaguely, but had forgotten whether the desirable Dervorgilla had been first Diarmait MacMurrough's wife, or Tiernan O'Rourke's. She had been kidnapped, that was all. He did remember how there was always that odd feeling from the old stories, the sense that she had not really wanted to return home to her first husband.

Strongbow's friends brought their Flemish foot soldiers and Welsh archers and settled on the land, like the Norse invaders before them. They married Irish princesses and eventually grew as Irish as the Celts themselves except in name. Since the English conquests, though, few FitzHughs spoke Irish. Since the Boyne, many had converted to the Church of England. After the Scottish Jacobite rising of '15, the old laws had been revived, and even fewer felt any strong compulsion to defy the English.

This was because Catholic lands and feudal baronies were traitors' forfeit to the English Crown. Most of the austere stone keeps the Normans had built five hundred years before were now ruins. Their massive square walls had provided nurturing shelter for hamlets to spring up all across Ireland, but many had been abandoned for centuries. The dark windows of roofless, crenellated, FitzHugh Tower, a few miles away, glared about at the glutinous countryside like the eyes of a skull turned upside down.

Icy trickles found their way down Richard's neck as he stood at Smithymans' door, and he shivered. The air of solid prosperity about the Smithyman farm, its tile roof and neat, whitewashed fences, made him uncomfortably aware of the contrast with the thatched and patched-up poverty of his own home.

He had just decided that he ought not to be here and had turned to go, when the door opened. A tall servant frowned at him. He partially closed the door, seemed about to send Richard away, when a small, stout woman with brown hair tied back in a bun appeared alongside, and smiled pleasantly at him.

"Yes?" she inquired.

"Good morning, milady," he stammered, blushing, "I—that is, would—is Billy at home, then?"

"Yes," she nodded to her left, "he's out in the shed doing chores. And you would be, let me guess, Richard FitzHugh, am I correct?"

He was surprised and could only nod. "Yes, milady, I live over yonder." He waved his arm vaguely in the direction of home.

She nodded. "Why don't you go around to the shed and get out of this terrible rain, Richard? I am sure William would be pleased to see you. Perhaps you can persuade him to come inside for biscuits, later."

Almost dumbfounded, he said, "Th—thank you milady, I'll tell him, I'm sure."

He stepped hesitantly backwards and then ran, shoes slipping in the mud, around to the shed. There he found Billy wielding an axe, making firewood.

He stopped, and extended his hand. "Hello, Billy."

Billy sank the blade of the axe into the scarred and mangled oak stump that served as his chopping block, and shook hands earnestly with a strong, dry grip.

"Hallo, FitzHugh," he said, somewhat solemnly, "And what brings you around today?"

To his discomfort, Richard found himself talking enthusiastically to the English boy. He sent a quick mental prayer to his ancestors for forgiveness.

"I, well, I just thought that perhaps we could do something together, Billy. Would you like to see the caves around back of O'Connor's? I know a great place for fishing, too."

Billy said, "I don't much want to go fishing in this wet, but I would like to see the caves, very much."

Richard felt the slight glow of friendship beginning to warm him. He gestured to the split logs, scattered where they had fallen from the axe. "Could I stack the wood?" Impulsively, he added, "Why don't you have a woodsman do this, like all the other English? I'm sorry, it's none of my affair, if you don't care to answer."

Billy smiled again, as he wrenched the axe free and placed another log on the stump. "No, it's quite all right to ask. I like to do this. It makes me feel good, for one thing. For another, my parents pay me the woodcutter's wage, one and a half pence an hour, and I very much wish to be a wealthy man when I am grown."

Billy swung the heavy, wedge-shaped axe down with an easy, balanced motion. The dark cylinder split cleanly, spraying moisture. Symmetrical halves thumped to the ground.

Richard gestured at the farm. "But you will inherit, and this is wealth, is it not?"

Billy shook his head. "My older brother John will inherit, and this is not wealth. Two or three years of bad harvests would quickly make me and my family poor Irish farmers."

He glanced at Richard. "English-Irish farmers, I mean. I would not be so subject to the weather for my life." The halves were halved again, and then Richard stacked them.

He thought a moment, and then asked, "And what would you be doing, then, Billy, to make your fortune?"

The answer came immediately. "I am going to go to America."

Richard was startled. Billy might as well have suggested that he was going to fly to the moon.

Later, they stretched their feet toward a small fire, in the caves behind Eva O'Connor's cabin. His new friend's certainty impressed Richard.

"But I hear, in America, there are savages who like to torture."

"Yes, it is very true that there are fierce fighters among the Iroquois and Ojibwa and the other tribes. Some say that the torture is a normal test of manhood among them."

"How do you know their names?"

Billy was getting excited now. "I read about America as much as ever I can. It seems like an amazing place. Did you know that some of the Iroquois chieftains came to London back in Queen Anne's time? I think one of them, at least, is still alive! It would be a truly wonderful thing to meet him, don't you think? I wonder what he would say about us.

"Some people say that the Iroquois have a very advanced government, that a great chief named Hiawatha was able to unite five warring Indian nations into one, many years ago." Billy noticed Richard's jaw drop. He paused and picked at his boot. Richard's astonishment at this enthusiastic flow of knowledge made Billy a little self-conscious. He shrugged and explained.

"My parents think learning things about the world is very important. My Uncle Harold is a Royal Navy captain on the North American station and he sometimes writes." He stopped and grimaced, briefly. "I am learning French and Latin as well, at school. I want to learn the law."

Richard scratched idly at the dirt. "Catholics can only become doctors or priests. I don't care about that. School learning is not much use on the farm anyway. Would you not be lonely, with your family still here?"

"When my father dies, this farm will belong to John. I will need to leave then, anyhow."

Richard shook his head. "I would not like to leave the land my ancestors fought and died for."

Billy looked at him. "Do you wish to stay here, where people like Stoatfester can force you to work like a slave, just to survive?"

Richard dropped his head and muttered, "What do you care about that? You're neither Catholic nor Irish."

"It just seems wrong to me. My father bought his land honestly, out of his settlement from the army. Yet there are people all around who used to own this land, and some now cannot even go to church without being persecuted like dogs."

Richard grunted and looked out at the cave mouth, where a rivulet fell and splashed across the entrance. "My grandfather said losing wars is not a good way to keep your pride or your possessions."

Billy nodded, "True, but a fight is an honorable thing. Rack-renting is just plain and simple bullying. Stoatfester and his kind make me ashamed to be English. It is not right to tread on people who have no way to fight back."

Richard poked some sparks out of the fire with a stick and flicked a sideways glance at him. "You are an unusual Englishman, then, Billy."

Billy grinned in the gloom. "Perhaps so. I intend to be a wealthy one some day, too!"

They watched the smoke twisting its way out of the cave for a moment. Billy warned Richard that Edward Stoatfester was plotting revenge. "Why did he not tell his father about it?" Richard wondered.

Billy laughed, "Because I think he was too embarrassed. I told him he should fight his own battles."

Billy sprang to his feet and walked to the cave mouth, where he looked up at the grey sky. "I think it's near time for my geometry lesson, which I have at home to stay out of arm's reach of that sodomite Grant at the Academy. Then it will be dinner time."

He turned and smiled. "I'll be going home, Richard. I'm glad you came by. I like the caves. Maybe we could go fishing next week, then." He waved, and Richard watched him stride down the hill into the thinning mist. *Eva was right. He is not like the other English.*

On his way home, Richard stopped by the O'Connor farm. Eva saw him coming and ran to meet him.

"Shall we go for a walk then?" she asked.

They climbed a gentle slope away from the house, fingers entwined, until they sank down together to shelter in privacy beneath a huge, ancient oak. Eventually they disentangled limbs and digits enough to talk, somewhat breathlessly.

"You were right, my love, yon Billy is likely to be a friend to us, and I like him more than a bit already, myself," Richard laughed. "He told Stoatfester it would be cowardly to get his father to fight his battles for him. I'm surprised that made any difference, but it seems he shamed him out of it."

Eva pushed a dark curl back from his forehead. "I think you owe him a debt then, Richard. Being his friend would be a good thing for you. You need some intelligent company that can talk with you about all the grand things in the world."

"He has knowledge of the great world, surely, and wants to go to America to make his fortune."

"America!" She shuddered, and moved her face to his, and talking ceased, for a time.

Then, she sat up, suddenly, as a notion took her. "We must find him someone, Richard, and I know just exactly who—Meghan McOrmond!" She leaped to her feet, and he, bewildered and a little frustrated, tried to tug her back down to the fragrant moss.

"No! Richard, let me go!" She pulled her hand from his grasp and took several steps down the hill, before whirling and gaily beckoning him.

"Come on, then, Richard FitzHugh, we can't dally here all night, else my father will be a-beating on your head, and my reputation will be all a-tatter."

Dinners at the Smithymans were quiet except for the clinking of knife on plate and the comments of the Smithyman patriarch, who frequently felt it necessary to point out to his three children the painful details of their errant ways. This nightly ritual was normally received with nods and "Yes, Father," spoken humbly and respectfully.

Billy's neck was particularly hot this night. Partly this was from irritation at the overbearing ways of adults, partly from suppressed teenage restlessness, and partly from the continual merciless needling of his elder brother and his younger sister, which ceased only at dinner. Everyone seemed joined in a conspiracy to make him writhe with frustration.

Finally, bursting with embarrassment, anxiety and prideful impatience, he could contain himself no longer. "I will not be a soldier and that's the end of it," he said, much louder than he had intended. "Using the law to make things better is, is, better by far than using a musket and bayonet."

Four pairs of eyes goggled at this treacherous departure from rectitude, and then three looked expectantly to the head of the table. The grim and mottled face of Magistrate Christopher Smithyman, Captain, Cockayne's Horse, Retired, glared like a basilisk at his younger son. Billy stared back without wavering.

For a few seconds the scene remained frozen, then Captain Smithyman's stony visage split open with laughter and he pushed his chair away from the table and stood up, grasping his cane.

"By God, I could not be angry tonight with a son who shows such true wisdom, and passion in pursuit of it. I took a musket ball from the French at Oudenarde to learn it, and it is all too easily forgotten. You are right, young master William, the way of the sword is both the way of honor and the way of sorrow." He turned and limped away from the table, chuckling softly and shaking his head. "Better by far, indeed, oh yes, indeed."

At the door he turned and poked his walking stick in Billy's direction. "You will have to study much harder, however, if you are to succeed as a barrister. Arguing before a judge requires knowledge as well as passion."

Billy held his tongue, but mentally rolled his eyes heavenward. *What a cursed fool I am, to give him another way to prod at me.*

His mother's face remained straight and stern, with not a twinkle in the eye to betray amusement at this defiance, nor the faintest sign of a mother's relief at its peaceful denouement.

"William," she said to him, "you must learn to control your temper and your tongue if you are to become a successful barrister, or anything else, for that matter. Wild indiscipline is not well regarded in either the army or a court of law."

Billy nodded at her, his eyes cast down toward the table. He fidgeted with his knife while a huge elation flared in his heart that his argument had carried the day.

"May I be excused, Mother?" he mumbled.

Anna Smithyman nodded. "You may go, William." She added, in passing, "Your Uncle Harold will be here sometime tomorrow, we expect, and I will require that you be here and have your face washed and your shoes shined for his visit. Perhaps he will answer some questions about the Spanish Main, if you act sufficiently civilized."

Five years of teenage struggle fell away from Billy's face in a second. An eager-to-please ten-year-old reappeared and said, "Oh, I say, Mother, I shall be very good, indeed. I should like above all things to hear about America." He rose and loped out of the room, all knees, arms and gigantic feet.

The next afternoon, a small carriage pulled up at the front door and Uncle Harold Holeybarth stepped down from it, resplendent in the blue and white uniform of a Commander in the Royal Navy. The driver set down a trunk, which the servant whisked off into the house. His sister Anna's children were in awe, as usual. He liked children. Anna had lined them up in front of the door in their finery and he greeted them warmly, especially Alexandra, who leaped into his arms over the objections of her smiling mother.

Captain Smithyman was also pleased to see his brother-in-law, although he, having seen considerable foreign service himself, was not particularly awed. They adjourned to the study after the excited greetings were finished and the beaming, gleaming children had been sent away.

"The children seem as intelligent as ever, I find," said Commander Holeybarth.

Smithyman nodded. "Brandy? We have recently received a small cask from that fine Irish distiller-in-exile, Hennessey." Receiving assent, he tugged once on a bell pull.

"John is dutiful and Alexandra is always delightful to be around. William? Well, William remains firmly set against a soldiering career and has decided that he is to become a barrister, it seems."

"That cannot be altogether displeasing to you, surely?"

"No, it is not. Speaking as his father, though, I'd say he might be one of those rare 'uns, Brother, who actually has both courage and brains, and might serve his country well in uniform. Certainly, when he is trained, I expect that he will be formidable before the bench.

"He seems, however, to have developed a certain, how can I say it, touchy sense of personal justice. This may yet bring him problems if he cannot bring it under control. The law is political, and politics is necessarily more devious than a simple sense of right or wrong might tolerate."

Commander Holeybarth smiled. "Hm. No, it is unfortunate that politics cannot be more like the Navy, where we all know our place and our duties." He paused to sip his brandy. "Although it is true, appointments depend very greatly on who you know. Even very great merit cannot overcome lack of friends at court."

Captain Smithyman eyed him, then. Smiling, he recalled his manservant to refill their glasses from the decanter.

"Surely, Brother, you're not suggesting that merit be the only criterion for success? That would be a damnably whiggish notion, indeed, even in these times when the King's Ministers seem more like kings themselves."

Commander Holeybarth laughed. "No, Brother, I do not for a moment suggest such a leveling concept, for then we of little talent would be lost forever. A toast, then, to our luck: May it remain with us and our families always." They touched glasses.

It tortured the children to wait until dinner. On the rare occasions when their uncle visited, he had always brought gifts for everyone in the family, and this, they had been told, was not to be an exceptional visit in that respect.

As the afternoon drew on, the aroma of a roasting goose gently infiltrated the house. At dinner, Captain Smithyman skillfully dismembered the bird, which vanished in an orderly fashion, along with several large lamb pies and two bottles of the Smithyman's best red Methuen, imported from London.

Commander Holeybarth held a goblet to the light. "This is dashed good wine, Brother! It is quite as good as many of the burgundies I've had the pleasure to capture."

Captain Smithyman smiled. "It is Portugoose wine, Hal, only two shillings a bottle. When we go down to Dublin we usually bring back a pipe or two of it. In Ireland, French wine, with the duties, usually costs something around eight a bottle and ranks, for us, as an extravagance. I am glad you enjoy it."

The first course was followed by Billy's sister Alexandra's contribution, a large mashed potato sculpture baked in the shape of a crown, on which the carefully constructed words, "Georgivs II Dei Gratia Rex" were almost legible.

Anna drew her brother's attention to it, "Hal, Alexandra was determined to make this for you, in honor of His Majesty's recent Coronation. She bought the potatoes from our Irish neighbors. We find them to be surprisingly good food —for all that many English are prejudiced against it."

Commander Holeybarth smiled. He winked at his brother-in-law and stood. "My dear niece Alexandra, I do believe such a royal dish calls for a toast. In the Navy, we are given permission to toast the King while seated. It is a wise and practical tolerance, for otherwise, ship's overheads become places where his maritime servants leave bits of their scalps. Ashore, however, it is different; we do not have to crouch, and as an officer I must stand."

He toasted, "The King, long may he reign." He smiled at Alexandra. "I'm sure that with such a warm and delicious tribute at its beginning, his reign will be a remarkable one, indeed."

Captain Smithyman rose to his feet and raised his glass, smiling. "The King, God bless him."

Alexandra blushed at this high praise. Harold smiled down the table at his sister and raised his eyebrows. She nodded and signaled to the servant. In a moment, he returned carrying a dark wooden box, a miniature trunk, with a curved top and iron handles attached to each end.

It was iron bound and iron studded, with intricate and elaborate brass work around the lock. Commander Holeybarth produced a key, and with a flourish he opened the lid, revealing several bulging muslin bags of varying sizes.

He said, "I should like to say that this was taken after an epic battle, but in this case, we took a pretty Spanish brig called the Santa Ana without much fuss. She was about 50 tons burden and carried ten guns, so might have given us some entertainment, but she gave up easily, after a very long and boring chase in light air, off Cartagena. I learned afterward that it was on precisely the same day that the Spanish armies lifted their siege of Gibraltar."

He paused, artfully, and Billy and John spoke with one voice, "Tell us about it, Uncle Harold."

Alexandra asked, diffidently, "What is a brig, Uncle Harold?"

He grinned. "A brig, my little pet, is a sailing vessel with two masts the same size and square sails on both of them."

He continued, "Now, it took us one entire day and night and the best part of another to come within long gun range—she was much lighter and handier than my sloop Beaver, but very green below with weed, which slowed her down just enough. Our bow chasers finally were able to fire a ball or two through her courses—those are the biggest sails at the bottom—and the captain struck her colors immediately. That is somewhat unusual for the Dons, they having a nice sense of honor about such things, but he had his wife and children aboard, as it happened.

"It also transpired that they were carrying this little chest locked safely away far below, full of pay for an outlying army garrison. As our party boarded her, my sharp-eyed midshipman saw the captain trying to sneak it overboard, along with their papers. He tackled him and that clapped a stopper on that. And so, I have some real Spanish gold and silver here, since the Navy also bought the brig. Beaver being the only cruiser in sight, there was also no necessity for sharing with the fleet, only the customary one eighth of the prize value to the Admiral."

He handed little clinking bags to Captain Smithyman and Anna and smaller ones to each of the children. They delighted in the shining heavy silver coins, and thanked him solemnly, with great feeling.

Commander Holeybarth took another sip of port. "That large silver coin is a peso, worth eight Spanish reales, so we call it a piece of eight. It's also worth the same as a German silver thaler, that we English call a dollar. They often cut them into eight bits in our colonies in the New World since coin is very hard to get there, so two bits is the same thing as a quarter of a dollar."

Anna got up and kissed her brother, and Captain Smithyman, smiling, limped around the table to thank him and shake his hand. Commander Holeybarth glanced at the children, who were noisily stacking coins on the table, and asked, "So, then, what do you want to do with all this newfound wealth, my niece and nephews? Come here, Alexandra. Sit on my knee and tell me what you think you will do?"

"I think, Uncle Hal, that I will keep three of these to give to my very own children when I grow up."

Commander Holeybarth laughed, "That's very farsighted of you, poppet. What of you, Master John?"

John weighed the coins in his hand. "I am saving my money for a truly fine fowling piece and I think this may just be enough to make it mine, Uncle."

Harold nodded and turned to his younger nephew. "Well, William, what do you think this Spanish silver is good for?"

Without hesitation Billy replied, "I will be making an investment, sir, to make my fortune."

"An investment, by God! And what sort of an investment do you think it is wise to make, William?"

Billy reddened slightly, knowing that he was being chaffed, but carried gamely on. "Well, sir, I believe that there is money to be made in trade."

"Trade! You would rather be in trade than a soldier or a barrister, then?"

"No, not entirely, Uncle. I believe a firm knowledge of the law would be an asset to making my way in the world in any case. But I would not be a soldier by choice and there are precious few barristers who seem to have wealth, whereas there are many traders who appear to be wealthy."

Commander Holeybarth nodded and waved his wineglass at Billy, then looked at the boy's father. "Well, Christopher, your children seem eminently sensible, each in their own way, do they not? I congratulate you and Anna for your success at raising such a brood. I aspire that I would do as well when I am married."

Anna smiled. "From your letters I get the impression that you have someone in mind, Hal?"

Commander Holeybarth said, smiling back, "Yes, I have met a rather delightful girl in New York. I am looking forward to returning there when Beaver's refit is completed."

"I also have the impression, from your letters, that her family is prominent in colonial society?"

"Sophia is the youngest daughter of a very erudite solicitor named De Vere. He sits on the Governor's Council and he is apparently one of the best educated inhabitants of the colony."

"She sounds very well suited to you, Hal. I do so hope that things work out well for you. Perhaps one day we shall have the privilege of welcoming her into the family."

"I hope so as well, my dear."

CHAPTER 3
The Stone Bridge, Leinster, 1730

Billy recognized the rider and his horse instantly, although it was half a mile or more down the valley to where they were crossing the little stone bridge. He growled inwardly, and would have turned aside had it been possible to do so unseen.

But the roadside and fields were mercilessly bare of trees and no convenient little copse or drift of fog offered shelter for himself and The Colonel, his four-year-old stallion. So he simply sat up a little taller in the saddle and stiffened his resolve to show neither contempt nor anger.

"Mind your manners," a mental voice told him, "else you'll be needing to explain things to the magistrate again."

His father was the magistrate concerned. It had been only eight months since he had been brought up to the bench by the constable on charges for knocking down Grant, the local schoolmaster.

His father had fined him five shillings and ordered him to maintain the King's peace for half a year. The irritation Father had shown at home had been worse. Billy winced in recollection, although he counted it a victory to be excused from further attendance at the Academy. He kicked The Colonel into a brisk canter, but before he reached the bridge, Edward Stoatfester placed his horse across the path. Billy reined up gently.

"And a good morning to you, Stoatfester," he said, evenly.

Edward Stoatfester spat, sloppily.

"It'd be a damn sight better morning if ye'd not be out usin' up all the good air, Smithyman."

"And what, in particular, would be a-chewing at your vitals this day, then, Stoatfester?"

"I've warned you before that you oughtn't t'be favoring the papist bog-eaters with your company, haven't I?"

Cool, stay cool, now. Billy consciously relaxed his grip on the reins. The Colonel shook his long mane and took a mild interest in the stalks of meadow grass lining the stony roadbed.

Billy leaned toward the other man and spoke in a low, intense voice. "I do seem to recall that we have had this conversation before, Stoatfester. It's nobody's business who I like to talk to. Do you have anything to add to your opinions that you would care to defend in court? If not, I do believe that you are obstructing a public route."

Stoatfester did not move. "Don't think that because your da's the Justice that you'd be able to swing any fancy lawyer tricks on the likes of me, old boy. A year or two studying an't going to be enough law to frighten me off."

"And just what is it that you're thinking of doing, Stoatfester?"

"I'm just giving a bit of friendly advice to a neighbor, Billy boy, mayhap for the last time. There's more'n just me that think you're cavortin' with the wrong breed o' cow up the hill, there."

Billy fought the sudden rage and brought The Colonel's head up, then urged him slowly forward. The roan stallion was two hands or more taller than the other horse. He was afraid of nothing at all, as far as Billy could tell, after two years of riding him. As horse and rider approached, Stoatfester grinned and moved aside. Billy stopped beside him, the horses facing opposite ways, and stared at the bulky blonde man.

"Let me give you a little advice of my own, Stoatfester," he said. "If you take it upon yourself to make any more comments of any kind on what I do, or who I see, you'll be given a long overdue lesson in manners, and be sure that I'll find it a very great pleasure, indeed."

He held the other's gaze for several seconds and saw a slow flush spread up Stoatfester's neck. Billy turned away and nudged The Colonel into action, walking towards the bridge.

A toss-up, whether he goes for me now, or he saves it for later.

He heard the loud, metallic click and stopped The Colonel. He swiftly turned in the saddle, saying, "Stoatfester, you'd be a great fool now, to shoot the magistrate's son, and me without arms, wouldn't you?"

The heavy pistol pointed at his chest.

Billy continued calmly, "I heard you bragging while you swilled at the Maidenhead in DeClare that you'd purchased a cavalry pistol, but from the gossip I think you need a bit more practice to hit as small a target as me, with something as big as that.

"If you think you can, though, you'd best get on with it. But by God, you'd better pray that you kill me, because if you don't, you're going to eat that horse pistol and your hand and arm along with it."

After a pause, Stoatfester shrugged, smiled, and lowered the barrel. "I was only seeing if you'd pee yourself when you saw it. It's only at half-cock now, you see. Can't fault a fellow for having a little joke, now, can ye?" He eased the hammer down and stuck the pistol back in his belt. He yanked his horse's head around and spurred it to a gallop.

Billy stared after him thoughtfully, then turned and rode hard across the bridge in the opposite direction. He was late, and Meghan would be waiting.

Anticipation of those perfect, soft lips on his made him hurry. His heart beat faster, but his excitement was tempered with a certain anxiety. Meghan did not like to be kept waiting.

Chapter 4

The Wedding, Leinster, 1733

Three years later, the wedding of Eva O'Connor and Richard FitzHugh excited the entire county. This was the old ways renewed, ancient Irish and ancient English lineage joined. One of the remaining wandering Gaelic poets was attracted to the event, even though it was only a wedding of poor folk, usually beneath the notice of such exalted eyes.

Billy Smithyman was the only non-Catholic to be invited. Although he was well known to be good friends with the groom, he felt dark looks from several directions over the course of the evening. A number of unfamiliar male faces quietly appeared, had a few toasts and danced awhile with the beaming, joyful bride, then edged quietly away again, in twos and threes. They had the look of men who had seen hard usage, and their watchful eyes darted here and there throughout the time they were present.

Billy asked Richard about them, and he shook his head, adding quietly, "Don't be asking questions about them right now, joy, it wouldn't be a healthy thing to do, friend of mine or no. Go and do the dance, now, Billy, with Meghan McOrmond, else she will die of despair, though the Dear knows what she sees in you."

The landlords and their agents were roundly cursed in nearly every conversation Billy overheard. Eventually, he was satiated from the feast and wobbly from drink. Meghan had left with her family and, realizing dimly that many also were waiting for him to leave, he bid farewell to Eva and Richard and left the torch-lit party, turning The Colonel's head for the dark track across the valley.

The Colonel walked slowly towards the gap in the hedgerow, his rider preoccupied. Billy cursed himself aloud as he found, annoyingly, that he was now a little too drunk to appreciate the warm, clear summer night and to think about its events.

"Damn you for a fool, anyway, William Smithyman," he muttered to himself. "Why would you drink like an English lord there, when you know you have enemies who watch your slightest move with the Irish?"

He supposed the men he had seen were some of the vanished Catholic brothers and fathers and uncles, the "Wild Geese" who had fled to Europe to soldier against England over the long years since the Battle of the Boyne.

But Meghan's hand in his had left a lingering warmth, and presently he found his thoughts returning to her with delight. A circlet of flowers in her long, brown hair, her dark-eyed, flirtatious fire and open admiration were still a dizzyingly pleasurable mixture.

Without the slightest warning, a huge blow to the side of his head knocked him out of the saddle, full onto his back. His wind burst out into the still, dark air. From a great distance, unable to breathe or defend himself, he felt fists and boots break bones, and teeth, and skin. After a time, through the pain and shock, he heard a familiar voice hissing, as if in a dream. "So you like the traitorous, papist potato-eaters, do ye? Well, then ye're a traitor yourself, and deserve what they get, only more. Have a good night, bog-eater." Billy felt his senses fade away, like the black shadow of the horse and rider moving across the moon.

During the grey of pre-dawn, nuzzled by his horse, he awoke on the cold, hard packed dirt of the track, spat teeth and clotted blood, and cried aloud at his first attempts to move. Slowly, he raised himself to one knee, then to his feet, clutching his right arm to his side to stop the terrible stabbing pains that came with each breath. Somehow, he found the strength to drag himself up onto The Colonel, waiting patiently. Billy clenched his teeth and held his breath against the agony of each separate movement. He was unable to prevent himself from groaning.

Alexandra Smithyman, sixteen years old, adored her brother Billy, although she often teamed up with her other brother, John, to torment him. She had waited up as late as she dared to find out about the wedding and had gone to bed bitterly disappointed.

In the morning, she was out the door early, to cut some flowers for the table, when she saw what looked like a muddy pile of rags at the gate, The Colonel standing nearby. Going closer with curiosity, she dropped the basket and shrieked in fright and shock when it moved, and again, hands to her mouth, when she realized it was Billy.

Her father and mother appeared, calling for the servants to help carry Billy into the house. A terrible anger flashed across his father's creased face, replacing anxiety when he realized that his younger son was not mortally injured.

"Get my horse, I'm going for the Constable," he bellowed, "By God, I'll have the bloody papists whipped to shreds for this."

Billy croaked, "No."

"Who, then, son? Who did this to you?"

"Stoatfester."

His parents looked briefly at each other. Billy sobbed for air through his battered, bloody mouth, "I...I'll handle it, don't say anything...to anyone." He gripped his father's arm.

"Promise me, Father, no word to Stoatfester."

"We'll talk about it later, then, son, when you have a little blood back in you. God bless us, why would he do this to you? Rest, now, rest, will you?"

Word of the beating did get out, of course.

Mysteriously, fresh baked soda bread, flowers, and bottles of whiskey appeared on the doorstep of the farmhouse for a week.

The Constable appeared, but went away, puzzled and concerned by the young man's insistence his assailants were not Irish.

"If ye say so, young Smithyman, I'll have to believe ye," said the Constable, clearly skeptical—and disappointed that an excuse for whipping a Pope-worshipper could not be found.

In a day or two, Billy was walking about again. After a week, the savage bruises and scabs began to heal, but his broken hand and ribs and the aching hole at the side of his jaw remained painful far longer. Long enough to nurse to flame the ember of a plan for justice. He needed to talk to Richard about it first.

"Stoatfester, was it?" exclaimed Richard. "The cur. We did not know, but in truth, joy, we did know that you sheltered us from the suspicions of the Constable, else some would have suffered. We must do something. Mr. Edward Stoatfester will have some serious pummeling to handle before long, himself."

Billy grinned painfully. "Nay, the Constable would know it was Irish work, by the cries of joy rising from every farm in Leinster. However, I am grateful for the thought, Richard."

"You cannot let it stand, Billy."

"No, I cannot, but there will be better ways to shake him and his people than simply breaking an arm or a jaw, for now. I won't call him out. There would be precious little satisfaction and no honor at all in shooting that worthless dog down. He thinks he is not identified, and I find in that some ongoing advantage. How many of your people work in the Factor's employ?"

Richard thought a moment, "Perhaps six or seven, around the house."

"If they could find alternate service, could they be persuaded to leave, d'ye think?"

Richard burst out laughing, "Sure and you're joking, Billy, they work there only out of love for the Factor, as you well know."

Smiling, but ignoring the quip, Billy continued. "I believe that many of the English farmers would be glad to purchase goods at somewhat lower prices than those the Factor charges at his emporium."

"As would all of us. The prices Stoatfester charges are usurious, but we Irish cannot by law buy a store, nor the land to put it on, neither."

"No, but I can, and living at home, I have no expenses to speak of, and years of woodcutter's wages to invest. My friend, I have done some thinking, and I will now give you my store of wisdom at no interest charge whatsoever."

In a few weeks, Smithyman's Merchanterie opened. It was instantly successful and quickly had to expand its line of goods. The Factor first protested directly to Billy, who shrugged and suggested that fairer prices were benefiting many in the valley, rather than a few in London. The man then rode off to repeat his complaint to the elder Smithyman, who simply stared at him malevolently and urged him off his property, "Before I forget myself."

Suddenly, there were no servants available to work at Stoatfester's, and for a time their indolent, spoiled son had to do the despised Papists' chores for his parents.

A month after the opening, Richard and Billy met in the cave behind O'Connor's. Richard brought a jug of whiskey. They lit a fire and toasted the successful enterprise.

"A wonderful thing, Billy, surely, and you're a genius to all of us, you know."

Billy grinned back at him. "A plan made in heaven, it seems. How are the girls finding it?"

"It's marvelous. They're being paid fair wages for a fair day's work, and they'd, any of them, marry you without even thinking twice."

"I'm even going to get my investment back, with a bit of a profit as well."

"Billy, you said that nothing could change here, but look what you've done by yourself." A pause, then, "Are you still thinking of leaving the valley?"

Billy nodded, somberly. "Nothing has really changed. I cannot be happy here. I must make my fortune, to be able to make things different, and Smithyman's Merchanterie is a step, but only a step to that."

"And what about Meghan?"

"Ah. My friend, I trust you are not about to carry tales back, but are merely making a friendly inquiry."

Richard's face warmed slightly, but invisibly, in the gloom, and he took a gulp of whiskey before replying. "You know well that I am no informer." He blinked. "I will allow as to the fact that her aunts, sisters, brothers, mother, father and uncles have asked me not less than twice a day what Mr. Smithyman's intentions might be, but Meghan does not ask. If you would rather I withdraw that decidedly personal question, I will do so, of course, and beg your forgiveness for intruding."

Billy laughed. "Love is a very dicey thing, indeed. I love Meghan truly and we are very happy together. But I must go, when I can, and she has given me to understand that she will never leave her valley family for the savage charms of the wilderness, the prospect of which I find so enticing, indeed, necessary."

Richard muttered glumly. "That is not a happy response for me to carry, even inside myself only. We all desire you to stay. I owe you a personal debt, and so does our entire community, Billy. If you leave, that must remain unpaid, and our future is far less pleasant-seeming."

"You know you owe me nothing, my good friend. What I do, I do out of conviction and love, not in hope of return. Except," he chuckled, "that I hope you will not begrudge me enough return to stay in business for us both. For Meghan and myself, I have asked her for no commitment, as she has not asked me, and so we are happy, and America remains a long way off, for now."

"In truth, Billy, she is committed, for all that, and her family...her friends wish her not to be unhappy and alone in later life."

"Aye, I know it but...." Billy shrugged and drank, then said, offhandedly, "I think I may ride up to Dublin for a time this summer."

Richard looked at him and said, quietly, "That can be a deadly place, I hear, for any man with pride."

Billy looked back. "Aye, I've heard that. It is also a place to learn. I would be going to see what the law reads like there. I might test my mettle with an introduction to some of my uncle's friends and find out what it might be like to live a fine gentleman's life in the city, for a time."

"You'll not be forgettin' your friends in humbler circumstances, would you now, Billy?"

Billy smiled broadly. "No, Richard, I'll be back in the fall, but I need to broaden my horizons. Besides, I've heard that one of my neighbors is now cutting quite a fine figure there, a sight which I'd not be happy to miss entirely, now."

Richard nodded, "I wondered where he had gone."

Billy took another gulp of whiskey. "I'm thinking that I might be able to take him somewhat off stride, and return that nice personal compliment he paid me after your wedding, since he still believes that I do not know it was him."

"I'd be happy to come down and help ye, Billy. It seems odd that the brute has been accepted into Dublin society, English though it is, beggin' your pardon, Billy."

Billy laughed, "He's been taking lessons."

CHAPTER 5
Dublin, 1734

Billy left the farm in the middle of June. By now, most of his training in the law was finished, and so he ambled down to Dublin on the back of The Colonel, passing several nights pleasantly in small inns placed at equally small crossroads. In summer, the roadside beggars rising from every ditch seemed less cadaverous, their paleness now browned and blending better with the dust.

He distributed a few pennies as The Colonel walked along, although his father had warned him this was stupid. He seemed to get away with it, but Billy realized that his father was right; he could sink himself without making the slightest difference to most of them. He still felt he had to respond to the most terrible of them, the ones with children as thin as themselves.

He was duty-bound to contact the judges and barristers his father knew, but by the time he reached Dublin, his first goal was to find out what Edward Stoatfester was up to and to make contact with the Dublin Irish.

Billy arrived in mid-afternoon, to be immersed in one of Dublin's two very different rivers.

He observed to himself, "The River Liffey is liquid and seems largely clean, but the human river is solid and exceedingly grimy." He threaded his way through herds of cattle and swine, ignoring the beggars, peddlers, and women in rags, and avoiding the carts rattling and creaking through. He kept to the middle of Thomas Street as he approached the Corn Market and the Gate to the Liberties. *To be sure, this is no place for Meghan, but I wish Richard had come. Dublin would be a place to make him think bigger thoughts than he is wont to do in the hills.*

Too, it would be good to have the company of someone in this city. Good to hear his comments on these fine, tall houses, with stinking slime and filth piled so deep at their feet you would think them sunk in a privy up to the windows.

He chuckled. *Like as not, he would tell me some funny story on why he thinks those brick Dutch Billies have their gable ends facing the street, but the rest of us put the broad sides of our houses to the street.*

He heard a whip crack and turned quickly in the saddle, hearing a harsh shout, "Way, there! Way! Make way, you scum!" A handsome ebony and buff carriage pulled by a matched pair of chestnut mares galloped madly at him, high wheels spraying muck left and right, driver cursing and lashing savagely.

Billy kicked The Colonel urgently into a side lane, frowning, as the leather-sprung coach careened by, but he caught a glimpse of an exquisite milk-white oval face with dark eyebrows, and a flash of wide green eyes under a flowered hat.

Taking advantage of the temporary gap in the crowd, he urged The Colonel back into the street and cantered in the carriage's wake for a few blocks. But when he came to Bridge Street he turned left down the slanting cobbles to the riverfront. Almost to the dockyards, he stopped at an undistinguished door under a battered, carved wooden sign without gilding or decoration.

He had heard about The Black Oak Tavern from Richard and his friends. More than a hundred years old, it crouched next to the dockyard, outwardly no different from many of the grimy warehouses. Inside, there was said to be as warm a glow as could reasonably be anticipated, if one was known to be a friend of Erin. They had given him a token to show to the proprietor, to demonstrate that he was no Dublin Castle spy.

Billy dismounted and handed a penny to the third urchin who approached, who looked slightly trustworthier than the rest. He told the child to hold The Colonel until he found his bearings.

"And mind," he added, "if you keep him dry and find him some oats, there will be more in it for you when I come out." The boy, wearing smelly, muddy rags, was perhaps ten. He smiled brightly as he accepted the coin. "Yes, Squire, I'll surely take care of him, beauty that he is."

The door was heavy, strapped and studded with iron. The doorway was low, its frame and sill considerably worn from, Billy supposed, a hundred years of staggering drunks rioting and scuffling with each other. A man stumbled out and stopped to urinate in the street. Billy stooped and walked inside, to be greeted by the reek of tobacco smoke. Through the smudge he saw candles, a large number of small wooden tables and chairs, and a polished, dark wood bar. Behind the bar, a portly, balding man stood in a leather apron, puffing on a long clay pipe and eyeing him alertly.

The floor was surfaced with cut stone covered by crushed and soggy rushes. A drain, perhaps a foot wide and several inches deep and apparently lined with brick, traversed the floor from the front corner on his left to the opposite corner in the back, where it became lost in the dimness and vanished under the wall. A murky, smelly rivulet coursed steadily through it.

Conversation ceased for a moment as Billy entered the room, and he was aware of many eyes on him, some suspicious and speculating, some indifferent, some curious and some instantly hostile. By the time he reached the bar, he had a companion at each side, and he felt the tiniest prick of a sharp blade at his kidneys.

A quiet voice filled with menace remarked into his left ear, "We've seen that you're a stranger in our fine town, I think, in your fine hat and with your even finer horse. Perhaps you'd like to let us know just how you blundered into this place, my fine gentleman." His new companion on the other side smiled sideways at him, and clapped him on the back, hard.

Billy said, "I'm glad to see that Dublin's legendary hospitality has not been a lie, my friends. I'm here from upcountry, and I expect you may know friends of mine named FitzHugh, from near DeClare." While they digested this, Billy spoke to the barkeep. "A tankard for my new friends and one for me, if you please."

He laid two coins onto the counter, one a shilling and the other a medallion whose meticulously inscribed runes he could not read, but which exerted a truly magical influence on the three men around him, all of whom immediately stared at Billy, respect replacing murderous intent. The point in his back was removed.

The two guardians picked up their beer and saluted Billy and the bartender before emptying the mugs with remarkable speed. Oddly, they exhibited no further interest in him and presently returned to the table where they had been seated before his entrance, as if the whole scene had never happened at all.

Billy retrieved the medallion, saying, "It is a curious thing, is it not, that one might find mortal danger so easily in such a civilized place as Dublin?"

The barkeep returned his look without much interest, scraping the remnants of a meat pie into a pot simmering over the fireplace at the end of the counter. "If you're from the country, you'd not maybe know that there are several hundred or more of the English gentry within a few hundred yards of here who'd as soon run you through or pistol your head off as say good morning, then."

"Perhaps some of us who are not raised in the ways of the English gentle folk, and aren't quite quick enough to see their true superiority on an instant, are becoming somewhat wary of well-dressed gents coming to this peaceful place."

Billy leaned forward. "And do you now and then see aught of a big, tall Englishman with yellow hair and fancy clothes and a way about him to grate your teeth even more than most?"

The bar man looked back with speculative eyes. "And what if I did remember a fellow like that, now? Also a friend of yours, perhaps?"

Billy slipped a silver crown onto the counter and nodded.

"I'd be grateful if you'd be able to find out where his lodgings and his ladies are, discreetly, you understand. His name is Stoatfester, Edward Stoatfester. He'd be the fellow who knocked me off my horse from behind and kicked out several of my back teeth in the dark. He fancies himself a fine hand with a big pistol."

The other man nodded, slowly. "I'll keep your description in mind, then, for when I see you next." The coin was gone and the man served another patron, then returned.

He spoke softly, "I'd not want to lose a friendly customer, now, but you'd likely save yourself silver if you'd inquire at The Eagle Tavern, up near the Castle. By all accounts, that's where the Hellfire Club bucks meet, before they go off to Montpelier Hill."

"I'll not want to inquire visibly there, myself. Someone would likely report such an inquiry coming from a stranger. This particular gent's not worth glorifying with a duel, although it would be a favor to the world to put a ball in his chest. Unless my information is sadly astray, he'd likely be wanting to outdo the highborn rakes, just to prove something. I shan't be part of his proof, now, no fear; there are better careers for a man than that."

The taverner met his eyes. "Then he'd be a right bad 'un. We hear those rich lads get into things a mite more deeply than just burning down Catholic churches. There's rumors that the Earl of Rosse and his high placed friends do the black masses and other evil things up there." He crossed himself.

Billy nodded.

"So I have heard, even in the hilly wilds."

He finished his dark beer and had another, along with a meat pie, before he went outside. The urchin knuckled his forehead in a rough salute and ran off to retrieve The Colonel from the stable. It was raining again. A squad of scarlet soldiers behind a sergeant marched in close order and more or less in step, down the right side of the street. They were keeping a safe distance from the building overhangs. They looked neither left nor right, and the few passers-by ignored them.

He gave the boy another penny for stabling The Colonel, who seemed dry and content. He buttoned his oilskin cloak more securely around his neck and walked the horse up the shiny cobbles, away from the dark and silent river.

The inn he headed for was one his father had recommended. There was a small fire crackling in a large stone fireplace in his room, and his bed looked deep and comfortable. The place was somewhat out of the way, but quieter than most, and he had paid a little more for privacy. He pulled off his boots and hung the dripping cloak and the rest of his clothes near the door. He fell back on the bed and immediately the face of the woman in the coach came to his mind.

He blew out the candle. His last thought was, *You'll not be finding the likes of her in The Black Oak or The Brazen Head, now, will you, Billy-me-boy?*

*****

As it turned out, they met accidentally, at the top of the steps of the Four Courts. His father's colleague had suggested he spend several weeks becoming familiar with the proceedings. At the trial Billy had been observing, the judge and one of the barristers of the Court of Common Pleas had suddenly adjourned to duel.

From his spot at the back, Billy had heard the judge brag loudly to the clerk that during his hunting the previous week, he had bagged three dozen hares before breakfast. One of the barristers, overly fond of his own wit, had sniffed audibly and giggled, braying, "I don't doubt it, your Lordship, but you must have fired at your wig, har har har har har."

A flung glove sufficed for words, and the judge made an adjournment. The onlookers straggled from the courtroom into the hall, and in a few minutes, with their seconds racing behind, the opponents dashed out through the door, jostling through the usual ragged and smelly crowd of civilians in their haste.

A slender figure wearing a broad-brimmed, floppy straw hat trimmed with green ribbons and pink roses was standing near Billy while he watched, amazed, as the duelists charged through the crowd. She was thrown against him and he flung an arm out and kept the woman from tumbling down the stone steps after them, into the squalor of the sunken lane called Hell. He then realized, with an involuntary intake of breath, that he had rescued the owner of the face from the coach.

She blushed prettily and curtsied slightly, having languorously extracted herself from his arms.

"I thank you, Sir, for keeping me from falling into Hell."

Billy swept off his hat.

"Milady, it would appear that some members of the High Courts in Dublin are in need of learning manners. Perhaps I can assist you to your destination, and on the way you can help me recover my wits, scattered by the presence of such stunning beauty."

"La, m'sieu, you are flattery itself."

The green eyes were boldness itself.

He took advantage of the situation and introduced himself.

She curtsied. "I am Mary Catherine Carlisle." She hesitated briefly and then said, "I cannot allow you to escort me home in a cab without knowing you, but perhaps you would be so good as to call on me at my house in the early afternoon some day, and we might get better acquainted over tea?"

"Milady, you may depend upon it that I will accept your kind invitation. What day would be most convenient for you?"

"I may be in, in the afternoon, tomorrow."

Billy looked at her tailored navy silk jacket, which emphasized a waist small enough, he thought, for his two hands to encircle. Her lace-edged wrap tucked modestly into the top of her gown, but enough tender pale skin gleamed through to attract his eyes like a compass needle. With a conscious effort, he met her amused gaze.

Their eyes locked, and the clamor, stench and chaos surrounding them vanished instantaneously. Without glancing away, he gestured at the dismal, wet, deeply sunken lane. Arches partly covered it, increasing the gloom, and it led west from Christ Church into the Courts, which were located in the ancient Dean's House. He spoke quietly.

"Pray, forgive me for asking, Miss Carlisle, but why would your immaculate self descend through this squalor to attend the court? It cannot be possible that you are a petitioner."

She looked about her, a secretive smile at the corners of her mouth, "Out of boredom, I sometimes come to the Courts to amuse myself at the foolish passions of men. You see, here in Hell there are also many shops with amusing playthings, and places for the court's business to be conducted outside of court. It is an...exciting place, a place with secrets, do you not think?"

Billy replied, with quiet conviction, "I would have imagined you'd see as much of the secret passions of men as your heart ever desired, without ever having to seek it in Hell Lane and the Four Courts of Dublin, milady."

Then he smiled into her eyes, "I must admit, though, that it is indeed the proper place for many lawyers to rent their apartments."

She laughed, a little breathlessly, and her slender body shuddered, a little quick motion like an eel swimming. "My dear Mr. Smithyman, you are very quick with your tongue, are you not?"

"Surely, I can usually rise to the occasion when required, milady. But you must allow me to escort you to find a cab. I insist."

At his words, she turned her face quickly away for a moment, but took his arm with a warm hand. He pushed forcefully down the stairs and along the sunken lane, striking out with his fist once or twice at the more impetuous beggars.

They emerged finally from under the last arch and came out into the yard of Christ Church.

He hailed a sedan chair for her from several waiting in front of the Cross Keys Tavern. Its crew of two picked up the handles and dashed toward them through the throng, knocking down two or three drunks. He helped her inside and closed the door, and she leaned out through the window, pointing to the Tavern.

"That place," she said, "used to be the meeting house of the Charitable Music Society, but they now prefer the Bull's Head," and sang a few lines as the cab dashed away, her hand gaily waving.

"Twas in those happy, halcyon, merry days,

That old Tom Ryan liv'd at the Cross Keys."

He bowed in return, smiling broadly, as the crowd swallowed up the cab. *I wonder whether the substance is made of the same stuff as that delightful wrapping.*

Billy had had enough of Dublin justice for the day, and mused about whether he ought to return to The Black Oak to check for news of Stoatfester. Lost in memories of his encounter with Mary Catherine Carlisle, he began to stroll slowly.

Sudden angry shouts and a loud, profane exclamation of disgust from a few yards in front startled him. He looked up to see a cascade of urine thrown from the second floor splash from the shoulders of a pedestrian who had refused to hire a cab. Shrieks of raucous laughter ensued from the amused crowd loitering in front of the tavern.

He immediately waved a cab over, determined to avoid a similar dousing. *First, however, I'd better ride back to my room and change from my court attire. It attracts entirely the wrong attention in Dublin.* He also was becoming aware of a certain feeling in his belly.

In his room, he gobbled down a cold squab, cheese with a pickle, and a half loaf of bread with a large ale. Having not eaten since breakfast, he didn't even wait for the tray to be set down. Waving one of the small squab legs, he joked with the maid who had delivered it to his room, "It's to reduce the chance that I might be tempted to purchase food nearer the waterfront, where I have heard that the rats disguise themselves as grey rabbits."

She giggled, shivering appreciatively in mock horror, and pressing one hot, thinly clad hip against his arm as she laid the platter on the little study table in front of the window.

My God, what a lecher I am becoming! I'd best purchase some armor soon for Mr. Cockerel, or I might be bringing a very nasty present home to

Meghan, from Dublin. He shook his head at himself and savaged the fowl. His appetite was very strong.

He left tuppence for the girl, knowing it was extravagant, but knowing also that it might help warm his bed, if not that night, then some other. He decided not to take The Colonel down to the Black Oak again, reflecting that by all logic the magnificent beast ought to have been stolen away during that first visit. Best not to press one's luck too hard. Also, best not to be so conspicuous down near the docks.

He paid the cab and moved quickly into the Black Oak. "A monstrous down-pour is it not?" he asked the barkeep, shedding his streaming hat and cloak. There was no reception committee escorting him to the bar this time.

After his second tankard of the black, still beer, and half an hour of discreetly assessing the temper of the evening, he slid a shilling into partial view and inquired about Stoatfester's whereabouts.

The man leaned towards him and said, "Your timing is good, Squire. He and the Hellfire Club are supposed to be riding off to Montpelier tonight in an hour or two, after they warm up enough. They're at The Eagle now, but they won't be there too much longer, since the cabbies tell me they've been there since twelve noon. It's the night of their weekly gallop."

Billy nodded his thanks. He decided that there was not enough time to get to his inn and have The Colonel saddled up, so he bid the bartender goodnight and walked up to Cork Hill. He found a darkened vantage point somewhat out of the way in the doorway of the Stationers' Hall. There, he could watch the comings and goings from The Eagle inconspicuously, after he persuaded the whores, children and thieves strutting or sneaking about to leave him alone. Billy dispensed a liberal shower of copper evenly and genially to the beggars approaching him, and he felt less conspicuous once the recipients had dashed off to bet at the nearby Cockpit Royal. He amused himself by reading the faded poster on the wall for the twelfth time:

> At the Stationers' Hall, in a warm room with a good fire, from nine in the morning to eight of the evening, is exhibited a painting by Raphael, and several fleas tied by gold chains.

Eventually most of the other street dwellers began to lose interest in his presence and seek shelter, leaving him to his single-minded focus on the entrance to The Eagle.

Suddenly, inspired by the seventh cold rivulet down his neck, he realized that if he hired one of the cabs waiting outside the door to The Eagle, he could wait in comfort and then follow his quarry, considering the possibilities at his leisure.

After a long wait, Billy glimpsed a large, familiar shape emerging from the pub, clad entirely in pale blue embroidered silk, flinging a cloak about his shoulders.

He said to the driver, "The big, blue boy there is the one I'd like to follow, but I expect most of them are off to the same place."

"Surely, and that'd be the Hellfire Club, an' a fairly good turnout it is tonight, considering the rain."

"Do you know well the usual way they go to Montpelier Hill, then?"

The driver nodded. "It's surely not a place I'd be going without business, though."

Billy said, "Let us get on our way there at a walking pace, now. When they overtake us, you can keep them in sight, but not too close. I'd not want to go in, but to stop there only for a moment and then return to my lodgings."

The driver shrugged and touched his hat, "It's your coin, Squire."

Billy watched the dark buildings go by for a time, thoughtfully eyeing the arrangement of the streets and alleys they passed.

In half an hour, they heard a troop of pounding hooves overtaking them. The driver called down, "Likely that's them, Squire. I'll pull aside a bit here."

Twenty or thirty men on horses galloped hard by, shaking the ground with their passage, long cloaks billowing back to reveal the gaily-colored silk plumage underneath. The cab resumed its progress at a faster pace.

After a quarter of an hour the driver called, "Not too far now."

They stopped at the iron-gated entrance to a long driveway, shadowed by twin rows of poplars. Beyond it, on a small rise, stood a massive brick house with ten or twelve chimneys. Dozens of windows glimmering with sparks of candlelight appeared for a moment, and then faded rapidly in the returning fog. Billy had a brief impression of swirling menace from the place, and heard a sound of low grumbling or muttering, punctuated by faint, high screams of laughter and muffled shouting.

Billy leaned out of the door and said softly, "An evil place, I think, driver. Let us return to the warm lights of Dublin."

"Warmer, I'd hazard, than anywhere in that place."

Close by them, as they turned, an insane yipping and shrieking came to them through the fog. The driver exclaimed in fear and the horses jerked.

Billy called out, "You're not from the country now, are you driver? That's just a fox family catching a rabbit, not the Antichrist himself. Not to worry."

The driver laughed shortly. "Squire, I was born in the shadow of the Castle. This is the closest I've been to the country in my entire life and if that's the kind of things go on out here, I'd just as soon stay in Dublin."

As daylight brightened his window, the singsong, hoarse call of the peat-seller's cart passing outside brought Billy to lazy awareness of the new day.

"Buy the dry turf, buy turf, buy the dry turf! Here's the dry bog-a-wood—here's the chips to light the fire, maids!"

He ordered breakfast and a large pot of coffee. He poured a cup for himself and ruminated on the night's events. The elements of a plan began to come together.

I'll get Richard's help. His friends can ensure that we are not interrupted. This will work.

He rose and put his shoes out for polishing and his hat for brushing. He checked that his white linen shirt, his breeches and his best bottle green wool coat and contrasting lemon-colored waistcoat embroidered with silver were spotless and pressed.

He sat at his desk, where his previous week's notes about law had accumulated in a neat pile. He picked up and examined one of the unused quills of the supply that he had ordered to be included in his rental fee, cut it and then scratched out two pages to Richard. Folding it inside another blank sheet, he closed and sealed the letter with wax. He would give it to the innkeeper on his way out to visit the Carlisle woman. He felt his pulse speed up slightly.

I'll have to visit the barber for a shave and for my usual hairdressing. No, it would have to be a bit more particular today—Damn!—No wig!

He was a little rueful, remembering his previous extreme reluctance to spend a pound or more on such a thing.

"By God," he'd reasoned, looking in the haberdasher's window, "the same amount might feed me steak and beer for nearly a month, and when a good brushing and powdering and a new ribbon in back seem to suffice under most circumstances...."

He shook his head. In any case, there is no time to find a decent wig and get it fitted in the next three hours. Brushing and powdering would have to suffice.

His hat and shoes were returned. He checked his supply of money.

It would not do to ride The Colonel up to the Carlisle's door, although he badly needs some exercise. This isn't the country. I'll have to hire a hackney. A gift? No, too presumptuous, on first introductions.

He took a deep breath. Time to go.

Three hours later he was presenting himself to the butler at the doors of an imposing manor.

"Mr. William Smithyman, Esquire, is it? And what would be your business at Carlisle House, then, ...sir?"

There was a distinct pause before the last word.

Billy replied, mildly, "I'm here at the invitation of Miss Carlisle, who asked me to call on her this afternoon."

The servant motioned him into the anteroom behind, locked and bolted the entrance, and vanished through a tall oak door on the left, which exactly matched one on the right.

Billy looked about. *This room alone is half the size of our farmhouse.*

The walls above the oak wainscoting were plastered and painted a pale sky blue. The walls to left and right held crossed sets of antique halberds and pikes. A red and black heraldic banner with the dust of ages on it trailed down the wall in front of him like old blood.

A plaster medallion spread itself across the twelve-foot ceiling like an octopus, and an iron chandelier hung from its center. Neither feature provided any sense of elegance to the room. In fact, the ironwork suggested a certain menace to those standing beneath. Billy shook his head at the fancy. A grim room, entirely, apparently designed more for defense than welcome.

Billy heard the heavy tread of the servant returning. The door opened and he was motioned into the house.

"Miss Carlisle will receive you in the garden," Billy was informed. He removed his hat and followed to an improbably bright, airy and green sunroom filled with plants, glassed in by hundreds of leaded panes at the rear of the house.

Mary sat, or rather perched on a tiny upholstered chair. She offered her hand to him and he bowed over it, brushing its back briefly and gently with his lips.

"La, William Smithyman, you are a large one, aren't you now?"

It was true; Billy's bulk seemed to fill the space between the greenery. He shrugged. "God has made me the way I am, but a healthy life in the country has helped, my lady."

Her eyes traveled frankly over him from head to toe and back as he looked about for a chair.

"Please sit, William," she demanded, gesturing to a chair.

Billy shook his head. "I expect that that poor chair is not made of stuff that would appreciate the weight of a woodcutter, Miss Carlisle. I would not crush your furniture on my first visit."

"A woodcutter!" She laughed huskily. "And a barrister too, I warrant, even if you don't live in Hell. What other talents lie hidden, sire?"

He eyed her steadily, and she returned his gaze. "I would not bore thee now with my ambitions, Miss Carlisle."

Her mood seemed to change, abruptly. She waved her hand impatiently, imperiously. "Please call me Mary, William. False modesty is not becoming in a young man, any more than braggadocio. I am sure I am not the first to tell you that."

Without a pause, she continued on, "I think it is a fine day to see the Earl of Meath's Liberties yielded to the Mayor, is it not?"

Billy had no idea what she was talking about, and tilted his head inquiringly. Her assertiveness bemused and entertained him.

Without waiting for an answer, she tugged on a bell cord. A servant appeared so quickly that Billy suspected he must have been actually within earshot.

Mary said, "Henry, Mr. Smithyman and I require the small carriage for the afternoon. Please be so good as to ask Franklin to bring it to the front for us, please."

Henry merely bowed and withdrew wordlessly, surprising Billy immensely. He looked at her. "Do your parents not restrict your comings and goings with strangers?"

She laughed briefly and extended her hand for him to help her to her feet. She brushed the daffodil-yellow silk of her hooped petticoats into order. Straightening, with a hint of that eel-like motion he had seen before, she said with a smile, "Do I look a mere girl then? Actually, William, through a twist of fate in the form of an East Indiaman, which was lost with all hands, including my parents, in the great typhoon of '32, I became an orphan at the age of 22. I own this house. So it is, indeed, no-one's prerogative to indicate when I might come or go."

Billy blinked at her speechlessly, and then offered his arm. "Milady, I am very sorry to hear of your bereavements. I am your devoted servant." She dimpled primly and answered, "Indeed you are, my sweet William, indeed you are," as they proceeded to the carriage.

Once they were settled, the carriage moved off to southwest Dublin at an easy pace. Billy remarked, "The first time I saw you, you were in this carriage, going like fury down Thomas Street. You looked to be enjoying yourself."

"And where were you, then?"

"I was the man on the large roan stallion who was forced to stand aside or be run down."

She giggled, "I was in a hurry and didn't want to be late for an engagement. And were you very angry with me?"

Billy nodded, "Yes, and I became on the instant determined to find you, to tell you how inconsiderate you were."

She put on a solemn look. "And when will you tell me this?"

"When the time is right, Mary Catherine. And since we are now introduced, you may call me Billy, if you choose."

The journey took nearly an hour through the crowded streets. For most of it, she entertained Billy with her account of the history of this bit of Dublin.

"I have gone to watch this affair since I was a child. It's Dublin's own traditional holiday, rather raucous and undisciplined, I'm afraid. The property was the possession of the Great Abbey of Thomas Court but was seized by Henry VIII and deeded to his Chancellor, William Brabazon.

"The Lord Mayor of Dublin has no jurisdiction here, except by permission of Brabazon's descendent, the Earl of Meath, and each third year this day, on the first of August, we celebrate the defense and opening of the boundaries of the Earl's Liberties."

They joined a short line of other carriages and came to a halt, still some distance from where the annual ceremony was to occur. The crowd was large and lively, although the Lord Mayor's party and sword bearer were not yet in view.

Mary untied the ribbon that secured her small hat and removed it. Then she leaned quickly across Billy and peered ahead through his window to see the Gates, her shining, scented hair instantly filling his awareness.

The carriage swayed with her movement. She was leaning on the window frame with her left hand and she had to balance herself against the gentle motion. She placed her right palm firmly on the spot where his breeches were already tight. Suddenly, they became mercilessly snug. She neither apologized nor withdrew her hand.

She said, a little breathlessly, "I don't think...It's very hard...Can we see from here? What do you...?"

Billy pulled the curtains shut on the carriage.

The rattle of drums brought their attention briefly back to Thomas Street.

"Billy!" she gasped. "OH!...It's...it's happening! Oh! We must see!" Billy quickly covered her open mouth with his.

On the return trip, it was dark. She peeked out and discovered a bright silver moonlight, then latched the soft leather screen partly up at the front, so that the glow gently penetrated the cab's still private interior.

She imperiously handed him her hairbrush, saying, "La, you have undone me, Billy Smithyman, now you must repair the damage, *n'est-ce pas*? One hundred strokes each side is what must be done, sir." She sat back and looked at him.

He reached up with the brush in his left hand and began. His eyes took in the perfect, moonlit globes swaying gently beside him, pale with their dark, raised centers. Then, his right hand moved across to caress as well, to weigh and lift the full softnesses and to gently compress the hardening nipples in the web between his fingers and thumb.

She squealed and slapped his hand away from her breasts, then grasped it with both her hands and squeezed it tight against her left breast for a moment, then released it again. His hand fell to her lap and continued its travels.

"I am all confounded, sire, and you are speechless!"

"With desire, my Mary, speechless with desire, you see."

"I see it very well indeed, there, sir. You ought to mind its manners more, do you not think? But no, I can see it has a head of its own, as it is with all men!"

He kissed her again, lingeringly, and their tongues danced and probed, striking urgent sparks of desire. His hand made her gasp, and quiver, and soon she moved to straddle him again.

When they arrived back at Carlisle House she said, "I will have Franklin drive you home, Billy, but you may not come in tonight, you know."

He grinned at her. "I may be going back upcountry within a week. Do I dare call again?"

She tilted her head on that exquisitely slender neck and considered for a moment, finger to chin.

"There is an opening in my calendar next week, Billy. The famous Mr. Handel is leading the first performance of his latest opera to be held outside London. It will be at the Tailors' Hall. You may escort me to it, if you wish. Thursday, I believe it is. Until then, M'sieu, and thank you for the Liberties today!"

He bowed and kissed her hand. "The pleasure was fully mine, Mary. I am very grateful for the opportunity to see such an important event in your company next week."

Now fully repaired and graceful, she rapped on the ceiling, and the driver opened the door and helped her descend,

Billy fell asleep more than once during the long return cab ride. Finally alone in his room, Billy flung himself on the bed fully clothed, and quickly sank into an exhausted slumber.

56

Richard's letter arrived two days later. He was required on the farm and would be delayed one week further.

Billy wrote to Meghan, a long, rambling letter that spoke of his attendance at the law court and about the "evils of the present establishment, which encourage only the most venal to power in Dublin since there is no real power there at all, only influence leading to meaningless government posts. These posts are generally given to individuals who prostrate themselves in the most disgustingly obsequious manner to the government. The real influence lies in London.

"The courts are instructive, and there is some witty back-and-forth. I wonder, my dearest, that any judges or barristers remain alive from the frequent duels with pistols, although, truly, it is probably because they are far better with words than weapons. I have only a few more duties to discharge here and I shall be returning after they have been completed. I hope you and your family are well and happy and remain your most affectionate and loving, if uninfluential, servant."

As he sanded the ink dry and blew the page clean, a vivid image from the Carlisle carriage filled his mind and he felt a tiny tweak of conscience, dismissing it almost instantly. *Dublin is not upcountry. Customs are different between here and there, and she probably knows about how the maids here behave, I'm sure, without me being such a brute as to remind her.*

A week later, after Richard arrived, he and Billy had scouted the route between The Eagle and the Earl of Rosse's house several times, and now waited patiently in the shadows of the dark and nearly deserted street they had picked.

Richard had been gloomy and snappish when he and Billy first surveyed the site.

"Billy, there are sixty or seventy starving Irish in every one of the little houses on all of these streets. Each room on every floor here has ten or twelve people living in it, like animals. Why don't we just kill the dirty bastard and be done with it? He and his kind have never had any mercy for the Irish, or with you either."

But when Billy announced the crowning touch of his plan, Richard had laughed out loud.

"Tis true, Billy, you are a genius! That will surely set him and the Hellfire Club at odds one with another for quite a time, I'd wager."

Billy had selected the spot carefully, and they had done a small amount of work to conceal their intentions. Richard had visited those living nearby, to mute their curiosity and ensure against interruptions. Then he had hired a groom who had contrived to see that Stoatfester's horse suddenly went lame on the appointed night. This delayed his departure from The Eagle and forced him to hire a cab for the weekly outing to Montpelier, a cab with a carefully selected driver.

Eventually the cab appeared, going at speed. The shocking appearance of a heavy cable rising suddenly from the cracks between the stone pavers and stretching across the road at eye height made the horse rear in fright as the cab careened to a grinding stop and almost turned over.

By the time Stoatfester, cursing the driver, had regained his seat in the hackney, two cocked pistols were at the windows and the masked assailants roughly pulled him out.

In a few swift movements, eerily silent except for muffled shrieks of rage and fright from Stoatfester, he was gagged and blindfolded and his hands lashed tightly to his sides. His breeches were slashed and pulled to his ankles.

Around his neck, they hung a crude but very legible sign, saying simply, "Papist-Lover," in English and Gaelic. They slung a rope loop under his arms and over a tree limb and hoisted him eight feet from the ground. It was all accomplished in a few minutes. After they had secured the rope end, they paused for a moment, surveying their kicking handiwork. Then, after a silent handshake, accompanied by the widest of smiles, Richard and Billy parted and the cab clattered off, vanishing into the night.

Stoatfester twirled in the darkness like a gigantic yellow chrysalis, his groaning top encased in tailored silk, his writhing, jerking, naked bottom half apparently struggling to emerge from its cocoon above. A large, interested and quite vocal group had gathered by the time the Constabulary appeared to cut him down, He was half-mad with frustration and the exquisite torture of his confinement by that time, and it did not the slightest good to see that three of his Montpelier companions had by then happened along, also late for the festivities, and thoroughly entertained by the sight of him thus entangled.

*****

Handel's new opera *Alcina* had not yet played anywhere outside London's new and fashionable Covent Garden, and so a glittering crowd of Ireland's elite had gathered at the Tailors' Hall. Mary and Billy sat near to several of her relatives from Ulster, who were icily polite to him and poisonously so to her. She flashed her eyes at him and with studied casualness verbally skewered the authors of several not very subtle remarks. They eventually left her alone, and a chilly silence surrounded the couple.

This suited Billy, for he found he enjoyed opera, and Mary's warm hand kept his attention close by. She was wearing a pale aqua silk gown without hoops and a velvet jacket. She showed him the printed invitation, placing one polished fingernail on a line at the bottom of the card.

She said, *sotto voce*, glancing at his lap, "As you can see, Billy, for reasons of space, the ladies are required to leave their hoops at home, and gentlemen are also requested not to wear their swords. But yours, I fancy, is still with you. Are you not a gentleman, then, Billy?"

Billy gazed at her admiringly. A huge, square-cut emerald hung from a gold chain deep between her breasts. He knew it shocked all the Anglo power structure, for green was the color of old Ireland. It was also well known that she had acquired the gem from a lover, who had himself brought it back from India. This in turn enraged the Protestant Irish business classes, who were reminded that imported, low-cost, high-quality Indian cotton cloth was ruining their own textile profits. The Dublin weavers in particular were being reduced to penury.

The Catholic Irish, of course, could only stare at the flaunted wealth and swallow their own envy and hate. When Billy commented on the beauty of the gem and the glory of its situation, she winked at him.

Now, she pointed her folded fan down at the conductor. "You would scarcely credit it, Billy, but the Opera has seen such enthusiasm in London these past several seasons that Mr. Handel there has practically caused the Royal Family to split apart."

Billy's attention was not fully on her words. He responded politely, "Oh, really?" His left hand gently caressed her warm right thigh.

"Yes," she said, after a sharp glance to see if he were paying attention, "The King and Queen and Princess Royal rather fancy Mr. Handel, you see. But the Prince of Wales, some say merely to spite his father, has gathered much of the remaining nobility to attend a competitor's opera house. There have been many insults exchanged, and even some rioting."

Billy smiled. "It does seem improbable that entertainments should cause such strife, does it not?"

"My friends write me that it has cost Handel nearly ten thousand pounds and that he is losing interest in writing operas altogether! He was unable to hire Farinelli away this past season, who has been the toast of London in years past.

"Farinelli," she added with a direct look, in answer to his inquiry, "is an Italian castrato who, it is said, has the voice of the ages."

Billy gaped a bit, then shook his head, "If I understand you properly, he sings well because he is..." Her hand gently closed, "Yes, sweet William, he has none of these."

"I would not choose such a career, I think."

Mary giggled. "No, you have different talents, if I'm any judge."

"And does the Opera come often to Dublin, then?"

She shook her head, "No, hardly ever, but we hear that Mr. Handel was invited here to perform *Alcina* because the Lord Lieutenant wishes to curry favor with the King by allowing Handel to recoup some of his losses."

Billy looked at the packed, sparkling, Tailors' Hall. "Surely, this will help his fortune, then?"

Mary agreed, "If he can make ten or twelve performances in Dublin, he will be well recompensed."

She added, looking around, "And he should, if I'm any judge. There are more men here than I thought had any musical interest in all of Ireland, but I expect they've really come to see Maria La Sallé dance in her underclothing. Handel brought her from Paris and, some say, let her write several of the dance parts herself."

Billy laughed, quietly. "The Opera is a much livelier world than I could have imagined. Upcountry, few have any knowledge of these things."

She dimpled at him. "You are learning many things in Dublin, then, Billy?"

He nodded. Now his large fingers gently, lightly, brushed up and down the fine hairs on her slender forearm. She shivered, and a deep green flash came from her emerald in its soft cradle.

Hours later, as the carriage turned into the lane at Carlisle House, she looked at him, smiling but wet-eyed. "You are going home, then, Billy?"

He nodded. "I will write, if you wish, Mary. And perhaps some day I will be able to invite you to visit me and return the gifts you have given me this summer in Dublin. I shall certainly never forget you."

She looked at him for a long moment, and with her fingers traced the shape of his mouth and his ears, as if memorizing his face. "I shall always look forward to receiving such an invitation from you, Billy."

He helped her reassemble her clothing. Looking out the window, she suddenly said, in a different tone, "You should stop at Donnybrook Fair on your way back and get something nice for your sweet Meghan, whom you have said nothing at all about. I suggest, perhaps, a lovely stylish hat. An expensive hat." Then, before he could get over his amazement, she gathered her cloak and was gone.

*****

The Colonel greedily accepted a carrot from Meghan as Billy dismounted. She would not meet his eyes and lavished her attention on The Colonel while Billy carefully untied the box from his saddle and presented it to her with a brief bow. He watched her face as she fumbled with the strings. Her smile was tremulous, but her face lit with pleasure as she caught sight of the hat within. She turned to him, at last, and he enfolded her and crushed her to him.

They walked, fingers interlaced, and he could still feel her nervousness. They sat on the crude bench that Billy had constructed, where they had a panorama that extended almost to Dublin. She said, "Have ye then come back from Dublin just to say farewell, Billy?"

He began to reply, but she went on. "I hear that the Dublin maids are very fair and generous with their favors."

Billy removed his hat and brushed off some dust. "Would I be bringing you a hat then, if I were saying goodbye?"

"Aye, ye would, if you wanted to let me down gentle. You're not a cruel man, Billy."

He put his hat aside and reached for her hand. "You know I would marry thee, Meghan McOrmond, but..."

"But do not ask me, Billy," she interrupted, "because we both have our fates. Oh!" She burst into tears. "What is the use of love anyway, except for misery?"

He put his arm around her and she moved close. They sat wordless for many minutes, her head on his shoulder. At length, he ducked his head and sought her mouth and they clung with lips and arms. His right hand slowly traveled up and down her flank.

She pulled back, breathless, and looked at him. "And do they kiss as well as me in Dublin, Billy?"

He laughed and shook his head. "There are no kisses anywhere sweeter than thine, my Meghan."

"Your flattery has improved in Dublin as well, I see."

Billy pulled her closer and she laid her head on his chest. He buried his face in her hair. His hands were slowly roaming.

"I missed thee, my Irish maiden," he said.

"And a maiden I'll be remaining, Billy, unless we're married," she murmured, but without much force.

In a silence, she squeaked a little, and then whispered to him, her lips brushing his ear, "But it is true that there are many...yes...many"—she was blushing—"things to do, which do not compromise any principles." Billy shifted his position slightly, and she bit her lip with her lower teeth. After a moment her lips parted and then she said, breathlessly,

"Surely, Billy, the priest will not have to hear me confess aught of this joy, except my love for a heathen Protestant, do you think?"

CHAPTER SIX

Smithyman Farm

In June of 1737, the post-boy from DeClare rode up to Smithymans. Billy answered the door and received from him a letter addressed to William Smithyman, Esq., closed with the seal of the Royal Navy and his uncle's name. The boy was apologetic and anxious about the fee. "It's dear, I know, Squire, but it's such a heavy letter, clearly more than one page the minimum, and ye see, here, it come all the way from New York by London. The Navy pays only if it's to a Navy man."

He looked at Billy and diffidently asked, "But you ain't in the Navy, are you, Squire?" Billy shook his head and paid the rider his shilling and four, with a penny tip, sending him away relieved and in good spirits. Billy had a feeling about the letter. His heart was fluttering like the wings of a lovesick sparrow. He broke the wax seal. "My dear Nephew William," it began, and by the time Billy had finished it, he had to sit down.

His sister discovered him sitting on the doorstep holding the pages. "What is it, what is it?" she clamored. Billy showed her the cover, and got the predicable response, "What does Uncle Harold say? I want to see!"

Billy waved the parchment at her, his mind flying far, far away. "Well, he's been promoted to Captain, but more importantly, he wants me to follow him to America," he said, "to manage his new estate, in His Majesty's Province of New York."

"Oh, Billy," she breathed, "It's what you've always wanted, isn't it?" Then she startled him by bursting loudly into tears and running away upstairs, slamming the door so violently that his mother and his brother came running.

At their inquiring looks, he could only hand over the letter. As comprehension dawned, they hugged him, laughing and crying together. Eventually, breathless, he begged to be able to go and think for a time and they relaxed their grip on him. Swiftly he made his way to the barn, saddled up and rode hard for McOrmond's farm.

"Meghan is with the cattle," her mother said, looking at him curiously. Billy tipped his hat to her and rode back through the coarse green-leafed mounds of the potato fields to the rough pasture higher up. At last, he could see a figure with a mane of long brown hair streaming away in the wind atop a light colored dress, near the seep on the hillside where the shaggy cattle drank from a dugout. He saw her arms begin to wave gaily, and his heart began to pound. He galloped up to her and jumped down into her arms and they kissed with a great passion.

Presently, she disengaged herself and dreamily sat down under an elm, patting the space beside her. "You have something to tell me, or you wouldn't be trespassing on this good Irish land," she teased. He took a deep breath.

"Meghan McOrmond, I would have you as my wife, dear. My fortune is made."

She drew in a breath, but idly plucked at the grasses, and would not meet his eyes. "And where is that fortune made, Billy Smithyman?" she asked, softly. "Is it in Leinster, where you have many friends, and family who love you?"

Billy felt a sudden sickness sucking at his heart, as if he were drowning. "No, sweet, it is not; it is in America. My Uncle Harold has asked me to manage his estate."

Meghan shivered, as if the summer turf had turned to snow, and her tone was calm and distant. "Then you have already received my answer, Mr. Smithyman, and we have no more to discuss on that account."

"Meghan, you cannot expect..."

She interrupted, "I expect nothing, Billy." She turned her calm face, now wet with tears, to his, and raised her hand to his cheek. "But oh, my sweet William, you must do what you must, and go where you must, but I cannot, must not, will not leave here. Do not torment me more; you know it cannot be. Leave, now, and remember Meghan McOrmond, who once loved you, and hoped you once loved her."

He reached for her, then, but she leaped to her feet and smacked her right hand hard across his face, then fled up the hill, "Go!" she screamed, wild in her grief, "You don't need me. Go!"

He thought his heart would burst from the pain, and then for months he hoped it would, to end his misery, although a much cooler, quieter voice in his mind chided him for a fool, that he had known all along that she would not go.

*****

Richard gloomily kept him company to Dublin, where he would board a ship bound for Plymouth, then another for New York. Neither man was talkative, and heavy sighs marked much of their progress. A distance was growing between them as quickly as the distance from home. They agreed that they ought to spend a last night out on a tear in Dublin, but Billy was eager to be on his way.

The bout of maudlin drinking eventually grew boring and neither man felt particularly enthusiastic about even the most attractive tarts who plied them with smiles and bold caresses. Billy thought of calling on Mary Catherine, but realized that he would most likely interrupt another conquest and he was unwilling to be unwelcome.

The men bid each other a dispirited and perfunctory good bye at the wharf late at night. They slapped each other on the arms, then grasped hands and held each other's grip, unwilling to part.

Billy spoke, softly, apologetically, "I must put my things below, Richard. Thank you for coming with me."

Richard looked at the dark harbour, at the rigging of the little ship and muttered, "I still owe you a great debt, my friend, even though you are now leaving me no way to repay your kindness."

Billy stared at the wharf planking and kicked at a large splinter.

"I've told you, you owe me nothing, but perhaps we may yet be able to help each other. If I think of a way for you to help me, over there, perhaps you will consider it?"

Richard looked at him.

Billy said, "Ships leave here every week for America. It is not as far away as you think."

Richard barked a short laugh and his eyes slid away.

"Surely, and that is the very truth of it, although I remember a person saying some time ago that it was actually quite a ways off. But it is farther than Tara, my friend."

Billy smiled, "I will write, and you must write back."

His friend nodded, muttered, "Yes, it's just that my writing is not up to much, now, Billy," then embraced him again, quickly, and walked away. At the end of the wharf, he turned up into the town without looking back.

"We know not whom to trust, for we are already so hemmed in by both English and French, that hardly a hunting place is left; so that even if we should find a bear in a tree, there would immediately appear an owner of the land, to challenge the property."

—Red Head, Onondaga Chief

CHAPTER SEVEN
New York Province, September 1737

A discerning eye could easily distinguish the three tall masts and precisely squared cross yards of Captain Harold Holeybarth's current warship, His Britannic Majesty's 28-gun frigate, *Panther*, as she rode at anchor in a choppy New York harbour. They stood out amid a reasonably large forest of other spars belonging to merchantmen, with yards dangling at various slovenly civilian angles. *Panther*'s long pennant, signifying a Royal Navy ship on active duty, streamed out from the main masthead like a ribbon, courtesy of a bitterly cold and gusty, whining east wind that occasionally hummed a much lower note through the ship's rigging.

The Captain was entertaining, as Royal Navy Captains in distant waters often have to do, but for Harold Holeybarth, this was usually a genuine pleasure. He liked the company of important people and he liked to make decisions. It mattered little whether these involved naval actions and official diplomacy or business.

His duties this day included the best of both worlds. First, a scheduled luncheon conference with officials of the Province of New York, followed by a meeting with his nephew Billy Smithyman, recently arrived from Ireland at his request, to manage his new 15,000-acre estate on the northwest frontier of the province.

The meeting with his nephew would be doubly, even triply, gratifying. Captain Holeybarth had purchased the land for a trifling sum during his last passage from New York to London from the grateful and flattered, but mildly confused widow of the recently deceased Governor of the Province. This newfound wealth was enabling him to satisfy his beloved sister's wish that he help her family.

According to correspondence from Billy's father, that young man was continuing to show signs of intelligence, steady character and no little courage.

He had become a leader in the local arena; he had earned the trust of the downtrodden Irish and had shown considerable ability in devising reliable ways to both earn and retain money. He seemed ideally suited to a life on the frontier, being unattached, eager to succeed, and accustomed to hard labor.

Now that Billy had come aboard, Captain Holeybarth thought his brother-in-law's description not unrealistic. The two men sized up each other as they shook hands, bent over in the height-cramped Captain's cabin of HMS *Panther*.

Holeybarth was older by fifteen years, short of stature and thin of hair, portly and, as his nephew remembered from his visits to Ireland, somewhat given to pomposity. He gestured to his nephew to sit down, while apologizing for the Spartan furnishings.

"The Navy makes no allowance for comfort, of course, so these brass twelve-pounders will just have to do," he joked heavily as he patted one of the side-by-side cannons pointing out the magnificent stern windows, "until you make my fortune, at least, Nephew."

"I'm extremely honored by your confidence in me, Uncle. I believe that I should be able to amply repay it from the opportunities on the frontier."

"And what sort of opportunities would you be thinking exist there, Billy? I confess that, being a professional naval officer, I know virtually nothing about how to make money, except to board 'em in the smoke, seize 'em and turn 'em over to the Admiralty Court for sale."

Billy smiled. "You have become expert at that, sir. I believe there should be many ways to improve your investment, particularly from tenants and freehold settlement, but also by trade—buying things for one price and selling them for a higher price."

His uncle wrinkled his nose, and took a pinch of snuff from the blue, white and red enameled brass box on his desk. "And you have a talent for that, do you?"

Billy nodded. "I seem to, sir, and my serious intent is now to put it to work to make my fortune, along with your own."

Captain Holeybarth looked sharply at him. "One of the reasons I asked for you was that you are family, and thus to be trusted with responsibility for my money. I do sincerely hope that you accept that responsibility without compromise. This opportunity that beckons is primarily due to your mother's —my sister's—interventions on your family's behalf."

The shouts of the Lieutenant of Marines exercising his men penetrated the closed companionway, followed by the rhythmic stamping of a platoon of booted feet.

"I do not wish you to risk my holdings in any way, so I am content with a return of a few percent; let us say three, for argument's sake. You may keep one-tenth part of that return for yourself, in addition to the fee I mentioned. However, I shall be sharply critical and shall not hesitate to terminate our arrangement instantly if I form the impression that you are sacrificing my estate's interests for your own. Is that quite clear?"

Billy nodded solemnly, although he was smiling inside. "Quite clear, sir, I would not have accepted it under any other guise and I am certain you will never regret your decision."

Captain Holeybarth eyed him a moment longer, then called out for his steward, who instantly appeared and opened a battered-looking cabinet. He pulled out a bottle, uncorked it and filled two large glasses with red wine. Holeybarth raised his to the stern windows and eyed the contents, saying, "We took fifty cases of this Madeira off a smuggler near Florida last year. It is the best I have ever tasted. A toast, then, to the success of our mutual business opportunities, sir."

"To success, Uncle."

"So, now," Holeybarth chuckled with renewed joviality, "what else do you need to set yourself up in trade here, Nephew, besides a large amount of uncharted forest wilderness filled with savages?"

After a further hour, and a certain amount of back and forth about the particulars and the costs, the negotiations over what Billy thought he would need were completed.

Holeybarth rose and offered his hand, "Billy, I am very pleased and proud that my nephew should seem so capable in the area of trade, where I am, I confess, completely unable to decipher windward from leeward."

Billy glanced at him as he put his jacket on. "Uncle Hal, you are dissembling. I find that you are tolerably well acquainted with the necessaries of this business."

Captain Holeybarth replied, "Well, thank you, Nephew, you flatter me, of course. I must ask that you call upon Mrs. Holeybarth during your stay here and, as it is now autumn, I should like to insist that you stay in our house until the conditions are more suitable for beginning our endeavor, in the spring."

Billy smiled. "You are very kind, Uncle. I shall call upon Mrs. Holeybarth within a few days and I should be glad of the accommodation and the company, indeed."

The ship's boat left him ashore at the wharf. Tucked safely into his greatcoat, Billy held his uncle's note for two hundred pounds, several crude maps and letters patent, along with letters of introduction to provisioners in

New York and Albany. He also carried away a determination that, whatever his uncle required as a return on his investment, he would better it.

He paid the dissipated-looking hotelier for a further two days' lodging and meals, and half a dozen candles, then trotted upstairs to the tiny room. Here, a straw mattress greeted him on a sagging wooden bed, topped with a graying pillow and some coarse, frayed woolen blankets, surrounded by an unfinished wooden wall with one small, un-curtained window.

He was oblivious to the surroundings, but fell on the bed and spread out the maps on the floor. He weighted down one corner with the flintlock pistol his father had given him, and his father's voice came to him, "You are sensible enough to avoid duels, Billy, and this might save your life on the frontier." The other corners he held down with a brass candleholder and several coins.

Fifteen. Thousand. Acres.

By most standards, including his own experience in Ireland, this made his uncle a very great landholder. In forest alone, it must be worth thousands of pounds, and two hundred pounds a year was a damned good income at home.

In the flickering light, he traced the broad line of Hudson's River, from New York one hundred and fifty miles north to Albany. Then, just above Albany, his finger turned left and followed the narrower northwesterly line of the Mohawk River a short distance.

There, fifteen thousand acres was a small square inked neatly in red on the map. Its northern edge fronted on the Mohawk. He guessed the distance to be forty or fifty Irish miles upriver from where the Mohawk emptied into the Hudson. Near the square, a stream labeled Schohariekill joined the Mohawk.

In flowing script, across all the area to the north and west of Albany, the map-maker had inscribed *Iroquois Territory*. Much of that part was blank, except for a few sketchy rivers and small lakes, and the vast blue of a large lake at the very northwest margin.

A lightly dotted boundary line separated Iroquois from British territory on the map. Billy noted immediately that it placed his uncle's land grant a considerable distance inside the blank, Iroquois Territory section. He pondered this until he blew out the guttering candle, and for quite some time afterward, in the dark.

The next morning he brought some cold water back up from the leaky iron hand pump downstairs and shaved, inspecting his image in the cracked mirror beside the bed. His mother had given him a silver-mounted shaving kit, saying, "You must not look like a barbarian, even in the wilderness where there are no barbers, Billy," and fifty pounds to invest for himself. He strode out into the streets of New York to find his breakfast.

Another grubby inn half a block away provided a large, rather tough beefsteak and two fried eggs, along with a quarter loaf of fresh bread and a mug of small beer. He handed over one of the precious shillings he had brought with him and found the unshaven, smelly proprietor more than happy to fill his mug again.

"We be very, very short of coin, my fine sir, that be the truth. Everyone as brings me real metal gets an extra fill or two, gratis. I don't like the paper that the gov'nor issues, that I don't."

He leaned close and put a finger beside his bulbous nose. "There's some that say the King's Ministers is a-trying to keep the colonies in line by starvin' us for coin, but I bain't made up me mind about that just yet. I'd guess from the look and sound of you, you just came in from England, what you say, then, good sir?"

Billy was startled. He had heard that there was some restlessness in the colonies, but he'd not expected discussion as frank as this from a total stranger. He looked up at the repulsive hotelier thoughtfully. "Now why'd the King and his Ministers be thinking such a thing? Are the colonies trying to get out of line?"

"No, sir, no, sir," he mumbled, "I don't think they are, but, ye know, many's wonderin' why the real coin allus seems to wind up goin' back overseas, for a-buyin' the English goods, and none of it seems to come stay here for the t'baccy or wood or fur we send out. It is passing strange, d'ye not think?"

Billy finished his second beer and rose, collecting his coat.

"Now, sir, I did not know that, before this morning, so you have very much opened my eyes, and I thank you for it." He smiled at the proprietor. "I'll be doing my level best not to send any more of it overseas than I have to, myself."

The hotelier chuckled and rapped him hard on the shoulder by way of farewell.

The name and address he had been given by his uncle was Turnbottle's, on Blue Heron Street. Eventually he found it, set on shaky-looking piles along the muddy east bank of Hudson's River—an isolated, ramshackle, unpainted warehouse with a tilting, narrow wooden wharf extending into the river at its front. A half-drunken guard posted at the street door took his card, then barred his entry with an ancient matchlock blunderbuss, the smoking match leaving a pungent smell in the still air.

After some time, the proprietor came to the door. He was a small Englishman with an expressionless face and black hair. He was wearing a heavy, knee-length, light grey wool coat with royal blue lapels and cuffs, and no collar. It was unbuttoned, and Billy could see a shoulder strap and belt underneath supporting a heavy cutlass and a pistol.

He stopped at the doorway and looked at Billy through tiny, cold, black eyes. Then he said very rapidly, all the words running together, "Do we know each other, Mr. William Smithyman? It's not a name, nor, now that I see it, a face that I recognize."

"No, Goodman Turnbottle, you will not know me, but you may recognize my uncle's name on this letter of introduction, sir."

Turnbottle extended his hand and took the letter, feeling the heavy parchment and looking at the seal with appreciation. He said, again very quickly, "You may wait here for a minute, until I return."

Billy nodded, touching his hat. He walked a little to the side and stared at the river, which he knew Henry Hudson had discovered for the enterprising Dutch more than a century before. Even this early in the morning, dozens of heavily loaded small boats and several larger ones were edging back and forth upriver against the current, whose swirls and eddies were visible everywhere. Most had sails set to seize the faint advantage of the light morning breezes. Others had long sweeps dipping rhythmically to propel them as well. It was low tide, he realized, from the height of mud showing along the shore.

Dozens more boats of various sizes were coasting down river, a few making their way to the three neighboring wharves, the majority heading around the bottom of Manhattan Island to the sheltered East River docks. The blue water of the river looked smooth as a lawn, covered with tan, gray, and red-winged butterflies of various shades, shapes and sizes.

A steady bustle of wagons and porters moved bits and pieces up and down the piers, like ants on twigs.

The autumn sun was quite warm on his shoulders in the tiny breeze. Across the river, a handful of houses dotted the endless green of the forest. At one point, he thought he could see a notch in the tree line, where a road crested the hill. Curious, he tried to imagine just how much of the opposite shoreline fifteen thousand acres might include.

Six hundred and forty acres to a square mile, he mused silently, as an itchy spot appeared over his right eyebrow. Scratching it eventually produced the answer, which caused his eyes to widen. He slapped one breeches-clad knee and exclaimed aloud, "Damme! That must be near five miles of shoreline on the square!"

Again, he did the calculation, heart thumping now with excitement. He looked around to see if anyone had taken notice of his exclamation, and thought a third time about it, silently this time.

Damme! I can't possibly be seeing more than five miles either way on the river. Everything I can see to the north, then.

He remembered how small the square had appeared on the map. *God's blood, Billy, ye lucky lad, this is a big place. Wait until Richard hears about this.*

He laughed aloud, and then stopped, mid-chortle, struck by a sobering thought, almost as if Meghan had overheard and was talking to him. "That's one grand piece of land, to be sure, me Billy O'Boy, and all of it well inside the Iroquois Confederacy line. You might well wonder, ye grand eedjit, what the warriors be thinking about the Great White Father across the big water giving their land away to his white servants. Mayhap making a pound or two won't be quite as easy as eating your mother's biscuits, after all."

He turned back to the warehouse, and the guard motioned him inside with his smoking weapon, pointing him to a cluttered office. A half-wall of rough-sawn vertical plank with a shelf nailed on top separated it from the stacks, bales and barrels of merchandise.

Mr. Turnbottle was standing at a desk along one side, making notes with a quill in a ruled ledger. When he saw Billy, he waved him inside.

"Come in, young man, come in. I thought you'd gotten knocked on the head —it's not a genteel crowd out on the docks."

His quick manner of speech nearly made Billy laugh, but instead he smiled and said, "No, no-one attempted to scalp me this morning."

Turnbottle gave him a sharp glance. "Well don't think they aren't able to, up past Albany, where you'll be going, if this letter is any indication. Do you know what it's like up there?"

Billy shook his head. "Only from books and my imagination, sir."

Turnbottle stared briefly at him, then shook his head in turn. "Well, I'll be glad to sell you trade goods for cash, but until you've been there a season or two, I'll not advance you personal credit, except on your uncle's signature. I will buy furs, and if you are looking for an agent for settlers for your uncle's grant, I'd be happy to act in that capacity for you as well."

He barked out a high-pitched laugh, "And if some savage brings in your scalp, I'll buy that too, an' sell it to your uncle, hee hee hee hee!" He stopped laughing when he noticed William staring at his coat.

"Well, what is it, Smithyman, what are you staring at? Just like an Indian yourself, it seems, gaping at things in here."

"That appears to be a French army overcoat, sir."

"Yes, yes, what of it, Smithyman? Régiment de la Reine, I think. I get all kinds of items in trade here, and these seem more comfortable than others, and even wear well, too. This one fit, as well, which is more than most can say, in any army." He giggled again. Billy was still studying the coat.

"Why, what's the problem, man? We're not at war with France, you know, nor have been, since Queen Anne's war ended in, what, the year thirteen? That's twenty-five years gone, now."

"No, no, of course not. It's just that my father fought under Marlborough and it's strange to see a coat like that on an Englishman. We don't see them in Ireland, you understand."

Turnbottle chuckled again. "No, not after the Frenchies invaded t'help King James, I'd imagine not. But you're going to see some things on the frontier that will make a French army overcoat on the back of an English merchant seem passing normal, young Smithyman—assuming you live to see any of them, that is!"

Turnbottle's humorous mood darkened suddenly, and he launched a rapid verbal fuselage. "The masters of the Board of Trade in London are far away and often make rules which are strongly resented. Did you know they forbid us to trade at all with our neighbors in the French Indies, but force us to ship all our goods to England? Does that seem to be a rule that any trader would respect?

"They have rendered all the colonial men of substance into a parcel of smugglers and sharp practising, furtive scofflaws. At the same time, they have turned every King's officer and representative here into sad, compromised wretches, half-heartedly trying to enforce regulations that they know perfectly well are not in the colonies' interest at all.

"It makes all the Governor's requests, however sensible, into simple objects for argument and obstruction from every colonist, whether he be a farmer with grain to sell, a drunkard who wants rum to drink, or a trader, who would buy and sell both."

Billy absorbed all that information silently. Turnbottle's irritation at his ignorance seemed to increase.

"Well then, do you need any introductions to the Albany traders? I'll give you a better price than they will, if you get good quality furs direct to me, but it's more convenient to deal with them upriver, for some."

"Thank you kindly, sir. As you may know, my aunt by marriage is a De Vere, and I am given to understand her family is prominent in the trading community in Albany. I will be staying with her over the winter, so I may well have an entrée to Albany through her."

Turnbottle gave him another sharp glance. "Yes, I'd imagine that would be true. Why, in that case, have you come to me, instead of dealing with them?"

Billy hesitated a moment, then decided to open his mind. "Well, sir, to tell you the truth, I had rather hoped that I would be able to break new ground, so to speak. As you pointed out, buying here and selling here brings better prices than Albany, because it's less convenient.

"So, in similar fashion, I'm thinking there might be an opportunity for a trader to be closer to the fur coming from the Upper Lakes Indians, through Fort Oswego on Lake Ontario. A post on my uncle's land would save a sixty or eighty mile round trip for them, and dealing direct with you here, I may have some competitive advantage."

Turnbottle's irritation had vanished. He whinnied, "You've put some thought into all this, I can see. You will be making enemies in Albany right quick. If you compete with 'em, they're not likely to be very friendly with you, family connections or no, young man."

Billy nodded. "We shall see whether they will tolerate a trading post on the Mohawk." He smiled, and withdrew a folded paper from his coat, handing it to Turnbottle.

"In any case, I imagine that it would be unobjectionable, even to them, for me to arrange for my first purchases here, especially since my uncle has directed me to you as a supplier to His Majesty's Navy on the New York station."

Turnbottle unfolded the paper and held it up to where the dim light fighting its way through the tiny windows in the wall at his back could fall on it. Years of dust, grime and cobwebs covered the thick, rippled, bubbly glass. He scrutinized the list of provisions closely, then seized a two-foot square, wood-framed slate hanging from the nearby post and made notations with a small lump of chalk, muttering under his breath as he worked for several minutes. A fine rain of chalk dust fell, adding to a thin pile on the floor. Finally, he returned to awareness of his visitor and, very rapidly, ran through the sums and pointed to the bottom line on the slate.

"One hundred forty-nine pounds, 10 shillings and thruppence," he said.

"Sell a country! Why not sell the air, the clouds and the great sea, as well as the earth? Did not the Great Spirit make them all for the use of his children?"

—Tecumseh, Shawnee Chief

CHAPTER EIGHT
Mohawk River, 1738

It was late summer, and Billy was relaxing for the first time in months. He had been punishing himself for a self-indulgent winter with unrelenting dawn to dusk labor, building a combined trading shed and accommodation out of the bush. He had framed two crude windows in it, which were equipped with canvas covers instead of glass, built a covered porch, and stocked the shed with the trade goods he had ordered from Turnbottle. He had also made several exploratory treks southwestward into the wilderness of the Pennsylvania mountains. He had left New York City in early May, and his first few weeks at his chosen location had been nearly sleepless. He had been warned to hoist his food into the trees at a distance from his tent, so that bears would not bother him at night. The guide who had brought him to his uncle's tract had chuckled at his greenness.

"I allus sleep with a good sharp knife ready to hand, y'see, food in the trees or no."

Billy had looked a question.

"Arr, no, it ain't to defend mesself," the guide laughed, "it's to cut a hole in the back of the tent to run through, when a bear comes in the door. Ye're all alone here, and no one to nurse you if ye're hurt in a fight. Best to avoid fights like that altogether. Tents can be stitched together easier than bellies."

Every night he had been visited, not just by black bears, but by whole families of masked, ring-tailed raccoons. It seemed that just as he would fall asleep, especially if he rolled over so that his nose was anywhere near the canvas wall of the tent, there would come that stealthy, curious sniffing, and little paws would try to pat the shape of his face through the fabric. His startled awakening would send them scampering, but they soon came back. Eventually he learned to ignore them completely.

The hissing growls of lynx and cougars downing prey in the forest became background noise much more slowly. He often awoke in a fright and spent a panicked hour or more, expecting an attack. The old forest creaked and groaned continuously at night, and even when the air seemed as still and humid as if he were in a bell jar, ancient, dead and rotting trees regularly fell with a frightening roar and smash, which never failed to jerk him violently back from oblivion to heart-thumping awareness. He learned to work so hard that only the jangling of the trade bells strung about his campsite could wake him. After the shack walls were up, he worried less about the wildlife.

When he paused for rest during the day, the noisy trees falling seemed much further away. But for the trees and small birds flitting about, along with some ravens and crows, and the occasional harsh scream of an eagle, the great forest seemed to be simply at rest during the midsummer days, slowly breathing in and out as the breezes sighed through the treetops.

Several times he had seen enormous, noisy clouds of wild pigeons moving from one spot to another, flocks that moved incredibly quickly, but were so large that they would take hours going overhead, darkening the sky. On his second trip southwest, he'd walked through one of their nesting sites.

For several days, he had traveled on a narrow trail through a thick hardwood forest, with hundreds of nests in each tree. The birds were attractive, plump, bluish grey with black markings and metallic-looking feathers around their neck, with a longish tail, rose-colored chest and white belly and red feet. He had caught and roasted several without much effort.

Worst of all in the nights were ferocious thunderstorms. Always coming from the west, they seemed to have a malevolent ability to creep up behind the mountains and then suddenly burst overhead in a terrifying display of power. A bright pink flash through his closed eyelids would be the first warning, followed immediately by the splintering crack of the sky splitting violently apart and a deafening roar.

Then the deluge followed, raindrops bouncing knee-high from the rocks and pounding a fine mist right through the sagging roof of his tent. Twice, hailstones the size of plums tore through the tent and forced him to shelter under a rock outcrop beside a little freshet. Those nights he clung precariously to the ground while the trickle became a raging, foaming torrent that plucked greedily at his feet and hands.

After three weeks, however, he had the walls up and began splitting shingles to cover the plank roof he had sawn and nailed up. It was easier after that.

Now it was late autumn, and he was writing to his uncle, relating that at this time he felt window glass would be an extravagance and that the small garden he had scratched out between the stumps had grown well, and peas, squash and corn had already been harvested.

"The pigeons will be a significant source of food if they come anywhere near me during their fall migration south. I estimated that there must have been hundreds of millions of the noisy creatures nesting in the one area I discovered in Pennsylvania, yet I have been reliably informed that it was not anything like the largest they know of in this country."

Billy set down the quill and watched his new housekeeper, Katrina, as she swept the floor of the cabin. He reflected cheerfully on his first winter in America, which had passed in a delightful blur of soft beds, willing women and elegant parties, undercut by the hard edge of ruthless power-seeking. He had been lucky to escape New York without seriously damaging his reputation, or that of his hosts, and alienating his Aunt Holeybarth.

He was relieved to be away from the heavy innuendo of powerful men attempting to persuade him to one political faction or another, and from the dangerous flirtations of their women. Not that he was exhausted. He smirked wryly to himself.

His Katrina, too, seemed not to have any hidden agendas. He had purchased Katrina's indenture from Voortman's overseer on the dock at New York, during a visit to Turnbottle's warehouse. Voortman's business dealing with slavery and near-slavery was extremely profitable. All the colonies were starved for labor.

Turnbottle had recommended the indenture market to Billy, detecting some element of loneliness. "Try Voortman's first, and see what you think, boy. The winters are very long and you will need a housekeeper to keep you warm."

She had been thin, but not at all ugly, and she had managed to keep some scraps of feminine pride—her blonde pigtails were clean and she had tied them with a scrap of ribbon at the ends. Her breasts jutted firmly under the thin shift, young and full on such a skinny frame. Sensing his interest, she had dared to meet his eyes briefly, and he heard himself bid on her services after the auctioneer held up her hand.

"Housekeeper, twenty years of age, fully trained in Europe, asking five pounds for seven years' indenture, as is, usual terms." When the auctioneer closed the bargain, Billy had paid seven pounds.

"My home vas near the great Rhine River," she said, in answer to his inquiry.

"My family is killed, except my brother, Johannes, slaughtered by the Catholic schweiner. We dreamed of escape to your England, where Protestants are safe, but when we got there, we were turned into slaves and sent here, because there were already enough English slaves and servants." Her eyes welled up and tears tracked down each pale cheek.

"He is only eleven, my little brother Johannes. When our ship reached Philadelphia, we were separated and I haf no, no..." she struggled for the word, "no knowledge, ja, knowledge of him now, for months."

She had stared at him, blue eyes turning suddenly apprehensive, then defiant, and finally, darkly challenging.

"If you beat me, Herr Smithyman, be sure you kill me, for if you kill me not, I vill kill you. I vill die, before I let anyone beat me more."

Billy had smiled gently then. "Katrina Pfalz, I will not beat you. Come, and make my shed in the wilderness a home for me."

When he had arrived home, he had scribbled a note to Turnbottle, instructing him to inquire for one Johannes Pfalz, age twelve, last heard of in Philadelphia.

He continued his letter to his uncle, the scratching of his quill mingling with the sounds of raccoons exploring all the possible entrances to the house. He was reporting on the season's activities.

I am happy to relate that I will return a small profit on your venture here, which I trust you will see as appropriate. I have leased parcels of your land to eighteen tenants since I arrived (accounts enclosed) and am pleased to inform you that the goods I brought from New York have been valuable to the tenants as well as to the local Indians, with whom I have begun a brisk trade for furs. The furs I will be selling to my agent Turnbottle, and as yet I do not know what profit we will receive from that activity.

I recommend, however, that to maximize your returns in future, it will be easier to do so through selling freehold lots from the grant rather than seeking tenants. Your forest property, as I previously described, is largely hilly wilderness, on the south side of the river facing north.

This necessarily gives it a less benign climate than the other shore, and I am reliably informed that the snow falls earlier here and remains longer. The main cartage track ends at Schenectady, twenty miles from here, making it more difficult to retain tenants, who tend to find the north bank grass perpetually greener.

For that reason, many of those who came by to see what was on offer here refused to stay to farm. The nearby Schoharie creek, which is more attractive, although there are many Indians there, is not part of the grant, and you have suggested that I should not attempt to purchase land on it.

Uncle, I intend to invest my small personal monies as well, over the next few years. There is a parcel slightly upriver on the north side, to which I believe I will be able to obtain title. It is backed by land which can be cleared and farmed, which also possesses a good creek to power a sawmill. This, I have calculated, has the potential to bring in a full forty pounds profit per annum, since I can then produce planking for settlers locally instead of buying from Albany or wasting time sawing and splitting by hand, as I did this year.

I would also solicit your support and investment in opening a new trading house in Pennsylvania, at a location which I recently visited. It is, I own, some two hundred miles southwest from here, but at a place on the Susquehanna River where the Wautegha creek joins the main river, called Oquaqua. I would expect trade opportunities to be better there than they are to my northwest, at Oswego. As I have previously related, Uncle, there are a group of rogues already in place at Oswego who have quite spoiled the trust and the attitudes of the Indians, since they offer very cheap rum but the prices they charge for durable goods are extremely expensive. At Oquaqua, on the other hand, there is the opportunity for a steady, if unspectacular, trade with the local Delawares and some Tuscaroras.

He finished and signed with a flourish, then sanded and sealed the letter and put it aside on the small desk. Katrina had taken a basket and was washing his clothes in the river. He tore off a twist from an inch-thick black rope of tobacco in his pouch and packed his clay pipe, lighting it from the fireplace. He had begun smoking the aromatic leaf almost as soon as he had landed in New York, it being seemingly a universal habit among the British and Dutch colonists, and a sacred ritual among the Indians, who cultivated it.

He poured a generous measure of rum from a small keg into a pewter mug and added a broken lump of sugar. He plucked several limes from the cask of them he had ordered from Turnbottle's and crushed their juice into the mug, stirring it with his finger, then went to sit outside on the plank bench underneath the overhang, to watch the long twilight shadows move up the hills opposite.

He liked to plan the next day's work in the calm of the evening. He would have to go to Albany again, tomorrow. The quality of gunflints that Voortman had sent with the most recent case of muskets was outrageous, and he could not allow the Dutchman to get away with it. If he sold them and they shattered on first firing, as had happened when he tried half a dozen, his reputation as an honest trader with the Mohawks would shatter with them.

Billy cursed himself, mildly.

I ought to have looked closer at the flints. I wonder where the thieving bastards got them. Now that I've seen them, they're neither amber-colored French ones nor our grey-black ones. Maybe Spanish or Portuguese? Stupid to buy from Voortman. Better not to have purchased anything from the Albanians at all. Even though I can claim family connections, they will not be honest with me.

He drew deeply on the pipe, savoring the smoke.

Not bad. He got up and looked for the invoice list. *Oh yes, Spencer's Best Roll and Carrot Tobacco.*

He puffed again. *This black Brazil isn't sweet like the Virginia leaf, but still, a nice, strong flavor. And that tight, smooth twist makes it very portable. It should be popular with the traders and the Indians, just as Turnbottle said. I'll write him and order another bale.*

He despised Albany, although he had to be careful, since his uncle's in-laws could damage him severely if he was too offensive. Albany was a bustling, self-satisfied and self-interested town, with filthy streets as bad as Dublin's worst, although outdoor privies at the back of the residences meant that human excrement did not usually form a part of the smelly mud.

Most of the smug inheritors of the grand old Dutch estates on Hudson's River conspired with local English merchants, and traders and trappers from Canada, to cheat everyone who could possibly be cheated.

Their other main occupation was to secure political connections with the Governor and his Executive Council, or, if it suited their interests better, with the elected representatives of the Legislative Assembly of New York. The great landowners and the mercantile houses made a formidable combination when they acted together, which years of incompetence and graft in the Governor's office had encouraged them to do.

He had detected the tone of hostile condescension from his aunt's relations from his first acquaintance with them in the winter. Subsequent meetings only reinforced his sense of being on the receiving end of their disdain.

He had traveled to Albany to see them very early in the summer, before he had bought Katrina's indenture and just after he had finished his shack and had shelter. "I apologize, Mijnheer Van Nes," he had begun "for my inexcusable delay in bringing greetings to you from my Aunt Sophia, your niece, but it was necessary to begin work to improve my uncle's investment immediately."

The patroon, whose great-grandfather had inveigled gigantic tracts of forest along the upper Hudson out of the hands of various small indigenous nations and the Dutch Crown, had smiled a long, thin smile, strangely at odds with his short, portly body. He puffed a cloud of tobacco smoke from the long clay pipe in his left hand.

"Investment, indeed," said Hendrik Van Nes, with a stage wink.

"It seems quite extraordinary, does it not, that the good Captain should get this large land grant from the late Governor's estate so quickly after carrying the grieving young widow home to England? It seems your Uncle Harold must be as good at boarding Governor's widows as he is enemy merchant ships!"

Billy remained outwardly relaxed at the offensively coarse jest and just said, drily, "With your permission, Mijnheer, I will convey your sentiments to my aunt."

"Oh tchaw, my boy, that is merely a joke between men of the world, y'know, not at all the sort of thing a woman of breeding would understand." His small blue eyes blinked rapidly for a moment, as if the smoke had irritated them. Billy made no response and the silence drew out.

"Ja. Well." The patroon, manorial lord over several hundred slaves, employees and tenants, cleared his throat and rang a small silver bell, replacing it delicately on the inlaid walnut surface of the low table beside him.

"What would you enjoy drinking, my young adventurer, while you tell me about Captain Holeybarth's investments up the wrong side of the Mohawk?" He spluttered a wet chuckle at the thought that the Captain might not have obtained the best land in the Valley.

"Patroon, I was admiring that silver tankard in your sideboard. Is that a European artisan?"

Van Nes looked pleased, and his eyes moistened slightly. "No, that one was made here in Albany by Konraet Ten Eyck at the turn of the century, for my father."

Billy stood and inclined his head to the cabinet. "Would you mind if I looked more closely at it, Mijnheer?" When Van Nes nodded, Billy walked over to the sideboard, squatting to look at it through the glass. "The detailing is truly exquisite, is it not? Ten Eyck must have been a wonderful smith."

He stood and turned, smiling disarmingly at Van Nes. "But to answer your question properly, Patroon, I have heard that the beer from your estates is the best in the colony."

The expected, transparent flattery from his niece's wet-behind-the-ears nephew achieved its desired object and the day's interview ended on a reasonably genial note.

"You must visit again, my boy, better yet, come to the estate and stay for a few days. I dislike coming to the office in Albany, but, alas, it is necessary to stay here from time to time. We could use a quick and clever mind like yours here. It is wasted, I believe you will soon see, out in the Mohawk wilderness.

Here we have achieved a delightful balance between the forces that threaten us, do you not agree?" The round blue eyes now were unblinking, the trap in plain view.

If he disagreed overtly with this powerful, crude man, Billy knew that Van Nes could easily create a very great deal of unnecessary trouble for him. Best to be diplomatic, and mask one's true opinions.

Billy bowed politely. "Patroon, I allow it is very clear that your family and friends have acquired great wisdom in managing the politics and the trade of New York."

A servant escorted him to the door and he spent that night in Schenectady. The next morning as he mounted up to leave, he noticed a native woman stumbling towards him. She was wearing a torn doeskin dress decorated elaborately with dyed porcupine quills and wampum beads.

She was carrying a babe swaddled in its backboard and she was sobbing piteously. As she reached Billy, she handed the little immobile bundle to him, saying, "English, be kind. They would take my baby, these devils. They would keep him from his family and his people, because we owe for the blankets we must buy." Wool blankets were a universal trade good that all Indians desired, for their hard-wearing, durable warmth and colorful dyes. They had quickly all but replaced many traditional items of clothing and the blankets stitched together from pelts, skins and furs.

Behind her, Billy saw several ruffians carrying clubs jog around the corner. He reached down with one strong arm and pulled the thin woman and her baby up onto the horse in front of him. "Hold tight, Mother, and we go," he said, as the men began to shout and run towards them. He galloped west towards Fort Hunter, quickly leaving the gesticulating pursuers behind.

He eased his horse to a walk after a quarter mile.

Not a patch on The Colonel.

He strongly missed the big, brave beast he had left behind. He had the woman move to sit behind him, and then continued along the road, occasionally cantering, deep in thought. No words came from behind him until they reached his shanty, long after dark on that side of the river, although there was still a faint glow high overhead, reflected on the opposite bank.

At the shed, candlelight emphasized her bruised and burdened face, eyes red-rimmed and hair matted. She was as wary as a wild animal. She gobbled down the smoked meat he cut and the hard bread and cheese he brought out. He dipped a mug into the barrel of icy water from the freshet that poured off the edge of the cliff nearby and she drank it down without stopping.

Then she pulled out one plump breast, instantly latched onto by a greedy mouth, while she stared watchfully at her rescuer.

At length, she spoke, low and intently, "I will not be your slave." Her eyes narrowed when he threw back his head and laughed.

He crouched by the fireplace and shrugged. "I can very easily buy cleaner, more beautiful, softer, rounder, stronger and childless slaves, so why would I wish to keep you? Where is your home, Mother?"

She jerked her head to her left and shrugged. "Canajoharie," she said.

He nodded. Kneeling on the stone hearth, he laid a fire and struck sparks to tinder, softly blowing the resulting tiny tendril of smoke into a delicate flame, which instantly seized the shredded birch bark and dry pine twigs. He began to add small split softwood sticks.

Billy made himself a rum punch and lit a pipe. He said, "The Upper Castle at Canajoharie is fifteen more miles, a half day's ride, and I cannot take you there tonight." He pointed to a corner of the room heaped with glossy skins of marten, otter, fox, wolf and muskrat. "You can sleep there, I will sleep over here. We will talk about this in the morning, before you go back to your people."

She gestured to the baby. "I have left behind things in Albany, but I must wash him now. Do you have, have…," she shook her head in frustration, "I need to wrap him up again, after."

Billy discovered that pieces of his oldest, softest shirt were required for the nether regions of the infant. She grimaced. "Your house is not a good home for babies. This will not last as long as our good dried moss, and he will cry more, but it may do."

Before she left, he learned that the Albany traders at times demanded children as hostages for credit extended to the Mohawks. Frequently they did not return them, claiming that the child had run away.

Interviews and local gossip, probed delicately for the truth, combined with his own observations, had given Billy a clear understanding of the Albany traders' preferred methods of doing business by the time he had lived a short time on his uncle's land.

The utter dogs, to snare and deal with these people as if they were simply vermin.

He made a mental vow. *I will return to Ireland, broken, before I live as those men do.*

Within a few months, he had intercepted a small number of the native trappers' canoes on their way down the Mohawk with furs to Albany. Through trade, he had become well known to the two larger Mohawk settlements. He was scrupulously careful not to take advantage of his customers' preference for the contents of his kegs of distilled 'English milk' as a payment currency for fur. He provided gifts and hosted them with rum but strictly limited the amount they could trade for.

The morning after a drunken debauch, they awoke and were at first astonished to find that only the fair cost of the small amount of rum they bought had been deducted from their credit. He refused to take back objects they had traded for the previous day, to satisfy their lust for drink. Billy had discovered that in other posts this was a primary source of profit, the objects bought back at a considerable discount from their sale price the day before. They were now used goods, after all.

Neither were his customers confronted, the morning after, with land sale documents they had signed while more or less insensible. When they realized that this was not just a whim of the moment, but his consistent practice, they became warmly appreciative.

Late in the fall, a tall, older Indian with a look of some importance and ferocity strode up to his post, accompanied by three other warriors. He seemed to be in his middle fifties, hard and virile-looking. The others were considerably younger, probably early twenties.

Billy stood to greet his visitors.

Now would be the time for a gift, me lad.

The four warriors muttered greetings and waved their muskets at him, somewhat half-heartedly, three of them refusing to meet his eyes, often a dangerous sign.

The leader, however, had not ceased to stare at him, unblinking and without expression. Billy saw his huge scar that stretched from lip to ear and realized that this must be Emperor Marten, a renowned Mohawk war chief. Billy offered them a pipe and some rum and gestured for them to sit down with him on the crude benches he had built. He greeted them with some of the Mohawk words he had learned in his trade.

"I have looked forward to meeting the most famous war chief of the Mohawks for many months. Please rest comfortably. I am unprepared for such eminent and important visitors, but perhaps some meat and drink would excuse my unreadiness."

There was a series of nods. Billy looked over his shoulder and saw, as he expected, blonde Katrina's blue-eyed face peering out the window. He gestured, hand to mouth, and it disappeared.

In a few minutes, she appeared on the porch, smiling and carrying a large leg of cooked ham to Billy, which he passed to the elder. Katrina then returned to the interior without a word. Billy caressed her hip as she passed. His visitors, who expressed evident, smacking appreciation, passed the joint from hand to hand.

After a second refill of the rum cups, Marten spoke. "I have heard some things about you which are surprising to my ear and to my people."

Billy drew smoke from the clay pipe, outwardly relaxed, but inwardly he felt a great excitement. He leisurely passed the pipe to the chief. "This is an astonishing thing to my white ears, which are admittedly ignorant of many important things. I was thinking that there would be very little that was surprising to a wise war chief, who is celebrated everywhere for his courage in battle, who is a guide to his people, and who had visited the home of the English Queen before I became a person on the earth."

The cold eyes moved from the glowing pipe bowl to Billy, and a small wrinkle grew between them, while a huffing sound emerged around the stem. At length, Billy realized that he had made Emperor Marten laugh.

Marten puffed smoke from his mouth, then smiled and spoke to the three other warriors. "I see that this Englishman has a very sweet tongue for his elders. You and your brothers ought to learn from him, to be as respectful as he."

Billy cultivated Marten's friendship, and in a few more weeks had persuaded him to guide Billy around the region.

*****

Marten looked up from skinning the buck when Billy called to him. Billy was lying prone, staring down across the end of a narrow lake from a steep, forested hilltop. They were several hundred feet above the water and more than sixty miles north of Billy's camp. Marten followed his gaze and watched a dozen large birch bark canoes emerging in a line from behind another hill, which was flat on top and somewhat lower. The crews paddled the canoes smoothly and swiftly to Billy's left.

Marten grunted and returned to his work. "That is only one of the many fleets of my cousins in Kahnewake, near Montreal, where they are called the Praying Indians because the priests have made them Christians. They are coming from the far northwest to Albany and avoiding Montreal. This is against the law of the French King, and yours as well. "You can see that they bring many furs that you will never see at your house. They make our enemies rich, both in Albany and in the north."

Billy said nothing, and Marten continued, after stropping the bloody skinning knife on his leather leggings a few times and checking it closely with his thumb for nicks.

"These furs do not come to you, my son, because few canoes pass upriver beyond Oswego, where the traders offer cheap rum in trade for furs. Many northerners also avoid Oswego because they tremble at the might of the Six

Nations Confederacy. Instead, they take the northern route from the French fort at the place the Ojibwa people call the Great Turtle, down to our relatives near Montreal, then to this place."

Billy turned to look at Marten briefly, and then resumed staring at the lake, where the canoes were rapidly passing from view. He said, "The northerners are wise, no doubt, to live in such fear of the terrible Mohawk warriors. But it puzzles me greatly that you allow their fear to profit your cousins in Kahnewake so much more than your sons and daughters and brothers and wives in the Mohawk castles. They too, I gently remind my old father, are at the mercy of that nest of poisonous snakes in Albany. Perhaps the great Six Nations are chewing off their own earlobes in this matter?"

Billy shaded his eyes to examine once more the two-hundred-foot bluff rising at the end of the lake. Although it was lower than his perch, it was high enough to tower over the lake and the creek at its foot. He lifted his eyes beyond it, following the misted gash between the hills, the slender lake shining, beckoning them northward.

On a clear day it feels like I could see all the way down the waterway to Montreal.

"We call that place Ticonderoga," said Marten behind him, "and we remember it well as the place where the French ambushed us and started the Iroquois wars, to their great regret."

Starting from the sand beach at the head of Lac St-Sacrement thirty miles behind them, there was an easy two-hundred-mile canoe highway through the trackless wilderness to Montreal.

The water gleamed in the afternoon sun like quicksilver, pooled deeply between the steep mountains, whose spines aligned from north to south like rows of steep green waves. They made travel from east to west nearly impossible.

Billy changed the subject.

"Do you not think, Marten, that it would be a fine place to build a fort down there, to pinch off the trade between Albany and Montreal?"

Marten shrugged. "Yes, it is, if you persist in thinking in that odd white way. We, the people of this land, realize that the river will always flow past the rock and we believe that it is wiser to strive to be part of the river.

"But, my forgetful English son, the warlike and active French have already built such a fort, Fort Saint Frederick, with many large iron cannons and a very tall tower of stone in its middle. It lies only fifteen leagues north of here, at a place where the second long lake narrows on its way to Montreal, that you call Crown Point."

He grunted, once, when the knifepoint marred the hide slightly, and muttered, "My wife, Oweraosorakehson, Wind-Through-the-Spruces, is much better than I at this work."

He went on, "I know that fort well. Before it was built, I was told by the Indian Commissioners in Albany that Crown Point belonged to your King's Governor in New York, our brother Corlaer, by means of a large and important Treaty which ended your Queen Anne's war with the French."

He added, with a glance to see if Billy was paying attention, "When I brought in French and Ottawa scalps clinging to my belt like burrs.

"But, when the French built the fort there, more than ten summers ago, in territory you English asked us to defend, not one small finger was raised against it by Albany or New York, although I heard from some traders that the Bostonians felt a very deep resentment, as we did on your behalf.

"It was very puzzling to us, my son, that Corlaer did not notice this insult and take action. It made us doubt that Corlaer would actually protect us, should the French and their allies attack us as they have in the past.

"Perhaps I will take you to Crown Point to see it, when we have finished smoking this meat, if you do not make your usual noises blundering through the forest like a blind moose."

Marten delicately sliced off some choice muscle from the deer's lower back, now very neatly stripped of its hide, and closed his teeth on the raw, dripping venison with great pleasure. He cut another slice and offered it to Billy, who left his viewpoint at the edge of the hill to take it and then sat, leaning against a leather pack.

Marten frowned now, and stabbed the knife northwards, mumbling through his mouthful. "Those canoes we saw will now return home with English powder, muskets and shot. Then, the northern nations, who have sworn war against us forever, will use it against us—and you, my English friend."

Billy smiled, he could not resist teasing his mentor. "You have not taken French scalps for many years, is it not true?"

Marten glared at him. "We have had no reason to break the peace."

He shook his head, as if his reflections were burdensome. "But the French are a virile nation, and now have great influence with the nations of the Iroquois.

"For they have built another stone fortress in Seneca territory near the foot of the great western falls they call Niagara, and you English have done nothing about that, either. This has impressed many Iroquois. And the other nations in the Confederacy are far more numerous than we Mohawks, the People of the

Flint, who guard the Eastern Door of the Longhouse." He pulled a piece of gristle from his teeth and discarded it.

"Although we are far greater in battle than they," he added.

A new thought struck him and he pointed the bloody knife at Billy. "We may soon travel to the warm south again, against the Cherokee and Catawba. We are now so friendly with our former enemies the French that we are in need of battle practice, and need to avenge last season's dead. You should go with us, the better to learn why the Haudenosaunee are masters of all between the great sweet water lakes to the north and the father of rivers to the west.

"I, Emperor Marten, a war chief of the Grand Council, will show you why the protective shadow of the Iroquois League extends to just a few days paddling from the warm salt seas in the south." It was a grand and generous offer.

Complimented, Billy nodded slowly. "This would be a pleasant diversion. However, who would then prevent the Albanians from stealing your children, my Father? Your warriors would be absent, and also myself."

"That is true. Perhaps it was a foolish thought."

He frowned and the snake-scar writhed. "And perhaps your lack of experience and skill would make this plan too steep a mountain for the other warriors to climb, they being far less tolerant than myself of white failings." He said this equably, and Billy took no offence.

Marten sliced some more meat and hung it near the fire.

"My son, we find it hard to understand why your clans, which I saw in England are capable of true greatness, send you over here to live, naked of any useful training. You make us rich by accepting used fur clothing from us in exchange for iron kettles, axes and muskets, and these fine knives.

"Yet, the English remain exceedingly disrespectful of us, the original beings, the Ongwehonweh, who are often called upon to save them, wherever they go. Even now, your governor wants our help to keep the French Indians away, but we receive no gifts to demonstrate the friendship he has for us."

He spat.

"Faugh! The French show much more understanding. They come to live with us in the forest and share our ways. We have granted the trading post in our territory at Oswego to the English, but you have seen that the fort there would not stop a child. You and your woman can easily walk through the palisade at Fort Hunter also, that the English say will help defend our castle there. The old Dutch fort in Albany has fallen down, and the Dutchmen have stolen their own city walls for firewood.

"If the French and the northern Indians go on the warpath, perhaps in this next war the Six Nations will join them, since the English do not care about us here, except to pretend to be our friends while they give us drink to steal our land."

Billy leaned forward and cut a piece of meat for himself.

"My Father, your words make my ears redden with shame. I can only say again that I am not on the side of the worthless English and Dutch you speak of. I am also sure there are many whose ears are open to the problems of your people. Sadly, I am at present only an unimportant trader and so I cannot make myself heard to the people who have the power. For now, I can only make things better for those who will trade with me and trust me."

The older man shrugged. "It is true that your trade is helping our people. As it grows, you will find that the Mohawks are a grateful and loyal nation. If war does come again, as we think it will, perhaps even the thieves in Albany may remember that they need our friendship."

Billy felt warmed by Marten's words. *The Albanians are fools. I want the friendship of the Mohawks even if they don't.*

CHAPTER 9
The Letter, 1741

Richard was recalling every phrase in what he and Eva called Billy's "land letter" for the hundredth time since it had arrived at his door in Ireland months ago, as if some word in it might be a clue to Billy's present whereabouts. It read:

Smithyman House, New York Province, September 12, 1740

Dear Richard,

I trust this letter finds you and Eva well and happy and that young Michael is enjoying good health. Perhaps he has begun to walk. I have not written you for several months, since I have been engaged in moving my establishment and myself to a new location across the Mohawk River, which I consider far superior in its attractions, in every way.

Richard, you will remember that when we parted in Dublin, I mentioned that you might possibly be of help to me, over here in America. I am now in a position to offer to you a situation, which I believe will benefit you and your family, and perhaps several others if you could see your way clear to supporting me in this venture.

I have recently acquired title to a considerable quantity of forest, through my increasingly friendly (and profitable) relations with my Mohawk neighbors. This tract has, I judge, considerable potential for both pasture and farmland once the forest is cleared. The woods are mixed hardwood and softwood. Some of it is marketable for masts for the navy, and if they are not buying, for potash. The ground is very rich, and I have been very successful in growing large quantities of peas, which bring in considerable money for a little sustained effort.

I propose that you might take possession of two hundred acres of this land and obtain full freehold title to it, after developing its potential fully in terms of its tillable acreage. I make this offer to you in respect of our friendship. That said, I fully hope and expect that you might assist my endeavors by attaching as many as twenty or thirty other families of your acquaintance, who might find this prospect interesting, under similar conditions, and also who might not be daunted by the task of clearing and cultivating the wilderness.

I can assure you that I am in every way serious about this opportunity. Richard, joy, I beg you to consider this deeply. There is vast room here, and good land to make your own, beholden to none for your security except your own fortitude and endeavor.

As you know, this area has been at peace now for a generation since Queen Anne's War and I hope that, unless the French decide to launch some provocation in response to our present war with Spain, it may remain at peace for some time to come.

Certainly, the local Albany people can be counted on to strongly resist any request by the Governor to vote taxes for defense or to fight their business partners in Canada, but that is perhaps beside the point.

Come, Richard, and let us prosper together as friends ought to do. I suggest that for your recruitment efforts you should earn an additional ten acres of freehold for each settler or family that you bring with you.

I look forward to hearing from you at your earliest convenience.

As always, Your true friend,

Billy Smithyman, Esq.

Today, seven months later, Richard was silently praying. *Dear Jesus, grant that Billy turns up soon, for we are surely the sorriest lot of pilgrims to America that has been, this hundred years and more.*

His arm was around Eva as they sat on the largest of their boxes, on the shore at Albany where the canoes and bateaux unloading the sloop from New York had deposited them. Their son and twenty-five others stood or sat amidst a small and disorderly heap of chests, furniture and miscellaneous boxes and belongings. Many were drooping with fatigue and the remnants of chronic seasickness.

It was just after mid-day and the June sun was a polished, heated weight on their anxious souls. After two hours ashore, however, its restorative warmth had inspired some to begin to convey their doubts, their very, very serious doubts, that their patron, Billy, might be still alive in this howling wilderness, and what would Richard be doing to save them all, then?

In a quiet moment, the complaining horde having withdrawn into sullen watchfulness, Richard pulled out another much read and much folded letter, his talisman through the voyage. So far, it had never failed him.

On the third page he read, once again, "My agent, Turnbottle, in New York, will communicate to me the exact expected date of your arrival in Albany after you contact him to make these arrangements, and I will meet you there. "

He folded the papers reverently once more and replaced them in the precious waterproofed canvas wallet that had accompanied him these thousands of miles, tied against his skin.

It was the appointed date. They had waited several days in flea-infested hostelries in New York for an arriving Albany boat. Trans-Atlantic seasickness abated with solid ground underfoot, but the reviving immigrants were taken aback by the appearance of the Albany sloop, *Hermione*, which Turnbottle had chartered for them.

She came suddenly into view on the Hudson, running downwind from the north, moving fast; close in to the east shore. Her tall, tan-colored mainsail and topsail were winged out to one side, her jib to the other. She was loaded so heavily that her deck was all but level with the water, making her black hull nearly invisible, and she had a large foaming bow wave, a bone in her teeth.

As she approached, Richard's party could see live cattle lashed to a wooden pole, which ran lengthwise from the mast back to the quarterdeck. They watched the sixty-foot boat brush by the end of the pier like lightning, driving down current on the ebbing tide. As the long quarterdeck passed the pier, they could see it was stuffed with kegs and freshly slaughtered hog carcasses. A crowded pen filled with loudly protesting sheep enclosed the helmsman on all sides. Suddenly, the topsail vanished like a conjurer's handkerchief, and the watchers gasped in unison.

Close by the pier, far too close, they felt, *Hermione*'s helmsman glanced their way and pushed the long tiller over firmly, turning her hard around to the left. Her wake creamed broadly and the river lapped green onto her starboard deck as she heeled outward on the turn.

As she reversed course, pointing up into the wind and current, her remaining sails began to luff, flogging heavily from side to side. Hurtling back upriver, she seemed certain to smash into the pier. *Hermione*'s jib slid smoothly down the forestay to pile on the deck.

A scant ten seconds later, the boat miraculously slowed. She nosed gently up to Turnbottle's wharf and stopped, her twelve-foot bowsprit poised motionless for a brief moment, two feet from the pier. Long lines flew through the air, uncoiling like butterfly tongues. One crewmember cast off her halyards, and the wooden gaff and the mainsail canvas it supported collapsed quickly onto the deck with a thump. Before she could drift back away from the dock in the current, the gang of waiting longshoremen muscled her alongside.

The immigrants waited in a dismayed cluster, watching the long line of wagons emptying the vessel's grain bins and deck cargo and wondering whether they were now to become the new deck cargo.

Richard walked over to the edge of the pier to introduce himself and his party, apprehensively inquring about the accommodations aboard. The grinning owner told Richard not to worry.

"You'll see, Goodman FitzHugh, old *Hermione* will be shipshape right quick, don't you worry about that!" And, sure enough, in very short order, the crew of four hands had thoroughly sluiced and scrubbed the decks with the salty river water, stowed the temporary fences and re-covered the produce bins in the hold.

Curious about the arrangement of livestock, which struck Richard as inconvenient, not to mention noisome, he asked the forthcoming owner whether there was a reason for it.

"Indeed there is! The sheep pen around the wheel keeps me warm on the run down from Albany and Newburgh, even in the freezing sleet of fall and spring. Besides, animals on deck are easier to clean up after than animals kept in a hold, and healthier too. They sicken in the dark, just like men."

Once aboard, the Irish were delightfully surprised. *Hermione* was astonishingly comfortable. The five-day cruise up the wide Hudson River was most pleasant, for those who could enjoy it. They ate delicious fresh-cooked meals, including a sturgeon weighing two hundred and fifty pounds that had simply leaped aboard in the middle of the day while they watched, amazed, as its brothers and sisters cavorted, making gigantic splashes in the river for as far as they could see. The cook, who doubled as deckhand and swineherd, apologized for the "Albany beef," explaining that it was "usually only eaten by the common folk, since it's so easy to get," but to the newcomers the flesh was truly delicious. They gaped at the sight of a brick fireplace, hearth and chimney. A polished wood mantel and mahogany paneling were unheard-of luxuries on land, let alone aboard a boat.

Gilt-rimmed mirrors hung in panels at the head of the berths and a very large mirror decorated the bulkhead separating the main cabin from the after state-rooms. The floors were hardwood, scrubbed white and clean. At night, a large, polished brass signal lamp lit the companionway leading down from the deck.

The continuing seasickness of many of the passengers had prevented them from enjoying the cruise to the full, however. This contributed to the peevishness of some, who were vaguely aware that they had missed enjoying one of the crowning experiences of their lives.

Now, Richard had calculated, there was enough of Billy's credit draft left for one night's lodgings for the twenty-eight intrepid immigrants, and then they were all truly cast ashore, with only Billy Smithyman's name to sustain them. And, by the grim looks and shaking heads of the merchants he had already talked to up in the town, Billy was not held in high esteem hereabouts.

It was a symptom of the immigrants' malaise that the appearance of three large dugout canoes, each manned by four or five nearly naked male paddlers, excited only mild interest. Most of the canoe men were shaved bald except for a topknot decorated with three feathers, and nearly all were weirdly tattooed and painted.

In the middle of the first canoe was one individual whose tanned skin was clearly a lighter shade. He was also missing the tattoos and ornamented piercings of nose and ears, and he retained a full head of oddly light-colored hair, cropped short, but partially covered with a peculiar sort of strapped-on cap made of thin wood strips and decorated with feathers and beads. When the canoes ran firmly ashore alongside them, several of the stupefied onlookers drew back in fearful amazement.

The European canoeist leaped out into knee-deep water. He was very large and broad-shouldered, deeply browned by the sun, wearing a pair of tanned leather breeches to the calf, where his companions sported only breechcloths. The be-feathered, half-naked savage strode up to Richard and clapped him on the shoulders with both hands, smiling broadly.

"Do you not know your old friend, Richard?"

Richard's eyes widened. "Is't you, Billy, is't truly you, joy, looking like such a savage as never was?"

Billy threw his head back and let go a heart-felt peal of laughter that brought a smile to several pinched faces.

Eva's look of fascinated horror changed by rapid degrees through blank incomprehension and incredulity to dawning awareness and delight, mixed with a certain amount of sensual breathlessness as she took in Billy's full Iroquoian splendor. Billy winked at her and she, too, laughed out loud, from relief and excitement.

In moments, the other voyagers had cautiously gathered around, returning Billy's frank gaze with various expressions ranging from curiosity to half-concealed disgust.

Billy turned to them and spread his arms wide. "Welcome to America, my friends. We have arranged wagons to bring you to Smithyman House, for those who have at present had enough of traveling on water." Several cheers rang out, a few loud, but some quite faint.

"For the others, I thought a few, at least, might care to travel with me on the river to your new home." He gestured to the natives standing by the canoes.

"The warriors you see here with me are our brothers, in the Indian sense, and before the next winter has passed, you will be as grateful as I am for their help and advice. Mark them well, these Mohawks, for they are men, and although this has been their land for many generations, they share it now, with us. Make them welcome in your lives and they will welcome you."

A creaking of wood and clinking of harness signaled the appearance of the first of eight massive wagons turning down the sandy track to the shore, and all heads turned towards them.

In their wake, a number of townspeople gathered, eyeing the newcomers, some catcalling in a hostile manner at the warriors. One in particular, a tall, blond man dressed more expensively than seemed common on the waterfront, caught the eye of Billy and Richard simultaneously. Richard said, "Billy, that's..."

Billy interrupted and spoke quietly to him. "I knew he had come here, Richard. Ignore him, and get your people and your things on the wagons; I will deal with that dog."

Edward Stoatfester surveyed the gathering and sneered. He strode up to one of the idle warriors near the water's edge, working up a bit of a swagger as he went. Four rough and smelly companions armed with cudgels trailed behind him.

He pulled a pistol from his belt and pushed it hard against the warrior's chest.

He shouted, spittle spraying straight into the warrior's impassive face, "Off the shore! Back to the trading huts where you belong, you filthy scum! This is not a place for savages!"

The Indian smiled slightly and nodded, making his silver nose-bob and elongated earlobes sway. A loud bang from behind them startled the little group. They turned, to look straight into the muzzles of seven leveled muskets in the hands of the wagoners. The eighth was busily reloading. The gang froze, clubs raised. Stoatfester gaped, slowly lowering his pistol.

Billy strode rapidly up to him. Stoatfester began to swing the heavy pistol. The warrior facing him effortlessly slapped the muzzle away with the back of his left hand. Stoatfester tightened his grip to keep it from flying into the water and it discharged harmlessly, spraying sand and mud from the beach.

Stoatfester now felt his right wrist seized with a grip of iron. A large knife appeared in the warrior's right hand seemingly without any motion, like a conjurer's trick, and the warrior, now grinning widely, waved it slowly back and forth in front of Stoatfester's face.

Billy continued his advance on Stoatfester and stopped very close. "Surely, you haven't forgotten my face, now, have you, Stoatfester? I fancy it is largely the same, in spite of your efforts to improve it at FitzHugh's wedding, in the old country?"

Billy waited a moment and smiled at the look of consternation on the other man's face. Then, as Stoatfester's mouth opened in shock and recognition, Billy said, "Remain very still, you fool, if you value your life." Billy caught the eye of the warrior and shook his head slightly, stepping back half a pace.

"You haven't yet learned when to show respect to your betters, have you, Stoatfester?" Stoatfester's eyes widened as the warrior made a quick motion upwards and he felt an extremely keen edge sting him from belly to throat. His clothes parted.

He glanced down in horror and saw a red line beginning to ooze between the gaping flaps of his waistcoat and shirt. When he looked up again, Billy knocked him down, unconscious, with a single huge blow to his face. Shaking the pain from his ham-sized fist, Billy scooped up the fallen pistol with his left hand and turned to speak to Stoatfester's followers. He nudged Stoatfester with one moccasin.

"You'll be wanting to be a bit more careful about choosing your friends in future, I expect. When you talk to this bit of filth next, tell him that Billy Smithyman just saved his life, if not his clothes." He leaned close to them and smiled toothily into each face, "and maybe your own, as well."

With his own large knife, pulled from a scabbard hanging around his neck, Billy herded the crestfallen gang to one side, where the grinning Mohawks set a guard over them, brandishing tomahawks menacingly. Two of the evidently drunken thugs began to weep.

Billy turned to the warrior and handed him Stoatfester's pistol. The Mohawk man turned it over admiringly and then stuck it in his waistband. He said, "This is a heavy thing, but well made, I think. This white is lucky to have a friend such as you, although I do not think he truly appreciates your kindness."

Billy chuckled and clapped the Mohawk on his shoulder.

"You are right, my brother, he is not particularly wise, and when I knew him before, across the great Eastern sea, he was the same." The warrior nodded, solemnly, and replaced his knife in its scabbard.

"We find that many whites are truly very hard to train, Brother, and this causes us great concern, that there are so many of them and that they act so superior and yet remain so ignorant." Not for the first time, Billy found himself in total agreement with his new brethren.

After the spectacle, the immigrants loaded the wagons enthusiastically. When Edward Stoatfester awakened, he was alone on the dock, neither friend nor foe to be seen.

CHAPTER TEN

Philadelphia, 1741

If he squeezed his eyes very tightly shut, ten-year-old James Haye could still feel the soothing warmth of his mother's gentle hand caressing his forehead. He could still see the gold buttons and braid on the big, comforting cuff of his father's red uniform. It was getting harder to remember, but it still helped to keep the tears from leaking out the corners of his eyes.

He knew the tears always got him into trouble. Even when he was angry and wanted nothing more than to pound his fists into the face of Elias Ruskin, his eyes would simply fill up. Then it was so very much harder, because they would see the tears and think they had him. And they did not have him. They did not.

A leather strap smacked down in front of him on the unvarnished oak with a desk-shaking explosion. "Haye!" The hard voice roared. "Haye! Are you asleep then?"

"N-no, sir," he stammered, "I had some d-dust in my eyes."

"Dust in the eyes, is it? Then perhaps you could show us all your sums."

James held up his slate for inspection. The numbers were, of course, correct. He loved the classes. Even smelly, bullying, fat Master Jacob was better than the dark, lonely halls and damp, cold, dormitory of the orphanage, filled with ambush, fists and kicks. The tiny New England Primer, *For the More Easy Attaining of the True Reading of English,* was his most precious possession. He pored over it at every available instant and preserved it against all abuse.

He could recite the alphabetic verses perfectly, his favorite being 'E' ("Elijah hid,/By Ravens fed"), although 'H' ("My Book and Heart/Must never part") also comforted him, and he clung to it with desperate little fingers. The tiny engraved picture of the Heart enclosing the book always reminded him of his mother. The Primer also had its own personal message, seemingly writ just for him: "I leave you here a little book for you to look upon,/That you may see your father's face, when he is dead and gone." Being best in class did not help much, he supposed, but since his parents had sickened and died from ship fever on the voyage from England last year it was the only thing he had found to do where he could win and keep on winning.

Master Jacob nodded. "Very good, Haye, correct as usual. Perhaps some of the rest of you might try to think as well." The Master's breath smelt of tobacco and something sickly sweetish. He gave James' ear a mean twist before turning away. "Next time, keep your eyes open. You'd be here to learn, not to daydream."

James wished the Master would not praise him. Elias Ruskin would just give him another kick. Two seats behind him, Elias was now repeating several problems on his slate, helped along by several twists of his ear, and James could almost feel the waves of hatred beating on his back.

Although the classes were his only safe place, James had become careful to get out the door first when the lessons ended. If he dawdled, the gauntlet awaiting him outside got worse. At least if he was out first, he could sometimes get most of the way back to the hall before Elias and his gang caught him. He knuckled his eyes again and gritted his teeth. The future stretched ahead endlessly, a long road down into a dark valley. He imagined Elias' nose on the end of his fist again. It made him feel better. If he timed it just right, he might get in a couple of good licks tonight before Elias' boys knocked him down. At least he had taught them that one at a time was not enough.

He couldn't expect help. His only real friend was his messmate Johannes Pfalz, who was too thin and timid to be of use in a scrap, although he was older, and his thick German accent concealed an extremely sharp mind. Johannes and his sister had come as servants to the Philadelphia docks and he had been abandoned to the orphanage as too frail to be useful, after his sister Katrina was taken away. He had no family anywhere else. The other thirty boys in the dormitory liked the fights—they got rid of the ever-present boredom— and cared not who won or lost. Most were also frightened for themselves, and as long as Elias Ruskin picked on James Haye, they were safe.

The founder and principal of Captain Jacob Drumgool's Philadelphia School for Boys had decided to run the dormitories like a British man o' war, and so each boy had his eighteen inches of hammock width at night. The fact that Jacob Drumgool had never been to sea bothered neither him nor his paying customers one whit. The city fathers paid him several pence per head per day to keep orphans alive. If he could instruct them sufficiently to sell them off as indentured servants or apprentices into the labor-starved Pennsylvania colony or farther afield, so much the better. He kept the profits.

Johannes occupied the next hammock, and he and James were able to talk after dark each night if they were very careful not to let others hear them whispering. They were going to run away as soon as they could. Mostly, they talked about how. It would not be easy, since Master Drumgool did not want them to escape; they paid for his rum and food.

"Class dismissed!" The sudden pronouncement came and James started in his chair. His heart began to beat harder. He realized that he had lost a few precious seconds of escape time. He always sat in the front to be close to the door. He collected his book and slate, tucking the book carefully into a pocket and eyeing Elias as he pushed his way to the door in the middle of the pack. Almost into the hall, he was stopped by the bullfrog voice of Jacob Drumgool.

"Haye! Haye, I say, Haye! Come here this instant!"

He returned slowly to the front desk. He noticed Elias Ruskin grinning, aware that any chance to avoid him in the hall was certainly gone.

"Haye, did you know that you are a very lucky young fellow?" Drumgool was in a fine mood. James had heard that he sometimes received a pound or even more to supply boys to apprentice. "I have found you a place to learn a trade and make your way in the world. What do you say to that?"

James felt a sudden lightening of his heart. "That sounds very good, sir. Where might I be going, then?"

Drumgool chuckled and pulled a jug from a drawer in the desk. "You'd be going off to learn about barrels, my lad, and at the knee of one of the best coopers in the colonies, so remember this: if you don't do me proud, after all the work I've put into you, I'll track you down and cut off your ear, just like the Spaniards did to that Mr. Jenkins. Then everyone will know what an ungrateful child you really are."

James swallowed and said, "And when—?"

Jacob interrupted, "At the crack of dawn, me lad, the crack of dawn tomorrow, so pack up your worldly goods and polish your face for it. Now off wi' ye to the dormit'ry, I've got better things to do than chat with the likes of you."

James' heart was pounding as he shut the door.

I'll be free! I'll never have to see this place again.

Hope lent strength and speed. As he approached the door to the dorm, Elias Ruskin's gang advanced to meet him. He saw them come, and he felt a fierce joy light itself within him. He dropped his bundle, he clenched his fists, and he smiled.

CHAPTER ELEVEN
New York City, 1741

Turnbottle signed the receipt for "214 bales of beaver furs, 2 of marten and fisher, 1 of lynx, 1 of mink, 1 of fox, 12 of muskrat, 2 of bear, 8 of wolf—prime condition, received from Mr. William Smithyman, Esq." and set the sheet aside to dry.

Billy remarked, smiling, "There seems to be an extraordinary feeling in the city today, a feeling of fright, one might almost say! I have been in the forest and have not had the occasion to read a newspaper for weeks, so Turnbottle, pray, what is the situation? Have the Spanish landed in the night and seized Wall Street by force of arms?"

Turnbottle gave him a bleak look. "Nay, Smithyman, what has happened is that a month or two ago a whore lied to save herself and as a result the entire city has been acting disgracefully, like it has wholly lost its wits. They are to break an ignorant old slave upon the wheel tomorrow, as an example to the others, for they fear an uprising."

Billy noted his tone. "You're not convinced, Turnbottle?"

"Indeed, and any sensible person would be unconvinced on the simple word of a whore, her procurer, and a tavern owner. It is a pathetic tale. First, a drunken plumber, not noticing fire after soldering a gutter, burned down the governor's house and the barracks. Then there were some other chimney fires about, that any fool can understand were accidents, including your uncle's roof in Greenwich. And then there were also a few fires that no-one can find any cause for, and then someone saw a frightened slave running from something, and suddenly every negro man, woman and child in the City is about to cut our throats. So, some more of those godforsaken black wretches are to be publicly executed tomorrow, on the word of three of the coldest liars in America."

He spat. "It's enough to make even the strongest stomach gripe. I will not go again, but you ought, Smithyman, to see what your masters are capable of when they listen to the foolish mob. Take Vesey Street from here up across the Broadway and then left along the Boston High Road, past the Common.

They've burned a dozen or so at the stake in the last month, a short walk from there. You'll see the crowds."

It was done with haste, Billy thought, as if to have the job finished before something caught up with them. He supposed that the Roman soldiers who crushed Jesus' hands and feet before spiking them to the wooden cross had worked with similar brutal efficiency.

The black man was spread-eagled, his wrists and ankles tied to the oversized cartwheel's rim, leaving his head near the hub. He had been mainly silent, until the maul shattered each arm and leg above and below elbow and knee. Then they untied his now sufficiently flexible limbs, and wove them through the spokes of the wheel before re-securing them. His cries were terrible. This pleased the crowd. However, he fell limp and silent again and ceased to breathe as the cart was driven around the block; and they were still eager for more death when the three others were brought to be burned. Billy turned away, nauseated, pushed roughly through the jostling crowd, and returned to the warehouse.

Turnbottle poured him a large brandy and nodded at his description of the ritual. "That is the English style. The French prefer to run the wagon wheels across the guilty limbs to break them, rather than use the hammer. Last week the civic officials were not so ceremonious, simply burning four of them at the stake without the preliminaries."

Billy swirled the amber liquid. "I'll not have forbearance with any who call the Indians savage, now."

The two traders looked at each other. Turnbottle spoke again, quietly, "Nay, but those who remember Queen Anne's War know that the same frenzy of hate and bloodlust swallowed all the colonies whole, then. It's easier to become demented with those who look and speak differently, and it's all too damned easy between brothers to begin with. Here's a prayer that we don't see war again, Billy."

Billy tossed the brandy back and the glass was refilled. "Yet war with Spain may mean war with France, sooner or later, will it not?"

The other man agreed, gloomily. "That is the usual way of it. Your uncle ought to know more than most."

Billy lit a pipe with a rolled up paper stick and puffed at it before answering. "Yes, I suppose he would. But Uncle Harold has been at sea this past seven months, supporting the expedition to attack the Spaniards at Cartagena under Admiral Vernon, and since he has perceived that I have developed a certain tendency to independence on the frontier, I am not quite so welcome in his house, it seems."

Turnbottle giggled a little in his high-pitched way. "Taking furs and trade out of your aunt's in-law's pockets probably diminishes their enthusiasm for your company, d'ye think? I have a strong recollection of telling you this, myself, about four years ago, although I do not say I am reminding you of that; nay, I am not a prattling preacher who says I told you such, before."

It was Billy's turn to laugh, a little ruefully.

"I remember the day very well, Turnbottle, that I do." He frowned. "But do you know what those Albany dogs have done, up in the north? Should war come, the Indian Commissioners there will have much to answer for. They have so much cheated the local Mohawks of land and fur that they now see no great advantage in trading with us or living with us, compared to the French, but play us off against each other.

"Even more grossly, Albany openly maintains trading links to Montreal and to the Christian Mohawks living there. In time of war, it is hard to see why our Mohawk neighbors would wish to block the intrusion of the French and their allies into the heart of the English colonies. Our own defenses hardly exist. I am convinced that the French and their native allies cannot be defended from, without we have the Iroquois Confederacy to block their passage and yet..." his voice trailed off.

Turnbottle blew his dripping nose forcefully onto the warehouse floor and wiped it thoroughly with the kerchief in his sleeve. He regarded Billy thoughtfully.

"You will need to cultivate your relatives again, to achieve any influence with the governor. Since your aunt's father and his family are powerful in the Albany trade and her brother is now Chief Justice of the Province, and him also married to the daughter of one of the most powerful patroons, you may yet be able to ally with them, or at least make your views better known. Even here in New York, I have begun to hear that the Mohawks prefer to trade with you. This is probably an asset as well as a danger, but you may have to swallow some of your pride."

Billy stood and paced restlessly. "Turnbottle, I am certain that your advice is wise, but I must first make sure the foundation of my fortune is standing. A penniless Indian trader will not be worth much, whatever his connections, and my relatives will continue to dismiss me entirely until I can demonstrate wealth to them."

Turnbottle handed him the small pile of receipts. "But you are making a fortune, Billy, and helping to make mine. If you can accept more advice, I suggest that you ought to look to the next governor as someone who may well be to your liking, in his attitude to the Province. I have heard, through my connections in London, that there will likely be a change in the next year or two.

"You may take this as you wish, my friend, but I have taken the liberty of putting your name in front of the Governor's Council as someone who has the larger interests of the colony at heart. We shall see what may become of it when the new governor arrives in the fall."

Billy felt a surge of unwarranted anger.

"Turnbottle, I imagine I ought to be flattered that you think I could deal sensibly with those who have power. However, I have always felt that some of the hardest hearts of all our worlds are in London. Coming from Ireland, and then seeing what they and their minions are up to here, it is very difficult for me to hear that I should solicit their ear, at present. Although, God knows why, I keep telling the Mohawks that there are those who will listen. Let me think on this as a possible way to improve things here, and I will write you presently about it."

He sat down again and tossed back the remaining brandy.

"I hope you do not think me ungrateful, but I have very little respect for most who claim power. I would distance myself from them and build a place that shelters my family and my people from such creatures. I believe they ignore the truly downtrodden, to their peril and disgrace in the end. I do not intend to make the same mistake."

Turnbottle bowed slightly and laughed his whinnying laugh. "I have a feeling that you may yet become more influential than you dream, William Smithyman."

He shrugged. "If they contact you, it will be up to you how to respond. As for our business, the New York privateers, especially *Royal Hester*, have done well with Spanish prizes, my friend, and I will be able to invest more with you soon. I have also seen your uncle's name associated with various great captured argosies. If I'm not mistaken, he sent in a Spaniard full of sugar and indigo last month worth fully nine thousand pounds!"

Billy said, "You wrote me that you were concerned about the flour shipments."

Turnbottle giggled. "The Navy is complaining." He searched through several piles of paper.

"Ah, here it is. The Jamaica quartermaster apparently enjoys his own wit." He sipped at his brandy and eyed Billy sardonically over the glass, then read from a letter.

"He writes, 'The Navy is well used to flour weevils, but the Admiralty generally requests that its servants ensure that there be more flour than weevils by weight, at the time of purchase'."

Billy smiled in spite of himself.

"I'll have to replace the damned cooper again. The Albanians lure away every one I bring to the Northwest. They don't like it there much, even if I offer them very generous terms on land."

*****

Billy bought a brooch and a set of dishes for Katrina from Turnbottle. The brooch was a pretty enamel and gold piece from India, the dishes a translucent blue and white pottery, from China by way of the French fortress harbour at Louisbourg, on Cape Breton Island far to the northeast of the English colonies.

Turnbottle had said, showing him a delicate blue and white cup, "These are pretty, are they not? They are from a place no one can pronounce, Chingdeshen or something like that. The French seem to have cornered the Chinese market for this new porcelain, and my Louisbourg connections say it is all the rage in Europe. Perhaps you would like to bring some home to the frontier. If we go to war, my suppliers on both continents will be cut off." He knew his customer.

The brooch was the greater success.

"Ach, Vilhelm," Katrina exclaimed, clasping her hands together and twisting them about. She would not touch it at first, and Billy had to wrap her fingers gently around it.

"Ach, Vilhelm," she said again, in that guttural German accent that he liked so much.

Now, she trembled with real pleasure. She turned away from Billy and, one at a time, unwrapped her fingers, red and rough from laundry and housework, to peek at the brooch hidden beneath.

She knew Billy liked her to be happy, and soon she sighed contentedly, feeling his large hands slide possessively around her hips and up her belly to cup and lift her breasts. Her nipples hardened against his palms and she could feel his demanding hardness pressed against her buttocks. Turning quickly, she flung her hands about his neck, moving her hips against him. They coupled urgently on the soft skins in front of the flickering fireplace.

CHAPTER TWELVE
Smithyman House, 1742

The huge iron axle and gear assemblies for the mill wheel were finally set in place, and the cogs all appeared to mesh properly. Billy nodded and waved his shirt and the men opened the sluice gate. Within a few moments, the ponderous eight-foot stones began to grind around with a satisfying din, and after watching the action with anxious eyes for an hour Billy gave over control to his miller, climbed down from the mill house and stepped out onto the grass.

He glanced at the river, a hundred yards away, as he did many times each day. It never failed to please him: its ever-changing self, the entertainment of passing traffic, or the interest of new arrivals or departures. He noted that two bateaux had arrived since the last time he looked. They were beached next to eight canoes. Several new bales of fur sat outside the store.

Their owners must be inside.

A thin tendril of smoke rose vertically from the ever-burning fire on the grass in front of the wigwams at Smithyman House. Several naked children chased each other around their mothers' legs next to it, waving small hatchets.

In the opposite direction, he spotted Katrina washing clothes at the edge of the sawmill pond above the house. There was a small, white-wrapped bundle in a basket next to her and his heart beat faster. He started up the slope to see Katy and his daughter, when sudden multiple whoops and the unexpected boom of a musket from the far corner of Smithyman House to his left made him stop and turn quickly.

Eight warriors in full Mohawk regalia faced him, faces and torsos painted using designs calculated to startle and intimidate opponents, nightmarish paint masks that rendered them inhuman in appearance, all brandishing tomahawks and muskets. One, his face blackened completely with grease and charcoal, except for two-inch circles emblazoned around his eyes, one in white ash and the other vermilion, strode forward. Billy and the black-faced Emperor

Marten grasped each other's shoulders, smiling broadly, while the rest gathered, also obviously pleased to see him.

Billy said, "I can see that you are going on the path of war, my brother. But I have not heard that we are yet at war with the French. Is it the southern Indians who will soon be giving up their scalps to you and your warriors?"

Marten's expression darkened. He grimaced and shook his head. "The Onondagas have sent chiefs to speak with Onontio, the Governor in Montreal, about the strong jealousy that the Six Nations see between England and France. The Onondaga Grand Council has agreed with the Clan Mothers and has again rejected Joncaire's request to establish a post at Tierondequoit, on the shore of the great lake near the Onondaga Castles, but we will not allow the English to build there either."

He gestured to his band. "Our people danced the war dance at Canajoharie and at Dyiondarogon last night. Our party travels south tomorrow for Catawba and Cherokee scalps."

He added, solemnly, "I do not fear that the Albanians will steal babies in our absence, however. The Gantowisas, the Clan women, have allowed only a small party of fifteen to travel with me, so that the Castles remain well protected against treachery. But let us speak about what is being said around the Onondaga Council fire about the English and their promises, so that you may better understand the feelings of the Six Nations."

Billy nodded. "I will have food and drink brought to our fire this evening so that we may pass the pipe and discuss these and other important things in comfort, Marten."

Katrina smiled at him when he reached her at the little wooden bench where she was scrubbing shirts. A squalling sound came from the basket at her side. "She did not like the sound of the musket, Billy."

He looked at the tiny face and felt an enormous surge of pride and love. He leaned down and picked the bundle up, rubbing his nose against his daughter's and marveling at the grip of the tiny hands which grasped it. "Anna Christine is very strong, is she not, Katrina?"

Katrina smiled broadly at him. The sudden intensity of her happiness caused her eyes to water and she turned away, pretending to concentrate on the linen shirt in her hands.

*****

The fire blazed up as they laid the huge spruce logs on it, the sparks swirling far up into the night. The five dozen men and women around it moved back into the cooler shadows, satiated with corn, venison and pork stew, along with catfish and turkey.

Billy signaled for Elijah, one of the servants he had purchased in Albany. The black man trotted across the grass from where the spit still turned. Billy beckoned him close. "Elijah," Billy whispered, "it is time to broach the special keg of rum we have prepared and serve it to the general party, but for our guests here and myself, bring us more of my punch."

Soon, a servant wheeled a keg from group to group on a wagon. Its dangling pewter cups clashed together with a hollow sound. Marten, Billy, and two women stayed together, moving to a small canvas shelter set up for them to one side. When the large pewter bucket of punch arrived, filled with sliced limes, Billy directed Elijah back to the stone house for the new pipe to be brought to him.

Once it was lit, he and Marten passed it back and forth in silence until the first bowl was finished. Then Marten handed the pipe to the young woman who sat beside Billy, who began to refill it, and broke the silence.

"That appears to be very like pipestone, Billy, but not quite the same color."

Billy agreed. "Yes, it has come from a Lake called Winipegon, far to the northwest in the Anishinabe lands beyond the Ojibwa country, where there is a mountain of it, I am told. Please keep it as a token of our friendship."

Marten said, "You are truly an Englishman who acts like a brother to us. We have not experienced such a thing from Dutch or English, for twenty years." He gestured to the women beside them.

"I have consulted with the Gantowisas, the women who govern the Clan Mother Councils. When I return from the south, we have agreed we will bring you to council to become an honorary Mohawk. My eldest daughter Onasawizio, Beautiful Feather, and my wife, Wind-Through-the-Spruces, who you know well, have convinced me that this would be a suitable thing for you. They have not yet chosen a name for you, however. This requires more dreaming." The two women laughed.

Billy said, "I would be greatly honored to be part of the Mohawk nation. How must I prepare for this?"

Beautiful Feather began to massage his neck and upper back. "I have chosen to be your advisor and guide your dreams. I will make the recommendation, and the Clan Mothers' Council will choose."

⸳They smoked another pipe. Billy said, "Father, it is too sudden to speak of concerns, but please accept my unnatural white man's rudeness in this. What are the views of the Council at Onondaga?"

"Your impetuosity is well known, my son," Marten sighed, "but I will relate to you the things that the Council is saying. These are to be discussed at a Six Nations Council called to meet in Philadelphia, before the leaves fly.

"There are complaints about settlers on the banks of the Juniata, which flows into the Susquehanna but was not part of the sale of that territory. These complaints had been sent to your brother Onas, as we call the Governor of Pennsylvania, but the magistrates that Onas sent to remove the settlers only made surveys for themselves, and they are in league with the trespassers."

Marten paused in appreciation and puffed on his pipe. Wind-Through-the-Spruces and Beautiful Feather were removing their dresses. In a few seconds, the men resumed their discussion, remaining cross-legged on the blankets, but now with warm, soft bodies pressed against their backs and long legs encircling their waists. Feminine arms and hands stroked and caressed, and hugged tight.

"Billy, the Joncaires are telling us that the governor of New York, that we call Corlaer, has been proposing to the French Governor Onontio a plan to unite your two nations, for the entire destruction of our people. You know that I am of the Mactegouche nation by birth and Mohawk only by adoption. The Connecticut and Massachusetts English have already destroyed my father and our people, and taken all our land away. There are many who think that what happened in the past to my people, and before them to the wampum makers on the Manhattan Island, and that now has also happened to all of the Hudson River Indians, is going to happen next to the Six Nations, at the hands of the Dutchmen in Albany."

Billy felt a deep rage, but spoke evenly and lightly, "My friend, these Joncaires are fine liars and even a moment's thought would remove this doubt. As you have often related to me, in your ancestors' time was it not the French who allied with your enemies the Hurons and attacked the Longhouse without provocation at the lake? How is it now that the Longhouse Chiefs listen so closely to such counsel from the same French?

"No, my Father, it is clear that the English would not do this thing, even if the French would pray for such an event, and will be laughing behind their hands to hear such talk. It is sure that this rumor is just a French trick, although it is also true that the Albany traders would certainly desire to do such a thing."

Marten murmured. "With their greed they get us drunk and steal from us what is not in our power to sell. We thought we were being paid to share the land, which we deemed a respectful attitude. But we were wrong. We find that your people think that they no longer have to share what they have bought. They have murdered us in our sleep, for our land is our life."

"Marten, I have been asked by some in New York who are concerned by these events to do more than trade. Some have asked me to help advise my country in these matters. I have begun to understand better that those in Albany often do not speak with the same mind as those in London or even in

New York. I will write to New York to find whether the time is a good one to begin such activities.

"But I now have a question, my good friend. It is said that the warriors of the Six Nations do not indulge in the pleasures of man and woman before battle, yet I can see that you are not hesitating in that respect?"

Marten smiled and murmured to Wind-Through-the-Spruces, who giggled and reached around him to re-pack the pipe. "Ah, my son, it is well known that Mactegouche warriors do not have the same evil feelings about making babies before battle as the Six Nations people do.

"In our culture we do not think it is a waste of a man's power, but instead it is a demonstration of his courage. For when a man is afraid, is it not true that his manhood can develop a shrinking illness?

"And is it also not better that a warrior should leave a seed planted before he goes to battle, in case he falls? It is true that many of the Longhouse people do not approve of my feelings in this, but, as you see now, even they are not unanimous at all times."

The camp had gone relatively silent, only snores coming from most locations around the fire. Marten cocked his head and listened for a moment, then said, "My friend, it is very still, is it not? How is it that I am rarely told stories of fights or killings or loud arguments when my people have come from meetings at Smithyman House? This is unheard of where you serve liquor in such abundance. Even the very meekest of the original people often find demons to fight, after so much rum. Yet here we never have a need to appoint one who is to refuse the drink and watch over his brethren who become maddened by the rum."

Billy's face was solemn in the firelight. "I will not often trade rum for furs, for that very reason. But, Father, you would be the first to admit that there will be no trading where there is never any rum. I will tell you the secret, my friend, if you first swear that you and your family will never reveal it, for although it is no magic thing, it is better, perhaps, that few should know of it."

Marten nodded, slowly. "I would like to know the secret of this quiet behaviour."

Billy leaned over and said, "There is a certain strong medicine, made from the sap of flower buds that only grow very far away, in mountains on the other side of a great salt sea that begins beyond the rocky rim of this world, to the west.

"When drunk in the proper quantity, this powerful medicine causes the eyelids to become very heavy with sweet dreams that cannot be resisted. The brandy and rum demons then cannot be easily awakened for a time. Unfortunately, it is extremely rare and costly. In the day's last keg of rum I sometimes put some of this special medicine, so that my guests and friends may sleep without having to fight demons."

"Haugh! That is impressive medicine, Billy. You have without doubt saved lives, then, at gatherings here. But you have placed a heavy burden on us to keep this secret. I now put the same burden on you. Do not let our enemies know, because they might find that it makes their ability to trick us much greater."

Billy smiled. "This medicine is known to many whites, but most could not afford to use it, even when they know it would further their evil purposes. It is dispensed in special stores in the cities, only by permission of our medicine men. Your people will remain safe from this, but I promise to you not to reveal this knowledge."

Billy felt a more insistent caress move across his back, down his sides to his thighs and further, and a warm breath murmured in his ear. "Enough talk, for one night! You men would talk until sunrise. The night is better used for other things."

*****

The next morning, Katrina brought little Anna toddling over to him and he reached out to seize her and swing her high above his head several times, where she gurgled happily, waving stubby arms and legs. Billy hugged her close until she began to squirm and released her back to her mother.

"Katy," Billy began, "I have been asked to go to Onondaga for the Midwinter festival and to receive a Longhouse name. This..."

She held up a hand, frowning, and said in a low voice, "It is not for you to explain to me. You know I do not enjoy sharing you, for you have made me happy beyond all, but I would not have you soothe me, like a milch cow in the barn. I am yours; just do not make me ashamed for that, in your house." She turned away without meeting his eyes and left the room.

Billy watched her go, in silence. In a few minutes, a servant appeared, and he asked for his gear to be made ready for departure the next day.

CHAPTER THIRTEEN
Onondaga Castle

Onondaga was one of the largest of the Iroquois towns or castles, and its people had seen no attacks for half a century. Nestled in one of the long, fertile lake valleys south of Lake Ontario, which point away from the big lake like the fingers of a spread hand, it was sheltered from weather and politics alike, and no palisades or guards appeared anywhere.

Here was the traditional meeting place of the Grand Council, where the 49 clan representatives governed the Iroquois League. The Gantowisas had selected these sachems to represent them, each from the correct mother's hereditary line. Five or six dozen 70-foot elm-bark longhouses were scattered about, and even in the depths of winter, it was clearly an important place.

Billy's party had arrived near the end of the nine-day festival; a blizzard having slowed their progress on the ten-day journey from Smithyman House. They accepted lodging in a longhouse reserved for out-of-town visitors, and the band of 40 men and women quickly established who would be sleeping where.

Muskets and other belongings went on the top of the six-foot-wide double bunks or hung from the joists and rafters. For a time after they had kindled their cooking fires down the centre aisle, breath still hung frostily in the air, but the warm furs covering the lower bunks beckoned seductively and many lay down to rest from the journey.

Emperor Marten, Beautiful Feather, Wind-Through-the-Spruces and Billy gathered about their fire after greeting and displaying Billy to a large number of their friends. Billy drew the Onondagans' attention as a candle draws moths. Fewer than a dozen white men had been seen in Onondaga over two generations, except as slaves or as prisoners-of-war to be adopted or tortured.

Over the fire, an iron stewing kettle full of corn, beans and venison hung suspended, just beginning to steam. It was moderately smoky in the longhouse, but the men had cleared the bark-covered roof vents of snow and slid them open, so that some of the acrid murk was beginning to stir upwards.

Marten went out for several hours. When he returned, an ancient woman preceded him into the longhouse. She brought a woven basket to Beautiful Feather, who added its contents to the kettle. Marten lit a pipe and passed it to Billy. "You will be named tomorrow. Faugh! We have missed almost everything. The Faces have already danced and the white dog has already been burned, although," he gestured at Beautiful Feather, "some of his meat has been saved for us."

Billy looked a question. Marten responded, "My son, the white dog sacrifice purifies our community and keeps it from harm, if there are no marks of injury on it. We strangle the dog, and then we make it more beautiful with paint and beads, ribbons and feathers, before we offer it to the heavens. This is done on a fire with tobacco smoke to carry it away, with our gratitude and prayers. We share the meat among us to bring the purity into our bodies."

He glanced upward to where he had carefully hung a black, wooden mask on a peg facing the wall. "I would have enjoyed having my Face talk with the others, but perhaps there will be a dream to tell during the next festival at Thanks-to-the-Maple time."

Billy said, "Would they not have waited for us? There are no other Mohawks here."

The three shook their heads and Marten replied, "No, English."

Wind-Through-the-Spruces explained, "The Ceremony must begin five days, exactly, after the first new moon following the time the Seven Star Sisters fly highest in the sky, or our seasons will be disorganized. Often there are no other nations here, so each one has its own ceremony to begin the New Year. We came only to let all the League know that they have a new white friend that the Mohawks recognize by a Longhouse name."

Billy said, "I will always be grateful for the honor you give me. It seems very difficult sometimes to see a clear way ahead. I am hoping that my new name will help me to see far enough to help my friends the Haudenosaunee." He paused a moment, then asked, in spite of himself, his eyes focused on the fire, "What is my name to be?"

The three Mohawks burst out laughing. "You will find out tomorrow, after the final Great Feather Dance. You are curious, English, like a child; it is true! If we had been here, perhaps we should have put your name forward during the boiling-of-the-babies, as we call the soup-ceremony when we name the newborn on the first day!"

Billy nodded, looking from one happy face to another and smiling ruefully. "That is a cruelty, to say my naming should be with the infants. Did I not fast according to the proper ways, and relate my true dream to you, that my guardian Orenda appeared to me in the summer, and that it is the spirit of the great cat-with-short-tail? Yet you will not tell me, and my soul strains to know, that I may make a proper reply."

Beautiful Feather put a hand on his arm. "It is not done, Billy. You must respond to your naming at the Council, without any prior knowledge of it, except from your Orenda or another dream. It is the way."

Marten huffed in silent laughter at Billy's torment.

At dawn, the Big Heads arrived, bringing the seventh and final notification of the New Year to each longhouse. Wearing long, shaggy bearskin coats and corn-husk masks, they danced up and down the aisle, accepting gifts of food and warning the sleepers to attend Council and reveal their dreams, or they would end up stuck-to-the-ceremonies, and spring would be delayed.

Billy stripped to a loincloth and high moccasins and they painted him from forehead to waist. He slicked his hair down firmly with bear grease. When he arrived at the ceremonial longhouse, he squatted with his friends, awaiting his announcement celebration, which Marten would lead.

His heart beat faster when the two drummers, straddling a battered wooden bench and wielding rattles made from three-foot diameter snapping turtle shells, began to bang out the rhythms of the Great Feather Dance. The splendidly be-feathered dance leaders commenced spinning and leaping about the longhouse.

Shouts and songs of praise to the Great Creator rose from every mouth. Suddenly, the drumming and dancing stopped as quickly as it had started. Marten got to his feet and strode to the center of the longhouse, smiling and waving in response to hoots from friends, occasionally calling something to them. He was wearing a buckskin dress, elaborately embroidered from neck to fringed hem with wampum and dyed quills. Billy heard him begin his oration, but many of Marten's words were lost and he could only stand, unprepared, when it became obvious at the end of the speech that he was being summoned.

"Behold! As I have related to you, I am honored to have been chosen to be a woman today by the Gantowisas of Dyiondarogon, to announce great tidings to the Great Council Fire at Onondaga." Marten paused for effect after each sentence.

"Here is a man." An approving murmur rumbled about the house.

"He has dreamed and found his Orenda." A cheer or two arose. Marten smiled broadly.

"He has given us his children, as many of our women can affirm." Laughter came from every corner.

"He has eaten of the white dog. And so, to all the Gantowisas of the Haudenosaunee, our honored leading women, who guide all our thoughts and provide light for our decisions as we travel our paths in the darkness, and to my family and neighbors, Councilors and sachems, he has shown himself a true friend to your brothers and sisters of the Flint People, who are the Guardians of the Eastern Door to the Iroquois League.

"So, I present to you, Onondagans, our Turtle Clan brother, who will now be known as 'Io'tonhwahere; The Waters Deepen for Him.' For truly, he has moved the waters at his house between our castles, our fortified settlements, to make great things. The stream now makes bread flour and wooden boards for houses, where before there was only forest. Yo-hay! We see that he seeks to gently turn the river of our people into new paths, to deepen the water for our canoes and to help us all, the same as our brothers the beavers have always helped us." Billy heard many shouts of "Yo-hay, our brother!"

And then Billy stood, and said only, "Katatenatons—I am called... Io'tonhwahere." And he danced his dance, blinded in the smoking torches, unknowing where the impulse flowed from, and after an indeterminate time he stood dripping with sweat, his arms flung wide, his head back and his eyes closed. His name dance was finished, and he had become an Iroquois brother.

CHAPTER FOURTEEN
The Van Nes Estate near Albany, 1743

It was not their style to meet as a group. They usually preferred quiet one-on-one settings to discuss issues that arose and to make decisions, but this was one of the rare exceptions. Jacob De Vere, father of Billy's aunt Sophia, had cajoled, wheedled and bullied the reluctant patroons and traders into a meeting at the Van Nes mansion to discuss the war.

The front of the Van Nes estate, its narrowest dimension, began a day's ride south of Albany. It followed the contours of the edge of the Hudson River for twenty-two miles. The guests arrived by boat, none of them willing to inflict the hardship of an agonizingly rough wagon road upon themselves.

Besides, the water route was infinitely faster, safer, more familiar, and far cheaper. All of their goods were exported or imported by water, and several of them had crossed the Atlantic more than once following up their business interests. The Albany sloops they built and owned were luxuriously outfitted. They would have regarded anyone taking the road as out of their minds.

Some arrived without their usual entourage of a dozen or more personal servants and slaves, it being understood, of course, that the host would provide all such amenities. Their wives relished this rare opportunity to exclude their husbands' mistresses, and they were enthusiastically greeting each other at the house.

Jacob De Vere, having persuaded his brother-in-law that the meeting must take place at his home, had promptly inherited the task of organizing it. His wife Judith bustled about with her mother, making sure that house guests were shown to their bedrooms in the spotless household and given an opportunity to rest.

Jacob greeted them all with the ease of long practice in the Courts, the Assembly and the Governor's Council. Honeyed phrases and knowledgeable banter helped to deflect the pointed grumbling of the burghers that business would suffer and the verdammt young scoundrels left behind in their offices knew nothing. The well-known expertise of the Van Nes cooking staff blunted any residual bad tempers.

"At least, Mijnheer," Jacob pointed out to Pieter Voortman, "you will not have to deal with the smallpox or yellow fever at Van Nes Manor."

Voortman's naturally dour face did not brighten much. Standing nearby, wearing a deferential air, was a tall blond man inclined to dandified clothing. Voortman nodded in his direction, "I believe you have already met my secretary, Edward Stoatfester?"

De Vere also nodded and smiled. "Mr. Stoatfester and I have discussed our growing problems with the Mohawks and their newfound friend, my nephew William Smithyman, more than once. I believe Stoatfester is rendering valuable service to our cause."

Stoatfester bowed slightly, unsmiling. De Vere waved them into the house, turning to see another boat pulling to the dock. "Please excuse me, my friends. Judith will direct you to your rooms where you may relax from your journey. We will meet after dinner to discuss these issues in detail."

Nearly twenty-four hours of feasting and carousing later, Edward Stoatfester was becoming impatient. He mentally sneered at the boisterous Dutchmen, who were now competing in a waterborne version of Pull-the-Goose, alongside a fair number of Van Nes's tenant farmers and their sons.

Will these childish idiots never get down to business?

He watched Voortman, smiling like a lunatic and as round as a goose himself. He was crouching on the broad plank that stuck out past the rowboat's stern, as the crew maneuvered the boat towards the bird dangling overhead. Voortman flexed his fat fingers in anticipation.

Out of the corner of his eye, Stoatfester saw lovely Anneke Voortman laugh. He relished the sight of her fifteen-year-old bosom bouncing as her father lunged upward and clutched, losing his balance comically as the big bird muscularly wrenched its head out of his grasp. Voortman fell with a tremendous splash into the river and the crowd roared with delight.

By God, I have to have her, there is nothing like her anywhere in the province!

Each of the guests had agreed to use another's boat and crew, in the interests of fairness. The crews rowed with vein-bursting, drunken abandon. Their job was to ensure that their master's competitor, perched at the back of their boat like a plump vulture, had the smallest possible chance to seize and carry off the bird as they passed beneath it. The goose was suspended upside down, its feet secured to a rope strung overhead between two sloops, with its head and neck barely within reach and liberally coated in grease.

The guests of the manor went first, of course, in an order of eminence determined by unwritten rules that had evolved through long association and practice. The host got first chance, then the richest of the guests, then the oldest, then the fattest.

After the first half dozen attempts had ended with every one of the drunken sportsmen tumbling off the plank, to the great glee of the audience and the exchange of some silver ashore, the desperate goose had usually determined from which direction its next tormenters would arrive.

Now the serious betting started. As the crowd's cheering increased, the next dozen men found their job more difficult—they had to shield their eyes from the goose's now well-directed beak as well as get an unbreakable grip on the eel-like neck. If the goose stayed tethered through the first two dozen attempts, they declared the match a draw, for it was considered unsporting to pull a dead goose off the rope.

The ancient Dutch governors had declared the sport an illegal, popish sort of activity a hundred years before, but it remained a very popular pastime, at least for many who lived up the river from New York. Some called it an English pastime. In any case, the British Governors had sensibly put a higher priority on leeching away some of the wealth of their Dutch constituents than imposing some dour Old Dutch or New Englandish sort of morality on them.

Stoatfester caught De Vere's eye at the other edge of the dock and inclined his head slightly towards the house. De Vere glanced about quickly as if to size up the gathering and nodded once, briefly.

The two young men preceded the raucous company. They each seized a glass of wine, then descended the broad steps into the garden.

"Damn them for a herd of children," Stoatfester began, "your patience is beyond my temper's hold."

The two men, one bulky and dressed stylishly in coloured silks and laces, the other slender, clothed in a very conservative manner, went strolling through the extensive grounds shaped by hedges that Van Nes's father had affected, following the style set in Versailles by Louis XIV's gardener Le Nôtre.

De Vere looked at him, amused, and said, "You would have them get down to the serious plotting immediately? I would not. After they have tired themselves with drink and play, they are much, much more malleable, my friend. Hot iron is far more workable than cold, is it not?"

Stoatfester grudgingly agreed. De Vere continued. "So, we are still agreed that we have four goals?" He held up his hand and ticked off his fingers. "First and foremost, we must protect the Albany trade with the French, or our friends and ourselves will face ruin. Our other objectives flow from this one.

"To protect the Albany trade, we must frustrate the governor in his ambition to ally with the New England colonies, who we know are being attacked by the French and their Indians. Such an alliance would make it more difficult to continue our trade with Montreal.

"Likewise, we must keep the Mohawks neutral and the Six Nations divided, trading with the Mohawk kin to our advantage.

"Fourth, we must discourage settlements northeast and northwest of Albany, which do nothing for us, but threaten the fur trade and provide wealth to our competitors. Do you agree?"

Stoatfester took a pinch of snuff into each nostril from a tiny gold box, his hands nearly hidden in the froth of lace about his wrists, before he replied. "Yes, I think those are sensible goals, and there is one man who is the key to our success if he can be brought low.

"We must seek a way to discredit Smithyman in the Governor's eyes and break him financially. If he falls, the Mohawks and probably all the Iroquois will remain pleasantly neutral. The French will have no need to disturb them in our region. Our interests in the Oswego fur trade will be strengthened by the removal of his competition as well, and his dangerous persistence in taking up the false land claims of those savage scum with the royal authority will be over. I think he is an important obstacle to our prosperity and security, sir."

"There are some faint hearts in the Assembly who tremble fearfully over the military nakedness of Albany," De Vere mused, "but I believe they can be distracted from action, or at least from decisive action. The presence of militia, forever looking nervously about for signs of attack, would make our normal back and forth traffic with Montreal far more visible than is healthy.

He nodded his head in the direction of the river.

"Our goal with our fun-loving friends, here," he said, "must be to persuade them to wrap the Assembly in their smothering arms and convince all that the old peace will hold."

The two men reached a dead end in the maze and turned. Stoatfester inspected his fingernails. "How will we convince the old farts to do nothing, then? They will certainly have heard of the massacres in Massachusetts and New Hampshire."

De Vere frowned and stopped for a moment, listening to a distant, drunken roar. "The goose is evidently plucked; we must return."

He gestured to the musket loopholes in the walls of the stone manor house, just visible over the hedge, and under the roof of the broad stoep surrounding the building.

"Yes, I expect that the Massachusetts colony will declare war shortly against the French Indians. Even as far south as here some might begin to look out for Indian summer again, like the old days, unless we can turn their heads away from the northeast and back to their own domains."

He smiled whimsically. "Did you know, my dear Stoatfester, why Indian Summer is the name of that warm week that sometimes comes just before winter, melting the first snows?"

Stoatfester shrugged. "I was not born here and cannot be expected to know all the quaint little customs in the colony."

De Vere looked at him. A small smile lingered at the corner of his mouth, but his eyes remained expressionless. "It is called Indian summer because snow on the ground normally ends the warpath season. Then for a week when the snow melts again, it allows one last time of scalping and massacres before winter makes the forest trails impractical for fast war parties. Yet it has been a long period of peace in this colony; so long that most people seem to remember only the comforting warmth of Indian summer and not the massacres. We must continue to soothe them, must we not?"

*****

"Tomorrow?!" Stoatfester ground his teeth.

De Vere flashed him a warning glance and responded quickly to cover up. "Of course, Mijnheer Voortman, tomorrow will be fine for our meetings. We must certainly allow time to bring clear heads to our group. We have important things to discuss."

Stoatfester waited just long enough for no perception of rudeness to be possible on the part of his employer, then stalked out of the room and strode down to the river, now reflecting amber and black from the hills on the other side.

It was dusk, and thousands upon thousands of waterfowl paddled about near the shore. Many still had a crowd of ducklings clustered about them, but now, at the end of summer, the young were almost indistinguishable from their parents. Stoatfester itched to get a fowling musket, but he knew that he would also have to get permission from Van Nes, and he was unwilling to do so. He took some snuff.

His frustration increased tenfold when high-pitched giggles reached his ear. He looked back and saw Anneke Voortman walking from the orchard up to the great house surrounded by a crowd of friends. She had braided her long hair and curled it up into a golden crown and she was carrying several dozen apples in her apron.

Unseen near the docks, he stared at her from darkness as she walked up the stairs and into the house. Almost bursting from lust, he cursed softly several times, and then walked back up to the house and around it to the

125

servants' quarters. As he turned the corner and vanished, a twenty-four-foot bateau rowed into sight from the north, heading for the dock with five people aboard, four rowers and a passenger.

It caught De Vere's eye and he waited expectantly. When the servant had brought word of the new arrivals, he thanked God fervently and hurried to the dock. *It was a damned near run thing. If the old bastard had not turned up in time, I might have had a very difficult proposal to sell.*

He embraced Old Cornelius and sent his extremely dirty, tired crew to join the servants in the house for food and refreshment.

They waited while the slave accompanying De Vere lit a torch near the path. De Vere dismissed him and poured the old trader and interpreter a mug of rum from the decanter on the large wooden table on the dock. They filled pipes and walked over to the torch to light them, then returned to the shadow.

Cornelius waved his pipe appreciatively, blowing the blue smoke up into the still air and leaning back in his whitewashed wooden chair. He lifted the mug and drained it.

"This is good rum. Have you another for an old man, De Vere?" Without waiting for a reply, he offered the mug for a refill, draining that as well. "I like your tobaccy, too."

He wiped his mouth and exhaled in contentment, grinning a gap-toothed smile at De Vere, who reflected that the Indian interpreter's mouth resembled the rotting palisades of Saratoga.

"You are a week late. Do you have news?" De Vere asked, controlling his impatience with difficulty.

Cornelius grunted assent. "Ja, Mijnheer, the Six Nations are not in panic, we need have no fear at this time."

De Vere rolled his eyes heavenward briefly in thanks.

"You have come at the perfect time, then, my old friend," he said, "with the perfect news. I have a place for you to rest, but you will need to present the observations from your tour of the Six Nations to our group tomorrow. Did they give you belts?"

No belts of wampum given after the meetings would mean that the observations were not to be depended upon. Cornelius squinted at him in the dark. "Ja, Jacob, they give me some small belts at Onondaga, with much ceremony. They are hiding something, but it does not appear that they will go over to the French."

"Good, good, that is good news. They are always hiding something, are they not?" De Vere smiled broadly. He gestured to the manor house, framed by torchlight at the corners of the stoep.

"Come! Come now, old friend, you have had a long journey of many weeks. You must come and get some true Dutch hospitality before tomorrow, but, I beg you, wait one more day before you take your pay. I require you to make this presentation properly to the patroons and the Indian Commissioners that are here, before your job is finished."

The lined, bearded old face winked and smiled. "Ja, Ja, I remember well, De Vere. I will finish the job tomorrow, you will pay me, and then, Albany is mine, ha ha! Maybe New York, even!"

*****

Now they were ready to talk. A huge roast of moose had vanished in an hour or so, along with turkey, pigeon, duck, goose and ham, dozens of hot loaves of bread, pounds of fresh-churned butter and several wheels of Van Nes's best cheese. As there was still something remaining in the cask of red wine, it trailed along behind the men on a wagon and was carried upstairs by four slaves. The men moved into the slightly smaller meeting room, removing their bibs and wiping their faces.

There, Van Nes's famous ebony table and sixteen matching chairs awaited them. Three large silver candelabra marched down the centre of the huge table. His grandfather had acquired the ebony logs from a cousin in the Dutch East India Company, the VOC. Craftsmen in Amsterdam had created the furniture to his order. Each of the chairs had the detailed Van Nes coat of arms carved into the back.

At one time, the patriarch's competitors tried to discredit him by spreading the rumor that it was not his cousin that he got it from, but murderous Madagascar pirates who had looted a Christian vessel, but such malicious gossip had only enhanced his reputation as a canny trader.

Voortman, as always, was the first to speak, in his curt fashion, after the scraping and creaking of chairs had nearly ceased. "All right, Van Nes, you have us all here, what is it you wish us to hear?"

Van Nes merely waved at Jacob De Vere. Jacob stood, elegantly bewigged and robed, as befitted the Chief Justice of the Province of New York, and began his speech.

"Gentlemen," he began, "friends, neighbors, partners," he paused, and bowed gracefully, "Patroons." A gust of appreciative laughter swept the room and he knew he could do it. He had hit the right note.

He spoke for an hour and then called in Old Cornelius, freshly scrubbed, to present his report. The Pennsylvania interpreter was well known to those present, and he punctuated his report by impressive flourishes as he tossed the several black and white beaded belts from Onondaga onto the table. When Old Cornelius was finished, De Vere took the floor again.

"So, my friends, Patroons, members of the Indian Council, that is my proposed path for us to follow, through the coming times. It is reasonably simple, but if we waver, it cannot work."

It quickly became clear that they were well on their way to being convinced. After some half-hearted objections, they looked at one another and agreed that it was a good plan.

*****

At the time of the guests' departure, the small matter of the Van Nes house slave with the broken arm and nose came up privately. Her foreman stood up for her. The injuries were apparently received when she had refused to allow one of the Voortman party to perform a certain carnal act on her. A modest note of payment dealt with this—Voortman bargained Van Nes down to twelve beaver pelts—accompanied by the shaking of older, wiser heads.

"The English are still barbarians, are they not?" So the discussion went. "But young men will have their way. He is an impetuous one, however, and we shall have to watch him in future. Truly, Mijnheer, good house slaves, even black ones, are very difficult to find."

To lead requires a skin seven thumbs thick.

—Iroquois Proverb

CHAPTER FIFTEEN
New York, 1744

"Your Excellency," Billy began, "I cannot pretend that my nature prods me into having much interest in furthering the general weal by way of political involvement. I much prefer to assist in improving my own situation and the state of those around me through direct actions. Unhappily, I now find myself in a position where I must do what I can to persuade you that action must be taken, or the frontier of the province is assuredly in peril."

The audience with Governor Clayton had been arranged through correspondence, Turnbottle's connections being effective and subtle. Billy wore his finest new wig and gold-laced pale blue coat, and round-toed shoes in the new style with silver buckles. *It is an extravagance, without doubt, but if I am to have influence, it may help.*

He restrained his ever-present dislike of the powerful enough to appreciate what appeared to be an inclination on the part of Governor Clayton to pursue the best interests of the colony, if only to increase his own income. He continued his presentation.

"Oswego was immediately abandoned by all the traders, my lord, when they received news of the declaration of war with France. This disgraceful exhibition of cowardice on the part of the traders has shaken all the Six Nations. For now, it has also convinced some of the northern nations, like the Ojibwa, that the French will win. Those who arrived at the post to trade in the past weeks found only a few soldiers there, and no trade goods or traders at all."

Billy thought it politic not to mention that these canoes had then made their way to Smithman House and had returned home rather more satisfied, in spite of the extra distance traveled.

"The Six Nations require some evidence to sustain their belief that we will defend them as well as simply depending on them to defend us. The women whom they call Gantowisas are very powerful and they will refuse to declare war against the French on behalf of people who will not fight even to defend themselves. Their men are true warriors, and also find it difficult to respect us."

The governor nodded, slowly. "What do you suggest, my good Smithyman?"

"Sir, I believe that Oswego must first be substantially reinforced. At present, there are fewer than thirty soldiers there. They cannot be expected to sustain a defense against a determined attack. The fort itself is not in repair. This post is a critical one, diverting wealth from the French in Montreal..."

The Governor interrupted, smiling slightly. "Diverting wealth into your pockets before it gets to Albany as well, I understand."

Billy colored a bit. *This Governor is better informed than I thought.*

"Sir, I will own that I have developed some trading partnerships in Oswego and that any fur trade that does pass by them I attempt to intercept on its way to Albany. If there is no military defense at Oswego, however, the French can sweep very quickly down the Mohawk Valley. All of the northwest frontier, and the Mohawk castles themselves, are very vulnerable."

He paused. "Not to mention Albany itself."

Before the Governor could comment again, he added with a smile, "It's quite true that my family and estates are vulnerable with them.

"But my second point, sir, is that the path south to Albany from the French fort at Crown Point is not defended, either. The advanced post at Saratoga is a rude joke, and I gather that the soldiers there must sleep in their tents even in the winter, since the buildings have all rotted. This fast and easy invasion route is wide open. I have observed also that there could be a fort built at the south or north end of Lac St-Sacrement, as the French call it, to counter Crown Point."

"And what of the Six Nations? Will they not defend their own homes, either?"

Billy permitted himself a smile. "They have for many years been persuaded that neutrality between the irresistible force of France and the immovable object of England is the wisest course. My goal is to have them accept that Britain must win; that she will win in the end, and that it is, therefore, in their own best interests to be seen as an ally." He stopped and glanced out the multi-paned window, then back at the Governor. "Sir, may I be candid?"

Governor Clayton waved a gloved hand. "Speak, my boy, I am not the King, only his humble representative."

Billy collected his thoughts for a moment. "It is possible that I may be able to engage the Mohawks on our behalf. This will not be easy or quick, and it is unlikely that the rest of the nations will follow at first, but I am prepared to undertake to do this. The Albany traders have treated them abominably, but they retain an almost incomprehensible loyalty to the governors and the Crown.

"If we can revive their trust in us and their interest in our success, it will further our ability to settle this frontier. They are relatively few, but they are truly exceptional warriors and also diplomats, in my humble opinion. I believe that the most far-seeing among them understand that their old ways will end, perhaps not tomorrow or next year, but they will end.

"Emperor Marten, their most respected war chief, visited London in Queen Anne's time, and again a few years ago. He knows, as few of his race do, that a few thousand of his people cannot hope to stand forever in the forests if the full flood of Europeans arrives, and he views us with some respect.

"I would help these people gain sufficient time to adjust their entire society to English ways. If they cannot adjust, they are doomed. Sir, they have been our friends, our trading partners and respected allies for a hundred years. They deserve better from our so-called civilization than to be extinguished as if they never existed. It is true that I am becoming wealthy because they trade with me, but, I submit, your Lordship, that they trade with me because they trust me. I would not betray that trust."

The Governor smiled and began to clap his gloved hands together, softly. He said, "Passion for the defenseless is an admirable thing, young man."

He met Billy's eyes with a long, expressionless stare. "Based on what I know, however, I have yet to be convinced that the Iroquois can be described as vulnerable. They claim too loudly to have such vast dominion over the lesser tribes. Nonetheless, you make a fine case that it is in our interests to engage them more fully in our cause."

He rose, and Billy rose with him. "Thank you for taking the time to acquaint me with the situation as you see it, Smithyman. I will consider it carefully with my Council before I next approach the Assembly. I trust your return to Smithyman House will be uneventful."

Billy bowed. "Thank you, Your Excellency. I am very grateful for the opportunity to speak to you. However, I suspect that for the next few years, my house will probably be known as Fort Smithyman."

Several weeks later, Governor Clayton was dining with his Chief Justice. They had left the table and were settling into the drawing room. De Vere, anticipating another opportunity to extend his influence, found the Governor suddenly redirecting their discussion.

"De Vere, I have received a letter from this Smithyman fellow."

"Indeed, Governor?"

"Yes, and it is a letter which tells me things I am not hearing from others, many of whom are supposed to be in a position to know. Do you not agree, De Vere, that we must do all we can to fortify the frontier?"

The Chief Justice of the Province of New York sighed. "Governor, we have had thirty years of peace on the frontier. The Indian Commissioners feel there is little chance of the French Indians from Montreal attacking us, since their blood relatives live here, on the Mohawk. There is thus little reason to expend taxes where no risk entails."

"This Smithyman seems to think that the French are seducing the Six Nations into hostility."

"He has been here only six years, Governor. It is difficult to believe, is it not, that he would suddenly have acquired more wisdom than those in Albany, who not only have been familiar with the savages their whole lives, but whose fathers traded with them as well?

"My Lord Governor, I have it on very good authority indeed that Mr. Smithyman is not to be trusted, nor is he in fact trusted, by any individual in Albany of substance who is engaged in trade or with the Indians. We also hear that he fled to New York ahead of Irish law, where he has comforted the papists and encouraged them into defiance."

Chief Justice De Vere was seated in a deep and well-upholstered chair matching the one that Governor Clayton himself occupied. A large crystal decanter, its contents quite depleted, stood on a side table. Liveried servants stood silently by, replenishing the glasses as needed. A dozen silver candelabras around the walls lit the room quite well, helped by reflections from the huge gilt-framed full height mirror, the polished walnut paneling and cherrywood furniture.

The Governor eyed his companion. "You are considerably more vehement about this young man than I expected, Jacob, especially since I gather that he is a relative by marriage."

De Vere waved one hand airily. "You can thus see that I hold no family biases when it comes to the good of the province, my Lord. I have confidential sources in Albany who are unimpeachable. You know, of course, that his uncle, Captain Holeybarth, is also somewhat taken aback by his nephew's independence of action in the Indian lands."

"And yet," the Governor reflected, as if casually, "we have the situation in the northwest, that the Iroquois are disaffected enough with us to send delegates to Montreal. Your Albany friends ought to know that if the Six Nations turn on us or allow the French to attack through their lands, we have very little hope of defense. Especially while the Assembly, which your friends control, refuses to vote useful funds for Oswego and the other forts. And, I believe he arrived here seven years ago, not six, is that not true?"

De Vere raised and lowered a dismissive hand, buying time to think while apparently acknowledging a trivial inaccuracy. "My Lord," he said, "as I have presented to you repeatedly, the Indian Commissioners believe that this will not happen, not after more than a generation of peace. We recently sent a trusted interpreter to visit all the tribes, and he has returned. He reported that no very great disaffection exists and that he was warmly received in every castle. The Assembly believes that they should not waste taxes on such unnecessaries as the expensive fortresses you have suggested, and on presents for Indians whose best interests are served by trading with us in any case."

"Hmmm." Governor Clayton beckoned a servant, who brought a box and opened the lid. The Governor selected a cigarro. "Would you like one of these, De Vere? I enjoy them better than a pipe. I believe it was Captain Holeybarth, in fact, who captured them and gave them to me."

De Vere shook his head. "No thank you, Your Excellency."

"I would hear, I think, from the Iroquois themselves what their sentiments are. Do you think we could call a council in Albany for the spring?"

"Indeed, Governor, by all means. A letter to the Commissioners instructing them to notify the tribes will be all that is required." De Vere paused. "Apart, that is, from the expenses of the Council itself."

"Oh, yes, gifts to the chiefs and suchlike."

"Yes, Governor, this will probably entail an expenditure of several hundred pounds to bring them. This expense, of course, must be approved by the Assembly, since the budget did not include it."

"Oh, damnation, De Vere, surely we don't have to go back to them for expenses so trifling! I am exasperated by their nit-picking impertinence on defense issues. Surely they can see that this is in their interest?"

"Yes, Governor." Another pause. *The old boy has a bee in his bonnet.*

"Probably they would, except that the Crown's Indian Commissioners are well known to feel there is no problem requiring such meetings at present. Also, your predecessor was very reluctant to share detailed expenditure figures with the Assembly for items falling under the Crown's prerogative, even when the funds were voted. In the absence of the accounts, there are some who doubt the funds have been expended with complete propriety."

The Governor frowned. "I should hardly think that building some earth and wood palisades and putting a few soldiers and cannon in them can be called constructing fortresses—especially when one considers the real fortress the Frogs have built around their entire town at Louisbourg, and their stone fort at Crown Point, which could quickly send attacks directly down the lake valleys to Albany and then down the Hudson River to New York itself. Do not forget that

I have fought the French at sea. Many of them enjoy war, and some are very good at it, indeed."

His voice was rising slightly in volume. He puffed and blew smoke explosively up toward the ceiling.

"Nor, with reference to Smithyman's character, does it seem that any of the Irish rose in any significant way to support the Scots in the recent Stuart rebellion. If Smithyman and others were encouraging them in sedition, one might have thought that some evidence of disenchantment would arise, not so? But even here, where he has brought many Irish to be settlers on his land, there seems to be no such sentiment. Nor have I received any communication that would indicate he is of interest to the Crown in that respect."

Despite the evening's apparent early congeniality, the Chief Justice was beginning to wonder if he might have overestimated the Governor's malleability.

"De Vere, I am forming an opinion that there is some dissembling going on in Albany, and with the Assembly. Are the political disputes which they cultivate over crown prerogatives and payments being allowed to interfere with the vital defense needs of the province?"

He leaned forward and pointed at the Chief Justice with his glass, emphatically enough for a little port to slop onto the floor.

"Surely, De Vere, the interests of the trading and landowning classes in Albany are not being allowed to cloud the vision of the Indian Commissioners as well? I hear regularly about land patent frauds from the Iroquois. They most certainly do not say that Mr. Smithyman is stealing land from them. However, they do not have the same opinion about the present Indian Commissioners, the traders in Albany, and the great Hudson River landholders, who are so very ably represented in the Assembly. I wonder, sir, at these bland assertions that things are all well, when clearly they are not!"

The Chief Justice gulped port and covered his surprise by holding his glass for refilling. His voice dropped to its silkiest. "My Lord, are you saying that you are leaning to trusting the word of an upstart Irish immigrant and some drunken savages over those of us who have so capably managed the affairs of business with the Indians for this many years? I find this very hard to countenance, as will the traders and the Assembly."

He sipped, to hide his growing anger, before continuing. "We have just recently expended hundreds of lives and thousands of pounds on the Crown's failed expeditions to attack the Spanish colonies in the south. The Assembly has formed an opinion that the Crown has not spent their hard-earned money or lives very wisely. Recently, for example, London sent us cannon, without powder or shot!"

De Vere sipped again, rather too noisily. "You should also remember, Your Excellency," he murmured, "that no emoluments for the continued support of the Crown have yet been passed by the Assembly for this or the coming year."

"Emoluments be damned!" cried the Governor. He rose to his feet. "This is not about bloody emoluments; it is about the good of the colony! Nor is it about what happened in the Spanish campaign. As you know, I have requested ammunition for the artillery the Board of Trade sent. The absence of powder and shot took me aback as well. However, you know as well as I do that the Crown has vast interests and responsibilities to defend around the world and some inefficiency is inevitable. Surely, the colonies must also take their own defenses in hand, or they risk losing those British liberties that they say they value so highly to an enemy who values them not at all."

"No!" Clayton said decisively. "No! For far too long, I think, I have listened to what I see now is just a pack of money-grubbing sharps slyly and cleverly avoiding their duty to the province and to their king!"

De Vere also stood then, swaying slightly, and spoke, fighting for calm. "Then, my Lord, I see you have lost confidence in my judgment. We shall see if the Crown or the Assembly's perceptions are better than mine."

He placed his empty glass delicately on the proffered tray and accepted his hat and cloak from the servant, who had silently appeared with them. He turned, and with naked malignity now apparent in his voice and his face, said quietly, "I swear by the Almighty that I shall do my utmost to ensure that your administration is an uneasy one in future! Good evening to you, Governor." He bowed and strode from the room.

Behind him, a glass shattered on the brick fireplace. "Go, then, and do your worst," the Governor called after him. "We shall see what may occur to your precious Albany townsfolk when the settlements are burning because they have refused to defend themselves!"

He shouted down the hall. "Roberts! Roberts! God damn and blast it all, where is that man when you need him? Roberts!"

A tall, slim individual with a neat, powdered short wig appeared silently at the door and bowed. "Governor?"

"Roberts, write two letters for me. One appointing whatshisname, Dalhousie, from my Council, to replace De Vere as Chief Justice of New York." He stopped and grimaced, striking his fist hard against his thigh.

"No, belay that! God help me, I cannot legally replace De Vere, since he holds the position on good behavior and I have no scandal to justify this. What in the good Lord's name was I thinking, to appoint him with such permanency?

"No! Call Mr. Morton to come to see me at his earliest convenience. Also, write a letter commissioning Mr. William Smithyman as Justice of the Peace for the Schenectady territory.

"And another letter, dammit! This one must go to the Grand Council of the Six Nations at Onondaga requesting them to send delegates to a council between the Governor of New York and their sachems, in Albany in three months—mid-July. We'll settle on a date when you bring the drafts back to me. That is all."

The Governor sat down again and bared his teeth, without humor, at the fire. He summoned another glass of port from the servant and crossed his right ankle over his knee, his brows knitted in concentration.

CHAPTER SIXTEEN
Fort Smithyman, 1744–45

"Billy," said Marten, "there is to be a Grand Council at Lancaster in the Pennsylvania colony this summer."

Billy looked up, surprised, from his accounts and stood to embrace his friend, a wide grin splitting his face from ear to ear. "Marten! I was hoping we would see you at Smithyman House before too long."

He stood back and looked him up and down. "You have been sleeping in your lodge, I take it, where no Frenchman can find you? You have no wounds or injuries that I can see at all!"

Marten smiled and replied. "No, my friend, I have no wounds, but my lodge displays several southern scalps. Unfortunately, the French continue to keep themselves quiet in the north. Still, I long for the opportunity to meet them in our own forests. The Joncaires seem to be keeping them from attacking. Perhaps the French are afraid."

His eyes wandered outside. "I see you are building a palisade."

Billy nodded. "If the Six Nations remain neutral, I expect that the French will raid at any time."

Marten looked away. "The Mohawks will not go to Lancaster, Billy, but I am hoping that perhaps you might, in our place. The questions which we talked about two years ago are to be settled, and perhaps some others. Some of our most famous orators from the other tribes will be appearing there.

"Corlaer has also recently sent belts which call Mohawks to a council in Albany, at this very same time. There we must go, but," he smiled mirthlessly, "perhaps there is not an invitation for you, as a mere Justice of the Peace, to the Albany Indian Commissioners meeting."

He spat.

"While the present Commissioners remain, such councils are a waste of time anyway. Tell me you will go to Lancaster and report what they say. I would have someone I trust tell me what is heard there, through British ears.

We can compare wampum belts and see which is to be most weighty for our people."

Billy thought for a moment. "Marten, I am not well disposed to leave my people for several weeks, when the French could fall on us at any moment."

Marten gripped his upper arms gently, but firmly, and looked into his eyes with affection. He spoke softly, "My brother, did I not just tell you that the Joncaires counsel the French at present to beware of offending the Six Nations? I, Emperor Marten, witnessed them saying this to the French Governor's priest, who was visiting Irondequoit on the Big Lake near Onondaga, only three weeks past." He shook his head slowly, smiling, "There will be nothing this year, and perhaps nothing until after the Thanks-to-the-Maple ceremony next winter."

Billy stared back somberly for a moment. "It is a true trust I am placing in your words, brother. My life remains here if I travel to Philadelphia. You know my second child with Katy is coming, and she seems less strong than with the first."

Marten shrugged. "My life too stays here, every time I go on the warpath to the south. You are family to us, Billy, and yours is ours."

*****

After the councils were over, Marten returned. The house was silent and the two friends walked down to the river. It was late fall, and nearly all the summer's visitors and traders had departed to prepare for the winter.

"Truly, Father," Billy said, "Cannassatego was a marvelous orator. I had never heard his equal, even you."

Marten nodded. "I am a war chief, not one that is chosen for his ability to speak and negotiate. I am happy that you found him so."

Billy continued, "There was much that I was not familiar with, but I understand that the ownership of the Susquehanna Valley and the back of the mountains of Virginia and Maryland have now been settled by payments, two hundred pounds of goods and one hundred pounds of gold. Nevertheless, the King is to be consulted before any settlements are allowed to the west of the great southern road."

Marten lowered his eyes and fussed with his pipe. "And what of the road itself? Is this, in English eyes, an agreement which the white governors are intending to keep, my son?"

Billy hesitated until Marten looked up and then held his gaze.

"Marten, the road belongs to the Six Nations. I believe the English governors do intend to keep the agreement, for they are aware that they need the Six Nations to keep out the French. It is a truth, however, that there are many settlers and important men, especially in Virginia and farther south, who resent the King's attempts to protect your lands and to restrain them from land speculation.

"For now, I think you will see fewer English crossing the mountains, except for traders. If the French appear in the Ohio Valley, on the other hand, many will believe that the Six Nations are siding with the French and against the settlers, for everyone has now agreed that much of that land is part of Virginia. This would be a grievous thing for your people and should strenuously be guarded against."

Marten shrugged. "The Council at Onondaga will decide if it agrees with these things. I think we will respect the English and the colonists if the English respect us."

He tapped ashes out of the pipe on his knee and met Billy's eyes. "Our Mohawk sachems who went to the Albany Council stated our position, that the Longhouse people will not allow the French to come through our lands to attack you."

"There was another thing," Billy began, and at his tone Marten looked up.

"There were some discussions about ending the Six Nations' war on the Cherokee and Catawbas and about some killings of whites on the great road, where it passes through Virginia." He paused and Marten's scar wrinkled slightly.

Billy continued, "I have heard that my father has brought back scalps from the great road south. Could it be that these scalps were from those whites?"

Marten smiled. "You have found a truth, my brother, for not all of my new scalps are Catawba or Cherokee. But what was the outcome of this discussion about the killings?"

Billy said, "The Governor of Virginia paid the Six Nations another hundred pounds, since it was determined that this war party had been attacked by the whites after they stole some cattle and pigs from illegal white settlers. The Six Nations gave several bundles of hides and furs to the governors to compensate for the dead whites."

Marten laughed. "The Catawbas are stupid and continue to insult us at their peril, but it should now be clear that the Six Nations can, and will, defend themselves. This road is ours, English, and I am glad the Council has affirmed it once more.

"We have already moved the road since my grandmother's time, from in front of the green mountains facing the sea, to their very top. In my mother's time we moved it again, to the foot of the far side of the mountains, all to accommodate the King's wishes in Virginia and Maryland. I think we will not be willing to move it anymore."

Billy shook his head. "My father must be mindful that killing whites will weaken the ability of the King to hold back the settlers from a war."

Marten's face became impassive, his eyes as unreadable as the shadows in a cave. He waved a dismissive hand. "Faugh! The Longhouse people understand that the King's men cannot always prevent invasions of our land. As the Council has witnessed, we, too, have problems restraining our young warriors from taking scalps, wherever they might find them." He leaned forward and added, softly, "Especially when they are attacked without warning."

Billy changed the subject. "What of the Albany Council? Were the words of the Governor pleasing to your people?"

Marten huffed his laughter again and said, "I think the Governor should appoint you as Indian Superintendent, my friend. His advisors, the Commissioners at Albany, are not changing any of their ways, and Corlaer himself seems to have lost friends in the white world, since only two of his Councilors came with him.

"The usual things were said on both sides about the great silver Covenant Chain which binds us to the English being renewed and polished, but Corlaer wished us to declare war on the French, and this we cannot do, not until we have been attacked by them.

"As we told Corlaer, for you whites war is clothing, that you put on and discard at will. I can understand this since I have seen in England how many of you there are, and your lives are therefore not valuable. For our people war is personal, to the death, and we are few on the lands compared to you, so we are not excited to take up the hatchet quickly, where no war already exists." This was exactly what Billy had told the Governor at their New York meeting.

"Still, I worry that the New York Assembly refuses to build forts where our women and children can go and be protected. We know the French and their Indians are formidable warriors. Who will then protect our families if you English will not, when we are on the warpath on your behalf?"

They began to walk back along the shore.

Billy said, "The French Indians in the northeast are raiding the New England colonies. I think attacks on New York province must not be far away. I would like to know what is going on with the garrison at Crown Point, since the New Englanders seem to feel they will shortly be attacked from there. My father, do you think that...?"

An echoing scream from the house ripped away his question. Both men turned and ran up from the river. A shaken servant pointed mutely at Billy's bedroom. His heart pounding madly, Billy burst in the door. Katy sat on the floor, her head fallen back on a chair, her eyes closed. Her legs were folded beneath her in a huge pool of blood, which had soaked far up from the hem of her night-gown.

Billy knelt beside her and instantly knew she was near death. Waves of mingled anxiety, pity and horror rose within him. He lifted her effortlessly onto the bed and covered her to the neck with her favorite quilt. With a sinking heart he ordered a servant to fetch the Dutch midwife who lived nearby. He knew that no physician lived closer than Albany, and the practitioners there were both drunken ex-Navy surgeons.

"Where is Anna Christine?" The thought of his daughter struck him with great intensity.

"Bring her to me, when the blood is washed up. She must not be alone tonight."

Marten placed a gentle hand on his shoulder and said, "My friend, we have a woman in Canajoharie who has treated female problems such as this many times for our people. I will send for her."

Billy absently nodded his thanks and Marten left. The midwife who had attended Katrina's first birth arrived and pushed her way to the front of what had become a crowd.

"Out!" She demanded. "Out! All of you, this minute, or you will kill her. She needs quiet, and rest, not a babbling bunch of foolish men."

She peeled back the quilt and winced. Calling back a servant, she said, "Bring clean linens, as quickly as you can."

In a week, it seemed that Katrina was to live, although the child she had carried did not. The midwife grudgingly admitted that the Mohawk herbalist had worked wonders with her potions.

"No, Goodman Smithyman, I do not remember seeing any woman who has recovered so well from such ailments, and so quickly." Her small brown eyes blinked. "You know I do not like the Mohawks—they are unbelievers straight from hell itself—but the savages may have saved your Katy."

Billy raged internally at such words about his friends and allies. But he held his tongue. She had, after all, helped his Katy live. And he had grown used to hearing such commonplace contempt. He knew that expressing his feelings to her would only increase the animosity that many of his neighbours felt for him, an Indian-lover. Her feelings were all-too-typical of the Dutch and, he knew, a very large number of British colonists as well, many of whom treated Indians as subhumans—a class of creatures even lower in status than their negro slaves —especially when the Indians possessed and occupied land the colonists coveted. Such attitudes, he knew, were fully encouraged by many religious preachers all the way up to the Pope, claiming that God Himself had decreed that those who do not cultivate their lands had no right to them. This pervasive white doctrine conveniently ignored the fact that the Iroquois were sophisticated farmers who had bred dozens of varieties of corn and had, centuries before, learned to cultivate corn, beans and squash together to improve the yields of each: the corn providing a stalk for the beans to climb upon, the beans extending the life of the soil somehow, and the hairy, prickly squash stems protecting them all from deer and rabbits. The lives of all the settlers depended on the crops cultivated by these "savages."

*****

The long winter passed without any attacks along the Mohawk, although New England was suffering considerably from raids by northerners spurred on by the French. Spring came and went, and one warm summer day, Billy was working in the log blockhouse that served as his office, an outbuilding near the mill. He tapped his fingers idly on the paper in front of him on the desk and stared thoughtfully out the window. A red-jacketed rider rode up, to be redirected from the house.

Billy emerged to receive the dispatch from the sergeant, wrapped in its tarred linen cover and sealed with the Governor's coat of arms. Billy thanked him and excused himself. He stepped back across the grass into his office, broke the seal and unwrapped the documents.

In a moment, his roar of delight summoned guests, servants and little Anna Christine, who struggled free from her nurse's arms and ran across from the house to where her father was, beckoning urgently.

"Papa, Papa," she cried, breathlessly, as he hugged her close.

"We must have a day of games to celebrate!" roared Billy to all who were in earshot. "We have taken Louisbourg! The French fortress on Cape Breton has fallen to Uncle Hal and the Massachusetts militia!"

He bent his head to his daughter. "It is a great day, my sweet one, a wonderful, amazing day! We will have a holiday, and games next week, so everyone can come!"

Anna Christine beamed back at her father, so tall and strong. She already loved the games days he organized, usually on a whim, when the daily routines had made him restless.

The games had become a popular entertainment among his tenants as well, when they realized it was their patron Billy who was the first to participate in the three-legged races and the sack races and whatever other silly pastimes he could think up.

Many of the most reserved settler matrons could be persuaded at these events to participate, even in the pig wrestle or some other dignity-destroying event, as long as everyone else was part of it. There was always a feast, with drink enough for all, and usually some exotic new foreign frivolity that Billy had become enchanted with since the last event and that he wanted to show off.

It was also a time to meet his homesteaders and their families without the usual constraints of business, a chance to take the pulse of his ever-growing dominions.

The day for the games came. Billy ran up, panting from his exertions in the tug-of-war, to where Katy was sitting underneath an umbrella. She smiled broadly to see him as energetic as a ten-year-old. She patted the grass and he flopped down beside her, beckoning to a servant for a glass of cider. He could see Anna shrieking with delight as she and a dozen other children ran about among the adults.

"How are you feeling?" Billy asked, and she reached for his hand.

"I am well, liebchen," she replied. "I think soon I vill be as strong as ever."

He nodded, "I thank God. You are no longer as pale as the winter moon, Katrina."

She shook her head and laughed softly, saying, "It is an interesting way to say this, for I am very sure it vas some of the things that Cloud-Hiding-the-Moon fed to me that made me better. You know, I could feel life coming back to me then, every time she brought something for me. The Mohawk are your—our—good friends, Vilhelm."

He nodded, picking some drying clumps from his mud-spattered chest and arms. "Yes, but I am concerned that they think we are not such good friends to them, Katy."

"But you are fair, they all trust you and listen to you," she protested.

Billy propped himself on an elbow and plucked a stem of grass to chew. "Most of them do trust me, but..." he looked at her and then pinched the skin of his arm, "I carry the stain of being a white, and so I am party to the crimes that other whites commit on them.

"There are still some chiefs, even among the Mohawk, who think I am only after their land. And the Albany people are working hard to bring me down. My old enemy Stoatfester has developed some influence there.

"The middle nations, even the Oneida around Oswego, are very much under the influence of the Joncaires. If the French Mohawks, the Praying Indians in Montreal, come here to attack tomorrow, will our clans fight them? Most of the Six Nations have little affection left for us."

Katrina looked about the grounds. "There are few here today, Villy, it is true, and they all do like a feast so much."

Billy agreed. "They are vexed that we cannot make more effort to defend ourselves, and them." He looked at the ground for a moment. "I think, too, that they do not yet trust me fully. I have not demonstrated my courage in the Indian way."

She started to argue and he put a finger gently to her lips. "I will have to do so, sooner or later."

"What do they need you to do?"

"They have not said it, but I will never be one of them until I have shown them that I am a worthy comrade in battle."

Katy's eyes narrowed and she smiled mirthlessly. "I do not think that would be a bad thing, Villy. I watched my family murdered by the white coat army in the Rhineland. Five of them raped me. If you must kill, then kill one of them, for my family and me."

Billy looked somberly at her. "I fought my father about becoming a soldier. I have always felt there was a better way. Now, it seems I will have to do what is most distasteful to me."

He threw the soggy stem down and plucked another.

"Moreover, it is a thing in which I have no training or experience whatsoever." He shook his head. "It is a foolish thing. I may not even be any good at it. I may get killed for my efforts."

Katy chuckled.

He said, in a low voice, "Maybe I'll be a coward and run away!"

She laughed aloud and clapped her hands. "You are very funny, Villy. You, a coward! Ha ha ha ha ha ha!"

He glowered at her a moment, then his mouth twitched in a smile as she continued to laugh.

He said, "I'm glad you have no doubts. I would not wish to be seen as a coward by these people."

He shrugged. "We shall see what might happen."

Squinting a bit, he scratched an itchy spot over his right eyebrow. "I think we are doing everything we can. I will write and beg the Governor to send a few of his soldiers here. Then we would likely be safe, unless the French send an army. He will send the soldiers because I am happy to feed and house them from my own resources, where others elsewhere will not."

Katy said, "They are fools in New York. The dummkopfen have forgotten what enemy soldiers will do if we have none to defend us."

"Yes, the Assembly and my relative De Vere are blocking the Governor's attempts to do anything, like spiteful children. They still do not see that the war is coming to them. They refused to send any men to assist the Massachusetts colony in the attack on Louisbourg, although afterwards they were shamed into sending some money."

Katy shrugged. "You cannot grow brains like peaches."

Billy looked about. "I am uneasy that the Mohawks are not here. I had hoped that Marten and some of the others would come. I must discuss the situation with them, soon."

Katy put her hand on his arm, rubbing the soft hairs gently up and down. She murmured, "Do not think more of the war today, my fine man. Enjoy your child and think of making more."

He returned his gaze to her, then. They began to smile at the same time.

The next morning Billy rode out to Richard's homestead. He reined up sharply outside a neat frame cottage, sided with ship-lapped, unpainted cedar boards, which the weather was already beginning to silver. It had four windows with heavy ironbound shutters and a mortared fieldstone chimney. Several children were playing a loud game of tag a hundred yards away, at the edge of the forest. Billy strode to the door and knocked loudly.

Eva answered, and when she saw him, smiled brilliantly and shrieked, "Bill-l-l-y! Richard, Billy's here!" She flung her birch broom down and her arms about him and clung, half-sobbing, until Richard appeared and added his embrace. Laughing, Billy disengaged and made a mock bow.

The children had heard the commotion and ran up, adding their own glad cries to the furor. Two of them danced up and down in front of him on tiptoes, waving their arms and fingers in supplication until he grasped one and then the other and swung them over his head and down again.

Eventually, the grownups sat together at the table. Billy passed his hand up and down the smooth surface of the walnut planks. "This is good work, Richard. Eva, you must be proud of him. You have both done well, have you not?"

They looked at each other and then wordlessly back at Billy. Eva got up and went to the corner, pulling up a trap door and reaching down into the cool, dark hole for a jug of cold cider. She poured some into three glasses. Billy looked closely at his and said, deadpan, "These are very nice glasses, you know. Where did you get them?" They held them up together, laughing at his feigned ignorance, for Billy had given them the set of glasses as a gift, several years before.

"It is you we toast then, Billy. You have given us a life here in the forest that is better beyond all measure than what could ever have been in Ireland."

He drank deeply with them, and then his smile vanished. He set the glass down and pulled a sealed envelope from his coat. "Richard, our Mohawk friends tell me that the French and their Indians are now collected at full strength at Crown Point. We shall, I fear, have to defend our lives and our families very soon. I have a task for you which could help save us all."

Richard bowed slightly and Eva moved closer to him.

*****

The Governor waved Richard into a chair in his Albany office with a smile, and signaled for some refreshments. He broke the now-familiar Smithyman seal and read.

My Lord Governor,

The settlers in the entire Mohawk Valley from twenty miles above my location, to thirty miles down river, with the exception of most of my own tenants, have now fled, following the traders into Albany. I trust that your Council or the Assembly will have made you aware of this already.

In my warehouses there are presently thousands of bushels of wheat and other grains which could be used to support our forces in the area. Only local militia, raised from the families who are resident on my own estates, now defend these warehouses.

These men, while valiant and quite capable of defending themselves against small forces, are utterly untrained in war and, in my view, inadequate, should the French send any significant force against us from Crown Point. This they may reasonably be expected to do, although at present they may hesitate, since it is well known that the Mohawks have developed some attachment to me.

I therefore beg Your Excellency to send us a small formation of soldiers to assist us in our defenses, and perhaps another to reinforce at least one of the Mohawk castles at Fort Hunter or Canajoharie. My house is now stoutly fortified and I have sent scouts out in an effort to ensure that we may not be surprised.

I am gratified to learn that my contract offer to provide all manner of military supplies, food and clothing for the garrison at Oswego, has been accepted by the Assembly. It is puzzling, however, that no arrangements or allowances were made for transporting the provisions farther than Albany at this time. Doubtless, this large expense was simply overlooked. I am sure the Assembly will find their way to reimbursing this to me at their convenience. In any case, I will organize and ensure the delivery of supplies to Oswego as agreed, and will provide the transport from Albany on account.

Given that the Mohawks say the French are preparing for an assault upon your province I look forward to your dispatch of army reinforcements for myself and the Mohawk settlements. The bearer of this letter being my trusted friend, I would be grateful if you would allow him to accompany the army back to the frontier.

We expect an attack daily; but unlike the New Englanders, who have evidently risen to the challenge, and in spite of your urgent entreaties, I hear from my contacts that the Assembly continues to bicker over the Royal prerogative. You have my sympathies, of course. I am convinced that those individuals will never give up their links to the French until the Governor of Canada breaks them himself, by a direct attack.

My Indian friends tell me this morning that a great panic has driven them to flee from the lower Castle at Dyiondarogon (Fort Hunter) yesterday. Some crossed the river to come here for shelter. They had heard that Albany had actually begun marching on their encampments to destroy them. It appears that this treachery is not actually occurring, but it is clearly believable in their minds.

The French appear to consider me important enough to put a bounty on my head. A friend in Albany has written me to say he hears it is because Captain Holeybarth is my uncle. I flatter myself that it is also because the Mohawks care to deal with me. I am confident that the reward will not be collected, if you can send some small number of men as I have requested.

I remain, Yr. Obedient Servant etc.,

Wm. Smithyman

The Governor looked up and beckoned to his servant, who gently awakened Richard, who had been leaning against the wall, dozing, with the brandy untouched beside him.

"Mr. FitzHugh, I thank you for bringing this important communication to me with such speed. I would be grateful if you would stay the night and accompany my answer to Mr. Smithyman in the morning. My servant will escort you to your quarters."

CHAPTER SEVENTEEN

Fort Hunter, Autumn 1745

The stupidity of it all was overwhelming.

Marten was angry, and his scar showed white against his dark choleric face. "Is your Assembly in New York afraid? Or are they in the pockets of the Albany traders?"

Billy shook his head wearily. They were discussing letters he had received from the Governor and from Turnbottle, letters which made it clear that the Assembly would leave the frontier defenseless for the foreseeable future. Billy had traveled down to Albany on business and stopped by Marten's home—a planked and whitewashed house by the river—on the return journey.

His news wasn't good.

"The Governor has asked them to take strong measures against the Albany trade with Montreal," he told Marten, "but before he can begin building forts he needs the Assembly to agree to spend the money. They did agree to buy presents for another general council in the fall—you should be getting wampum belts about this, soon."

"We will come," said Marten, "but the English would be wise to show that they can do more than talk. We will not fight your war for you, my friend."

Billy understood. "New England has declared war," he said. "They are being attacked all along the frontier. I am told that they will come to the council in October."

Marten was not impressed. "New England is angry, but New York does nothing. Some of our people recently returned from Saratoga, north of Albany. They say the English soldiers there are so ragged that their private parts are naked. The soldiers said they will not stay to sicken and die in canvas tents there all through the winter again. Our people told me they were able to push down some of the wood palisades with one hand. Fort Hunter is the same, and I have also seen Oswego myself. Will you attend the council?"

Billy grimaced. "No, the Indian Commissioners in Albany still refuse to allow me to participate. Fort Smithyman, at least, is now walled and garrisoned."

"Then I cannot see that anything but more talk will come of it. But we will go to hear the talk, at least."

Billy asked, "What of Crown Point? Do your people have a sense of what the French intend?"

Marten glanced at Billy. He said, "This is for your ears and perhaps for Corlaer, but not for the Albany people, my friend." Billy nodded.

"We hear that the French now grow impatient for revenge, since the English victory at Louisbourg. They begin to believe that the Mohawks will not fight for the English. We hear that they will soon be sent south into New York from Crown Point, perhaps after the corn-harvest festivals."

The two men sat quietly for several minutes as the smoke from their pipes curled and mingled.

Billy broke the silence. "Perhaps God requires that blood be shed before humans understand their duty."

Marten chuckled in his wheezy fashion. "It is not Manitou who requires awakening by bloodshed, my white son. The ground must first be fertilized with blood before the seeds of true human wisdom will grow."

Billy shook his head. He pointed the stem of his pipe at Marten. "Your people will suffer much, will they not, if the French and their Indians attack in New York?"

Marten smiled. "My son, why do you think that no attacks have yet been made on this province, although New England is bleeding badly? The French and the Northern Indians are not foolish. If they attack the Longhouse itself, they will feel the weight of our vengeance.

"But, they also know that we and the River Indians were long ago cheated out of our eastern lands along the North River, that whites now call the Hudson. We have sacred healing places there, places that no white man has yet discovered. We would never have sold them knowingly. You and your Governor know this very well, my brother, for we have complained many times, yet we always hear that nothing at all can be done."

Marten set his pipe down and reached behind him for the musket leaning against the wall. He cocked it against the powerful spring and triggered it twice, looking closely at the frizzen and pan action as it slammed open and sparks flew, before putting it aside.

"I will have to give that one back to the English gunsmith, my son, I cannot tell why it misfires so often. I have cleaned the flame port well as he instructed me, but it still is not reliable, although it looks proper." He set the gun down and sighed. After a lengthy silence he continued.

"Billy, the English will now find that nothing can be done by the Six Nations people. We have been forced to move away from these eastern lands because your people claim falsely that we no longer possess them. Now even a child can see that Longhouse blood will not be spilled to defend them."

Billy nodded, slowly, reluctantly, at the logic.

Marten stood up. "That is enough politics for this day. It is truly unfortunate that some will now have to suffer, but it is also true that the Great Turtle who carries the world causes the sun to rise whether we will it or not. Will you stay, although dinner will be late tonight because of the harvesting?"

Billy rose also and smiled at the warrior. For the first time, he noticed some gray hair in Marten's topknot, and the deep wrinkles from each nostril to the corner of his mouth seemed much more pronounced than the last time they had met.

"No, I must leave," he replied, "but I did want to hear your words about these things. Thank you. Are you well fed, Marten? I see neither your wife nor your daughter here today, and you remain as lean as a fox."

Marten pointed behind him with his thumb and said, "They have spent the day in the fields harvesting the corn and criticizing men. We will feast very soon." The great scar wrinkled slightly.

"As for my leanness, you know, English, foxes stay lean because they have to hunt rabbits that sometimes can run faster, although the rabbits are not so smart. Farewell for now, my friend. I will come to see you after the Council."

Upon Billy's return home, his servant Elijah insisted on seeing him urgently on a personal matter.

Elijah, Billy knew, rarely got upset. It made his plea that much harder to resist.

"I would not leave you at this time, Lord, but I beg your permission to go to Saratoga. I just learned six months ago that my sister was there. This made me very happy, and I was content to wait until my jobs here could spare me, but now she has sickened from a terrible fever. I would see her before she has died."

Billy hesitated a moment, then said, "You are admirably stubborn, but I am not your Lord, as I told you when I paid your manumission, your liberty paper, in Albany. I do not wish to seem cold, but she may already have died, Elijah. In any case, I don't wish you to bring the fever here."

The tall black man nodded vigorously, but argued, "I will stay in Albany for three weeks before I come home, Lord, so that there is no danger. I know a safe place there for negroes. But I must see her; it has been more than twenty years since we were parted in New York."

Billy finally relented, although he hated to lose another man who could use a musket. "Elijah, go, and return as quickly as you can, for we need you here. If your sister is better, and you wish to take care of her, bring her here with you. I will send you by bateau: it is not safe on the road now." He scratched a hasty note on a scrap of paper and handed it to Elijah, pointing out the door.

"Take this to the wigwam there; let's see, fourth from the right. Do you see it?"

Elijah nodded again.

"Good. They will take you across to the Lower Castle, and from there they will make sure you get to Saratoga. They will wait for you too, but they will not wait longer than two weeks. And don't mention that you work for me as you pass through Albany. They might keep you there just out of spite, I think."

Billy walked Elijah to the door, and the river caught his eye. It was an icy cobalt blue flecked with silver. The sun seemed to be quickly receding, as the afternoon shadows grew longer. A sudden gust of the cold north wind whirled yellow and orange leaves high up into the air in a perfect expanding spiral before releasing them to drift in a collapsed cloud into the river.

A perfectly clear sky; we will get the first hard frost tonight.

He sent up a brief silent prayer for Elijah's safe return.

CHAPTER EIGHTEEN

Fort Smithyman, November 1745

Billy had to suppress a smile. He and Marten were sitting on a log bench outside his office. Marten was boasting. "I made quite a good speech, my English son, you would have been proud of me. I think it was nearly as good as what Canassatego might have done," Marten thought for a second, "except that I am perhaps more direct and not as subtle as he, as becomes a warrior chief."

Billy watched his servant fill two large shiny mugs with rum punch, and the two men each drank a deep draught and offered the cups for refilling.

Billy said, "Do you like these cups? I have now settled a tinsmith nearby; his work is quite good, is it not?"

Marten eyed the flimsy, lightweight mug. "It has not the solid feel of the other metal ones, my friend; I do not think it will be popular with our people."

Billy said, "It will be much easier to carry. The traders will take many of them to the northwest."

Marten said, "It is true that ten of these would not weigh the same as one of the others."

Billy agreed, grinning. "Yes, and the price is the same as the weight. Even better, now I can bring sheet metal and make them here. It will be far less expensive than buying them in Albany or New York and then paying to have them shipped to me by wagon or bateau. I think they will be very popular, and I can now sell mugs for much less than the French or even the Albany traders can."

Marten shrugged, a bit nettled that Billy had changed the subject away from his diplomatic exploits. "You are usually right in these things, Billy. I would not be such a good trader. You are pleased with yourself, I see."

"I am very pleased, Father. I have increased the value of my settlement here and taken money out of the hands of those who hate me while doing it. What more can a man ask? But tell me more of the Council. You said there were many of your people there, and I saw many of their canoes pass this place."

It was Marten's turn to hide a smile. *I expect many more stopped here than passed by, my friend.*

"Our brothers, the ravens," he said, "have the finest eyes in the great world for shining things. If I ask them what they have seen, they would tell me that many of the more foolish Longhouse people are carrying home these flimsy cups, along with tales of how wonderful a place Smithyman House is."

He paused and looked at the darkening sky, then continued. "You will not have seen any Seneca among these people, however. The Keepers of the Western Door had a serious and strange type of malady. None could come to this Council in Albany, although we counted that there were nearly five hundred others present to hear Corlaer and Emperor Marten speak about the Covenant Chain.

"That terrible sickness," he continued, "was peculiar, for although it prevented Senecas from sending any delegates to Albany, it did not keep them away from Onontio's recent council in Montreal."

Billy tilted his mug and drained it before he responded. His eye met the servant's and his cup was refilled almost before it had ceased its downward swing. He wiped his mouth on his sleeve.

Returning to Marten's earlier pokes at him, Billy said, "My Father, the prices that those wise and discerning individuals found here are better by half than those in Albany or Oswego, which is why they come to spend their beavers at Fort Smithyman."

Marten flapped his hand dismissively and continued his story. "One chief was particularly eloquent, as I have mentioned. He suggested the great Covenant Chain binding the English and ourselves was forged because we were assured that the English would always work to provide us with goods at fair prices."

Billy nodded, "And it is true that Oswego and Albany have doubled their prices since last year."

Marten kept his eyes modestly looking at the mug as he continued.

"The remarkable orator that spoke these things brought tears to the eyes of all present. He pointed out that the ancient chain binding our peoples, which was created in the time of the Dutchmen, is now quite tarnished and considerably weakened by the prices we must pay for powder, shot, clothing and guns. We are destitute, so we must keep what we have for the hunt, unlike those who can afford to go to war."

Marten raised the mug and gulped rum.

Billy said, smiling, "It sounds as if that orator was very eloquent, indeed; but I hope that not too many Seneca families are mourning."

Marten made no reply, except an ostentatious gesture of examining his pipe bowl, which was no longer smoldering. Billy's servant ripped off a twist and presented him with more brown, compressed leaf, along with a burning stick from the fire in front of them.

"This leaf is kinder, Billy, than the black rope," he said.

Billy agreed, "That is so. It is also much more expensive."

Billy drew on his pipe and puffed a cloud of blue smoke into the night. "The Governor, I heard, at first presented very angry words to the Haudenosaunee," he said.

Marten nodded almost imperceptibly. *He insulted us.*

Billy continued. "But then later, I was told, he defended the Six Nations from the anger of the Bostonians. It is surprising, is it not? He would have been very disappointed that the Six Nations publicly refused to dance the war dance against the French."

"It did surprise us. But we told him we are a patient people, and loyal friends to Corlaer in spite of the English abuse of our people, and we would polish the Covenant Chain to a perfect shine once again, and remove all the rust from it, and that should the King's Forces be attacked at any time after we received this hatchet, we would take it from our bosoms and strike their enemies with it."

Billy nodded.

"However, we must consult with our tribal allies in the west, before we can make this decision to begin a new war on the French. This is a very weighty matter, for it was to end just such a war, one begun by their war chief Champlain in the time before Corlaer arrived here, that we and the French signed a great peace with many other nations in their castle in Montreal when I was very young. This will take us two months. We are a great people and our influence must be carefully weighted before we take the warpath."

"Truly, these are serious matters, Father. What did the men from Massachusetts and Connecticut say then?"

"They were unhappy and angry, and they said many things about the despicable Albany men, especially when there came word during the Council that the French had attacked and burned their fort at Great Meadow.

"This caused them to agitate for Corlaer to press us to revenge them immediately. Corlaer pointed out, however, that this attack took place before the agreement at the Council. Therefore he had no choice but to support us in our decision."

Billy was silent, digesting this news for a moment.

Marten got up. He walked a few paces beyond the fire's light and urinated. When he sat again, he wrapped himself tightly in his blanket and stared moodily into the flames.

"Corlaer told me, and left belts with me that said he would again urgently demand that your Assembly in New York take emergency action to defend the province. He will ask them again to build a stone fort at the Great Carrying Place between the Hudson River and the waterway to Montreal, as soon as he returns to the city."

He turned his grave face to Billy, who was equally somber.

"Billy, while I believe that Corlaer is being truthful with us, why is it that he, the King's man here, can neither do away with the Assembly nor order them to do the King's bidding?"

Billy met his gaze. "Marten, it is the same with us as with the Longhouse Grand Council at Onondaga. You and I know that there are still some sachems nearby in Canajoharie and even Dyiondarogon, whom the French have almost convinced to break the Covenant Chain.

"The Governor cannot order the Assembly to spend its own money. Nor does he have the forces or the permission of the King to do all of these things himself. He has, I think, done as much as he can do, and has committed large sums of his own private money. But even these small actions anger the Assembly. They will not agree with anything he proposes."

Marten shook his head. "Your Assembly acts like a jealous wife that sees someone else preparing a meal for her husband. She thinks only that her position and powers are being trampled and not that it is her own absence from the cooking fire that has made her husband hungry."

The two men noticed movement and looked up at the same time. Out of the black sky a few huge glistening snowflakes floated down, lighted from beneath by the fire. In minutes, there were more than a man could count.

They fell perfectly straight, and they kept falling for three full days and nights. Then a howling northeast wind blew for a day. When the thick cloud had passed, snowdrifts crested gracefully to the eaves of Billy's now cave-like office, creating sparkling, painfully bright rainbows in the sun. Only by clambering to her father's shoulders could Anna see out of the windows on Smithyman House's main floor. The intense snow light made the upstairs rooms brighter than summer. The Prussian blue room almost glowed, and even the dark green music room and study seemed to come alive.

No canoes or bateaux remained beached in front of the house near the river, of the dozens that had been there only two weeks before.

A velvety silence descended onto the New York frontier. Twelve thousand jittery settlers and a handful of soldiers were scattered along the banks of the

Mohawk and Upper Hudson. They sent prayers of thanks in several tongues to surprisingly different versions of the one God. Then they slept deeply and soundly for the first time in months.

Billy began to chuckle and Katy looked up quickly from the mound of soft furs in front of the roaring fireplace, where she was playing with Anna. Billy had not been chuckling a great deal this fall and winter. She smiled and raised her eyebrows inquiringly.

He was sitting at his great desk reviewing his accounts. Ever watchful of his moods, she had seen him lay down his quill and shake his head, then turn and pick up a book from a stack on the floor.

He pointed to the one he was holding open and said, "This man Franklin is a highly amusing fellow. He's been publishing *Poor Richard's Almanack* each year for sixteen years now, and each time he comes up with new sayings that seem quite wise. Here he says, 'Laws like to cobwebs catch small flies, Great ones break through before your eyes.'

"He means that powerful men break laws without being punished; but small flies, unimportant people, are the ones who are always caught." Billy set the book down open and picked up another. "This is last year's *Almanack* —'God heals and the Doctor takes the fees,'" he read with a laugh.

Katy smiled her agreement. "That seems very true, but does he not offend people when he writes these things?"

Billy laughed again. "He does, he does, my sweet, and it seems to run in his family to want to irritate powerful people—my New York agent Turnbottle has told me that Ben Franklin's brother James was imprisoned for a time in Boston for such writing."

He waggled the book back and forth. "This is a useful book, full of true information about the calendar and the stars and suchlike, and very accurate."

Katy said, "I have always been curious about such things. "How can they be predicted so surely? You have pointed out those planets to me yourself that he writes about in his book, and they move about the sky in ways I do not understand."

Billy smiled affectionately. "Ah, my Katy, these things have been shown to move on physical principles that ensure you can measure them and predict them far into the future. The Navy uses such calculations to tell where a ship is at sea, where the only landmarks are the sun and stars, as if they are landmarks as fixed and reliable as the mountains."

He looked back at the book he was holding and frowned. "It is puzzling, though, that this man Franklin and his brother do not support the science of smallpox prevention. I find the stand they published against pox inoculation quite ridiculous and dangerous, even irresponsible."

"I remember well, Billy, that you forced me to do that disgusting thing to myself and to Anna."

He nodded. "But it is true, is it not, Katy, that we have not suffered here from that disease? You know well that many die from it each year in the cities and nearby. And it carries off Indians like wild pigeons.

"It is insane. It can be stopped, yet very few follow this practice because of simple prejudice and fear. I will persist, with our people, and we will see a change, I am convinced. At least our family and those that depend on us will not die from this."

He waved the book. "It was years ago, and I think Franklin has changed his mind somewhat, but such an influence has probably contributed to thousands of unnecessary deaths."

Katy smoothed her daughter's hair and kissed her. "How can you be so sure that it works, liebchen?"

"It has been well known in knowledgeable circles in England for nearly a generation that inoculation works to prevent infection. My friend in Ireland wrote me of this. She says that many of the wealthy and noble born are doing this, now. It was first observed by the wife of the Ambassador to Turkey to be a commonplace practice in the East, where they do not now suffer overmuch from this dreadful plague."

He stood away from his desk and went over to the hearth. Anna looked up as he bent and swept her up into his arms. She began giggling, shrieking with delight, arms and legs flailing, upside down.

"No," he said, pretending to chew her nose, "we will not get sick from this, will we, little tweedlemedee?"

She pretended to scream in fright and struggled to get away. He hugged her harder and then set her down and returned to the accounts spread on his desk.

He flipped again to the last page of the thick, hardbound ledger. He had read this page before, and it had shocked him into putting it aside for a few minutes. He read again the sum, so carefully printed there by his clerk. The expression on his face hardened. He seized a sheet of paper and made some furious calculations with his pen, then suddenly crumpled it into a ball and flung it at the fire with a curse.

Katy looked up, startled at his change in mood, and read his face. She turned to Anna and said firmly, "It's time for bed now, Anna Christine, go and give your father a goodnight hug, a big, big hug."

Billy stood to receive his daughter and squeezed her hard. She squeaked, and when he set her down she beamed shyly and curtsied her prettiest curtsey, saying, "Goodnight, Papa."

"Sleep tight, liebie," he said, and she ran out, followed by Katy.

When Katy returned, Billy was still writing.

"It is very late, Vilhelm," she said, standing behind him and rubbing his shoulders.

"Aye, Katy," he replied, "it is late, but I must get this letter off to the Governor tomorrow."

"You are so upset, Billy. Can you tell me what is wrong?"

Billy sighed. "It is business, only money, Katy, but it is very serious. I have been foolish. Those wretches in the Assembly will not pay any transportation expenses to supply the Oswego garrison. Even the regular transport cost me several hundred pounds more than they paid me last year."

He cursed, quietly, but let her continue her massage.

It is good to be able to tell someone, even if I am confessing my own idiocy.

He said, in a low voice, "But since the war began, the bateaux men will not leave here without armed guards. I am now spending two thousand pounds a year of my own money to make sure the garrison gets food and supplies. Soon I will be ruined, because I will have to borrow, and then those dogs in Albany who hate me, and their friends in the banks, will have me where they want me."

He shook his head. "I can only hope the Governor will pay for these expenses."

Chapter Nineteen
New York, December 1745

The news of a massacre at Saratoga shocked the province, which had seen nothing like it in New York since the last century.

Governor Clayton had called an emergency meeting of his twelve-man Executive Council. At present, he rested his cold gaze on Hendrik Van Nes, who had been invited to attend.

A fast cutter and a squad of marines detached from the Royal Navy patrol frigate in New York harbor delivered the invitation. It was pro forma only—the Marines had received instructions to bring the named individual along, whether he wished it or not. They had been mildly disappointed when he consented so readily.

"You had assured us, repeatedly, mijnheer, that the frontier was safe."

During his naval service, the Governor's booming quarterdeck voice had easily reached his man-o-war's crew even in the teeth of North Sea gales and flapping canvas. It rose to a shattering roar in the room of his house that he used as an official meeting chamber.

"The French would not dare to attack us, you and the Indian Commissioners said, because they fear to offend the Six Nations. The French are a pragmatic race, you yourself told me, and there is no good reason to stop making money from each other, as war would surely make us do."

The object of his wrath crossed his legs and opened his mouth as if to answer, and Governor Clayton held up his hand. In the brief pause, the scratching quill of a nervous clerk could be heard as he scribbled frantically to record the Council minutes.

"I am not finished yet. No, not nearly finished yet! How is it," he raged, "that I, and my personal advisors, appear to know far more about what is truly happening on the frontier than you and your accursed Indian Board, with all your years of experience and your expert judgment?"

He pointed a gloved finger at the seated Van Nes, who closed his mouth impassively.

"You, and those other Albany people, and that prancing popinjay, your brother-in-law De Vere, have used your influence to set the entire Assembly against any sensible action, against any precaution which His Majesty's administration suggested, either from me or from this Council. As a result," he sputtered, "this, this, this dreadful slaughter at Saratoga is on your heads. Thirty settlers massacred and scalped; all the houses and Van Beek's blockhouse in Saratoga burned and a hundred prisoners taken away.

"Who are we now to believe, you and the other Indian Commissioners, or those that you and the Assembly said were children, frightened of shadows? You, and the Assembly, rejected every advice from His Majesty.

"Establish a common defense with New England, we urged you. Build and garrison a fort at the Great Carrying Place. Even, we implored you, just supply Saratoga so the garrison could survive the winter, much less repair the fort, God forbid.

"Build a common league with the friendly Indian nations to the west. All were refused. In its foolish, embarrassing, dogmatic parsimony, the Assembly refused to offer any aid to the campaign against Louisbourg either, until long after it was successfully concluded.

"Now you refuse even to send word to the Six Nations that I am calling them to take up their hatchets against the French!"

He shook his head. "I cannot understand this pusillanimity. Captain Philip Van Beek, whose father was a great soldier for this province, fought and perished in Saratoga. His gallantry in volunteering to remain—although we withdrew the eleven soldiers under his command into Albany to shelter for the winter—shows a sharp contrast to the attitude of the Assembly, does it not?

"The like was never known that one part of a government should be left in this fashion, to be butchered by the enemy without support from the other."

The Governor paused in his tirade, and held out his glass to his servant. Van Nes sat calmly without responding. After pacing the length of the room twice, Governor Clayton began anew, his tone low and menacing.

"You are well advised, I think, to remain silent, mijnheer. As you know, the Assembly has now decided to spend its bloodied money, that it so suddenly saw was its clear duty to raise, but not for a stone fort at the Carrying Place. Instead it will go on a set of tiny blockhouses, scattered miles apart, not much better than poor Van Beek's."

He gulped some wine. Van Nes brushed at imaginary flecks on his coat. The Governor began again.

"This will not even improve the morale of the Indians. They will see, rightly, that the French will take and burn these cabins without a moment's pause, should they conceive it desirable to do so. Should a force of five or six hundred descend on us again, it might well not have much trouble even with Albany itself!"

He made a sweeping gesture at the room. "Even New York might well tremble at such a force. Our puny wooden palisade across Manhattan Island at Wall Street could not prevent such an army from attacking.

"Furthermore, Albany says it will not even provision the Fusiliers which I sent to guard that city and Saratoga. I am again using my personal monies, to send them some minimum of supplies. It is appalling! Why should I do this, or request any further support from His Majesty's forces, which must sustain this war all around the world, when the inhabitants of this wealthy province, quite unlike our neighbors in New England, refuse to lift a finger in their own defense? It is useless for the Assembly to agree upon what bounty will be paid out for French scalps of each sex, when our natives will not go to war."

The servant refilled his glass.

"There is one last chance for you and the Assembly to save the situation. I have summoned you to hear it as I lay it before my Council, with witnesses and minutes, so that no man can say later that the Crown is keeping important secrets from its people.

"In my address next week, I will be asking the Assembly to support a campaign in the spring to invade and take New France, once and for all. This is, at this point, entirely secret, as the plans are developing. However, the general shape of the campaign will be a two-pronged attack, one from Louisbourg to attack Quebec City, and the other from here to attack Montreal.

"Mijnheer, you must consider your reply carefully. I cannot over-emphasize how much rests on a positive response from this province to participate fully in this plan. Even our Iroquois allies may forsake us permanently unless they see us to be interested in holding this province and our future out of the hands of the French.

"I expect, when you leave this meeting that you will endeavor to persuade your friends to influence the Assembly that this is in their best interests.

"Now, sir, what say you to this plan?"

The portly Dutchman stared stonily at the Governor and a prolonged silence fell in the room as he contemplated a reply. He puffed gently on his long clay pipe. Eventually the clerk ceased to write and the only sounds were that of the street, which came faintly through the brick.

Suddenly and unexpectedly, Van Nes smiled, but it did not reach his eyes.

"Governor, you have the right of it. All of us lost staff and investments, if not family, in Saratoga, and Van Beek's death is a terrible blow. The French Indians skulk around the outskirts of Albany taking scalps and our people have abandoned their homes everywhere on the frontier. I am certain that the Assembly will heed your desire to attack the French, without reservation."

He drew on the pipe again and glanced sharply around the table at the other Councilors, shrewdly taking their measure, then locked his eyes with the Governor once more.

"I trust, Excellency, that London will provide the necessary support for this venture as they said they would at Louisbourg, or is it a risk that we must undertake on our resources alone?"

The Governor shook his head. "Governor Lindsay has met with Rear-Admiral Holeybarth and is assured of the enthusiastic support of Royal Navy assets under his command.

"Our portion is to be an assault on Crown Point and Montreal. The Duke of Newcastle has directed all the colonies to cooperate and has written to say that five battalions of regulars will be coming from England and two more from Gibraltar. London will pay for the militia, and Parliament has voted to reimburse the colonies for Louisbourg. All this, of course, is to remain in absolute secrecy until our official announcements."

The Dutchman nodded. "As I said, Governor, I will advocate support for this venture, and I have no doubt that others will concur."

Van Nes was saying all the right things, but his eyes remained unexpressive and something of their coldness entered the room. After an awkward silence, the Governor put his glass of claret aside and stood.

"Very well then, mijnheer. If you care to stay for dinner we would be glad to see you again after the Council discusses some other private matters."

Van Nes rose and bowed slightly to the Governor and Council. "Your invitation and your confidences are welcome. I will carry them home with me now and look to better days ahead, Governor."

Governor Clayton walked him to the door and summoned the scarlet marine who was standing outside. "Take him home as soon as possible, Lieutenant. He is needed there as much as here."

He offered his hand, knuckles up, to Van Nes in farewell. Van Nes took it limply between forefinger and thumb and bowed slightly, insolently, again. He straightened, turned and swept away down the hall without another word, marine in tow and with his large felt hat, decorated elaborately with lace and feathers, firmly replanted on his head.

CHAPTER TWENTY

Albany, 1746

A bright flash of moving color below caught the eye of Edward Stoatfester, and he glanced out the third floor office window of the new brick Albany City Hall.

It is ridiculous, typical of this insane place, that everyone still calls it the Stadt Huys, in spite of the fact that the colony passed from Holland to England two generations ago.

Without being aware of it, Stoatfester began to grind his teeth again. Dressed immaculately in the current French style, he was taking notes at another of the endless meetings between Voortman and De Vere. They were adjusting their tactics regarding the Governor and Smithyman.

It being a hot spring day, the third floor of the building was stifling, even though all the windows—the highest in the town—were open. Stoatfester's attention was already wandering when he caught a glimpse of Anneke and her mother below. They were walking up Handlaers Straat, which the English officers in the fort were now beginning to call Court Street.

By leaning slowly forward and then gradually backward, he was able to keep the two women mostly in sight as they crossed the bridge over the still-lively Ruttenkill stream, until they turned onto Jonkheer Straat and passed the Dutch Church.

As always, Anneke, waving her hands about and laughing freely posed a lively contrast to her dour, practical mother. Her large gold ear-hoops flashed in the sun. Her mother doted on her, but frowned at her effervescence. Anneke's scarlet petticoat vanished around the corner, just as a silence fell in the room and Stoatfester realized that he was the subject of focused stares from the two other men.

"And is your interest in what is outside so incomparably greater than in what is going on here, that you cannot do your duty, sir?" De Vere seemed particularly choleric today.

Stoatfester knew this was partly because the Legislative Assembly had responded with uncharacteristic enthusiasm to the Governor's call to arms for an invasion of Canada, although De Vere had succeeded once again in restraining them from voting any money either for Indian affairs or the transport of supplies for the campaign beyond Albany.

He met De Vere's gaze steadily and responded politely, dipping his quill and wiping it carefully.

All the while, his mind was screaming at him. *Yes, certainly what's between that little blonde vixen's legs out there is more important than anything in this stuffy room! Don't you know my cock's about to break off in these breeches, you idiot?*

His thoughts continued to boil inside his skull while he wrote.

Although there is one thing, and these fools are the means to get that. When I have finished helping them to destroy that self-righteous poseur Smithyman, there will be time enough to get revenge for all these little insults. Time enough.

"Do you have anything to report, Stoatfester?" De Vere's question broke into his thoughts and his mind again focused on what he was helping to plan for Smithyman.

"Yes, in fact I do, sir. I have contacted the most disaffected Mohawks from the Lower Castle near Fort Hunter, and some Oneidas. They will act on our behalf to embarrass Smithyman and disrupt his negotiations with the tribes. I believe we shall soon see some results from this initiative."

De Vere nodded thoughtfully. "That would be useful. Smithyman seems to be able to hold the Governor's attention far more than is healthy for us. Please encourage them to do as much as they can. Do you have enough money?"

Stoatfester shook his head immediately. "They are extremely grasping, sir, as you know only too well. It would be more comfortable if I were able to offer them enough to eliminate any temptation to deal with Smithyman and their other tribal brothers, which would obviously be to our detriment in this."

De Vere and Voortman glanced at each other and Voortman shrugged and said, "It is well to invest some small sums in this. Smithyman's fall would be of great value."

Voortman waggled a fat forefinger. "But, Stoatfester, you must be quite certain that this is not traceable to us. If the Governor got wind of it, we would be in a difficult position."

Stoatfester smiled. "I do not deal with the savages myself at all, mijnheer. There are many, many in Albany with good reasons to visit Fort Hunter and Oswego to talk with these people. So far I have found one or two of them that I can trust, but they, too, require payments of coin, not paper."

Voortman frowned. "Coin is difficult to come by, and for that reason more visible than notes of credit. But I shall do what you request. You must come to the house for this, however."

Stoatfester's mind raced.

A coup, indeed! A chance to find Anneke alone, perhaps, and some substantial coin for rum, which will greatly improve my chances to obtain a land patent from the savages, as well as wreck Smithyman.

He nodded, meekly. "I will attend upon you at your convenience tomorrow..."

Voortman cut him off. "Not tomorrow, but Thursday after mid-day I will see you."

"As you wish, mijnheer."

"Just be very sure that those kerels you deal with never know where that silver comes from, Stoatfester, or your situation here will be ended."

"Kerels, mijnheer?"

"Rascals, Stoatfester, rascals. The unscrupulous dregs of the gutter, who take our money and usually deliver precious little of value in return."

De Vere pointed out, brightly, that the current outbreak of smallpox in Albany had not only forced dozens of its citizens into quarantine, but it was likely to continue through the summer and disrupt any Grand Council of the Chiefs that the Governor might be planning in Albany.

"Ja," said Voortman, "most of the savages know whose side they should be supporting. I hope the rest all get a fever and take it home from any Council."

The Voortman's Albany residence was on the west side of Jonkheer Straat. It was a substantial two-story building with old-fashioned stepped gables, its narrow end facing the street in the Dutch way. Its glazed yellowish and reddish bricks alternated in a pleasing checkered pattern. Voortman's private office occupied a back room on the main floor.

He and Stoatfester passed the central staircase, bright and gleaming from its spotless white tiles imported from Holland. The heavy office door was built of three-inch oak plank, reinforced with iron straps and rivets. The room was illuminated during the day through one multi-paned window equipped with iron bound, loopholed shutters. In the centre-bottom pane was a colorful stained glass representation of the Voortman coat of arms, which matched four others in the front windows of the house.

There was a flintlock blunderbuss racked beside the door. When loaded with goose shot, its bell-mouthed barrel was deadly at short range in a crowd. It looked ready for use, and so did the pair of basket-hilted cutlasses hung beside it, the edges of the heavy blades glinting in the afternoon sun.

Voortman made no comment on these aspects of the room, neither when he ushered Stoatfester in, nor when he bolted the door behind him. Voortman's grandfather had boldly built the place in the days when Albany was a mere cluster of fortified wood houses in the forest, most of them belonging to the Dutch West India Company and their agents and partners in the fur trade with the Iroquois.

Then, the residents sheltered from French and Indian raids in the shadow of the comforting twelve-foot high, sharpened wood palisades surrounding the city. By ordinance, each resident of Albany had to build and maintain his own section of the wall. A few of those rotted ancient stakes still stood, like crooked fangs. During a generation of peace, residents had stolen most of them for firewood.

A hundred yards farther on, Jonkheer Straat passed the foot of a low rise, which was surmounted by Fort Orange. Just below the south bastion of the fort, the wagon road passed through what had once been a gate in the town's palisade and then climbed a little farther before winding twenty miles west to Schenectady, where a ferry crossed the Mohawk River.

The main wagon road then continued, increasingly rough and narrow, along the Mohawk's northern edge for another hundred miles. It passed fertile flatlands where German immigrant farmers prospered, and led through the silent, forested hills to the Oneida carrying place at the head of navigation of the Mohawk River. Most travelers and almost all commerce used the river.

The alarm in the community at the slaughter at Saratoga fifty miles north of Albany convinced the Assembly to go through the motions of reinforcing the Albany fort to reassure the townsfolk. Masonry walls had begun to rise at a leisurely pace and one or two of the most decayed sections of the old wooden palisades around the town had been replaced. Nowhere had the new ramparts been finished, however.

Voortman hauled out a dusty, padlocked chest from behind a heavy mahogany screen, painted with a depiction of a ship belonging to the Dutch West Indies Company, the WIC, under full sail. Selecting one of the long iron keys from the ring in his hand, he opened the lid, pulled out a small bag of coins and closed the lid in one smooth motion. Even Stoatfester, standing nearby, had little chance to see the contents.

Voortman counted out ten pounds in various bits of silver, retied the deerskin bag and locked it back in the chest. Before giving the silver to Stoatfester, he pulled a massive bound ledger to him across the desk, dipped a quill and wrote in the sum. Stoatfester initialed the entry.

Anneke's tinkling laugh floated to them from the grand front parlour.

"Oh, hello, Stoatfester," she said, as the two men walked through the sumptuously furnished voorhuis toward the front door.

"Have you met my new tutor, Mr. Livingston?" She continued, "He is endeavoring to teach me my sums, but I am afraid that I must be too simple-minded, for I never seem to get them right."

The pimply, thin young man stood. Stoatfester nodded distantly at him and gushed at her, "He must be a poor teacher if you have such trouble with counting, for I have seen you assisting your father in the business, myself."

Anneke's bright blue eyes rested on him for a moment, appraising, then dismissed him. "Fie, Stoatfester!" she said. "That is mere accounting, not to be compared with, what was it called now, Livingston, algebra?"

Stoatfester flooded his mind with a vivid picture of himself feeding Livingston one of his own eyeballs on a stick, as he had heard occasionally happened to Iroquois prisoners. He smiled warmly. Voortman opened the door and he then had no more excuse to linger. When he glanced back, he could see only the back of Anneke's slender neck and her tightly wound golden curls.

He stepped down into the dusty street and turned right, toward the waterfront, scattering the foraging chickens with his boots while dodging cattle, pig and horse excrement. Voortman's neighbor was re-roofing and Stoatfester had to walk around high stacks of red clay tiles, which were piled halfway across the street. A loud argument had broken out between the tradesman and a wagoner, who was having trouble passing.

"In court, Jans! You and the Philipses will be in court before I put up with this again!" The wagoner shook his fist in the face of the unimpressed roofer. Stoatfester strode past, unhearing, down to the track along the Hudson River known as Dock Street.

Albany's owners deliberately turned the backs of their houses and businesses to the river's dockyards. Their hirelings, however, reached grasping fingers into the pockets of sailors and boatmen in every smelly tavern and rooming house along the river's edge. Stoatfester knew this area well.

He cared not at all that his money was considerably more welcome in the half-hidden brothels than he was. No one on the muddy path wished to risk offending the patroons by informing on their brutal protégé, much less by more direct actions, but dark looks and unheard curses rained silently upon him, whenever he appeared.

CHAPTER TWENTY ONE

Warpath, 1747

Billy was trying hard to improve his friend's mood. "I see that you have a new gus-to-weh headdress, Marten." They were seated near the gate, inside the palisade that now surrounded Smithyman House.

It was late evening, and the fire in front of them burned brightly. A resin pocket in the two-foot diameter hemlock logs occasionally exploded in a violent shower of sparks. Many of the Lower Castle Mohawks had begun to consider this as one of their council fires and were meeting here in preference to the official Albany location.

A few yards away, the new thirty-foot flagpole stood, its lower portion fitfully illuminated. It was simply a pine tree, barked and limbed. Since the Governor had sent a platoon of regular troops to help defend Billy's fortified house, mills and warehouse, it was now a semi-official British establishment. Each morning and evening, a soldier formally raised and lowered the union jack.

Marten's hard expression softened for a moment, and he reached up with both hands and removed the sumptuously feathered skullcap, made of bent ash strips stitched together.

"My daughters have favored me with this. You see, here, the three eagle feathers of a Mohawk warrior. They are set into wooden spinners that my daughters carved. The porcupine quill overband and beadwork on the front is also their work."

He admired it for a few seconds and placed it on the ground beside him. "It is pleasing to have daughters who respect their father."

His face returned to its look of stony resolve, and his obsidian eyes stared into Billy's.

I must take a great risk with this white man, now. If he does not respond properly, I will be shamed. Many will call for my replacement as war chief, and they will be right.

"Your Governor's Indian Commissioners have called for a great council in Albany again. At Onondaga, the sachems have decided that none shall attend this council."

He tossed down the remainder of his tankard of rum and licked his lips.

"The Gantowisas have tired of your dishonorable play war, where you ask us to fight but will not fight yourselves."

At Billy's gesture, one of his servants refilled their pewter mugs with punch.

Billy said, "The Governor will present a plan to drive the French from these lands forever and has been promised thousands of troops to help."

Marten eyed him skeptically. "This has been tried before, when I was a very young warrior. It came to nothing, although I personally brought home many French scalps, and it hastened the deaths of many fine warriors. Yet the Albany dogs remain as Indian Commissioners. We cannot understand this. We do not believe the Governor's words either. We will not go to Albany."

Billy was silent.

Marten slapped at a mosquito attempting to drill through the impermeable layer of bear grease on his arms. He began to speak again, quietly. "My son, if Corlaer arrives at Albany and none of us are there to meet with him, this will help to discredit the Albany Commissioners. We hope that perhaps great Manitou will then open Corlaer's eyes to see that those Commissioners will never speak the language of the Longhouse, as you do."

There seemed little point in pursuing the matter further, so Billy changed the subject.

"What do the scouts say about Crown Point?"

Marten ignored the question.

"At Onondaga we hear that our enemies, who now live in what was once our land north of Lake Ontario, may be turning away from the French, since they say that the French trade goods are becoming very scarce and expensive."

Billy said, "Good. This is because we took the fortress Louisbourg last year. Since then the Navy has been able to stop French ships from bringing trade goods and weapons across the great eastern sea."

Marten said, "That may be so. The Ojibwa have begun to send more canoes to Oswego. We do not like this and we will see that Albany does not equip these people with weapons to attack us, as they have already equipped the Northerners and Easterners."

Billy smiled. "I am sure that the French like to see their allies coming to Oswego even less than you do."

He repeated his question. "Have you heard any news from Fort St. Frederick?"

"Fort St. Frederick? Not much has changed there. The prisoners from Saratoga that were not given over to the Northern Indians have been moved to Montreal."

Marten held up his hand to forestall Billy's next question. "I have not yet heard that Elijah was among them, although there were many black men and women. As you know, those you sent with him did not see whether he lived or died before they escaped. No one saw his body. A few of the French soldiers went away with them, but the garrison at Crown Point is large. Many of the Northern Indians have now left, however."

Billy frowned. "I am paying well to keep scouts there; I hope they will not sleep when our enemies are present."

Marten smirked a little. "You must understand, Billy, that the lands of others are not our concern. If there are worries about those lands, their owners should be providing for scouts to warn them of any danger. I do not know if that is being done."

Billy remarked, glumly. "Nor do I know, my father. It is shameful. The New York Assembly and the Indian Commissioners have shown many times they do not believe that the French will attack. Even now, after Saratoga has shown that they are fools, and the French and their Indians are taking scalps everywhere around Albany, they still will not act as though they are truly at war."

Marten shrugged. "I have told you that the Frenchmen, the Joncaires, father and son, are continuing to speak to any who will listen, in the western Longhouse."

He sent up a cloud of smoke. "There are now many who do listen carefully when he tells them of the treachery, greed and cowardice of the English."

He slashed his hand down, "But it is still certain, even now, that no French force, nor any English force, will travel through the Longhouse without our permission and knowledge."

I must trust my instincts, and those of my women and warriors. This man is to be trusted with our lives. He shrugged mentally. If he is not, then better to see this, now.

Marten held up his pipe and the servant quickly refilled it. He puffed on it for several minutes and a dense cloud of tobacco smoke engulfed him for a moment.

Then, he stood and took the war hatchet from his belt. He turned his head to hold Billy's gaze. The hatchet's edge gleamed as he turned the weapon back and forth in the firelight. He let his arms fall to his sides and turned again to the fire.

"Billy," he said quietly, without turning around, "you know that the Onondaga Council speaks for the Longhouse and that we will not now go to war for your Governor or your Albanians. I myself, however, thirst to bring in a French scalp. I have spoken to Wind-Through-the-Spruces and Beautiful Feather about this matter. They have consulted the other Gantowisas at Dyiondarogon."

Billy stood, knowing that he must reply, but before he could say a word, Marten suddenly swung his right arm back and threw the hatchet across the fire. It flew thirty feet, turning twice in the air, and its blade chunked deep into the flagpole.

He turned to Billy and said, "You see, I have struck the hatchet that our people at this time carry only in their bosoms. I, Emperor Marten, war chief of the Mohawk, will take our people to war against the French, but I do not go for the Albany people, and I do not go for Corlaer, nor do I go to preserve the ancient Covenant Chain between our peoples. I go to war because you say it is right, my brother, and our clan women, and my young warriors agree with you."

Billy put down his mug and walked to the flagpole. He plucked the hatchet from the wood in one strong motion and then struck it in again, deeply.

He turned to Marten and said, "It was the Mohawks that the French struck first, without warning, in your great grandfather's time. I would not have it said about me that I ask my brothers to fight where I will not. Let us go together, my brother, so that the French begin to understand that we are not all like Albany, in this place."

Marten nodded.

I hoped you would say that, my brother, but it is a great gift to us that you have done so.

"Now is a very good time for you to become a Mohawk warrior as well as a brother. I will find five of our best warriors from the Lower Castle, and we will go hunting."

In a week, the seven men were resting on the tall hill overlooking the foot of Lac St-Sacrement. They observed two canoes making their way down toward Albany.

"They slip down to sell things to the Dutchmen in ones and twos these days, to be less visible." Marten said. "But, as you know, many of these canoes are paddled by our cousins in Montreal, and so we must leave them alone, for now. When they have passed, we will cross to the east of the long lakes. There, we can lie in wait for a party of the Northerners and Frenchmen as they go or return from Fort St. Frederick."

Four days later, they crossed a trail showing evidence of recent use. Marten squatted and conferred with the others in Iroquoian. By now, Billy could follow almost all of what they said.

"Nine or ten, perhaps eleven, outbound." was their conclusion. "Two days ago."

They scouted the trail carefully until they found a place near the summit of one of the hills, where a giant pine had been lightning-shattered. A huge portion of trunk and limbs had fallen across the track. Some of the sturdier branches and a few remaining stump fibers, bent double, suspended the four-foot-thick trunk precariously, high above their heads.

Marten stopped them. Billy could see his eyes gleam as he briefly looked up and down the faint trail.

"Here," he directed. "We will take them here."

Billy felt his heart begin to pound. He held out his right hand and saw a very faint trembling. As if Marten had read his mind, the war chief grinned ferociously at Billy. The huge scar writhed on his vermilion and black cheek. He walked over and clapped him on the back.

"You are worried, my son, about your first kill. Be not afraid. I, Marten, have seen into your heart. I have consulted my warriors. We would not trust you to be with us if we thought you were unfit. We are not foolish, Billy. There is always some risk in war, but we have much experience in this.

"It is true that they have more men than we do, but they will be tired from climbing this hill. Some will be carrying things taken from the New Englanders and some could be wounded, for the New Englanders are not asleep. The trail is narrow and they will be single file. We will drop this tree in their middle and take them down in halves."

Marten gestured at their little band. "Unlike what I saw in London, where your people are as numberless as mosquitoes, the Longhouse people are very few, but very wise. We do not simply throw away our lives to demonstrate our courage, as you foolish whites seem to prefer to do."

They prepared the tree and readied themselves. Then they waited. There was no practical way to set up a warning system reaching farther away than their own ears and eyes without losing a warrior from the ambush, and they were outnumbered perhaps two to one already. Three days and nights they remained in place, sheltering under stacked evergreen boughs.

Each morning dense cloud shrouded the hilltop. The second and third day a cold rain fell on them. They talked very briefly in low tones. They lit no fires and smoked no pipes. Billy chewed on his dried meat supply and ate some ground maize, squirming as he tried to keep the larger rivulets of icy water making their way through the branches away from his neck.

"You must be as patient as a toad that waits for the fly," said Marten quietly. At dawn each morning, they recharged their muskets with dry powder.

"Do not worry about the waste of powder, Billy. We will have only a very small warning. There will be time for one shot only, but the shots must be good." Marten's scar writhed briefly, "After that, we will have their powder, and their hair."

The French officer leading the band of ten was alert. He heard the thump of the hatchet stroke that freed the tree overhead, and he motioned the party to stop, but that was a mistake. Two of his men were unable to dodge the deadfall and its thick, brittle branches speared them as the trunk smashed them to the ground. Nearly simultaneously, six musket shots exploded.

The officer had turned away in sudden alarm, just as Billy pulled the trigger. The usual fraction of a second delay, between the flash in the pan and the ignition of the main charge in the barrel, seemed to take an hour.

Billy, his heart now pounding in earnest, saw the French officer was still standing. He dropped the musket and picked up his hatchet, his hand suddenly sweat-slicked.

You missed, you fool, and now you will have to make the best of this.

He stood and charged blindly through the smoke, teeth bared in fear and rage.

However, he had not missed. He nearly tripped over his victim. The three-quarter inch lead ball had smashed into the left side of the Frenchman's chest and he lay dying on the track, wide-eyed. He gulped blood quietly for a few seconds and then was gone, staring at the sky.

A few faint groans and some thrashing in the bush marked the fall of four other men. Three remained on their feet, two in front of the tree and one behind. They were Abenaki, French allies from the northeast nations, whose former territory was now being invaded and occupied by the settlers of New England.

Snarling defiance, they dropped sacks of plunder and reached for hatchets and knives. Surrounded, surprised, and outnumbered two or three to one, they were quickly knocked down and overwhelmed by the Mohawks before Billy could tear his eyes away from the dead Frenchman.

One of the Abenaki had a weeping flank wound, wrapped with grimy blood-stained linen. They killed him immediately with a hatchet stroke to the skull, along with those wounded by the fusillade. The two survivors were subdued after a brief but fierce resistance and bound tightly with rawhide strips.

Marten was gleeful. Billy watched the warriors scalp the dead Indians, and then knelt beside the dead French officer.

This is a test. I must do this well.

He seized the officer's gilt chest plate and yanked it off, snapping the light chain holding the gorget around his neck. The man was not wearing his uniform coat or hat, but only a blood-soaked linen shirt, baggy woolen pants, and leather Indian leggings and moccasins.

Billy tossed the French musket to one of the warriors and rolled the corpse onto its face. Drawing his knife, he mimicked the Mohawks and made several quick cuts down to the bone around the man's hairline, then put his foot on the small of the man's back, seized the hair and pulled sharply upward. The scalp ripped free, spraying blood.

Billy thought it sounded like a stump being pulled from a swamp. The glistening, bloody dome of the French officer's skull flopped back onto the ground. He turned and held up the skin. He felt nauseous and his hand was shaking. He was having difficulty breathing.

"Yo-hay!" they called out, grinning. "He is a warrior in truth, today." After a moment, he could smile weakly back at them, although his legs remained wobbly.

He tucked the dripping flap of hair and skin into his belt and stripped the corpse of its cartridge case and officer's sword. The Frenchman carried no papers. One by one, the Mohawks came up to him and clasped his arms; Marten last of all. He looked Billy in the eyes and nodded. "You are a Mohawk warrior, my son. This is a thing that we will remember forever."

He gestured at the leather and wood cartridge box that Billy held. "But we do not need their cartridges, my brother. We have other things to carry and we must now leave before a patrol comes to find out about the shooting."

They headed south along another ancient trail, just below the ridgeline. They stopped frequently to listen and look for signs of pursuit, but none appeared.

The two Abenaki prisoners remained silent, not responding to the occasional kick or taunt. They were yoked to each other by the neck and to one of the Mohawks. They received no food and only a small amount of water during the three-day return journey to the crossing between the long lakes.

They left behind several bags, but carried away the silver trays, most of the silver knives, forks and spoons, a matching silver cream jug and some curiosities, such as a gilt-framed oil portrait and several mirrors.

Their arrival at Dyiondarogon caused a sensation. Billy was recognized by the clans there as a Mohawk warrior. He traded the French officer's scalp and gorget for the silver tray and jug. The two prisoners ran a hastily convened gauntlet course. A hundred Mohawk men, women and children, armed with knives, clubs and spears, formed a running path.

The Abenaki impressed the participants with their agility and endurance during the first run. By popular demand, they were then allowed the unusual honor of running a second time. Both were severely wounded by the time they finished their second passage, but families who had previously lost sons now adopted them.

Two of his warrior companions then paddled Billy back to the beach at Smithyman House, where the mill creek entered the river. They raised their paddles in salute and shouted their praise at him, before pushing off again. As he washed off his war paint and a few remaining splatters of blood, Katy asked but one question, "Did you kill any Frenchmen?" Billy nodded, and she was content.

He showed her the silver pieces and said, "This is not for us, Katy. We will, in time, use it for something more valuable than serving tea." He pointed out the engraved insignia and initial in the centre of the tray and on the cream jug.

"I will find out their former owner, but I am very certain that I have seen some similar insignia recently, on silver in one of the great houses in Albany."

She was shocked and said, "But that is infamous, Vilhelm, that means they are buying things stolen from murdered New Englanders."

He nodded, grimly. "Put it safely away for now, my sweet, and bring me some tea and all the news. Is there any mail from Turnbottle? Where is my little Anna doll?"

"She is with Richard, but will be home tonight." Katy's eyes traveled from Billy's broad shoulders down his naked body. Her voice grew slightly husky. "You need a hot bath, my Villy." She called out and in a moment was instructing the maids to heat the water.

*****

A week later, Billy responded to an invitation to return to Dyiondarogon.

The deep gashes inflicted on one of the Abenaki in the second run of the gauntlet unfortunately had became infected, rendering his left arm useless. The usual herbal remedies had failed, and gangrene had set in.

His adopted family had little choice but to reject him as unsuitable. They were reluctant, for he had shown courage and a willingness to adapt to Mohawk ways. However, he and they were consoled, because he had earned the right to die bravely under torture.

Billy was invited back to enjoy the rather rare spectacle of a warrior's death song. After more than thirty years of relative peace in the north, there had been few captives. Generally, Catawba and Cherokee prisoners did not survive the long run back from the south. As a result, several hundred excited onlookers surrounded the stake where the prisoner was tied, and the adjacent fire.

Billy sat next to Marten in a place of honor. He was restless, apprehensive, and squeamish, and muttered as much to Marten in a low voice. "It is a great honor to be asked, Father, but I am not sure that I should have come. It will be difficult for me to witness this without disgracing you and myself. My culture teaches that these things are very cruel."

Marten smiled affectionately at him. "My son, you whites do not understand us in this respect, but it is not complicated." He waved his hand at the throng about them. "We are all humans, born to pain. So there is much honor and true nobility in rising above the pain. This," he pointed at the warrior, "this allows us to measure the honor and nobility of an Abenaki warrior."

He met Billy's eyes. "But it would be a truly savage act, to us, to lock up any one of the people you see here in a room with no sunlight or freedom. That is far more cruel than anything we will be doing. Many of our people, even warriors such as myself, or this one you see in front of you, who may have great physical courage, would die, broken, from just a few weeks of such treatment. Yet I saw in London myself that you whites consider imprisonment normal, even for ridiculously trivial things like stealing food. I was told that some are kept in prison for years." He spat, and pointed at the Abenaki.

"Faugh! You can see, this man is calm. He is not a victim, he is not a child, he is no slave. He is proud. He understands what is ahead. He has been prepared for this since he was a child. Many are warriors and some are chosen, but most are not." Marten shook his head sadly. "It is simply that your training is poor. Our honor is precious to us. He can earn honor today for his people and he knows that."

The Abenaki warrior was a man named Rough Foot. He sang well and defiantly in his own tongue for more than three days. For many hours, the listeners could not hear the slightest waver in his tone, even around noon on the second day, when one of the matriarchs succeeded in chewing two fingers and the thumb off his good arm.

Billy drank a great deal of rum. He looked at his own hands, trembling, and fought off nausea and an overpowering urge to flee. *How can he stand it? I have known since I was a boy that they do this but I can't really bear to watch it.*

Billy suddenly remembered the slave he had watched broken on the wheel in New York, and the outrage he had felt and expressed to Turnbottle. He turned the memory over in his mind, partly as a distraction from the unimaginable stoicism of the man tied to the post. He drew strength from contemplating the memory.

I was right then. That slave was innocent. Worse, he was never free to choose any fate whatsoever. As much as we can choose any of our fates, this man on the post chose to be a warrior and, knowingly, chose to war on the Iroquois. Our own ritual savagery, murdering ignorant and innocent slaves in cold blood, was just as bad as this, however much we sweetened it up with hypocritical official processes and paper. Maybe worse.

Rough Foot did faint once, later that afternoon, when the youngsters inserted sharpened burning sticks into various new and existing orifices, and the festivities adjourned for several hours, while he recuperated. They fed the children and opened new kegs of rum.

In the evenings, Rough Foot was given water and a little food if he desired some, and allowed to rest. Near the end of the third day, however, and especially after he had received his wire necklace of red-hot hatchet heads, his voice suddenly weakened quickly. All regretted this, since it necessitated ending his song.

This they accomplished by hacking off his head, which was accomplished fairly quickly, to Billy's relief. The Mohawk children then paraded the dripping blood-drenched object around the Castle on a spear. The clans judged the warrior's bravery had been sufficient, especially considering that he had been weakened by his gangrenous limb, and they threw his head into a boiling cauldron, along with his uninfected, sectioned limbs and heart. The warriors who had captured him ate his liver raw.

When portions were served to the celebrants, Marten observed offhandedly to Billy that it had been a respectable performance, although by no means outstanding.

"When I was very, very young, just before the grand peace treaty with all the nations was signed in Montreal in your year 1701, I remember seeing one of the truly great ones.

"He was an Ojibwa named Blue Snake. We captured him with six canoes of the finest winter furs, which we sold in Albany. He was on his way to Montreal from the sleeping giant country far to the northwest."

He chuckled, "For a time, the French traders had been listening to Ojibwa lies and thought we were no longer able to guard the lake. However, none returned to Montreal from that brigade to boast that the Longhouse people are weak, or sleeping. Our Upper Castle, Canajoharie, celebrated this victory for many moons, because the French and the Ojibwa fought well. It was a very honorable victory."

He fastidiously ripped a large piece of wrinkled skin from his meat and tossed it behind him. The pack of ever-present dogs snarled at each other over it.

Marten nodded his head upriver towards Oswego and continued his tale.

"Blue Snake lived a full week, at the Oneida Castle, and sang strongly, until his tongue was cut out. Many of the elder sachems and Gantowisas in the Longhouse remember him quite well." He shook his head ruefully. "He should have been Mohawk."

"But that was the old days. Sometimes, it seems that the young warriors today are softer. Or perhaps our people have lost some patience since those days. It is an art to help the warrior sustain his song. We do not restrain our children, and perhaps we do not train them as well as our grandfathers did."

He glanced at Billy, who shakily lifted his slab of soaking, half-cooked man-thigh to his tightly closed lips for a polite ritual taste and then quickly put it down. Billy looked back at Marten and apologized, "My people have a horror of eating man flesh."

Marten nodded, chewing. "It is a wasteful and disrespectful horror, like many white ways. The Longhouse people only eat flesh from men that have earned such an honor. We feel it strengthens us."

He smiled slyly, the snake-scar moved up and down, and he continued. "It is difficult to understand why your people find this practice so revolting. Do your priests not tell us in all your churches that we should eat of the flesh of your Jesus God and drink of His blood as well?"

Billy had a coughing fit.

Marten talked on. "It is still very puzzling to us that so few whites can sing death songs as well as our warriors, since we know many whites are strong and brave."

He shrugged, "As I have mentioned, we have decided it is simply a fault in your training."

During the revelry, several visitors quietly departed. An Oneida went down river. A Cayuga and an Onondagan went upriver.

CHAPTER TWENTY TWO
Albany Council, 1747

The anchor chain rattled out through the hawsehole, but that wholly familiar sound barely registered in Governor Clayton's consciousness. He had been awake since dawn, when the Royal Navy cutter, *Arcturus*, sailed into view of Albany. He was now fully dressed in his old-style uniform as a Rear Admiral, and the commander of the *Arcturus* was ever mindful of Governor Clayton's status with the Navy.

He had half-expected to see the smokes of a ruined town, but all appeared well, no slightest sign of war anywhere. The fort on the hill still showed its red, white and blue union jack waving gently on the top of the tall flagstaff. The town appeared intact, sleepy, in fact. There was nothing but what appeared to be normal cooking fires, anywhere in sight.

A jet of white smoke from the side of the fort, followed ten seconds later by the boom of a gun, signaled the beginning of his salute. Five minutes later, the lookout called that a boat was putting out from shore.

By the time the bateau reached her, *Arcturus*, too, was shrouded in smoke, banging a reply back from the six brass four-pounder cannon on her deck.

The Commander of Fort Orange, Major Itcheson, clambered up the side. He came to attention on deck and saluted smartly. Clayton returned the salute.

They went to Clayton's cabin, sparsely furnished and small. They had to remove their hats before going below and sat, knees touching, across a narrow folding table. Clayton summoned a bottle of claret and said, "I'm afraid this is all the Navy could spare for me. I will be entertaining on the sloop we chartered, but I think for now we need to conduct official business here, away from civilian ears. Do you agree, Major?"

The Major nodded and accepted a glass of the red wine from the Governor's steward. "Yes, Sir, it is somewhat difficult to know who to trust in this place." They toasted His Majesty and he continued, "They are not over-enthused about the war."

Clayton sniffed. "Tell me what you know about the situation here, Major."

"Well, sir, the first thing is, we have smallpox in the town since two days ago, and I would strongly advise that you remain aboard until we can isolate the sickness and be sure that the contagion is not in the fort."

Clayton cursed, a colorful seaman's oath, which mildly startled the infantry major. "More delay. Our campaign against the French is not beginning auspiciously. Have any of the tribes arrived for the Council?"

Itcheson shook his head. "We've seen no sign of anyone other than the usual trade canoes, sir."

Clayton drained his glass and called for the steward to refill it, then waved him away. "Just leave the bottle, Ridley.

"Once again, only two of my Councilors have accompanied me for this Council. I think the Assembly has put their wind up. It is insufferable. What a boon it would be to have a real command again, even one as insignificant as this."

He slapped the hull, "At least here an order is something to be obeyed, not nibbled and quibbled to death with polite insolence."

"Indeed, sir. Civilians are pitiable creatures."

"What of the French?"

"Except for small parties of their Indians around the outskirts of all the communities, who scalp and kill an unwary farmer now and then, they stay at Crown Point, so far, sir."

"Could you defend the fort? Against a force like the Saratoga attack?"

"We would defend ourselves stoutly, sir, but I confess that a determined assault by a force of six hundred would be very difficult to hold off for long. We have not completed repairs to the walls and our garrison is only eighty men. We have only five serviceable cannon and three mortars."

"I can send you nothing from New York, but I might be able to persuade *Arcturus* to part with a couple of four-pounders, for what it's worth."

"I would be grateful, my lord. However," Itcheson gestured out the port light, "most of the people here seem to feel the French would never dare to attack Albany itself."

He added, "They are most grossly inhospitable, hostile even. And the prices they charge for provisions and goods are outrageous."

The Governor sighed. "We'll just have to put the best face on it we can. I will be moving to more spacious quarters on the sloop today."

He reached for a pile of papers and pulled one out, glanced at it, then scribbled a signature and date and sealed it. "I would be grateful if you could inform the Indian Commissioners that I would meet them there on the sloop, all the ones that are presently healthy, that is, on the morrow in the evening, for dinner. You are invited as well, sir and—do you have a wife in Albany?"

"No wife, my lord."

"Very well then, Major. Bring yourself, at least. Perhaps you have an officer who would enjoy being out of the fort for an evening. I would be delighted with the company of men who understand what wartime means."

The Major rose, and bowed. "I thank you, sir, and perhaps there will be some better news by tomorrow."

The Governor waved a dismissive glove and the Major left him alone.

A week later, a Lieutenant, a messenger from Major Itcheson, appeared over the side of the Governor's sloop and saluted.

"If you please, my lord, Major Itcheson wishes you to know that no new cases have appeared among the garrison since the outbreak began ten days ago, so we believe that it is safe for you to disembark. Your quarters have been made ready."

"Very well." Clayton growled and dismissed the Lieutenant, saying, "We shall be there forthwith. We will require some wagons at the waterfront for our baggage. The marines will escort me into Fort Orange and perhaps you may be able to find quarters for them as well, since you are under garrisoned."

"Very good, my lord."

The Governor of His Majesty's Province of New York unofficially opened the Albany Council of 1747 on the morning of July 22. Of all the nations summoned to the Council, from a population of perhaps twenty or thirty thousand, two Onondagans and one Oneida appeared, late in the afternoon. However, they presented two fresh French scalps to Clayton, with a very warlike speech by the Oneida, who was their leader.

"I cannot any longer prevent myself from avenging all the murders of the French upon my people and yours, in ancient times and now," he said. "I determined to open the path for my brethren."

He gestured at his companions, who shook their muskets. "We took these scalps on the very doorstep of Fort St. Frederick at Crown Point, Father Corlaer. The French troops all ran out after us, but forgetting their guns in their haste to catch us, they had to return, and so we were able to escape."

Clayton consulted briefly with the two Councilors who had accompanied him from New York and who, with the local garrison commander, were the minimum required for a quorum. Four Indian Commissioners sat on his left, his Councilors and the fort commander sat to his right. The encrusted, unstretched French scalps lay on the table in front of him like squashed rats. Governor Clayton stood, and gracefully doffed his gold-laced hat.

"You are our honored allies in the war against the French and we are very grateful for your efforts on the warpath."

With ceremony, the silver bounty payable for the scalps was counted out and presented.

"If you return at this time tomorrow we shall have further tokens of the King's gratitude and appreciation ready for you."

The Governor pointed to the keg of rum standing just outside the door of the tent, where a uniformed, musket-armed marine stood guard.

"Please accept our warmest hospitality, my friends. You will find plenty of excellent food around the back of the tent by the fire."

The Council transacted no other business on the first day.

On the second day, four Indians turned up. The Governor presented the three from the previous day with colorful bundles of wool strouds for making blankets, and cocked hats trimmed with lace. The Oneida, whose name was Wooden Fish, also received a silver gorget to hang about his neck and a fine, laced coat.

"We have a new name for you as well." Governor Clayton gestured to each side of the long, mostly empty, table. "From henceforth, in our eyes you shall be known as the 'Opener-of-the-Path.'"

Wooden Fish responded with enthusiasm. He held up his gorget. "I see the face of the King on this silver badge," he said, "and I am his brother. My friends are determined to go again on the warpath against the French and, as you see, one of the River Indians has already joined them. If Corlaer desires, I will go again to lead them."

He took a breath, "Or, I could go among the Six Nations to tell them that they are late for your Council and that the war will be over if they do not hurry." The Governor frowned slightly.

Wooden Fish insisted, "I will bring them, Your Excellency, or you may take these gifts back when I return."

Clayton turned to his Councilors, who shrugged and nodded.

"Go then, Opener-of-the-Path, and bring your brethren here to our Council Fire. We are patient, but you know well that the French have strong forces still at Crown Point. We believe that they may fall on your villages and on ours at any time."

The Oneida grinned and ran out the door of the tent. He and his companions whooped boisterously outside, drank deeply at the keg and cut large pieces of pork from the spitted roast at the back. Then they trotted at a mile-eating pace out the newly repaired gate of Fort Orange, carrying their muskets. Three of them disappeared north up the eastern branch of Fox Creek. The Oneida went west, to Schenectady.

At the table, the Governor called for wine. He pursed his lips and steepled his fingers. He said, "It would seem that no one in the Six Nations is afraid that the French will attack again. Neither does anyone in this city seem to be nervous enough about it to persuade the Indians to talk to us."

He tapped papers on the table. "Yet Smithyman up the Mohawk writes to me that his Mohawk patrols say there is such a large force at Crown Point that they expect they will attack. My garrison commanders say the same thing."

His large fist suddenly pounded the draped plank table. Two wine glasses bounced and capsized. Servants scurried. "I have been here for almost two weeks. Why do the tribes not come?"

Theatrically, he held a glass pitcher of water to the light streaming in through the door of the tent. The water was a golden, speckled brown. Clayton sarcastically suggested, "Perhaps it is because the water here is full of swimmers? I have had this pitcher filled up one-third with rum and yet, as you can see, there are still hundreds of these little creatures taking baths.

"I have seen water kegs kept two months in the bilges of man o' war not so alive. Has Albany been pressed into the Navy?" he joked.

The Indian Commissioners suddenly and unfortunately recalled that they had sent no wampum belts concerning the meeting to the Esopus people, or the Minisink tribes, or the clans on the upper Susquehanna River.

De Ruyter, head of the Commission, ventured to downplay the lack of action. "These tribes, which we call Mohendars, are not numerous, my lord, nor reliable in our cause, and we determined this would be a waste of time and the colony's resources."

It was a minor thing, but it was the last straw for Clayton. He cursed loudly, and roared at his secretary to take a letter, which he dictated in the presence of the Commissioners.

"To William Smithyman, Esquire, Smithyman House, for immediate delivery." Clayton took a gulp of wine and wiped his mouth with the linen napkin, thinking furiously.

"You are hereby appointed Indian Agent and Head of the Council of Indian Commissioners of His Majesty George II's Province of New York, effective immediately. You are charged with the immediate and urgent recruitment to the present war of the Six Iroquois Nations, and with the most strenuous encouragement of their representation at the present Council at Albany. Please respond immediately, or delay at your peril. Signed, Clayton, Governor. Copy to His Majesty, to my Council, the Assembly, and the Commissioners by name, dated today."

His secretary finished scratching and bowed, going to his office to make the good copies.

A shocked silence prevailed at the table.

That'll fox 'em! thought Governor Clayton.

He stood, and the table stood with him. He put on his laced hat and turned on the Commissioners with a scornful quarterdeck rasp heard all over the fort.

"You well know, you blackguards, that the Assembly voted no funds whatever for this Council or Indian affairs. I am funding this Council entirely on my own account, not on the Colony's, nor on the King's penny. The Colony's resources be damn'd!"

He bowed slightly left and right, and exited the tent without another word.

*****

Billy was breathless with excitement and pride. Katy smiled to see him in such an elevated mood.

"I am going to Dyiondarogon to talk to Marten, Katy, I will probably be back tomorrow," he had said.

She and Anna Christine waved at him from the house as he went out through the heavily timbered gate. The iron hinges screeched as soldiers hastily pushed the doors shut behind him. The huge hardwood bar thudded with finality into the sockets inside. It was dusk, almost dark. The stillness of the summer forest outside was oppressive. Billy could hear Anna Christine crying. She was missing her Papa. She sounded very far away.

An army detachment of four redcoats under a corporal marched stiffly into the bateau behind him carrying their muskets and looking grim. The rowers also kept loaded muskets at hand. They demanded double wages to take him over the river to the Mohawk castle.

"It be very, very dangerous out there," the boat captain had said, shaking his head dourly. "My cousin Joshua, just down the river across from Schenectady, had his neighbor murdered and scalped right there in his bean field, just Monday last."

Billy paid in advance, making a mental note to log the expense when he returned.

When he arrived at Marten's home, Beautiful Feather and Wind-Through-the-Spruces ran to him. He dismissed the boat's crew until the next day, admonishing them, "If you delay me here past dark tomorrow, you will get half wages only."

He beckoned the corporal. "Wainwright, you may allow two men leave tonight, but you and the two others must remain to guard the bateau. Keep proper watch."

An arm around each woman, he strode off to the neat, whitewash-planked house that Marten had built outside the Castle. Its front porch overlooked the river, and from its back door stretched a flourishing vegetable garden with a small apple orchard. Here, the brooding hills retreated half a mile from the river. Beyond the vegetables, broad fields of ripening corn extended to the hills.

On a pole by the front door hung several dozen scalps, many ancient and decayed, but some obviously recent. They were all stretched on circular bent wood frames and decorated with paint and wampum beads. A few hundred yards away, the ramshackle stockade of Fort Hunter leaned, overlapping the punky wooden stumps of an ancient Mohawk palisade. A few red coats were visible above the wall from time to time. The black silhouette of two small swivel cannon topped the new, timbered corner bastions.

A small fire flickered in front of his home and Marten himself sat on a stump smoking and talking to a stout man with long brown hair and an extravagant moustache, dressed in fringed and beaded buckskins. Billy felt an additional surge of excitement as he recognized Henry Chilton.

Henry was one of the traders who successfully risked their lives penetrating west beyond the mountains, into the hardwood forests and fertile valleys and plains of the Ohio River and its tributaries. He had enormous experience with the peoples and customs of the west. Billy had risked a few small investments with Chilton. He had been amply repaid, and so the men's greetings were cordial.

Billy smoked a pipe and drank rum with them as the darkness grew. They spoke about many trivial things. The women sat beside him but sensed that this visit was something out of the ordinary.

"Io'tonhwahere has news, is it not so?" asked Wind-Through-the-Spruces. Billy turned his head slowly and solemnly to look at her and puffed on his pipe. "Why would you think that?" he asked.

The two women burst out laughing. Beautiful Feather spoke, "Because we can see that you are bursting with it, although you think you can conceal your feelings like a Mohawk."

Now they had attracted Marten's attention and he looked more closely at Billy. "It is true, my brother, I think that you must have received an important belt."

Billy frowned. "I would not be so transparent to my father and sisters."

Even Chilton began to smile, although his face was notoriously difficult to read. Many suppliers in Philadelphia had found out to their chagrin that Chilton's disappointed frown at having been worsted in a deal often disguised the elation of an entrepreneur.

"Out with it then, man," said Chilton, "they have found you out! What is this burning message you bring?"

Billy said, "I have been appointed Head of the Indian Commissioners for New York."

Marten let out a whoop and pointed his pipe at Billy. "Did I not tell you we should ignore the call to the Governor's Council? This is joyful news, indeed!"

Wind-Through-the-Spruces and Beautiful Feather looked at each other and then pressed themselves close to Billy. His heart was pounding.

Chilton extended his hand in congratulations. His grey eyes were piercing. Billy heard the familiar lilting Irish accent, "Perhaps we can be of some help to each other, my friend. I can bring you news of the west, and with your connections at Oswego you can warn me of Frenchman on their way there."

Billy nodded, thoughtfully. "Perhaps we can be of even more use to each other and to England than just as news bearers, Henry."

Chilton winked, owlishly. "English goods and fair prices can be very persuasive. Since Louisbourg, the French have almost nothing to offer to the western tribes. I heard in the spring that a Frenchman was tomahawked to death near Pickawillany, for offering only one ball and a powder charge for a beaver."

"One ball!" Billy exclaimed. "I don't blame whoever it was for being insulted."

They absorbed that news, shaking their heads at the fatal folly of the trader. Billy asked, "But haven't the Miamis always been friendly with the French?"

Chilton shrugged. "That is true. Partly because there have not been many English in their country. There is also a story that hundreds were poisoned to death by brandy they bought at Oswego."

"When was that?" Billy asked.

"Awhile back, before I came from Ireland, which was in '40. I've heard various dates, but it seems likely to have been the summer of '32, near as not.

"The story goes that the Miamis came all the way to Oswego themselves and carried 400 kegs of brandy back to the Ohio country. Then, many of them started to die. When they broke open one keg, they found the skin of a man's hand floating in it. Not the whole hand, mind you, just the skin. It put them off Oswego. The French, of course, were very pleased to tell them to stay away from there as well. Makes you wonder."

Billy stared at him. "Could it not have been smallpox?"

Chilton shook his head. "Nay, it seems that the French Commandant at Fort Miami investigated and actually saved a few of the local chiefs with doses of this Orvietan medicine that he had brought from France for curing various things. But Orvietan doesn't work on smallpox, and he saw no signs of the pox at all."

"Hundreds died?"

"Three hundred Miamis, aye, but probably many more, because the brandy was taken to some of the other tribes as well."

"Oswego had only been built six or seven years before," Billy mused. "It's not likely they'd be wanting to kill off customers they had just taken away from the French, and who'd just purchased hundreds of kegs of brandy, d'ye think?"

"Not likely," Chilton agreed. "Seems like someone must have poisoned 'em on purpose, though."

Billy was silent. He caressed the smooth brown thigh of Beautiful Feather, who was kneeling beside him. She kicked him, gently.

He shook his head and puffed on his pipe. "I expect that the distillers made a bad batch and then sold it off cheap for the Indian trade. The Albany traders always know a bargain when they see one. They water it down at Oswego anyway, probably figured no one would much notice. That is likely where the skin came from. It must have floated in when they were refilling the kegs with the river water, stripped by the current from someone drowned under the ice all winter."

Chilton looked at him, and then at Marten, who had been listening intently. "Yon Smithyman is a smart one, is he not?"

Marten smiled. He inclined his head to Billy. "Our Gantowisas would not love him so much if he were senseless like most whites, is that not so, women?"

Beautiful Feather was braiding colored quills and wampum into Billy's hair. Wind-Through-the-Spruces massaged his back. They ignored the other men.

"Henry," said Billy, "you should come to stay with me for a week at Smithyman House and we can talk about the western trade." He paused and addressed Marten. "For now, though, I need help to bring in the Haudenosaunee to the present Council at Albany."

Marten huffed his gasping laugh. "An Oneida named Wooden Fish, dressed in a very new, laced red coat, passed here ahead of you on the same mission, Billy, only a day ago. If we come in, now, he will boast that it was his influence."

Billy was startled, but smiled and said, "I care not who gets the credit, Marten, if the Six Nations come to Albany, we will all have joy to spare."

Chilton appeared to smile again. "There may be more than just the Six Nations thinking about coming in. On my way up the Susquehanna River from Croghan's Fort, I fell in, for a time, with twenty Chickasaw warriors. They were going to ask the Senecas to show them the way into Canada."

He chuckled and slapped Marten's thigh, nodding and grinning at Billy.

"You would have enjoyed, them, my friends—truly, they were warriors! They told me that a French force had come against them in their own southern lands four years ago, and had very kindly left behind four hundred muskets and many scalps, but the muskets were now worn out."

He started to laugh and spluttered out the next sentence in gasps.

"They told me that since the French had not thought it proper to bring them any more muskets, they would like to go into Canada and bring back some new ones, themselves."

The three men and the two women chuckled grimly at the vision of the Chickasaw obtaining their new French muskets. Chilton wiped his eyes, weeping with laughter at his own story. Wind-Through-the-Spruces refilled their tin mugs.

Marten eyed Billy and said, "The Onondaga Council thinks that we Mohawks are out of control, since you and I raided east of Crown Point. But many tell me that they know that the Mississaugas north of Lake Ontario are now also very unhappy with the prices of French trade goods."

He puffed thoughtfully before continuing, his fathomless dark eyes resting their gaze on Billy's face during the silence.

"I think, Billy, that since you have become head of the Albany Commissioners, that the Chickasaw," he inclined his head to Chilton, "and the Mississaugas may now shame our shy brothers in the Six Nations into coming to talk to Corlaer about war against the French."

Marten suddenly threw his head back. His whooping ululation filled the night air with wildness.

*****

The two columns of warriors joined reluctantly at Schenectady, becoming a parade of feathers and fearsome painted visages, half a mile long. The children, sachems and gantowisas followed. The Mohawks led the way, as was only proper on their territory. Billy rode at the front on horseback, with Emperor Marten and several other Mohawk war chiefs. As usual, with feathers on, he was nearly indistinguishable from the rest except for being slightly taller, along with the fact that he had no dangling silver nose-bob or copper ear hoops. Garish body and face paint hid his white skin and lack of tattoos.

At first, there had been an extreme amount of grumbling between the nations as they collected. Many of the Six Nation people were deeply offended at the way the Mohawks had manipulated them into attending the British Council of War, through the unauthorized attacks on the French and their allies. They standoffishly insisted on walking down the south side of the Mohawk River from the lower castle. On the north side, the column included Senecas, Onondagas and Mohawks, plus the band of Chickasaws looking for Canada, and two Mississauga Ojibwas, who had heard about the Council while at Oswego.

Billy had feared that the insult exchanges and catcalling between the two factions might erupt into serious violence, but somehow, sensible minds had prevailed. Once the two groups were forced to travel together down the road into Albany, most of the ill will seemed to disappear, apart from a few scuffles and some minor bloodshed. Billy refused to provide any liquor until they reached Albany and the proper ceremonies could be completed.

When they came in sight of the fort, they began to fire their muskets into the air. Almost immediately, the much deeper boom of the replying salutes from cannons on the ramparts lightened their mood considerably. With a great noisy, exuberant display, they set up camp. Governor Clayton strode out to greet them in his Navy uniform and invited the war chiefs and sachems into the fort for refreshments. Billy returned with him to his office for private consultation.

The Governor took off his hat and sat heavily into an upholstered chair. He looked Billy up and down. "Well, sir, you do indeed look the part. I am very glad to see you, I cannot quite say how much."

Billy grinned. "Our labors are not done yet, Governor. There remain one sachem of the Lower Mohawk Castle and two in the Upper Castle, one from the Tortoise clan and one from the Bears, who are unpersuaded. They have been talking a great deal to the French, I expect, since they have close cousins at Kahnewake near Montreal. Before we begin the public conference, we must bring them into the fold."

The Governor grimaced. "These are endless negotiations, Smithyman."

"Yet, my lord, but if we are successful, we will have an invincible force to fall upon the French, or, conversely, to protect us should they fall upon Albany."

Clayton beckoned and a servant presented a large platter of smoked meats, cheeses, breads and pickles. He stabbed a pickle with a fork and waved it about.

"We can't dawdle around here all summer, Smithyman. Newcastle has ordered a campaign against Crown Point and Montreal this summer, and the provincials are going to start arriving here very soon."

He picked up a glass of water, started to drink it and cursed, spitting out a mouthful and emptying the rest of the glass onto the plank floor. "God Almighty, with these things swimming in the water I wonder that half the city hasn't died by now. Vile, it is, simply vile. When do you think we'll be able to start the Council, then?"

"It's very hard to say, my lord. They do not want to make war on their relatives."

Clayton groaned. "All of the cost of this Council is from my own pocket, Smithyman. It is truly an achievement to bring so many, sir, but now I have to feed and entertain them!"

In the end, another ten days elapsed before the formal start of the Council. The Governor caught a fever and one of the two members of his own Council from New York had to present the opening speech.

The New York Indian Commissioners then refused to attend and sent in their resignations, saying they had lost all influence over the Indians, but Clayton refused to accept their resignations, for the second time. "Damn your souls," he said to them, "You cannot play at being Commissioners just when you want to, you incompetent devils! We are at war now, and I will have you Albanians charged and gaoled if you refuse to serve now, when everyone I could replace you with is working elsewhere for the good of the Province!"

"It was a good speech, for a white man," Marten admitted. Billy and he were reviewing the opening day's events.

"Corlaer's man was very effective reviewing all the terrible history of our wars with the French. It will be a good thing when your armies attack Crown Point and Quebec, and when that happens many of the nations will have more confidence that it is wise to support the British.

"He was masterful in his timing, when he threw down the war belt. I am sure the decision will be to take up the hatchet, but they will have to deliberate for three full days to ensure they maintain the dignity of the decision. What was all the shouting about, in the streets near the water?"

Billy chuckled. "The Governor needs two hundred boats built, to carry the army to Crown Point. The Albany bateau builders refused to make them, saying they were busy with other projects, so he had the Navy press them into the service and under his command."

Marten was curious. "Press? This is a new word to me. What does this mean?"

Billy explained. "It means that they were forced to do it or be put in jail."

A death sentence would be easier for our people than that confinement, Marten thought. Cautiously he said, "But would that not affect the quality of the boats they might build?"

Billy laughed aloud. "A very good point, Father. I expect the Governor will be placing guards to ensure that they do a proper job. If the boats do not float, men will be whipped or imprisoned."

Marten shook his head. *More white insanity.*

"If they will not even build boats for him, why would they go to die for him?"

"There are yet enough," Billy replied, "although perhaps not from this place, who feel that driving the French from the north is a good thing to do. Perhaps when they arrive, they will inspire the New Yorkers, as the Senecas were inspired by the Chickasaw to come here."

Marten grunted. "I think we should show the French that the Longhouse people are awakening. I will take a war party to frighten them in Montreal. We can be ready to depart soon after the war hatchet is raised up."

Before dawn, on the sixth day of the conference, Marten awakened Billy and Beautiful Feather. They were staying in a wigwam next to the large canvas marquee that Billy had ordered set up outside the fort, for war councils with the Six Nations and their allies.

Billy had refused the Governor's invitation to stay in the fort, "If I am to be their agent, they must see me as one of them, my lord."

Governor Clayton had smiled ruefully, "You truly live the part, do you not, Smithyman?"

The Haudenosaunee sachems had returned to the Council in three days. Their speeches indicated they were convinced that the British were in earnest about defeating the French and that this made them rejoice. They agreed that the attacks by the French had been sufficient cause to make war on them in return. They renewed and polished the ancient silver Covenant Chain between the British and themselves. They took up the hatchet and accepted the war belts. They danced the somber war dance with enough feeling to please the Governor, and he ordered the distribution of generous presents, to the great satisfaction of all the nations.

Now, Marten gently grasped Billy's shoulder, to wake him. "There is smallpox again in the city, Billy," he said, urgently. "Our people must leave quickly before it infests us." Billy awoke Beautiful Feather and insisted that she must go as well.

He said to Marten, "I cannot go, my father, I must remain here for many days to make arrangements with the Governor's staff. Get your people to safety. I will come to see you in, let us say, two weeks, and perhaps the worst of the contagion will be finished. Some time we will also talk again about the invisible fence that can be created in your people's bodies to prevent this death from taking them."

Marten grimaced. Like many Indians, he had heard the rumors that inoculations were a white way of spreading disease to his people. "When I see that building this fence in your blood is becoming common practice among the whites then perhaps we can talk about it again. For now, I see that white people all around us are afraid and die of this disease, almost as much as we do —although I admit your own family appears to have the protection of Manitou."

The unfortunate Mississauga Ojibwas lingered too long, in the midst of wealth that they had not seen for many years. They both became infected. One of them spoke to Billy as he was dying, "I am unhappy not to be able to strike the hatchet with you, but you must send a French scalp to my mother to console her."

Billy nodded, "This will be done, Brother, you must not worry." The Senecas agreed to take the red-painted war belts and the Ojibwas' share of the gifts back and present them to the Mississauga nation on their behalf.

The Governor summoned Smithyman to his quarters in the Fort. "Smithyman," he said, "You have done well to bring the tribes in, and indeed some who seem well disposed to us are arriving even now from the Juniata Valley. I need your help now with a related matter before you go back."

Billy was in a somber mood. "The conference has been successful, Your Excellency, but many of the warriors who attended are now dying. It will be difficult to gather them again this year for any large campaign."

Clayton nodded. "Yes, but I see perhaps some small scale activity for them, at least. In any case, Smithyman, the Albany scouts I am sending out from here seem singularly unenthusiastic. They demand extra pay and some even seem to have been warning off the enemy by firing muskets before we can execute an ambush.

"It is intolerable, that several hundred Frenchman and their Indians can descend on Fort Massachusetts as they did this month and none of us know anything about it ahead of time."

"I have scouts out," Billy replied, "but they report back little about parties that do not seem intended against the Mohawks."

"My plan," said Clayton, "is to entrust you with organizing some scouting parties of our own which can move through the forests like the natives, and harass the French, bringing prisoners and intelligence back to us. I leave it to your discretion to name the individuals. You can pay them from the Indian Accounts."

Billy was silent.

"Yes, yes!" the Governor rasped, "I know that the Assembly has not voted any funds for the Indian Accounts, Smithyman. Just keep track of the expenses and we will recover them somehow, from the Crown if not from the province. You agree we cannot just let the French be, now?"

Billy bowed. He said, "I will do as you suggest, my lord. I do agree that we must try to put them on the defensive. I think I have someone in mind who would be able and interested in doing this." He hesitated.

"Well, what is it, man? Speak up! I must know what my officers are thinking."

"A fellow named Rogers, sir. Also I have Walter Butler in my employ at Oswego, who might be useful in this sort of business, but I have a question, Your Excellency, that you may wish to hear and answer discreetly."

"What, Smithyman, what sort of question?"

"Sir, have you heard any rumors about the entire campaign against Canada being cancelled?"

"Canceled? What do you mean, canceled? What have you heard, and from whom?" He was clearly astonished.

Billy said, "My business agent in New York wrote to me, saying he has it from reliable sources in London that Lord Newcastle has recalled Admiral Holeybarth to England and will not send any regulars. The Massachusetts colony has also withdrawn its support from the attack on Quebec, because the French are sending a fleet to retake Louisbourg and to attack shipping and facilities along the coastline."

The Governor read Turnbottle's letter quickly, his brows knitting. "God damme!" he exploded, "Why have I not heard anything official of this? And the militias keep arriving, so New Jersey, Maryland and Pennsylvania have not yet had news of this, either."

Billy said, "I can keep this from the Mohawks for a time, but not once it becomes public, which in my estimation, will be very soon."

"Too true, Smithyman. Well, if it is true, it cannot be helped. Why, though? Why in God's name Newcastle would reverse course like this I cannot fathom. He was one of the most enthusiastic advocates, judging from his previous letters."

"My agent says that the Admiralty is concerned about an invasion of England itself at present." Billy flipped to the fourth page of the letter.

"Here it is, you see, Governor. Although he goes on to say that there also appear to be powerful individuals in England who have become jealous of the success of the colonies against Louisbourg." Billy had carefully kept back the page where Turnbottle described the Duke of Newcastle as an incompetent nincompoop.

"Smithyman, I thank you for this information. I will write immediately for instructions."

Governor Clayton bellowed for his secretary.

"Worse and worse," he growled. "I have to victual a thousand and a half militia men around Albany, none of whom has yet received their complete enlistment bounty or any other pay since arriving here. And now it appears that I will not even be able to do anything with them against Crown Point, lacking any army regulars or artillery."

He looked at Billy. "At least you, sir, deliver on what you say." He laughed harshly. "It is a painful virtue in this world, I warrant. Is it not, Smithyman?"

Billy nodded. "Your servant, sir. I will see what can be done with our allies and some rangers." He bowed and turned to leave.

"Oh, Smithyman, one more thing." Billy stopped and turned back.

"I nearly forgot, with all this other business cropping up. The Frogs have returned your servant Elijah, with some other parolees, from Montreal. He came up from New York last week, and I sent him on up the river to Fort Smithyman. Didn't think you would need him in your wigwam, you see."

Billy paused a second, absorbing the sudden news. He blinked, and then smiled happily and said, "I thank you, Your Excellency. I shall be extremely glad to have him back."

A thought struck him. "He may also have obtained some interesting intelligence for us on his travels. Many whites think black people are witless, and it may have made his captors careless. I will write to you as soon as possible about it."

"O Mother of Christ, have pity," shrieked the women in despair.

"This is no time for praying," cried the young Madeleine Verchères.

"*Aux armes! Aux armes! Les Iroquois!* Quick to your arms and guns,
Fight for your God and country and the lives of the innocent ones."

—*Madeleine Verchères*, William Henry Drummond

Chapter Twenty Three
Raid, Summer 1747

The raid that Marten had assembled was returning south, paddling hard and fast up Lac Champlain, through a narrow gap separating a rocky point and an island. Thousands of green lily pads of various shapes and sizes reached almost from shore to shore in the calm, dark water. Huge dragonflies, 'Devil's Darning Needles,' flung themselves violently about over their heads. Smaller damselflies hovered at water level or rested on the lilies, their blue and green coloring so bright they seemed to glow.

Billy was daydreaming a little, watching the stems and leaves swirling past, in eddies created by the powerful stroke of Wooden Fish's paddle in front of him. A blue heron stood in the shallows near shore, reflected in the mirror of the lake between the lily pads. It flapped heavily into the air as they passed.

A sense of exhilaration filled the four-canoe brigade. Yo-hay! Marten's plan had succeeded perfectly. They had even been invited for an audience with the Governor of Montreal! Of course, Billy and Marten did not go, they were too recognizable, but two Mohawks, with relatives in Kahnewake and good French, so ably convinced the Governor and his minions of their friendly disposition that they were entrusted with dispatches to Fort St-Frédéric!

On the return journey, they had fallen on an unsuspecting French post near the rapids at Lachine, on the south side of the river. The Mohawks had insisted on conducting the assault themselves. There was a brief skirmish, but the astonished and terrified militia and their family inside the palisade could put up little resistance after the gate was forced.

None of the attackers were injured. As they returned out the gate to the trail, Billy saw one screaming woman pursue them, the flames silhouetting her waving a large knife. The frightful looking Mohawks laughed. One shot her, and her scalp joined her husband's.

Then they trotted through the forest to where the Rivière Richelieu exits from Lac Champlain. There they boarded canoes secretly purchased and left for them. Nearly a dozen scalps now swung at the warriors' belts. Four prisoners sat, bound and gagged, in the last canoe. One was a rather attractive young, blonde woman. Another twenty miles up the lake, a few hours at most, and they would drag the canoes into the forest and run along the ridges past Fort St-Frédéric, towards home.

Their speed undoubtedly helped their situation, but the first volley that exploded from the trees at this narrow spot was perfectly aimed. The leading canoe simply dissolved into bloody foam and flying bark fragments. Not a single swimmer remained visible in or under the wreckage when the next canoe desperately raced through the red water only seconds later. One broken paddle tilted into the air, still gripped firmly by a severed, submerged arm.

At the same time, three balls found their mark in the second canoe. Billy distinctly heard one of them smack into flesh just behind him, a second after the noise and white smoke of the volley shot from the trees. He turned in alarm as Marten missed his stroke and lurched sideways, clutching his left arm. The sudden motion caused Wooden Fish to overbalance, just as he put his shoulder into the stroke. He tumbled right out of the canoe, surfacing briefly six feet behind them, flailing the water and choking, then sinking again.

Billy knew that a second fusillade was less than thirty seconds away. He looked at Marten and then back at the two other canoes now overtaking them rapidly. He spoke in urgent tones to the stern paddler in Iroquoian. "Keep going quickly," he said, "If we are separated, I will meet you at the St-Sacrement carry, on the hilltop."

Without further comment, he dove cleanly overboard, finding the feebly moving body of the drowning Oneida deep below and far behind.

He grasped the scalp lock firmly and hauled him to the surface just as the last canoe was approaching. As it came alongside, strong arms heaved them aboard, even as another, less well-aimed volley banged out and splashed among them. One paddler collapsed, his head flying to pieces, gushing bloody brains across the water as the musket ball exited. They rolled his body out into the lake without ceremony. Most of the other seven paddlers did not miss a stroke, knowing that their only chance lay in quickly increasing the range.

The unseen attackers got away two more volleys before the three surviving canoes were safe. One more warrior was hit in the last canoe, a ball penetrating the fragile birch bark and cedar ribs and shattering the man's knee. The canoe wavered in its course, but the rhythmic disciplined paddling of the unhurt crewmembers carried it away before they suffered more damage. The crippled warrior stripped off his loincloth and stuffed it into the spouting hole in the canoe hull.

An hour later, they drew the canoes into the trees on the west side of the lake, twelve miles north of Crown Point. They posted lookouts a half-mile from the camp, two farther up the lake, two behind and two in the forest to the west.

They gently brought ashore Marten and the man with the shattered knee. It was very clear from the floppy nature of the warrior's lower leg that he would never walk again. Three other warriors were less badly injured and it appeared that they would recover without much difficulty.

Billy examined Marten's arm in the failing light. The ball had passed through, and the arm was not completely shattered, but some splinters of bone poked out of the exit wound. Billy ordered a fire lit, against the advice of Marten and Walter Butler. Billy had appointed Butler commander of the new Ranger Company he had created to harass and probe the French.

In the flickering light he plucked white slivers from the oozing wound, then ordered the arm bound to a splint and then to Marten's chest.

"I will have the healers fix that, at Dyiondarogon," said Marten. "Who else is wounded?"

"Yellow Knife took a ball in the knee," Billy told him. "He cannot walk. He will lose the leg. There are three others with minor wounds, but none at all survived from the front canoe."

Marten grunted, "He must stay behind."

Billy said, "He will die."

Marten nodded. "That is so, but it will be a warrior's death. He knows this already." He grimaced as his arm spasmed. "Why did you jump out?"

Billy said, "Wooden Fish was not injured. When I saw he could not swim I thought we should not waste a warrior."

Marten met Butler's eyes.

Butler said, in a low voice, "The French used a swivel cannon loaded with grapeshot in that ambush, not just muskets. We were lucky the French gunner hit only one canoe."

Billy nodded, somewhat dazedly. "Yes, lucky."

Marten broke in. "Billy, these cannon are heavy and they needed time to carry it there. Yet there could have been no alarm given until after we attacked the outpost yesterday, and we have not stopped since then. A canoe will outdistance any man running. There is a traitor."

Billy shrugged. "It could be one of many who have kin in Canada. Not only the Albany devils love the French. Wooden Fish is an Oneida, but he was the first to go to war, of all the Longhouse people."

"So it appears, yes, but we must be very careful now."

"Yes, certainly. What must we do?"

"They will likely follow by canoe," Marten predicted. "We will cross to the west side of the ridges as quickly as we can from here and go south. We will leave Yellow Knife south of here at the edge of the lake, with four muskets."

"South?"

"Yes, it will confuse them into thinking we continued farther by canoe. They will take much longer to realize that we are on foot, and they will look in the wrong places."

Yellow Knife was in good spirits when they carried him into the canoe. They paddled him two miles farther up the lake, towing a second canoe, which they concealed only partially by the shore, as if in haste. They had splinted his leg firmly.

He spoke to Billy before they left him. "I am content, my brother. If I am lucky, I will have the chance to kill several more before I die and the great pleasure of fooling them again. If not..."

He shrugged, "Then I will sing my death song to the forest and to Great Manitou alone, and it will also be good."

"I will deliver your scalps to your lodge," Billy assured him. "They will praise you, as I do, my brother."

Yellow Knife smiled. "That is good. Go now; I am impatient to be alone."

He began to sing his song as Billy and Marten left him.

That night the survivors of the raiding party abandoned their canoes, crossed the mountains and headed south to safety. The soft concussions of sporadic, distant musketry was heard the next morning, for a time, then all was still in the forest once more. Yellow Knife's song had ended.

Although they stopped and checked several times for the French, there was no sign of them, and they concluded that their ruse, and Yellow Knife's death, had succeeded in fooling the pursuit. After a day or two, the likelihood of them being overtaken was reduced to a negligible risk, and they relaxed.

But it had been an expensive foray, with not much success to boast of. The intelligence gleaned from the routine dispatches and the meager haul of scalps and prisoners did not begin to compensate for the loss of so many warriors.

Billy and Marten agreed that smoking out the presence of a traitor on the raid would slightly balance the scales. Time alone would tell.

CHAPTER TWENTY FOUR
Fort Smithyman and New York, Autumn 1748

A year later, Billy received a letter from New York, so very far away from the inconclusive but bloody military campaign of raids and skirmishes he was operating in the north out of Fort Smithyman. He read the letter from Governor Clayton for a second time. He began to chuckle at the irony of it all, then threw back his head and laughed uproariously.

I shall write Father immediately, although I know not whether he will be pleased. No, that is not true. He will be pleased. I know not whether I should be pleased!

Katy was telling a bedtime story to Anna Christine when she heard him laugh. She tucked her daughter in and kissed her on the forehead. When she came to the door of the great room, he looked up at her from his desk. She was wearing only her shift. He had stopped laughing but was still smiling.

"Come here my pretty," he beckoned, "Come and see what great honor is done your husband today." She walked slowly over to him and stood behind his chair, one hand on his shoulder and the other lightly fondling his hair. He held up the parchment with its royal seal.

"Governor Clayton has appointed me Colonel of the Indian Forces of His Majesty's Royal Province of New York. There is a salary and a red coat officer's uniform to go with it, my lovely. Gold lace on the waistcoat, and silver in the waistcoat pocket."

She moved slightly to the side of the chair and her right breast gently nudged his shoulder. Her right hand moved to his neck and she bent and kissed him hard on the mouth. The paper fell to the floor and he stood, turning, and pulled her roughly against him while their mouths remained locked together.

His large hands each seized one of her buttocks, squeezing, and then his right hand found its way between her thighs. She groaned with pleasure and her head fell back. He picked her up and carried her to the big canopy bed down the hall.

"Liebie," she whispered to him later, in the dark, "Vilhelm, you vill be always, for me, the only man in the world." She was leaning on an elbow, gazing at his sleeping face. He was snoring lightly.

"I know that you will never marry me, but my dearest man, when you called yourself my husband last night, I was the very, very proudest woman in the world, and you do love me, I know it. And I do not mind, truly, that you also love the others. You have given me a wonderful daughter and we will make more. Perhaps even now we have made one."

She put her head on his chest and closed her eyes tightly against the tears.

Shortly after dawn, the sounds of the military encampment outside were beginning, as they had every morning now for a year. She listened for a moment and then leaped from the bed and dressed, rushing to the kitchen in the basement and harassing the cook for their coffee and morning bread and preserves.

When she returned, Billy was sitting up, grinning at her. She smiled back and placed the coffee on the side table, handing him a cup. He quickly set it down. She tried but failed to avoid his reach and squealed as she was unceremoniously heaved onto the bed across him. She stayed a moment, enjoying his caresses, but then stood and wagged her finger at him.

"You have a very busy day today, Colonel Smithyman, do you not?"

He pretended to scowl for a moment, then sighed and drank some coffee.

"You are right, my sweet German girl, I have now even more things to do. And the first is to write the Governor to thank him, and tell him that he must send supplies. It is insane! We now have nothing of any kind to give my warriors in return for their work bringing in scalps. They will soon think that I am just as disgusting a liar as any Albany trader.

"This is good coffee. You must have beaten Irene particularly hard this morning." He eyed her. "I heard you scolding her, down there. But you must tell her also when it is good, you know."

She tossed her head. The days when she had been brought here as a servant herself were becoming for her a faint memory. "Cook would make things only her way if I did not make sure she has respect for her betters."

He swung his feet to the floor. "Perhaps I should go to New York myself. The raids are fewer now that the summer is over, and perhaps I can discuss details more easily with the Governor in person than by letter. Yes, my sweet, I think I must go there for a week; it will be better than writing."

She nodded, smiling. "You must order your proper uniform there, Vilhelm."

He laughed, delightedly. "You are right, you are right, that is an excellent idea."

*****

"Smithyman, how very good of you to come and see me. Do come in, now." The Governor offered port, claret and beer with a large selection of cheeses and fresh bread and, "a very hot pickle indeed, Smithyman, from a place in India called Madras. They have the very hottest food in the world. Do try it, but only a little, else you will not be able to discuss events with me, ha ha!"

Billy laughed at the Governor's little joke. He sniffed the green relish, which seemed innocuous enough, and used the tiny silver spoon to place a small amount on his plate. He spread a sample on his bread and cheese and took a bite. It filled his mouth and nose with delicious fire and he gasped, then ate more.

"An amazing experience, Your Excellency, I have never tasted the like."

"Have some beer, Smithyman, it seems to complement it best. The relish is good, ain't it? I have become quite fond of hot pickles and chutneys. I first had some in Gib, years ago, from a friend in the East India Company. This is the first good supplier I have been able to get here. But I am sure you did not come all this way to sample my pickles, Smithyman!"

Billy smiled. "No, Your Excellency. I wanted to thank you in person for the honor of my appointment as Colonel. I have a report about what we have accomplished on the frontier in the past weeks and our plans for next spring and summer. But also, I wanted to discuss supplies."

Governor Clayton frowned. "Smithyman, I have nothing to give you. First, I have pledged myself to the hilt to the banks here for this summer's Indian Council in Albany, for which the Legislative Assembly has now had the gall to accuse me of pocketing money. My own money, by God! The Assembly has also refused to pay the back wages or feed the New Jersey-men and the other militia who will be over wintering in Albany and Saratoga. These men, not surprisingly, are now threatening to mutiny. The Assembly will not pay anything for the Fusiliers either, unless they garrison themselves in Saratoga, to replace the Jerseymen.

"Captain Wilson has had to break into the provincial storehouses in Albany to get grain to feed his troops. Now the Assemblymen, led by your blasted relative De Vere, have chosen to view Wilson's action as an affront to the rights of all Englishmen. The whole thing is well on the way to beggaring me. I am sorry, Smithyman, you have been taken advantage of by the Assembly for the transport, I know, but my hands are tied."

Billy bowed. "Governor, my apologies, you misunderstand me. I do not hold you responsible for the Assembly's debts of honor. I contracted to supply Oswego and I will do so, whether the Assembly sees fit to pay for that service or no. I conceive it is my duty. No, the supplies I am referring to are for the service you have now commissioned me to do. We will get to that in a moment, with your permission."

"How is Emperor Marten?"

Billy smiled. "He is a very poor patient. His wife and daughters are becoming angry at his demands. However, I think he is well on the way to regaining use of his arm, although it will now always be weak. There was, thank God, only a very little corruption, and that was healed, thanks to the skill of the Mohawk herbalists. They are quite remarkable, although some of their nostrums seem irrational to our eyes.

"With respect to our activities, Governor," he continued, "I have the great honor to present the following report."

He removed two pieces of paper from his waistcoat, examined them, and read from one. "A small party of six of my Mohawks returned the morning of my departure for this meeting, with seven prisoners and three scalps." He looked up. "As you may know, this is a remarkable performance for so small a band.

"Lieutenant Butler and his Rangers have brought in six scalps and nine prisoners from Crown Point since my last correspondence. Likewise, a Canajoharie party has brought in three prisoners and two scalps. Gingegoe and his group have brought in another seven prisoners and three scalps."

Billy gestured to his leather case. "I have written certificates for these so that your books may show the bounties as a reasonable expenditure. I believe that we are shocking the French and they may reduce their attacks on us because now they will need to defend as well as attack."

After a moment's silence, Governor Clayton said. "Smithyman, this is the only activity at present which can be taken against the French, and I find it impressive. I offer His Majesty's thanks."

He added, "I believe I can speak for His Majesty as well, that you should be highly commended for risking your own life on the raid into Canada."

Billy smiled. "I thank you, Governor; I will carry your message back to the Mohawks. I believe that none could do better than they, in our service."

Clayton laughed harshly. "If it was up to our elected Assembly, I daresay we'd all be speaking French by now. Smithyman, I have made up my mind to tell them that unless they do their duty and fund the militia, I will order the Oswego and Saratoga garrisons back to Albany. I think they ought to chew on that. Feeding and garrisoning those soldiers' mouths on their own doorsteps, instead of on the Crown's or your account, and abandoning Oswego's fur trade and the Saratoga frontier to the French and their Indians might be a stab painful enough to their pocket books to bring them to their senses. Nothing else seems to work."

Billy smiled, and opened his mouth to comment. Clayton raised his finger. "I will not bandy words about concerning this, Smithyman. The Assembly is out of control and someone has to rein it in again."

Billy closed his mouth. *Closing Oswego would be insanity. Even Newcastle would have your guts for garters, Governor.*

He unfolded the second piece of paper.

"Your Excellency, the supplies I referred to a moment ago are used to reward and supply the scalping parties that I have sent out and that are coming in daily, at your orders. As I have reported, the Mohawks are working hard in our interest, but their families are very poor now because war parties cannot hunt or trap or trade for furs.

"I require silver to pay them, and muskets, powder and ball to equip them, along with some trifles such as clothing in large quantities, which will make them happier in our service. These I refuse absolutely to purchase in Albany— those dogs will make the excuse that they have none to sell me, in any event. There is also three months back pay due my officers and men. While it is less urgent, I am also now feeding upwards of two dozen prisoners."

The Governor nodded and interrupted. "I think that you ought to send a unit of Mohawks to surround and protect Saratoga, especially if the levies refuse service there."

Billy shook his head, "With the utmost respect, Excellency, this is not the thing to do with them. They do not tolerate garrison life well with Christians, and we are keeping them from the hunt. Their only pay is for scalps, prisoners and whatever else they obtain from the enemy. They would quickly leave, and all our patient efforts to persuade them into war would be forgotten."

The Governor sighed.

Billy continued, "Cutlasses, blankets, and a dozen other things are needed to continue the campaign, else they will go home, for they need these things for themselves in any case."

Governor Clayton waved for his clerk.

CHAPTER TWENTY FIVE
New York to Voortman's Warehouse, Albany, Autumn 1748

"...vermilion, blue camlet, red shalloon, good lace and white metal buttons." Turnbottle looked up inquiringly from the list. He was standing by his chalk-board wearing a long black coat, which gave him a somewhat sinister air.

Billy said, "For the Senecas. The French have usually given them these things and we have promised to continue."

Turnbottle went back to writing the list on the board. "...Thirty good castor hats, with scallop lace in white or yellow. Thirty wad extractors, three dozen axes, and sixteen tomahawks. Four dozen leather knives, gunflints, kettles, tobacco, ten dozen half-moon needles."

He laid down his chalk and looked at Billy. Billy waved the Governor's draft. Turnbottle reached for it and eyed it skeptically.

"The Governor has pledged a great deal," he said. "Did he also give you some idea when the Crown might pay?"

Billy shook his head. "No, but in good faith they must pay, do you not think, Turnbottle?"

"There are many who think good faith and government are things not of the same world, my friend."

"But you are not one of them, are you, Turnbottle?"

Turnbottle put down his lump of chalk. "I think we should go for food and drink, now. We'll continue this later."

Billy agreed. "A capital idea, Turnbottle. Also, I need to see a good tailor here, if there is a good one."

Turnbottle raised his eyebrows. "Tailor?"

Billy stood and drew himself up to his impressive full height, puffed out his broad chest and squared his shoulders.

He said, smiling, "Ah, for once I know something ahead of the well-informed Turnbottle. Governor Clayton has appointed me Colonel of His Majesty's Loyal Native Allies and of the militia of Albany County. This warrants a proper gold-laced colonel's uniform, does it not?"

Turnbottle stared at him a moment, then offered his hand in congratulations. "Billy, you have come very far in nine years, have you not? Without doubt, that also deserves a bottle or two of the finest New York has to offer. This uniform should come from London, however. We will arrange for a temporary one until it arrives."

He called to his assistant. "We will be out until tomorrow. Do not sell to any new customers until I return."

Turnbottle took Billy to his favorite lair, the Oar and Whistle Tavern, on the Broad Way. He waved his hand and a girl brought a pitcher of beer with two pewter mugs almost before they sat down.

Turnbottle looked dubiously at the beer and stopped her from pouring. "Billy, would you prefer we celebrate with the finest, to start, perhaps? Then we can get to the beer when our palates are numbed. What say you?"

Billy grinned, "I am at your mercy, Turnbottle; your wisdom is renowned, whereas I am a mere forest trader."

Turnbottle giggled his high-pitched laugh and turned to the waitress. "Sissie, take these back and bring two bottles of my very best claret from the special cupboard, please." He dropped a shilling in one of the mugs and she tipped it out into her hand, curtseying low enough to draw both men's eyes quickly to the deeply curved shadow above her stays, before departing on her mission.

"So, Billy, are you officially here, or are you still avoiding your relatives?"

"Can we avoid them here? My Uncle Holeybarth, at least, will not be present."

Turnbottle eyed him. "No, indeed not. I hear he has bought a borough and retired an Admiral of the White after heaping himself with glory and prizes. The victory with Anson off Cape Finisterre was not enough; he then captured the entire Santo Domingo convoy of French West Indiamen! Sixty-two of 'em, they said."

"He no longer corresponds with me, alas. I hear these things from my brother and mother. The family is thrilled, indeed, as we ought to be."

"De Vere does come in here sometimes, but he generally does not have eyes for anyone in this corner. He and his friends usually meet at the table in the other room. If your ears are sharp, there is usually a lot of politics decided here, however."

"If I remember aught, I will try to enlighten the Governor."

Sissie brought the wine and showed Turnbottle the little silver tag hanging around its neck. The men watched her avidly as she pulled the stopper from the green, onion-shaped bottle. The motion threatened also to release the quivering pink breasts above it. She filled two glasses.

"Sissie, you lovely, lovely thing, you have brought me the new glasses, without being asked," Turnbottle said.

He lifted one up against the candlelight. Billy admired it, prompting Turnbottle to hold forth, "You see, this is what we call the mercury twist in the stem, because it looks like quicksilver in the light."

Billy said, "How can they do that?"

Turnbottle smiled at him. "It is very attractive, is it not? The glassmakers introduce air into the molten glass and spin it in such a way as to make this pattern. Isn't it curious, the way taxes can have unexpected consequences?"

Puzzled, Billy asked, "What do you mean? What possible connection could taxes have with this exquisite glass?"

Turnbottle whinnied. "There is an excise tax on glassware, which is charged by the weight of the glass. Air in it means you pay less tax. Very simple. And so, voilà, we have these elegant things for our wine, instead of the usual lumpen jars."

They sipped. Billy liked the wine. "Turnbottle, you must send a pipe of the wine and four dozen of the glasses to me. Katy will love the glasses, and I love the wine."

They sunk the first bottle and traded gossip. Billy told Turnbottle about the Governor's resolve to threaten the Assembly with closing Oswego.

Turnbottle shook his head sadly, "He is a fool, a brave man with proper intentions, but an ignorant fool nonetheless, and evidently not over bright. Did you point out that this would instantly be used against him by the Assembly and Newcastle both?"

Billy said, "He refused to discuss it with me. He would likely lose the Six Nations, as well, if he gave Oswego to the French on a platter. It is mere bluster, I expect. But I fancy it is generally unwise to make hollow threats, is it not, Turnbottle?"

Turnbottle nodded, gloomily. "It will cost England greatly if she persists in sending such unsubtle sea-dogs to America in positions of authority. This is not Ireland, or even Scotland. The Board of Trade does not know what they have. Look at yourself."

It was Billy's turn to laugh somewhat bitterly. "The New York Assembly is well on the way to bankrupting me, Turnbottle. I do not see myself as an example to be emulated."

"You are wrong, Smithyman, quite wrong, you know."

Turnbottle giggled and nudged Billy's arm. "Else I would not advance you the credit that I do. Have some more of this, now, and admire Sissie's assets with me. She always drives away the glimglams.

"By the way, speaking of Scotland, did you hear what the Duke of Cumberland did to the wounded Jacobite Highlanders at Culloden?"

Billy said, "I haven't read details of the battle."

Turnbottle said, "It is true, as you once said, that no-one has an exclusive license on cruelty. Cumberland, who is George's son, you know, had the prisoners bayoneted. They say he burned down a building filled with wounded. Some officers refused to order their men to do it."

They were silent for a time. "Do you think, Turnbottle," asked Billy, "that it is the most savage side that always wins?"

Turnbottle beckoned Sissie, who emptied the bottle. He asked her to bring another and proffered another shilling between thumb and forefinger. She took his hand and placed the coin in the warm valley between her breasts, pressing his palm down slightly. He released the coin and squeezed gently. She giggled and pushed him away.

Turnbottle raised his glass to Billy. "To Sissie and her gender," he said. "She, at least, seems not to be savage at all."

Then his face darkened. "If they try those games on the colonists, Billy, the game will be lost. There aren't enough troops in all of England to hold the colonies down if they rise."

"Do you think they will rise, Turnbottle?"

Turnbottle shrugged. "It may never happen, but to prevent it, the Ministers and the King must realize that this is not England over here, it is a new place and they need new ideas to deal with it. The question is, can they do that, Billy-me-boy, and will they do that?"

*****

Voortman burped and snapped his fingers to have the great silver trays of fruits and cheeses removed, but as the servants picked them up he plucked one last ripe, red apple. Voortman, Stoatfester and De Vere were meeting in his office on the second floor of his warehouse in Albany. Through the windows, opened in the early autumn warmth, they could see a great deal of activity on the river. Heavily loaded bateaux were being poled and rowed up and down. Half a dozen river sloops pointed upriver at anchor just offshore.

"If the war goes on another year," Stoatfester gloated, "Smithyman will be bankrupt and in our hands, and so will the Governor. The cost of placing guards on every shipment to Oswego is hundreds of pounds a month. The

Governor himself is also paying for provisioning hundreds of troops, and borrowing the money from us."

Voortman nodded. "Ja." He began to chuckle, a deep, belly-shaking rumble. "De Vere, you have been brilliant."

He raised his wine glass in salute to De Vere across the table.

"The Assembly blocks the funding for defense in the name of economic prudence, and then blames the Governor for all the failures. The little settlements and traders outside our estates are discouraged, so we maintain our control here, and the French are not defeated, so our power and profits grow."

He began to peel the apple in his hand with a little wooden-handled knife. "Because of the blockade, the French are so desperate that they will pay almost anything to us for trade goods. And to prevent a full-scale rising in the west," he went on, "Governor Clayton has to pay our prices to feed the militia. It is wonderful. Simply a wonderful time."

A new thought struck him and he spluttered with laughter.

"And it is all done in the name of defending the God-given rights and liberties of our poor downtrodden American Englishmen against the monstrous and evil encroachments of the English Crown. It is truly genius. Even another Dutchman could not have done this better."

He threw the peel out the nearby window and bit deeply into the apple with an audible crunch. He closed his eyes with pleasure.

His mouth was full of the sweet fruit as he gestured and mumbled at De Vere.

"But how will you be able to persuade those with influence in London to see you as the next Governor yourself, if you persist in taking the Assembly's cause as your own, hmmm?"

De Vere smiled thinly. "I have no ambitions to be Governor, mijnheer."

The Dutchman returned the smile. "No? Well, perhaps it is a good thing that you do not, then,"—he licked his fingers—"for I think that you have personally stoked up fires of outraged liberty in the Assembly and among the people that will burn up many ambitions in the years to come."

Voortman abruptly turned to Stoatfester. "And what of your spies, do they have news of Smithyman?"

Stoatfester said, "He has stopped going out on the raids, since the French nearly took them all on Lake Champlain."

"Do they suspect anything?"

"I do not think so. Smithyman, the fool, actually saved the life of one of my men during the French ambush. It seems they have detected nothing yet. That one also reported that he has heard that the French may be setting up a new post halfway between Montreal and Fort Frontenac. It is to be where the Oswegatchie River joins the St. Lawrence, above the rapids. A priest named Picquet wants to divide the Iroquois by offering Christian converts food, shelter and trade goods, and good farmland. They will use the place as support for Fort Frontenac. It is very hard to approach from here. Any attack by land would have to go across all the mountains of the Adirondacks. So, they will be safe."

"It will threaten Oswego, as well," said De Vere.

"Increasing the price of guards yet more!" Stoatfester laughed.

"So, gentlemen, I take it we are in agreement, then," said De Vere. "We carry on as we have. The war is neither being won nor lost. The militias sit idle and eat the Governor's grain. We gain profit and supporters every month that the French are undefeated, while our enemies in New York lose money and respect. The Crown seems to have lost interest in the war. Our new agent in London may well be having an effect. We will try to ensure that he has the time to maximize it."

CHAPTER TWENTY SIX
Katy, Autumn 1748

When Katy's labor began, Billy sent immediately for the midwife, and to the Mohawks for the herbalist woman who had nursed her through her previous miscarriage. The latter arrived with an assistant, her daughter.

Through a day and night, he paced outside the bedroom, sleeping only fitfully. Katy's groans seemed weaker now, but still the women would not allow him entry.

Suddenly, Katy shrieked and Billy crashed open the door. In the arms of the midwife was a squalling baby, but Billy's eyes were for Katy in the bed. He knelt beside her and kissed her forehead. Her skin was a cool, waxy white that he had never seen or felt before. The herbalist was working below her waist. Katy's eyes flickered open briefly and she seemed to recognize him. A faint smile moved her lips. She did not speak, and in a few minutes, she stopped breathing.

The Mohawk woman stood wearily, covered to the shoulders with sticky redness. She met Billy's eyes and shrugged. In her own tongue she said, "She is gone. She was very strong, but no one can live who has no blood. I could not keep her from going to the spirit world. I tried mugwort first, and also milkweed and baneberry and alder, and spiders' web, but none of it was enough."

Billy's eyes filled with tears and he nodded. "I am sure, Mother, that no-one could have helped her more than you. Thank you for your kindness."

The herbalist's tall daughter, Laura, looked solemnly at Billy. Her dark eyes flashed. "You have a warrior to teach now." She looked about twelve in her beaded, loose-fitting overdress, but was seventeen.

Billy turned and his son squalled again. He stroked the infant's head. "Thomas," he said. "She wanted to call him Thomas if it was a boy."

The midwife said, "I will take care of him, but he must have a wet nurse. There are many in the settlement who would be honored to do this for you. I will find a suitable one."

Billy nodded. "Yes, that would be good." He leaned his forehead on the door-frame and closed his eyes against his grief. After a few moments, an insistent tug on his sleeve made him open his eyes again and look down. The black eyes of the herbalist's daughter rested on him.

"You must rest now," she said. "This part is over, but you have much more to do." *He looks at me and sees a child, because his loss blinds him. When he has ceased to mourn I will make him see me as a grown woman.*

He nodded. "Yes, I will go to bed now. Thank you." He walked slowly and unsteadily to the study, where he fell to his knees, and then onto his side on the soft skins piled there.

*****

Elijah woke him gently. "My lord, I have breakfast for you." The very pleasant aroma of grilled chops and fresh coffee came to Billy's nose, but when he stood up and went to the table, he found that his appetite had vanished. He picked at the food and drank some coffee, then pushed the plates away. "How is Thomas?" he asked. Elijah smiled, "He seems strong, and the midwife Mary says he is very healthy."

Billy fell silent. Finally he roused himself and said to Elijah in a dull tone, "Have them fetch the preacher from Fort Hunter. Katy wanted a Christian burial. She will have a spot where she can see the river."

After the funeral service and interment, Billy spoke to the midwife, then talked softly with Anna Christine. She wailed and clung to him, but Eva and Richard, who had moved their family into Fort Smithyman, eventually persuaded her to come with them. Then Billy vanished for a week.

On the eighth day, a gaunt, deeply tanned white man appeared at the gate of the fort. He was clothed in a worn blanket and loincloth, decorated Indian leggings and moccasins. He carried an axe and a musket. A war hatchet, skinning knife, powder horn and a small leather bag hung from straps. The guard challenged him harshly, then recognized Billy and saluted.

"I'm sorry, sir. Welcome back, Colonel, sir."

Billy grinned at him. "It's not a redcoat uniform, but a uniform nonetheless, isn't it? Any Frenchmen about?"

The sentry frowned. "No sir, none here. I heard they killed forty woodcutters down near Schenectady, though, the dogs. Begging your pardon, sir, are we going to win this war?"

Billy said, "I'm sure we will, soldier, but it's sometimes hard to tell, isn't it?"

"That be the very truth, sir. Very sorry about the missus, sir."

"Thank you, soldier. She was a fine woman, and she truly wanted us to beat the Frogs, so that's just what we'll have to do, isn't it?"

"Yes sir, I expect so, sir."

Billy strode up to the house. Inside, the word spread quickly that he had returned. Anna Christine came running and he swept her into his arms. She was sobbing and he realized his leaving had frightened her severely.

"Where did you go for so long, Papa?"

"I told you I'd be back, now, didn't I, sweetness?" She nodded wetly into his shoulder. "I went away to say goodbye to your mother. I built a little house in the woods with my axe, to be alone with her spirit for a while, and I will show it to you sometime." The wet nurse brought Thomas in then, and for a time Billy soaked up the presence of his son and daughter.

"Are you happy to have a little brother, Chrissie?"

The big sister, now almost seven, nodded, but said, "It would be nicer if Mama were here too."

Billy hugged her. "Yes, you're right, it would be, but Mama is looking down on us from heaven now, and she is expecting us to go on and be strong, like she was, don't you think?"

Elijah drew him a bath and then Billy had him summon the household staff. Billy found his eyes moistening again when he told them that he had gone away for a time to grieve for his wife, but that now things must go on. He thanked them for their support and help for Katy. Several of the women, including Cook, mopped their tearful eyes. When he dismissed them, he asked Elijah to send for his clerk and for Richard. Elijah bowed and started to leave, but then returned.

"My lord, I have not had the opportunity to properly thank thee for my deliverance from the French," he said.

Billy shook his head, "Elijah, I thank God that you were spared. It is nothing, nothing."

"No, Lord, I will never be able to repay your kindness. I wish now only to give you the name of my protector under French care, who was a very young French officer, a child named Hippolyte St. Remy. But for his alertness I would not have been able to communicate with thee."

"Elijah, were there many other prisoners in Montreal with you?"

"Yes, Lord. There were, I believe, as many as two or three hundred. Many were white, but some were black and some were Indian, and I believe those Indians were suffering much, confined in the chains. They released only a few with me. Other than that I was able to observe very little, except that they have a stone wall entirely encircling the city."

"I hear you are getting married, Elijah."

"Yes, Lord."

"Is she a good woman?"

"Yes, Lord, and she takes very good care of me."

"You shall have twenty-five acres as a wedding present."

Elijah was stunned. "That is far too generous, Lord. I am undeserving. The other servants will be jealous."

"I expect you can handle them. Besides, if we lose this war, you will not own it long."

"That will not happen, Lord."

Billy looked him in the eye. "I hope not, Elijah."

"I will go now, Lord, and get your men."

An hour with the downcast clerk was enough for the accounts. It was all too clear. Another few months and Fort Smithyman would belong to Billy's creditors like a repossessed musket—lock, stock and barrel.

My only luck is that my biggest creditor is Turnbottle.

Billy sent the clerk away, with a kindly pat on the back. "It's not your fault, Muir. But are there any letters?"

There was one from Chilton, in his usual illiterate scrawl. "I have found a Johannes Pfalz in Lancaster. I think that he is the brother to your Katy. When I spoke to him, he told me this. I have copied this to Turnbottle. If you wish to act, write me at Whyte's in Philadelphia."

Billy's eyes watered and his guts clenched. He seized a quill and wrote immediately to Turnbottle, "Please purchase this man's indenture and have him sent to me here."

While he waited for Richard to arrive, four Canajoharie Mohawks came in with a scalp each and two prisoners. Billy counted out the scalp bounty in silver and wrote a brief note, handing it to them and telling them to show it to the soldiers outside and replenish their powder and shot from the Army stocks. He sent the prisoners to the little roofed stockade, now beginning to overflow. He got up and paced the room. Because of the war, there was no trade and no income.

You idiot. You gambled that you would be able to supply Oswego at a profit. Even worse, you vain fool, you accepted the Indian Agent's job, knowing that the Albany people hated you and would undercut you with the Assembly.

Richard entered and stopped dead as Billy turned and glowered at the interruption. His blood froze. *Jesus, Mary and Joseph! He looks as if Satan himself were at the door!*

"Billy, you sent for me. Is something wrong?"

Billy relaxed and made a wry face. "I was cursing myself for a fool when you came in. It is nothing, Richard. Have some rum and sit down, I would hear the news."

"I am glad of the drink Billy; ye looked as though ye were going to run me through, just then."

He poured himself some lime punch.

"It is much as before," Richard began. "The papers all say Lord Newcastle approves of the preparations to attack Crown Point but now wants the colonies to abandon the project and pay off the levies, except for the minimum required to defend the frontier. He refuses to send troops. He has recalled the Navy. Some of the Jersey militia and their officers have mutinied and gone home."

Billy rolled his eyes.

"There was a battle at Fort Number Four in New Hampshire, and the commander, Phineas Stephens, was given a sword by Admiral Knowles, for his heroic defense against overwhelming odds."

"Knowles replaced my uncle."

Richard drank some punch. He half-smiled and said, "What is it, do you think, with Admirals? Your uncle offended the Bostonians by taking credit for the capture of Louisbourg. Admiral Knowles has now provoked most of Boston into open rioting because he press-ganged some merchant sailors. I read that the mob besieged Governor Lindsay and took some of Knowles' own officers hostage. They forced him to give up the sailors."

Billy shook his head, slowly. "Pressing is good enough for Englishmen, but don't try it over here, hmmm? How are Eva and the boys?"

Richard smiled. "They are well and safe in here. It seems you have wrapped your estate in armor, and nothing is being attacked between Fort Hunter and the Upper Castle."

"The Mohawks are having fun right now. It will not last much longer. I am going to run out of money and supplies, and at the same time all the colonial militias will go home. Then the Mohawks will see that we are not going to attack Crown Point after all, and I won't be able to jolly them along anymore."

Richard frowned. "Will they go over to the French, d'ye think?"

Billy said, "Perhaps not the Mohawks, but all the rest might. They will think we lied to them again. They will not be happy. I'm not happy," he said with emphasis.

"What will you do?"

Billy shrugged and threw up his hands in exasperation. "What can I do, Richard, except what I'm doing, writing a letter a week to His Excellency and another to my agent, begging both for supplies and money. I have no connections in London that will help. I won't write my family about it."

His misery was apparent as he looked at Richard. "I remember telling you back in the Old Country that I'd not want to be indebted to far-away landlords, nor be a soldier, and look at me now! What a joke I am."

Richard said, in a low voice, "It's not the same, Billy, and you know that."

Billy got up and clapped his friend on the back. "Ahh, you're right, Richard, I should not be so low. It's just that without Katy, things seem so much worse."

Richard gripped Billy's arm. "Yes, surely, but you still have your children and your friends here. That will never change, Billy."

"I am embarrassed to be a beggar to anyone."

Richard began to protest, but Billy cut him off.

"I fear my uncle was right to snub me. I have let my sense of duty mix up my sense for what is good for my business and my family."

Richard shook his head. "Thanks to you, we are all freeholders beholden to none." *Even we Catholics, Billy, for which we will be forever grateful.*

"And everyone knows that what little defense there is against the French is thanks to you and the Governor."

Billy said, slowly, thoughtfully, "We have never seen the French attack Albany. Maybe in their own way those thieves were right, all along."

"You, of all people, Billy, ought to know better."

CHAPTER TWENTY SEVEN
Peace, Autumn 1748
(Entr'act)

Peace finally came in the form of the Treaty of Aix-la-Chapelle, confirming lengthy discussions between the French and the English, and a host of others, that had actually concluded in an agreement at the Dutch town of Breda two years before. Everyone was dissatisfied with it, and everyone knew it was only a truce of sorts.

But ending the long and bloody stalemate known to history as the War of the Austrian Succession came very late in the year '48. There was no chance for warriors to transform themselves back into hunters before winter set in. However, Billy's credit became more elastic as the prospect of a revival of the fur trade thawed the hearts of the counting houses. He extended his own credit to the Longhouse in the form of blankets, food, and the usual winter supplies.

There was quiet satisfaction in Albany at the profits from the war, mixed with mild frustration at not having finished off Billy or the Governor. On the frontiers, there was profound relief.

But there was only apoplectic rage in Boston, for the British Tory government gave the fortress at Louisbourg back to the French. "*Status quo ante bellum*," Billy read in the newspapers.

A heavy official letter arrived, with the familiar seal of the Governor of New York. Billy opened it carefully. "My dear friend," he read, "I am joyful at the opportunity to replace the recently departed Mr. Livingston, may he rest in peace, with yourself, on my Executive Council, should you wish to take up this responsibility in addition to the heavy weight you already bear for the welfare of the province." Billy felt his pulse quicken at the explicit praise, and a little of his depression lifted.

Beautiful Feather came for a time during the winter, but she was restless in the big house. She was fond of Anna Christine and little Thomas, but the little girl remained distant, missing her mother.

In the spring, Beautiful Feather was pregnant, and she left Smithyman House. "I do not like how the English stare at me, Billy, and I am happy at Diyondarogon," she said. "You will always be welcome there, but English ways are not my way, and I wish to raise our child properly in the ways of our people."

Two months later, at the end of June, Billy traveled to New York to be inducted into the Governor's Executive Council and remained for nearly two months.

When he returned, joyful news awaited him, and he went to visit Beautiful Feather and their newborn son, whom he named Adam. He rejoiced in holding him, but although Beautiful Feather and her family were happy to see Billy, she would not return to his house, nor permit him to take her child back with him.

Fort Smithyman seemed empty, and he organized a games day, hoping the activity would shake loose the grey cloud he felt enveloping him. After the final tug-of-war had ended, he and Anna Christine were coated, as usual, in mud. Holding hands and laughing, they walked over to watch the local militia officers compete at riding skills on the course set up behind the house.

After lancing hoops at full gallop, the winner, an officer unfamiliar to Billy, was trotting by the stables when a young native woman wearing a brightly embroidered blue cloth blouse and a buckskin skirt decorated with silver ran from the crowd and vaulted effortlessly up onto the horse behind him. The animal reared in surprise, but the girl held on as the officer delightedly spurred his mount to a gallop and circled the camp twice at full speed before slowing down. When he did, she lightly jumped to the ground. The young officer bowed formally from the saddle and the girl flashed a smile and glanced at Billy before disappearing again into the crowd.

Marten had come to visit. While he had recovered well from the injury, his arm would never be the same, and his belly was beginning to show signs of a magisterial roundness from the care lavished on him. Billy turned to him, his mouth open to ask a question. Marten had been watching, and forestalled him. *He has the eye of an eagle for women.*

"She is Laura Silverbirch, the daughter of your herbalist from Canajoharie. She is one of my nieces and a shameless show-off."

Billy said, "Is that so? She has changed much, since Katy died."

Marten chuckled. "She has changed little. It is your eyes that have changed, my son."

The militia officer handed his horse off and strode up to Billy. He held out his hand and said, "My Goodman Smithyman, what a delightful event! I can see why you are famous in these parts. My name is Stephen Crowell, and I would have a word with you, if you can spare a few minutes."

He had a firm grip and a big hand. Marten got up, not without effort, and said, "I must go and see what Wind-Through-the-Spruces is up to."

He grimaced. "If I am not around, she forgets just who she is married to."

Crowell and Billy laughed, and Billy slapped his good shoulder. "We will speak again later, Marten," he said.

Billy studied Crowell a moment. Then he said, "To state the obvious, you are not one of my officers from the Albany County militia, Lieutenant Crowell."

Crowell bowed. "No sir, I am from the Orange County companies. However, I wish to speak to you about that, among other things, Colonel Smithyman. I am moving to Albany and I would be delighted to join your regiment, if you would have me. I have references, sir." He produced a sheaf of papers from his map case.

Billy accepted them. "You came prepared, Crowell. I like that."

"Thank you, sir. I would also be interested to engage in your civilian life as well. I have heard that you are one of the pre-eminent traders to the native population in this part of the world."

"Some in the region do not think this is such a good thing, but I do attempt to make a living, it is true."

"My family in England are becoming wealthy from making cloth fabrics using new shuttles that multiply the labor of our workers a hundredfold. Perhaps we have interests in common."

Billy stared at him briefly, and then nodded. He gestured at the mud now drying and falling off him in flakes. "Crowell, I would like to come to Albany to discuss this with you when I am more presentable. When you get settled, send a message to me and we can discuss this at leisure."

The bewigged officer smiled and stepped back. "I will not salute, sir, since you are not in uniform, but I will be in touch with you very soon. Thank you for your time."

That man has energy and boldness, as well as respect. It is an attractive combination.

A heavily laden bateau poled by several men came into view and tied up at the little wooden wharf. Two passengers were helped out by the bateau men, and Billy noticed in passing that here was an odd pair. One was quite short, while the other was tall and young-looking. Something in the slightly foppish mannerism of the smaller one struck Billy as familiar. Suddenly he began to chuckle and made his way down to greet them.

"Turnbottle!" Billy exclaimed. "Whatever possessed you to come up here into the wilds?"

The small man turned to look up at him, took a step backward, and then spoke very fast in a high pitch. "Who are you sir, and how do you know my name? I am looking for Mister Smithyman here. I am told this is Smithyman House, and I see a great p-p-party and outlandish savages parading about."

Billy became conscious again of the drying muck covering him from head to toe. "Ha ha, Turnbottle! I have fooled you in my disguise as a swamp creature. It is I whom you seek."

Turnbottle peered closely and then cackled with glee and slapped his leg. "A good joke, Billy Smithyman, upon my word, a great joke. You always were one to throw yourself into things!"

The taller man was dressed in very frayed and patched homespun. He looked to be about twenty years of age. Turnbottle followed Billy's gaze and then thrust the young man forward. "This is Johannes Pfalz, Billy, whom you told me to rescue from Philadelphia. I thought I would come up with him, to see how my investments are making out."

Billy shook his hand. "Johannes, I am very glad to welcome you to my community. This will now be your home, if you find you will be happy here. I am so very sorry that we did not find you a few months sooner. Your sister, my Katy, is gone, but she was very dear to me, and you have a niece and a nephew now."

The young man said, confusedly, "I am honored, Sire—Your Excellency— Herr Smithyman." His accent was fainter than Katy's, but the resemblance was close and Billy felt a pang. He smiled at Johannes, and he felt the mud cracking again on his face. He turned and waved at the house and Elijah instantly acknowledged.

"Come, now, come. Elijah will find you a place to rest. I will clean up and we can talk at supper."

Two days later, Turnbottle was ready to return to New York. "It has been a rare party, Billy, for I find that you have more interesting guests than most do, down in New York. I must go. I don't trust the idiots to run the place for more than a day or two without me." He added, gloomily, "Like as not I'll go back to find just a few smoking piles left sticking out of the water."

Billy changed the subject. "I think I'll take your advice and buy a house in Albany."

Turnbottle said, "And I will find out about this Crowell and what he might have to offer. It may be interesting enough for me to dabble in it with you."

"Don't forget Chilton might also be interested, if the cloth is cheap."

Turnbottle frowned and waggled a finger. "Oh, I don't doubt it's cheap, Billy, but is it good? There's the question, is it any good? Oh, I had another letter from Chilton recently. I forgot to tell you. As usual, he mangles the

King's English almost to the point of opaqueness, but he does say the Mingoes tell him the French are stirring things up in the west again.

"He writes that some large expedition went west as far as Pickawillany from Montreal, frightening the Indians and trying to kick the traders out."

He giggled. "According to Chilton, they all agreed to leave and then continued about their business quite as before. The Frogs were very annoyed, he said. Perhaps you have heard similar things—aren't Mingoes Iroquois too?"

Billy nodded, "That is what whites call the Iroquois when they are living in their hunting grounds west of the mountains. It is not what they call themselves. Some of them have returned recently, and what they told me agrees with Chilton. The French are also agitating again closer to home among the Iroquois. And there is a priest at Oswegatchie, northeast of here, who is seducing them away from us."

"I think you were wise to invest in Chilton again."

"Yes?"

"Especially since he did get some indemnities and debts forgiven by Pennsylvania for his war losses. But I would be careful to invest in small doses. He does strike one sometimes as a remarkably unlucky soul."

He gave Billy a direct look. "Speaking of unlucky, it seems everyone but you is to be compensated, then, does it not? When will you be coming again to New York?"

"The Governor will want me at a Council meeting sometime, probably in the fall. Lack of compensation, and support for Indian affairs by the Assembly are on my agenda. I mean to bring Marten with me, so that afterwards he can tell the Longhouse personally what was said."

"Hmmm. Good to have a friendly witness, what?"

"Yes, especially if there is news of the French."

"One more thing, Billy. Have you heard of the Ohio Company?"

Billy hesitated, repeating the name to himself, and then said, "Oh, yes, the Governor of Virginia is part of that group, isn't he? They are petitioning the Crown for some land west of the mountains. Six Nations land. Up to now, also Pennsylvania land." He shrugged. "French land. Who knows?"

Turnbottle chuckled briefly. "Virginians, yes, Billy. The Washingtons, and Lees, and their English partners are looking for a royal grant of 500,000 acres."

Billy's eyes narrowed. "So much?"

Turnbottle nodded. "Aye, large enough, and if they simply build a wooden fort on the Ohio and settle a hundred souls near it in seven years, they get to keep it, too! Think on that, Billy."

Turnbottle climbed gingerly into the bateau and raised a hand to Billy as they pushed off. "Until the fall, then, my friend."

*****

His Albany house had a wonderfully strategic location, at the corner of Market and State streets, Billy thought. It was a Dutch style two-storey building, narrow-fronted and immaculately clean inside. Billy installed a used desk, a chair and a bed, and he hired a maid to keep the house dusted. After standing for a time in the echoing, empty front room, he wrote to Turnbottle to order some furniture.

Katy would have liked to set this place up.

Crowell's residence was only a few blocks away. He welcomed Billy warmly and showed him about his similarly Spartan house. "I am a bachelor," Crowell apologized, "so I cannot offer you much in the way of domestic luxury at present. I take all my meals out."

They talked about the new process of cloth making, and the young businessman showed him samples, of a uniformly high quality and an impressively low price. Billy saw a drawing of their machines. After an hour, their talk turned to military topics and Billy suggested they walk up the hill to Fort Orange to pay a visit to the new Commander.

"Colonel, I have been acquainting myself with a bit of the correspondence and minutes of the Indian Commissioners here, just to get a bit of footing, you know, and I am puzzled."

"Stephen, we are not on duty yet, please address me as Billy. You may save Colonel for our upcoming official visit." Billy chuckled and continued, "There are many puzzling things about the Commissioners, what is it in particular?"

"There are many references to individuals like 'Corlaer', 'Onas' and the like. Am I correct in interpreting this as their way of naming the governors?"

Billy nodded. "You have the right of it. Corlaer is the governor of New York. Onas is the governor of Pennsylvania. Onontio is the Governor of Canada. Corlaer was the name of one of the Dutchmen in the old days that they liked."

"Thank you, it is a small detail, but it is nice to be sure."

They turned up Jonkheer Straat, making a detour around the heaps of manure.

"Have you made acquaintance with many of the good burghers yet, Crowell?" Billy asked.

Crowell shook his head; "They have been a bit stand-offish so far, I find. A clannish bunch, it seems."

Billy nodded. *That's putting it kindly.*

Major Itcheson was absent. The acting Fort Commander was an older man, seemingly overwhelmed by the minutiae of an under-funded peacetime garrison command. From the odor on his breath he was also a drunkard. "Colonel Smithyman, Lieutenant Crowell, good morning. How may I be of assistance, gentlemen?"

"This is merely a social call, Captain, but perhaps you could entertain the idea of a ball, to introduce Lieutenant Crowell to society here?"

The older officer stared at Billy as if he had never heard of such a thing. He hiccupped. "A...ball?"

"Yes, Captain, you know, those events where one has music and dancing and refreshments, that sort of thing? I would have thought that this was well within the purview of the garrison commander at Fort Orange. Good for relations with the civilians and all that. Lieutenant Crowell here is an eligible bachelor, and these stuffy Dutchmen don't want to let him meet their daughters."

The captain's brow darkened. "Well, I don't... I mean...."

Billy interrupted. "I imagine that Lieutenant Crowell might be entertained by organizing the thing as a sort of exercise in logistics, Captain. If you could lend him the support of a clerk to write the invitations and some men to help decorate this place, it would give them something more to do than complain about their pay arrears. Raise the Crown's profile in these parts in a favorable way. You can report to the Governor that it was your idea, if you wish. He likes to hear of such things going on." Billy raised his eyebrows.

"If you put it that way, Colonel...."

"Good, I knew you would be supportive, sir. Crowell, please be sure to send me a few invitations as well. I haven't danced in a very long time."

On their way back down the hill, Crowell grinned at him. "I admire your style, sir. That incompetent couldn't organize his own latrines."

Billy smiled back. "One must do what one can to keep things going. He's not under my command and I'm no trained officer, but I shudder to think of that man defending us against the French. I hope Itcheson returns soon from wherever they have sent him."

They returned to Crowell's house and Billy agreed to purchase cloth, "The red and the blue seem to be preferred, by my Mohawks at any rate. You may bring it in to Turnbottle and he will attach it to his regular shipments to me."

Crowell offered his hand. "I thank you for your patronage, sir. May I take you to dinner to celebrate our new business? One of the things I have discovered about Albany is that the Dutch truly know how to cook."

*****

The ball took place six weeks later. None of the Albany patriarchs could resist their wives' and daughters' insistence on attending. Packages containing hundreds of yards of silk and lace were anxiously unfolded in Albany houses. Several invitees attended from New York itself.

Billy brought Elijah, Richard, and Eva to Albany with him and felt a surprising excitement as he dressed for the event. He had decided to wear a white silk brocade coat and waistcoat with gold lace trim rather than his uniform. Richard had been reluctant to join in until Billy virtually ordered him to get Eva a gown and a proper new suit for himself.

"I don't want to go to this affair without some friends of mine there, Richard, so consider it a duty to me, d'ye hear? I know the clothes are expensive, but you'll put it on my account, now, so I want to hear no more about it!"

Under Crowell's direction, the soldiers had erected a gigantic marquee, covering nearly the entire parade ground within the walls. Billy was the centre of attention, being the only one present from the Governor's Executive Council, as well as the tallest man present. Dozens of uniformed army and navy officers provided colorful contrast to the elaborate gowns of the women.

The Dutch community had risen to the challenge. Their younger menfolk appeared in the latest fashions, while the elders maintained a more traditional appearance. Stoatfester was present, always near the Voortmans' tables. Billy made his social rounds as the senior government official present, ignoring Stoatfester. Albany society was coldly polite. De Vere had chosen not to attend, his wife not being well.

Anneke Voortman moved gaily about under the marquee among the lanterns and stretched ribbons, surrounded by a swirling vortex of young men whenever a dance ended. She was now twenty-two, on the edge of becoming too old to be considered marriageable in polite society, nearly a spinster.

Her parents were almost in despair, for she gloried in her freedom. Her blonde hair and décolletage, set off by a scarlet silk gown covered in layers of silvery lace, were the envy of every woman and magnetic to every man who didn't have a woman's close eye on him. Late in the evening, Billy was able to achieve one dance with her, and murmurs swept around the entire tent as they completed the sedate steps of the minuet. Billy bowed deeply and became conscious, as he straightened, of her bright blue eyes on him. A minute twitch of her fan, invisible from more than a couple of feet away, sent a clear message.

Billy was amused, flattered and instantly aroused. In spite of his interest, he tried to think clearly. As his tight breeches began to betray him, Anneke smiled knowingly at him. He knew that many of the eyes on him would also notice.

If I bed this delectable girl tonight, what do I risk? It's one thing to anger the Voortmans politically and in business, but this would make it personal. Do I need them to hate me more than they do already for a few moments of pleasure, however flattering and satisfying?

When the next dance began, he went to speak to Stephen Crowell.

"Stephen, he said in a low voice, "I need your help to rescue me from myself."

He slipped out to the privies and returned shortly. A few minutes later, a uniformed soldier appeared at the entrance to the marquee and brought a note to Billy, who frowned as he opened and read it and then bowed to the crowd as he left, winking inconspicuously at Stephen. He went into the officers' quarters and shut the door, remaining there for half an hour as if in a meeting. Then he left the fort and returned to his house. He was half beginning to doubt that the signal he had seen was real, although his own had been evident enough to all.

Stoatfester had witnessed the whole thing and at the end of the evening his hands were beginning to tremble.

That unbelievable whore!

An overwhelming rage filmed his mind with a red haze. He walked, unseeing, out of the fort, went to open the door of his lodgings, then changed his mind and made his way like an automaton to Water Street.

The woman he hired there did not have an opportunity to cry out or defend herself. The moment Stoatfester felt himself released in her, a vision of Anneke bedded with Billy flooded his brain. The red mist descended again, he got up from the bed, turned, and then without any warning frenziedly smashed his fists into the whore's face, breaking her nose and jaw and dropping her into merciful unconsciousness. He continued to indulge his fury.

When he was finished, the wall above the bed was covered in blood. The woman had not made a sound, and his grunts of exertion were similar to what was usually heard from those rooms. Finally, the red tide and the roaring in his ears subsided as his rage was slaked. He dragged her battered corpse over to the open window, outside of which the river flowed by silently in the darkness. The heavy splash of the woman's body, like a sturgeon leaping, was quickly gone. Stoatfester used her garments to wipe the blood from his face and arms. Then he threw them into the river as well.

When he descended the dimly lit stairs, few would have noticed the remaining smears, dribbles and spots. In the event, none was there to see him, but had there been a careful observer, the red madness remaining in his eyes would have been plainly visible.

By the time he met with Voortman and De Vere the next day, Stoatfester's demeanor gave no hint of the terrible thing he had done. De Vere opened the meeting with a summary of his views on the political situation, ending his report with, "And so, I believe we are headed for war again."

Voortman used a sliver of birch to pick his teeth. "Our position is good, then. We may be able to finish off Smithyman this time, as well."

Stoatfester jerked slightly at that, and a drop of ink flew from his quill, but no one noticed.

De Vere nodded. "The Assembly remains ours, and it will not pay Smithyman's expenses from the last war. Governor Clayton foolishly continues to goad them with his insistence on long-term funding. They will not have it, and Smithyman is, of course, seen as Clayton's man."

Voortman asked, "And the Iroquois?"

De Vere grimaced. "A double-edged sword, as always. They prevent settlers from moving west and northwest, which is good, but they support Smithyman."

Stoatfester lifted his eyes from the paper where he was recording the discussion. "The Iroquois are not at one with Smithyman, even now. The Mohawks, yes, but the western nations resent them, and Smithyman's influence over them."

"Pfah!" Voortman spat. "They are all irrelevant. The savages and the French together in the last war never directly attacked Albany, much less New York. I think we can continue to ignore them. If the natives turn on us, they are only a few thousand at most, and becoming fewer," he chuckled mirthlessly, "even if Smithyman is trying to impregnate every squaw in the wilderness."

Another inkblot splashed onto the minutes.

De Vere began to say, "If they side with the French..." but Voortman interrupted. "The French be damned! Are the French going to be able to take Albany or New York? The English colonies outnumber them twenty to one, perhaps more. Never! Certainly, the settlements will burn. But what is that to us, except good news? If the Iroquois do turn, perhaps they will burn Smithyman out, while they are at it!"

The thought cheered him on. "The French could no more hold down these colonies than England could, if a million rose against them. We are realists, here; I think we need waste no more time discussing the Six Nations or the French. If war comes, we will sell to the army, whichever army it might be. In the meantime, we keep those pliable ignoramuses in the Assembly in our grip, and that will be the beginning and the end of it, gentlemen."

He rose from the table, and the meeting was over.

CHAPTER TWENTY EIGHT
Laura, June 1749

Dinner was less than an hour away and Billy's houseguests were still delighting in the charms of the bottled lightning in his new Leyden jar.

No-one has yet been electrocuted.

He leaned against the front doorway of Smithyman house smoking a pipe, half-engaged in conversation, watching a blue heron stalk minnows along the riverbank beyond the wigwams. Then he saw a slender figure detach itself from the blanketed group that was feasting around the fire and walk toward him. Something about it made him excuse himself and step from the verandah down to the ground.

As the young woman walked, she passed in and out of the long shadows cast by the trees, so she seemed to appear and disappear, a creature of the forest. As he watched her approach, he swallowed. Her soft deerskin dress flowed about her figure, emphasizing hollows and curves. She stopped, only a few inches away, and her clean, natural scent surrounded him. Her long hair was black and shining and tied into two braids. A smallpox scar near one eyebrow and three others on her chin seemed only to emphasize her extraordinary beauty.

She said in Iroquoian, "My uncle told my mother that you asked about me."

He nodded.

She smiled up at him. She was half a foot shorter than he, but her personality seemed to shimmer visibly, like the heat waves rising from a candle flame.

"It is good that you did so. For although I am a Mohawk woman and should obey my mother's wish that we be man and wife, and all the other Gantowisas agree that it is a good match, I would not be sent where I am not welcome."

Billy was silent. He was unable to ask the question his soul demanded. His cowardly heart hid from the answer. However, she dropped her dark eyes and then looked up again into his.

"It has been my wish also, since I first saw you."

Billy breathed again. He found his voice and said, hoarsely, "You are beautiful beyond all women, Laura Silverbirch. I have been searching for you since I was born."

He embraced her and kissed her and Laura raised her arms to encircle his neck. When he could speak again he asked, "I have learned many things from the Guardians of the Eastern Door, but this I forget. What is the custom of your people for marriage?"

She smiled and said, "I will use English now, Billy, for if I am to be your woman I must be excellent in it." She glowered at him a little. "You must correct me when I go wrong.

"Mohawk men and women need only love. Death requires much ceremony with us, but marriage very little. If I did not know you, or if your family was here, there would be more formal arrangements between your mother and mine, but," she shrugged, "Gakwarinnionton requires only that you carry me inside your house."

Billy grinned at her and instantly picked her up, as effortlessly as if she were made of starlight. He turned to carry her into the house and exclamations of joy went up from dozens of throats around the fire behind them. Laura laughed softly.

"You see," she said into his ear, "there are many witnesses here that we are about to be married."

His European guests made way, some with mouths rudely gaping and eyebrows raised, but Billy and Laura ignored them entirely. He carried her down the central hall to his bedroom. He kicked the door shut, and they did not emerge until the next morning, when Elijah hammered insistently on the door, shouting, "Lord, Lord, you must eat, and the children are afraid."

Billy, smiling broadly, swung the door wide. He crouched, spreading his arms wide for Anna Christine who walked in holding Thomas by the hand. He lifted them up and nodded to Elijah over their heads, "We will all have breakfast in my room, Elijah. Bring plenty, for I am now a married man, with many responsibilities."

Very quickly, the household realized that Laura's orders were not to be ignored. Those who were unable to take direction from the brown Lady Smithyman, as Billy's European guests began to call her, found new employment. Those who showed disrespect through sloppy work or churlishness either improved or else they also left Smithyman House.

Anna warmed to Laura, as she had not to Beautiful Feather. Laura's English was good to start with, and she rapidly became fluent, whereas Beautiful Feather had not been comfortable in English. Anna had inherited a love of reading from her father, and when Laura challenged her to teach her, they began to spend many happy hours together. Laura's younger brother Matthew, who was ten, became a frequent visitor; and Billy made sure that Johannes, who was tutoring Anna, included Matthew in lessons whenever possible, as well as Richard and Eva's sons. Thomas fell under Laura's charm immediately.

She delighted in the lively Celtic dances and music brought over by the transplanted Irish as well as in the more sedate parlor musicians that Billy hired to entertain his guests and himself. Billy's commercial and official business fascinated her; she mostly sat silently with him for hours as he managed his affairs, sometimes making private comments to him about what she saw in each individual who came to the office. She was determined to learn to write and joined the classes given by Johannes, whose aptitudes for English and mathematics had brought him clerking opportunities in Philadelphia.

At the same time, it soon became very clear to Billy that Laura had already become an herbalist of considerable renown and success along both sides of the Mohawk Valley. She was beginning to match and occasionally even eclipse her mother in her instinctive ability to diagnose and treat subtle diseases. By the end of the summer, a new and growing stream of supplicants, both native and European, was finding its way to Smithyman House seeking to avail themselves of her skills, not his.

Billy encouraged Laura to wear European dress if she wished, and although she was always excited about the next little doll showing the latest European fashions, she refused to wear them.

"I am standing with my feet in two worlds, Billy," she explained once to him. "While I wear my people's clothes, one foot can remain in the Longhouse, even though I am your woman and live with you and your people. When I begin to wear your clothes as well, my Longhouse self will have difficulty breathing. For others this is not the same, but for me I feel it strongly."

She looked slyly at him, cocked a hip and pretended to pout. "Do you not like me in my deerskins and feathers any more, Billy Smithyman?"

He shook his head slowly. "That was never a thought that entered my mind." He listened for a moment, but the household was quiet. He stood and closed the door to the study, turning the key in the lock. He walked toward her. "Perhaps I can demonstrate how much I enjoy the way you look, so that any doubts you have may pass like smoke in the wind."

She clung to him, molding her body and her mouth to his, and his hands crept between them and unbuttoned his breeches. As their clothes fell to the floor, he lifted her up and then let her gently down. As he slowly entered her, her mouth opened and she sighed with pleasure. It sounded to him like the wind in the treetops.

*****

The problem of the prisoners was proving unbelievably difficult to solve. Billy had written the Governor many times urging him to allow Billy to negotiate directly.

> I still have nearly two dozen French nationals here eating our food, and while they are admirably high spirited and civilized for the most part, the Iroquois daily demand that their people come home from Canada, and they cannot understand why an exchange has not been done.
>
> I must add that none of the native people take well to confinement in white prisons, such things they have never encountered in their culture, and if more die there, it will make our problems here much worse. Many Iroquois have gone over to the French at Oswegatchie, and some formerly loyal Mohawks have become Christians in Kahnewake, because the French have persuaded them that it is we, not they, who are intransigent in this matter. I will come to see you later in the fall as you requested and we should discuss this further in person if no success can be reported before then.

Laura was clearly impatient with the status of the prisoners living at Smithyman House as well. There was a yellow-haired young woman among them who was working very hard at holding Billy's eye.

Laura suggested that she and Billy might go away for a time and visit some of her people's former hunting grounds north of Oswego, across Lake Ontario. "There is a sacred place there for our people, at a very deep lake which is on top of a mountain. It is a good place to collect special plants, and it is a place for lovers."

Billy's interest in exploring this country encouraged her, and a hunting party had been organized, when alarming news intervened.

Marten himself came to tell Billy. "The French have convinced several of the Onondaga chiefs to allow a French post near Onondaga Lake, my son. I was there only last week and the Jesuits have coated everyone with French honey.

"Pthah," he spat. "They are sickening with their smooth lies, but many believe them."

Billy instantly acted. He wrote a letter to the Governor outlining the situation and set off through the cold autumn rains on horseback to meet the Onondagans, organizing bateaux from Oswego to follow along the shore, carrying gifts and food.

When he arrived, the surprised Onondagans hurriedly provided Billy and his party with a guest longhouse. Billy observed one of the black-robed priests moving out of the castle and summoned the chiefs to a Council on the spot. Having caught the Onondagans openly doing what they had promised not to do, he was determined to press his advantage.

He dressed in his formal red British officer's uniform, trimmed with white and gold and bright brass buttons. He put on his Colonel's gold-laced hat, and he passed out twists of tobacco. The gathered sachems smoked with him, grim-faced. After two pipes, Billy began.

"The Longhouse people have for many generations and through many difficulties kept the silver Covenant Chain with Corlaer bright. Nevertheless, today I find it fouled with slime and almost broken, here in the very heart of the Longhouse. The great chain that has bound your people and mine together, that we both took up freely, for our mutual benefit, you have let fall into the dirt and you have trod it under with French shoes from the black robes. You have shamed the great Confederacy of your nations, who once recognized its value."

Changing tactics, he smiled warmly at them then and held up both hands.

"But I recognize that Corlaer has sometimes presumed a great deal on your friendship, and that you have in many recent years been unable to hunt because your warriors were gathered to fight the French, at his request."

The first of the struggling bearers from Oswego had appeared at the edge of the clearing with a large bundle. Two dozen noisy sheep and a similar number of pigs and six cows, then a dozen more bearers, followed him. Billy realized he was losing his audience.

"So, let us now make a feast, of food that I have brought from Oswego, from Corlaer, and we will tomorrow discuss this terrible shame again and what you can do about it. Perhaps then we will have a reason to truly celebrate."

The two dozen sachems, all of them selected by the women of the clans to represent their collective wisdom at the Onondaga Council, and some of whom also represented Onondaga at the Grand Council of the Iroquois Confederacy, stood and made to go and tell their people, but they were too late. The news was spreading very quickly already, because Billy had spoken in Iroquoian. The fires were stoked up, and within minutes hundreds of Onondagans were gathering.

Billy allowed no rum, although he had several kegs brought into his longhouse, draped in canvas.

Next afternoon, a huge crowd gathered to hear him speak to the sachems again, in the early afternoon. This time, he wore Mohawk clothing with the headdress of a warrior. He paused and looked about without speaking, then lifted one arm and circled it slowly around the ring of his audience. He ended the gesture by pointing over the long bark houses at the narrow lake beyond them. It sheltered among the hills, still, silver and black in the falling rain. Then he let his arm fall slowly to his side and the chattering audience grew silent.

"I call upon Onondaga to make the Covenant Chain bright again, by actions which will be of comfort to Corlaer, actions that will tell him all of the Longhouse people remain loyal to him. Actions that will cast out those who are neither his friends nor the friends of the Longhouse, but enemies who seek to make you shame yourselves by their sweet and false words."

The chiefs sat frozen in their places. Billy raised his smoking pipe and pointed it at the lake. His other arm he extended wide.

"Hear me, for I am one of you. Do you not call me 'Beaver Dam'? Was I not named here, in your midst? Have I not married one of your daughters? Like the beaver, which also makes the waters rise, my work is for you, yet you have taken many sticks away from the dam that guards the waters, and given them to the French. This must end, or the waters will be released and the great covenant will be broken.

"I call upon the Onondaga nation, in the name of the great Covenant Chain and your friend and father Corlaer, to grant him this lake and all of the land around it for two miles, so that you may never again be able to give in to the temptation of the sweet-tongued French, without Corlaer's consent.

"To recognize this great symbol of your devotion, Corlaer has asked me to give you many presents and to pay the Onondaga nation three hundred and fifty pounds in gold, which I have brought with me this day. Do the French offer this? Do the French offer anything for the right to build a fortress here, but sweet lies? I have heard of no great gifts here from them. I see only the vanishing mist of their words, and I know that you would soon see a stone fort rise here, like the one that the Seneca, in their innocent confusion, allowed the French to build on their country at Niagara.

"Then, you would have nothing at all in return for your betrayal of the Great Confederacy's covenant. You have my word that Corlaer will never build here and neither will he allow anyone else to build here but the people of the Longhouse, whose land this is."

A silence fell on the gathering, followed by a murmuring that sounded like muttering of far-distant thunder. After fifteen minutes, an aged sachem rose and walked to Billy bearing a pipe. It was over.

Billy produced a parchment and a desk and sat down to receive the signatures and marks of the sachems and every one of the adult Onondagans present, who lined up for several hours to sign the deed. As they passed, he greeted them cheerfully in Iroquoian and invited them into his longhouse for presents and for rum.

CHAPTER TWENTY NINE
Government House, October 1749: Roads to War

Billy took Marten and Richard with him to meet the Governor in Albany. He wore his London-made Colonel's uniform. Marten wore his Mohawk war chief regalia and weapons, including a red coat of his own, while Richard was attired in his most formal jacket, waistcoat and breeches.

The Governor received them in his house inside the fort in the late morning. After a few pleasantries, he offered tea and invited Billy to speak.

"I am not a complicated man, Your Excellency, and I will come directly to the point," Billy began.

Governor Clayton nodded and smiled. "No one would accuse you of being a dissembler, Billy."

Billy set his teacup down and removed a multi-page document from a stiff leather case.

"Your Excellency, here is my resignation as Indian Agent and Superintendent of the Indian Council. You will already know my reasons. Without belaboring them, I spent over seven thousand pounds during the war and the Assembly has reimbursed less than seven hundred. It has nearly broken me financially, and it is now obvious that the Assembly is not going to either honor its debts to me, nor is it going to budget any funds for Indian Affairs.

"They have diligently worked to find every possible way to evade both obligations. They have ordered payment to me from funds they knew were exhausted. They have continuously cut down my bills and returned them. Now, like they did yourself, they have accused me of pocketing my own money spent on supplies. I cannot therefore continue to accept the responsibility of this post."

The Governor sighed.

Billy continued, "However, before I do resign, Governor, my last act is to present to you this deed for the land around Onondaga Lake, which, as I described in my previous report, was signed by every adult present in Onondaga Castle."

Billy smiled grimly. "I expect that it may at least prevent the French from encroaching even further on your province, in the heartland of the Iroquois."

He unfolded the heavy papers and pointed to the last paragraph. "As you see here, I bought this land with my own funds on behalf of the Crown, three hundred and fifty pounds, and when the price has been reimbursed to me, the Government of New York will have legitimate title to it.

"I trust you, and your successors, will use this gift from Onondaga wisely," Billy paused and then continued. "And I thank Your Excellency for the honor of his trust in me, which has empowered me to do what little I can to help the Six Nations and ourselves keep this ancient friendship intact."

Billy extended the papers to the Governor, who sighed again and reached out a gloved hand to take them.

"Smithyman, this resignation is not entirely unexpected, as I am sure you are aware. I feel dreadful about it, but you know that I have been petitioning Newcastle and the King for redress. They have consented to return to me only about nine thousand pounds out of the fifteen thousand I have expended during the war, else I would reimburse you myself. Your service has been truly exemplary, and your name is favorably regarded in the Ministry, I can assure you."

He turned the papers over in his hand.

"Alas, however, there is a new government in London. They may replace the Duke of Newcastle. As his protégé, my influence is now minor, at best. I have asked them to replace me, as well."

This was news to Billy. Even Turnbottle had apparently not heard this yet.

The Governor continued, "Unfortunately, the provincial assembly has become even more obstinate, and your enemies now predominate there, especially since you have joined my Council."

He looked curiously at Billy. "Although they have offered to give you freehold title to Onondaga Lake as compensation for the last war."

Billy laughed harshly. "Big of them, since I own it already."

Governor Clayton shifted in his chair and addressed Marten. "What say you to his resignation?"

Marten's lined, unsmiling face with its great scar appeared cut from stone. *I should not have gone to London. Seeing your English millions corrupted my soul.* He spoke only briefly.

"Our people will remember that Corlaer has supported our friend. But if the Albanians again become Indian Commissioners, then as Manitou makes the sun rise and the rain fall each day, many will begin to think that you no longer value the great Covenant Chain."

His speech slowed to a deep guttural growl and he spaced his next words for emphasis. "The Haudenosaunee will not report to those monsters ever again. They are devils, not men."

The Governor looked at Billy and asked, almost plaintively, "Smithyman, will you then continue as a member of the Executive Council and as Colonel of the militia and native auxiliaries?"

Billy saw a very tired and frustrated man. He nodded slowly. "I believe I can still be effective in these posts. If I continue to have your ear on the Council, the King and the Board of Trade will surely get better information about our friends. Should war be coming again, I also feel more comfortable being able to direct at least some part of our defenses, so that it is not left entirely to my enemies to protect what we have built here."

The Governor crushed the parchment in his left hand, then rose and bowed to Billy. "I am grateful for what you have done, Smithyman. My only regret is that it seems I cannot now return the favor."

The four men shook hands firmly and parted.

When Billy and his friends emerged from the fort, it was early evening, and there was frost in the air. After some discussion, they decided to eat at one of the Albany inns and stay overnight at Billy's town house.

The morning was bright but cold. They shivered, and their breath steamed, as they left the house shortly after dawn. As the three men walked to the stable, only Marten noticed a shadow moving on the roof above them, but he was able to shout a warning and draw his tomahawk as four men dropped on them. One went down immediately, twitching, as Marten uppercut the weighted blade through the chin and spine of his attacker. He jerked it free, pivoted and sank the bloody hatchet deep into the neck of a second man, who was slashing at Richard.

Billy had looked up at Marten's shout and tripped backwards, away from a man with a long blade. As Billy rolled frantically over in the dirt, his long, heavy coat flipped up and caught the blade, twisting the killing stroke away. Billy caught the man's wrist and kicked hard at his groin, and kept kicking with his boots, as he tried to pin the knife arm.

The staring eyes of the painted face looked implacably into his, and Billy started with recognition. It was Wooden Fish, who smiled evilly as he saw Billy's awareness grow, and then tried to switch his knife to his left hand.

Rather than weakening him, the shock galvanized Billy. "You!" he shouted, and kicked him again. "You!" This time his boot connected with bone somewhere and then Billy twisted and got one knee into the man's belly under his entire weight, while his whole being focused on controlling the knife hand. Then a hatchet blade blurred past Billy's eyes and buried itself into the man's face, spraying blood and bone, and it was over.

Richard's second assailant cut once more at him then backed away and ran. Richard took a step in pursuit, then his left leg collapsed under him and he fell, cursing and writhing in pain.

It had all taken only a few seconds. Billy and Marten were unhurt, but panting with exertion and the aftermath of mortal combat. Marten had to go down on one knee to recover his breath. They cut away Richard's breeches. He was bleeding profusely from a painful stab wound in the thigh, but it was not pulsing—the thrust had not found the femoral—and after Billy tied a tourniquet, they were relieved to find the wound, though dangerous, was not mortal.

Marten scalped the three men. He waved Wooden Fish's dripping hair at Billy. "You should have let this one drown. It would have saved us much trouble."

Billy nodded. "You have saved our lives. I will listen much more closely to your advice in future, Father. Who is paying them, do you think?"

Marten glanced after the long-vanished fugitive and shrugged, "We will know. The one who ran will be recognized and we will know then."

He looked at Billy and said, "But I think we must know already, is it not so?"

They returned to Billy's house and bound up the knife wound properly. Richard was adamant that they should not stay. "I can travel, and I will not spend another hour in this hellhole, nor go to an Albany doctor. Let us go home, my friends, and leave the Albany dogs to clean up their own messes."

*****

The news of Billy's resignation as Indian Agent, and the failed attack in Albany, burst like a thunderbolt over the Six Nations. Delegation after delegation arrived at Smithyman House, traveling through the icy rains of late fall to express their anxiety and uncertainty.

Billy, with Laura at his side, was able to reassure many of their friends. They feasted with the delegates twice a week. Gradually, as the tension relaxed, the upset sachems went home calmer, to face the winter with some optimism. Billy was not going to abandon them after all.

CHAPTER THIRTY
The Tannery, Albany, 1751

James Haye was a long way from Philadelphia. He was now a trained cooper's assistant, but did not have the all-important reference from his journeyman master, so he was unable to hire out his skills. As a result, he was standing waist-deep in the muddy Hudson River on Albany's stinking waterfront with a smelly cow-hide in his hands and a stack of fifty even riper ones behind him on the shore. The hides had been soaking months in the noxious tanning liquor. He was feeling sorry for himself.

He liked washing the hides, for it was the only time the stench of the tannery seemed to thin a bit, but the rest of the job was dreadful, and dangerous. Quite apart from the poisonous chemical soup he had to bathe in to do his work, anthrax had infected two of the last four laborers. They had died. However, since he could not get work with a cooper, James was forced to hire on with the tannery as unskilled labor. He hoped to save enough to homestead somewhere, or better yet, set himself up as a cooper on his own.

When he heard a paddle knock on a gunwale, he looked up, from deep within a tortured daydream. He saw a small, much-patched bark canoe gliding by, nearly within spitting distance. In bow and stern paddled two of the dirtiest, hairiest traders that he had ever seen. In between them, where normally there would be stacks of baled pelts or trade goods, there was only a pair of sacks made of black bearskin, with all the hair still on. The packs contrasted sharply against the pale cedar ribs and honey-colored birch bark of the canoe.

He stared as the canoe swept past the tanning yard and beached below the Voortman store. The bowman leapt over the side of the canoe and, shin deep in the river, unbuttoned his fly, closing his eyes in relief as the stream of urine arced into the water. His companion from the stern, now similarly occupied and standing beside him, said something that made them laugh uproariously.

James saw that both men carried at least two large knives, slung from shoulder straps or under a belt-like sash. The stern paddler had slung his musket and appeared to have a tomahawk on his left hip, tucked into an army bayonet carrier.

They conferred briefly, and the stern paddler removed his black, shapeless, wide-brimmed hat and dropped it into the canoe, revealing very long, greasy hair as black as any Indian's. He grinned at his companion, then strode up the beach to cross the plank deck into the trading office. In a few moments he re-emerged and the two men hurried back into the canoe and paddled furiously along the riverfront to the nearest of the dozen wharf taverns.

As the afternoon wore on, James worked his way through the stinking cow-hides. He suddenly had a strong feeling that he would like to talk to these men. They were among the first traders seen in Albany, in the spring of 1751.

They were sure to have tales to tell about their travels and adventures, he thought. At least, it would be better than eyeing the Albanian Dutch girls, who were as unattainable as the moon for a tradesman without a shop.

Better than the agony of thinking about Lucy being married, too.

The wound she had made in his heart still ached, although no longer badly enough to make him want to moan her name aloud.

It had worked out well at the Philadelphia cooperage for several years. His lop-sided, plucky smile had charmed the cooper's wife enough to give him a chance to overcome his ignorance of manual skills. He had learned quickly, and the frequent beatings he received for minor mistakes or inattention were lighter, and briefer, than those delivered to some of the other apprentices.

His quarters in the attic had been dry, he was able to change the straw monthly, and his bed remained somewhat above freezing all winter, since the chimney formed the middle part of the stone wall next to his bed. Later, the ardent attentions of Lucy, the cooper's daughter, had warmed his bed even more.

Now, nearly a year after he had last touched her, the memory of her little gasps and shudders of release forced him to pause in his work and ease his breeches. Even alone, he flushed a little, remembering the first time Lucy had noticed the effect she had on the skinny fourteen-year-old apprentice.

She was then a flirtatious seventeen, betrothed to Henry, the smith's son. She had made James' life a torment for months. Until one night, that is, when the cooper and his wife were late returning from a neighbor's dinner.

As usual, James had taken the broad pine stairs to the attic after his meal, not before Lucy had allowed him a long look down her suddenly loosened neckline while she was clearing the table. He had once again fought for sleep against the raging stiffness below his belly. Often, he had awakened in the morning to the shame of damp stickiness down there. Sometimes, the violence of his unconscious thrusting had startled him to appalled wakefulness, fearful that someone might have heard him downstairs.

Sleep had come, eventually. However, this night he had awakened to a presence beside him. He sat up, startled, but she had put her fingers to his lips, then slid her hand lightly, slowly, down his neck, and chest, down to his belly. He had groaned when she gently but firmly grasped him, and then began to stroke. In a few seconds, he had bucked uncontrollably against her hand. In silence, she had risen and returned down the stairs. Life had been quite different after that, until the inevitable happened.

When she discovered her pregnancy, his descent into hell was instantaneous. Having known no other, he had a limitless passion for her, but her scorn for him was infinite. Abruptly, her marriage to the far preferable Henry was duly completed. He actually had prospects, and a future, and he was sufficiently bedazzled that he failed to notice until far too late that his young bride's belly was swelling perhaps a bit early. But the cooper had sensed something amiss, with all James' mooning and sighing. He had drawn the obvious conclusion and turned him out with no reference.

The bruises from the kicks and curses of the cooper had healed quickly. They were nothing. He was used to beatings. But Lucy; oh, sweet Lucy's stony-faced rejection had wounded far deeper. In his misery he had fled, scarcely sensible of where, until he had run out of money in Albany. Stunned and agonizing, he presented a less than pleasing appearance to the coopers there.

"No work for you here, boy," was the universal response when he could present no references. A tanner was hiring unskilled labor, however.

James had been daydreaming that Lucy really still loved him and he would win her back when he had made his fortune. He finished washing the stack of hides and decided to try to find the bushmen before they left Albany again.

Finding them proved surprisingly difficult. They seemed to have vanished into the waterfront, and James spent three evenings in the taverns, buying a drink here and there for aggressive merchant sailors who wanted to fight, but would rather have a rum flip.

Finally, he saw the bowman staggering out of a whorehouse, looking even dirtier than when he had arrived. James walked over just in time to keep him from falling into the liquid mud, steaming where he had just emptied his bladder. A pair of small, close-set, bloodshot eyes focused slowly on James. The trader mumbled a word or two of thanks in a nearly incomprehensible drawl, then said, startlingly clearly, "Friend, mayhap you'd like to share a bowl of flip? It's the least I can do for savin' me from bathin' in me own pee, now what say ye?"

James nodded and agreed, "A kind thought, friend, a bowl of flip it is, then." They headed for the Duck's Foot.

A cacophony of loud voices greeted them as they approached the tavern, occasionally graced with the strains of some common fiddle air and loud clapping as one or other of those present danced a jig or a hornpipe. Often the whores would dance with each other or a customer, but frequently two of the men embraced each other with great drunken glee. The audience applauded uproariously if they completed the steps without knocking over a nearby table and its patrons.

The trader elbowed his way in and spotted a table that appeared to have enough room, if not enough chairs. On the way he shouted, "A bowl of flip over here for me and my friend," pointing to their table with his right hand. The barkeep looked up to see the trader seize two clay pipes with surprising precision from a nearby rack with his left hand. He nodded, then caught the eye of a barmaid, jerking his head in their direction. James dragged over a vacant chair and they sat.

The room was a hot, humid contrast to the cold night, where it felt like a late spring frost was on its way. It smelled strongly of ancient stale sweat, vomit, and urine, spiced with spilled beer, hot rum and a dense pungent smoke from candles, rushlights, and tobacco. James pulled a twist of tobacco from his pouch and offered it to his companion, who pinched off enough to fill his pipe before handing it back.

"Thankee, my friend, thankee. And what be your handle, then? I go by Ephraim," he shouted.

"James Haye. And from your speech you're a long way from home, Goodman Ephraim."

Ephraim smiled drunkenly. "Yes, that be true, since my Pappy raised me at the river end of the Chickasaw Trace, down in what used to be Natchez country. He was a trader there, one of the first of us English to cross the mountains and set up by the Mississippi, near where they massacred the French in Fort Rosalie, back in '29. I learned about the trade from him."

"So, what brought you up here to the New York Province, then?"

The trader spat. "It's too hot and feverish there for my blood. Besides, the French allus seemed to be stirring up the Choctaw and Cherokees, and there still ain't more than half a dozen English down there. Up nearer the top of the Trace there is more, where that Irishman—what's his name, now? James Adair —is at."

He leaned closer and put his finger beside his nose, "T' tell ye the truth, friend, there are far too many poisonous snakes down there for me, too. Cottonmouths and copperheads. I have a bit of a horror for them. So, maybe five years back I heard tell of an Iroquois war party that traveled down the war trail against the Catawba and brought some scalps and slaves back. One of the Chickasaw thereabouts—they hates the French, ye see—he told me that

Mohawks is very friendly to the likes of us English, so I walked up the Trace to the Cumberland post on the Tennessee, where I met my partner, Peter Martin."

The bowl of steaming flip arrived, in the hands of a young barmaid. Her breasts jutted and swayed enticingly in her low-cut linen shift. She was wearing no stays. With evident reluctance, Ephraim pried a coin from his leather pocket and, when she took it, reached up to fondle her. She laughed and slapped his hand away, leaning down to reveal the deep, inviting valley, and said, "Ephraim, you'll need to pull out a lot more before you get any of this."

He grinned and seized her hand, bringing it down to his lap, "How about pulling that out, then, Annie, my belle?" She slid her hand away, apparently reluctantly, James noted. Ephraim turned to James and winked. "She loves me, Annie does, but she won't admit it, Jimmie, me boy."

Annie tossed her head and flicked her eyes over to James. "If you bring your handsome young friend Jimmie along," she said, locking eyes with James, "you'd get a special rate, for he looks a lot better than you, Ephraim."

Ephraim roared with laughter. "Aye, Annie, but judging from the look of him he has no coin, you know, and old Ephraim and Peter just sold last winter's furs to Billy Smithyman, didn't we, an' I ain't sharing you with nobody." He pulled out a golden guinea and spun it in the air, catching it and putting it back in his pocket. James noticed that Annie's eyes followed the coin as if it were magnetic. "So, my Annie, what will you do for Ephraim for that, d'ye think?"

She shook her head and tucked the payment for the bowl inside the pocket underneath her shift. "You're too drunk to please a lady, Ephraim. Come and call when you've cleaned yourself up a bit." With another sidelong glance at James, she went back to the bar.

Ephraim lifted the bowl to his lips and some of the rum ran down the sides of his face. He handed it to James and continued his story, "So, Peter and me, we two been in business t'gether ever since. I get along up here in Albany," he added, after a contemplative puff on his pipe, "an' between Peter and myself, we know pretty much ever' beaver pond from here clear up to the Frenchie fort at Rainy River. An' best of all, there're only rattlers up here, and they're polite snakes, givin' a warning an' all." He paused, and eyed James narrowly.

"Now, it seems like I've run right off at the mouth about my business, so, Goodman Haye, what brings you to Albany yourself? I ain't seen you here before." Suddenly, a long-bladed knife thumped into the table and stood quiver-ing between them. "If'n you think you'll be able to take my coin away from me, young'n, be warned that there's a few Cherokee, a Shawnee or two and even an Ojibwa that tried their hand at it and found it bitten right off by my friend Wolf, here."

James started slightly, but took a puff on his own pipe and stared back at the trader. "I'm lookin' for something to take my mind off a girl, Ephraim, not lookin' for trouble."

"How old are you anyway, boy? I'm thinking that you're awful young to be down here in the Duck's Foot, now that I got a clear look at ye."

James shrugged. "I'm twenty, an' my parents are dead. I learned the coopering trade out of an orphanage in Philly."

He looked across at the trader, his mind made up suddenly. "But I want to go with you and Peter when you go to trade next time."

Ephraim guffawed, and clapped him on the back.

"A girl, is't, Jimmie-me-lad? Hawhawhawhawhaw!" He slapped his knee and laughed until he began to cough. James found himself a little stung, and it showed on his face, in spite of himself.

Ephraim laughed heartily again. "Don't take it wrong, lad. Ye Gods, wait until I tells Peter that ye'd like to go to the wilderness t' forget a girl. Here, now, let me do another bowl and don't be looking so cross. Whoohee, now, you are the serious one, ain't ye?"

"Annie!" Ephraim bellowed, turning toward the bar. "Annie!" and waved his finger at her.

Then, James saw the stern-paddler surge through the doorway. The flip and Peter Martin arrived at the table at the same time.

Ephraim gestured, "Peter, this here's Jimmie—he wants to go next trip wi' us, to forget a girl." He began to chuckle again.

Peter smiled at his partner, and then looked at James, sizing him up quickly. After a few seconds he said, "We won't take you. You can't paddle, you 'ave no investment and you look too bloody English to come north of the Lake." He had a faint accent on some words that James could not place.

James began to reply, but the trader held up a large, meaty hand. "We can talk some other time about this. I know from looking at you that these things are true."

James was learning to hide his feelings better and merely shrugged, leaning across to seize the candle and re-light his pipe.

For several weeks, James haunted the taverns. He waylaid the senior partner, Peter, nightly, to hear stories of the trapper's life in the wilderness, hoping Peter would change his mind. James was fascinated, and his youthful, open admiration won the amused tolerance of the older trader, more used to being shunned by the farmers and merchants and their families for his Indian looks and ways.

Finally, the trader had had enough of the Albany fleshpots, and one night told James he was leaving.

"I'm going to lay up awhile at my cabin at Lake Oneida for a spell. There is probably some call for a cooper up there, maybe you would 'ave time to set yourself up before winter sets in. You are not ready for tripping to the wilderness yet and I ain't ready for another partner anyway, but you might like it better than Albany, if you want to forget your girl. I'm looking for the quiet, now, and my woman, Caroline, is probably looking for me, too."

"What about Ephraim?" James inquired.

Peter spat and grinned. "Ephraim's done got 'imself a lair 'ere for the summer, I don't doubt, and if it's not 'ere it's probably in New York. 'E knows where to find me."

"When will you go?"

"Two days." Two deep furrows appeared between Peter's eyebrows. "I've got some business arrangements to complete, first. Be at Voortman's landing day after tomorrow and you can bow paddle us up to the Oneida carrying place."

He glanced at James, and chuckled briefly. "Then we'll see what your shoulders are made of. I can give you a 'and building a shanty up there, if you've a mind to, and I will introduce you to Billy Smithyman on the way. He might buy some of your barrels once you get set. Maybe Fort Oswego would buy some, too."

James sensed the quickening of his pulse, a feeling he thought he had lost. He nodded, wordless.

Peter got up to go, then stopped and returned. "You'll need some gear, boy, but we'll get that at Smithyman's post. Just bring your money, your tools and a blanket or two, and that will get you there."

*****

Smithyman House was a three-day paddle against the Mohawk's current from Schenectady. By the time they arrived, James felt as if someone had filled his shoulder joints with powdered glass. Peter was amused and told him that they would rest for a day or two before continuing. "We've got about a week's more paddling, up to the Oneida Carry" he said, to James' inward groan. At Smithyman's he purchased, on credit, a musket, axe, knife and sundry tools, food, blankets, a small tent, and cooking items for basic homesteading. When Peter vouched for him, Billy accepted his word, payment to be in barrels the following spring.

When Billy invited Peter and James to dinner, James found himself seated at a lively table of sixteen on the spacious second floor hall of Smithyman

House. The tide of conversation surged powerfully back and forth throughout the meal. As the youngest present, his social skills were not quite up to the task, but he watched the constant flow of Billy's friends and neighbors coming in and out of the room, and up and down the stairs. Some of them were clearly officials of the Provincial Government, some, visitors from overseas.

At the opposite end to Billy sat a young Indian woman of striking beauty. She was dressed in richly decorated buckskins and was issuing commands to the servants, while kissing and then gently shooing away a young white girl, who had an even younger boy by the hand.

To James' right was an older Indian, with earlobes pierced and stretched until they rested on his shoulders and a silver nose-bob dangling over his upper lip. Across his left cheek from mouth to ear was a gigantic, raised scar. He wore a red coat with brass buttons.

Peter sat across the table, flirting with his very blonde neighbor, who looked to be the wife of one of the visitors and spoke heavily accented English. James overheard someone remark that she was Swedish.

Next to the Swedish woman there was a tall, thin man roughly the same age as James.

Where have I seen him before?

Then the thin man spoke, and with a flood of amazed joy, James recognized his faintly accented voice and blurted out, "Johannes! Joe! Is't really you? It's James Haye!"

The man looked at James blankly, then with recognition.

"By God, it is you!"

The two young men leaped to their feet, ran around the end of the table and clasped each other in an affectionate hug, to the amusement of all.

Johannes laughed and explained, "James was my brother in the orphanage in Philadelphia. We plotted together many times to escape, and he took many blows from that bully Elias Ruskin, on my behalf."

James nodded enthusiastically. "If I had not been sent away to become a cooper we would have escaped, too, for Johannes is very smart."

Billy interjected from the head of the table, agreeing. "That is why we have him teaching classes here, but it is very good to have such an unsolicited recommendation!" Everyone roared with laughter.

The two young men punched each other lightly. James said, "I am going to homestead up at the Carry, but I will come down to see you as soon as I'm settled in properly."

Johannes smiled happily, and said as they returned to their meal, "I'll look forward to it, James." He looked at Billy. "It seems this place is doubly lucky for me! I have found my old friend here, as well as a home"

The plates, piled high with meats and vegetables, came, were emptied and removed, and returned, replenished, until even James could hold no more. Wine and rum punch and local beer overflowed, and the roar of interested discussion rose ever higher.

In a brief silence, James timidly remarked that the prices Smithyman charged were less than he had seen in Albany. Billy laughed, uproariously, "Yes, my friend, and they do not like me for it, do they, now? But I purchase direct from my agents in England and New York, and I fancy they work very hard for me. You will find, young James, that I purchase here at fair prices also, and I will be very pleased to look at your cooperage products when you are ready to send some to me. Good journeymen are hard to find here in the northwest."

Billy shouted across the table over the renewed babble, and shook a drumstick at the older Indian sitting next to James. "Marten, Marten—I have more information about this smallpox inoculation. If you still think you are a warrior, you must try it with me and we will protect your people. It is now common in England. Even Mr. Franklin in Philadelphia, who was nearly arrested in Boston for opposing it, is now supporting it. We must do this, my old friend. I hear there is a new infection that started in New York last month; they had to move the meeting of the Assembly and the Governor away from my uncle's former house at Greenwich."

Marten bobbed his head in agreement. "Billy, your words say that I must be as much a man as you. If my Mohawk sisters and their babies are to be trusted, this will be a true challenge." Marten paused for dramatic effect and then continued, smiling, "But, Billy, I must tell you that I have had a dream, a true dream, that you had given me your green coat."

Billy seemed taken aback for a moment, then recovered and roared again with laughter. He stood, stripping his coat from his back. He strode around the table and placed it over Marten's shoulders.

"Marten, I trust your true dream, my friend. I know that you will respect that it is a hardship for me to fulfill your true dream with my best new coat, that took six months to get from London, and that was made with the very best English cloth and gold lace."

Marten smiled with satisfaction. "It is as you say, William, our people know that your heart is with us even when it causes you true pain."

Eventually, James grew dizzy from the heat, the din of conversation and drink and the extraordinary mix of people. He saw that Johannes had left, unobserved, sometime earlier, so he, too, quietly wandered away. Peter and the blonde woman had also disappeared at some point, without anyone apparently noticing.

A smiling servant opened the back door and he slipped out into the cool night. He walked around to the front, where a large fire burned amidst a circle of half a dozen bark wigwams. The palisade and gate that had faced the river were gone, although the other walls were still in repair. Upwards of two score Indian men, women and children sat around the fire roasting rabbit and deer, their canoes to one side on the grass. When James reached his canoe, he unrolled his blanket and looked back at Smithyman House, where the light of dozens of candles blazed out of every window. Even the musket loopholes through the ground floor masonry revealed slots of the welcoming yellow glow.

The next day, he visited with Johannes for several hours and they found that the old bonds remained very strong. They swore that they would remain in touch, now that fate had reunited them.

When Peter and James departed, their combined purchases meant that they had to leave the small canoe and transfer to a larger one. Peter simply selected one from a group set to one side and let the trading office know. As they loaded it, James asked about who owned them and how anyone knew what was where. He was surprised to hear Peter tell him that Billy kept meticulous track of these.

"Yes, my young friend. Slips of paper with his signature are legal ownership documents up and down the entire river, from Oswego to Albany. Some canoes are lost, but everyone knows that trading has its hazards, and very few are stolen." Johannes nodded. "Billy does his best to make trade happen."

Billy came to see them off.

"Visit soon, James," he called as they pushed off. James waved and smiled happily, then put his shoulders into his stroke.

They stayed close to shore, where the current was weaker and occasional back eddies boosted them on. Many times, they pulled the canoe through shallows or rapids. Each night they would haul the canoe ashore at some sandy beach or otherwise convenient site, unload it and use the upturned hull for shelter, combined with an oilcloth. It was a time of relative peace on the northern frontier, and they shared some of the campsites with other traders and a variety of Indians from several nations and clans, mostly Iroquois. They also encountered several canoes of Ojibwa. Peter seemed to be friends with many.

Around the fire those evenings, James peppered the older trader with questions. Peter's amusement increased. As they paddled up the river, their relationship gradually grew into a more solid friendship.

One night James asked him about his background. After a moment, the trader chuckled, and his accent broadened perceptibly.

"To all that I know, hereabouts, anyhow, I'm Peter Martin. But, t' tell ye the truth, my father and stepmother named me Pierre-Martin and my father's name was de Saint Rémy. And if my true mother 'ad her way, I'd be a-runnin' around the forest like her family, with the name of Crow-with-One-Eye, or some such. She was Ojibwa, and so I can pass among them north of the Lakes as a brother."

He leaned forward and re-lit his pipe with a twig. "Now, all this is between you and me and Ephraim, and you'd be putting me at risk to tell anyone. My younger half-brother, Hippolyte, 'e's in the French Navy. I think 'e is going to be posted commander of all the vessels on the big lake this fall, if I got it right. Maybe I'll go see him, and I'll get Hippolyte to donate some good French brandy to the trade."

He chuckled. "My Indian wife, Caroline, she's a Seneca. So, you see, I can swim like a fish between the English and the French and the Indian nations, and as long as I can do that, I'll be doing alright, don't you think, young James?"

But the only response was a snore, for James, exhausted from the lond day's exertions, had fallen asleep as he listened. Peter chuckled again, and puffed on his pipe, and stared at the indifferent stars.

*****

When they arrived at the beginning of the Oneida Carry, they made camp and then walked to the fortified tavern called Stobo's Inn, where they spent a pleasant evening drinking Stobo's local beer. James' shoulders were beginning to improve.

The next day he walked the rough and rutted track across the height of land that divided the Great Lakes from the Mohawk River watershed. After a wide circuit about the area, something impelled him to pick a spot which had a nice view overlooking the Mohawk, but which was not far from the landing or the beginning of Wood's Creek, which led northwest to the big lake. There was a good stand of mixed hardwoods on a hillock there, and the swamps grew cedars. Together they promised easy access to the raw material he would need for his trade.

The entire hamlet huddled close to the short wagon road that led across the Carry—a few scattered shanties and one or two small farms, along with Stobo's place and some rapidly disintegrating palisade works left over from the recent war.

Peter helped him get a shanty started, then disappeared into the woods for several weeks after a slender, attractive woman suddenly appeared. He introduced her as Caroline.

James still knew little about the various tribes and bands that he saw coming to trade or passing on the river, other than what he had gleaned from his long conversations with Peter and from the usual tavern gossip and occasional newspaper story. The Indians he saw here bore no resemblance to the drunken, dirty, shambling wretches he had seen in Philadelphia and New York. These people looked like they might be very dangerous if provoked.

James had had his share of fistfights in the streets of Philadelphia, and he had won several fights with the drunken farmers and sailors around the settlements and in Albany. But he had no desire to have to fight for his life with these men. He had a distinct feeling that skill with his fists might be less of an asset in the wilderness than skill with a tomahawk or knife.

When Peter reappeared, he invited James to visit his camp, near where Wood's Creek joined Oneida Lake, and then he vanished again. After Peter left, James finished erecting the shelter and felled several oak, maple, ash and hickory trees, along with a few sweet-smelling cedars. He cut and split the logs for seasoning. Then he finished building a lean-to attached to his shanty to serve as his workshop. He was ready for a rest.

One morning he walked the fifteen miles over to Peter's cabin, which he had dug halfway into a dirt cliff overlooking Lake Oneida. It was nearly invisible except for a curl of smoke winding upwards from a rudimentary chimney. The trader was in an expansive mood, and invited James in for rum. Caroline was nowhere about. James took a gulp and raised his mug to the trader, asking him why he went off to the wilderness.

Predictably, Peter laughed. "Mostly, now, Jimmie, to make a living off beaver, you have to go up to Ojibwa or Cree land to the northwest, or damn near as far as the Mississippi to the west, because they've been trapped out around Iroquois land here for a hundred years. Only problem is, the Indians think that they're the only ones have the right to catch game out there, and all the nations except mostly the Iroquois think that the British are out to push them off their land. An' they're right, too."

James asked, "What about the French?"

"Frenchmen, now, we, they, don't do too much in the way of settlin', except right around the forts for supplying the garrisons and the traders, and downriver in Montreal an' Quebec and old l'Acadie. Frenchmen also act a lot more like warriors, to the Indian way of thinking. They set up forts as tradin' posts, with some soldiers an' even cannons in 'em, some of 'em. On the other 'and, the English usually can offer better trade goods and better prices for furs than the French-men, so many of them are 'appier to trade with English connections."

He turned to rummage in a box, pulled out a silver bracelet, and tossed it to James.

"Y'see these bracelets, now, all the nations love to wear 'em. They all know that the English ones are purer silver than the French, too. I carry a few pounds of 'em upcountry every fall, and I can sell 'em for two or three beavers each and still make a decent profit. The Frenchies ask ten pelts for theirs at Niagara and Toronto, and even at Fort Frontenac. Up at Michilimackinac they charge even more, for it's farther to ship. The civilian governor takes most of the money, anyway. That's why unlicensed coureurs de bois like me exist.

"But my brother wrote me from Montreal last fall that the governor is so upset about the trade all going to the English, that 'e has ordered all the posts to match English prices. I don't rightly know if that's happening, yet, but that will surely madden all the licensed traders at the magazins royals—those are the royal stores—for there goes away their own profits." He paused and rubbed his forehead, as if in pain.

"My own father was too honest to make profit out of the fur trade. 'E was twenty years at Fort Niagara. Too many flour barrels filled with stones, and muskets with bent barrels or broken locks coming up from the crooks in Montreal and Quebec to make good money. The English Oswego post took most of the lower lakes trade away anyway, when they started selling rum, cause the licensed French traders weren't allowed to, officially, on account of the priests."

James asked, "Where is your father now?"

"Died, last fall. He was drowned when the rotten old ship and the slovenly captain that they sent for him sank in a storm. But it was maybe just as well for him, because I think 'e had a broken heart already. Intendant Bigot, the civilian who runs the affaires of the colony, lied well enough that 'e persuaded the military governor to recall Papa to Québec, and 'e would have put him out on the street with nothing because 'e wouldn't turn crooked and pay Bigot and his partners, who are cheating the King." Peter fell silent for a minute or two, brooding. He puffed at his pipe and scratched underneath his homespun shirt, then continued.

"Up in the upper country in the northwest, farmin' ain't much of a way to make a living. To tell the truth, most of the land don't seem much good for it, being mostly trappin' an' huntin' land—rock and swamp and trees growing out of pretty thin dirt and sand. The Six Nation Iroquois, on t'other hand, have good land here below the lake. They understand farmin' more like the English, and they grow maize and beans and squash just like any regular farmer. Fact is, they showed those plants to us."

They drank another mug of rum together, in companionable silence. Then Peter asked him, "How're you set for the winter, boy?"

James had to admit that he had not yet planned or put away any food for the winter, other than the barrel of flour he had purchased.

The trader was grimly amused. "I fancy ye'll be yet leaner by springtime, then. Ye'll have to come a-hunting with me in the fall, an' we'll lay in some smoked meat. You can borrow my fishnet, and if the wild pigeons come down nearby you can net them and smoke 'em. There are a couple of places north of here where you can spear big salmon out of the streams and smoke them down. If you get some dried corn and beans from the Mohawks and a hundredweight of dried peas from Smithyman, you'll survive then, mayhap. But it's a long winter here, mon petit garçon'."

CHAPTER THIRTY ONE
Onokenoga, Lake of the Gods, 1751

Finally, the vexatious French prisoners were successfully exchanged. The blonde vixen departed with her compatriots, and the Mohawks returned by cargo canoe from Montreal, permanently broken. They were physically sickened and spiritually dead, simply from their long confirnement.

Laura had been waiting impatiently for this conclusion, and the opportunity it presented to get Billy away from business so that she could have him all to herself for a time.

She and Billy were standing at the edge of a precipice. Three hundred feet below, the wind spirit softly blew across the rippling waters of Skaniodorio, the great lake. It gently mingled the forest reflections with the glittering sun and water and dashed flashing emeralds into their eyes.

They were side by side, arms about each other, and they hugged their bodies tight together, as if hips, flanks, torsos, and shoulders could meld into one. The crisp, clear fall weather was intoxicating, but their minds rarely turned to anything but the nectar of each other's presence. Their souls reveled in it, splashed and swam through the unbelievable drenching pleasure of it.

The warriors who had escorted them north across the big lake from Oswego had now drawn off, in part to allow them some privacy but also to maintain a protective cordon around the hill. This was not Iroquois territory; it belonged to the Ojibwa, and the Ojibwa remained friendly to France. There were still occasional raids happening here and there in New England, and one had to guard against surprises.

However, this place, Onokenoga, the Lake of the Gods, was Six Nations land for several generations after the war with the Hurons, and it remained sacred to them. The still, black waters were only a few dozen steps behind them.

Mohawks traditionally made several pilgrimages a year to the Lake-on-the-Mountain, to throw sacred tobacco onto a ceremonial fire. This expressed their people's thanks for the generosity of the three spirit sisters of the Iroquois—Corn, Beans and Squash—who lived in the inky depths of Onokenoga.

How the water got into the lake, which was at the top of the highest ground for several day's travel in any direction, was one of Great Manitou's mysteries; that it stayed there, and the cliff leaked hardly a drop except in springtime, was another.

Later, Laura rose above Billy in the tent, and their fire by Onekenoga's shore silhouetted her. She swayed, and panted, and told him the love story of the Lake on the Mountain. How the young couple had eloped, against their mothers' will, and had come here and were caught, and in their disgrace and despair they threw themselves into the lake to hide.

But the maiden was swept out over the cliff by the swift water that falls there in the spring, and her brave warrior, who dove into the lake with her, never surfaced. And the angry Gods impounded their spirits irretrievably, because they had violated the sacred waters with their bodies and their sins.

"But..." she gasped, as he reached up to caress her, and her eyes and teeth flashed fiercely at him in the gloom, and she seized his hands and crushed her breasts with them.

"...but in the end, the three sisters took pity on the lovers. They started a leak in the cliff wall, and.... she giggled and sighed, and then continued, after a time, whispering, "...then, with his powerful warrior's hands, he was able to widen the little crack into a breach and escape, to fall with the spring waters into the narrows below and join his beloved, forevermore." She lay herself down on his chest, and they slept.

In the morning they made love again, and then cooked some whitefish and ate corn bread with berries, and she went off to collect herbs while Billy lay back and watched lacy white tendrils creeping slowly across the sky from the west.

When she returned, they could not stop from caressing each other. They clung together exhausted at night, entwined like the stems and fruit of the wild grapes; so closely that at times they could not easily tell whose fingers were whose, and Laura yelped once, then laughed breathlessly after leaving tooth marks in her own arm, thinking it was his.

The next morning, the beautiful, delicate mares' tails etching the sky were being replaced by a thickening grey film, creating a huge, pale yellow ring around the sun, with two brilliant sun dogs glowing like coals at opposite sides.

Skaniadorio, the big lake that was so beautiful in the sun, had become a flat, grey-and-black mirror, and the warriors returned to strike the camp. They gambled that the weather would hold for the day, and set out to paddle directly across it back to Oswego, rather than take the long way around the end of the lake. It could save them at least a full day of traveling, maybe two; for it was clear that the first of the violent fall storms was now on its way.

By the time they left the shelter of the mainland behind, a faint wind had begun, riffling the water, and when they were two hours offshore and out of sight of land, it was driving a chop that occasionally threw spray into the two canoes. The afternoon sun then vanished into a deep murk and whitecaps began to appear all around them.

After another hour, the waves threatened to capsize the canoes, and the stern paddlers had to yell commands and steer carefully as waves as tall as a man's legs heaved sideways against them. They had a further hour of paddling ahead of them before they could rest on one of the group of islets that provided shelter in the middle of the lake.

The warriors were growing worried, for the wind was still rising, and some shouted debate occurred. Several were insisting that they should turn away from the wind and give up trying to reach the islands. They conferred with Billy, and after a few minutes decided to press on. They sacrificed one of the dogs they had brought, cut its throat and threw its body overboard, in a traditional ritual to ease the anger of the lake gods. It wasn't a white dog, so it wasn't a good sacrifice, but it was all they had, and it would just have to do.

Billy and Laura both were bailing constantly with leather buckets, but the canoes gradually grew heavier, and the water sloshed back and forth inside them. As the day grew darker, the white spume on the water seemed to glow weirdly blue-white, and the canoes rolled from side to side, their crews desperately striving to keep the gunnels from going under. The warriors all peered anxiously ahead for any sign of the low islands, which would mean they were safe.

Billy's eyes met Laura's. She was exhilarated, laughing as the wind whipped the spume into her face, and she grinned at him, tossing a bucket of bilge water at him. He smiled back, felt his heart thumping, and thought it might burst with the joy he had found with her. His eyes filled with tears and he was glad for the storm.

For the first time in many years, he prayed sincerely to his Irish-English God that they might survive. He picked up the pace of his bailing, although his arms groaned, and for a time they seemed to gain on the cascading storm-slosh.

In another half hour, however, it was clear they were losing the battle. Billy's arms were on fire and he could not imagine what the paddlers felt like, although there had yet been little change in their steady thrusting.

Suddenly, a shout came from the lead canoe and it started to turn sharply to the left. A huge rogue wave loomed, and the exhausted warriors redoubled their efforts. They turned the canoes just in time for the hissing swell to raise the stern and pass underneath them, the crest boiling over into the canoes as it passed.

They laboriously turned back on course and then Laura called out, pointing ahead, where suddenly a wall of white water a quarter of a mile long sprang into the sky and fell back. Cries of relief went up, for this marked the long flat reefs to the west of the islands, and they all felt a resurgence of energy. In a few minutes more, they were safely into the calmer water between the long, sheltering arms of the curved eastern beach, gliding to a halt on the grey pebbles.

During the night, the wind's moan rose to a demented howl. Under the upturned canoes it felt as if the entire island was going under water, for the sheets of horizontal rain were indistinguishable from wave tops. The big canoes themselves stirred restlessly in the gusts, and they had to stake them down.

The storm raged over them for two more days before blowing itself out. They managed to get the canvas tent and two wigwams erected and tied off securely in a wooded campsite that had served Laura's people, and others, as a place of shelter for generations.

Billy and Laura twice walked around the island during the gale. They stood on the western shore and watched the surf fly white into the sky as far as they could see. They smoked their clothes dry over the fires and gloried together in the beauty of their bodies and in the immensity of the feeling that flowed between them and around them.

The winds finally shifted northward and gradually died away, but left behind mountainous swells on the lake. It was another day and night before they could safely depart again for home. In the times when they rested from making love, they made plans.

"Uncle Marten said that you have a vision that will allow our people to prosper in your coming world, Billy."

Billy nodded solemnly. "I know there are huge pressures in England for people to come here, where they think there is unlimited room for all. Marten knows; he has seen that the English are very, very many hundreds of thousands and the Mohawks are only a few hundred. And so the Haudenosaunee and all the rest, even acting all together, will never be able to throw us back into the sea."

"What is our future, then, Billy?"

"For your people to thrive forever, they must understand our ways from a young age. That does not mean abandoning the Indian ways, just as you and I have not abandoned our own ways. The Keepers of the Eastern Door are very intelligent and disciplined. So, in a different way, are the Europeans. You can master both."

Laura thought awhile, then said. "It is a frightening thing to leave behind the forest and the old ways."

"Some of us do respect your people, my sweet forest woman. My uncle has donated much money to the school in Stockbridge, and they seek my advice often. It is not to change you, but to make you able to survive in our world. In our lifetime and our children's lifetimes much that is in place now, much that you have grown accustomed, to will pass away.

"Some things have already gone. This is not all bad, is it? Which of your people would now prefer to cook with stone knives and clay pots rather than steel and iron?"

"We would wish to have the liberty of the forest and the wealth of the English, both," she summed up.

Billy laughed and caressed her face. "Aye, my sweet, such is everyone's wish—my wish too! And for a time that has been true and will be true for a little longer. But when the forest has become farms, your people must become farmers to survive. It is not a disgrace; the Six Nations know farming very well already."

When they returned to Smithyman House, they had decided. Laura's younger brother Matthew would go to the Stockbridge school, or perhaps the one Reverend Wheelock was establishing in Lebanon, Connecticut, to learn white skills. Billy's son, Thomas, would learn Mohawk ways. They would make many more babies, starting now.

CHAPTER THIRTY TWO
Smithyman House, 1752–53

The following summer, Uncle Harold Holeybarth died. Billy received a letter a few weeks later from his mother:

> Our dear Hal had come home from the Navy Office, where he had just been appointed Vice-Admiral of the Red, and promptly caught a fever after coming here, which took him off in a mercilessly short time. We are all devastated, William, but I am so glad that you and he had been able to make up some of your differences over the years. After your appointment to the Governor's Council, I think he was able to see, although your methods were not the same as his, that the two of you had the same goal in mind in the end.

Laura finished reading the letter aloud and looked at Billy in inquiry. Her English was amazingly improved; it was now as good as many educated Europeans, and she had stumbled very little. He removed his large hands from where they had been resting on Laura's belly, feeling the tiny stirrings of life within.

He took back the letter and grimaced. He said, "Well, Uncle Hal had a fine run of it, certainly. He gave me my start here, and for that I am forever in his debt. We shall see if this might have any local effect. Chief Justice De Vere is Uncle Hal's father-in-law, and now one of his executors."

Billy scratched above his eyebrow. "Perhaps now that he has lost one of his main sources of influence in London, De Vere will need to change his tune in New York. Perhaps that is why the Governor has summoned his Council."

But Governor Clayton had other things on his mind.

He opened the meeting in a good mood. In a low voice, to avoid being over-heard even by the servants, he said, "Now, gentlemen, I tell you this in all confidence; no one else is to know until I make the announcement. You are all aware that I have been petitioning the Board of Trade on this, but I have now received a letter that the King has agreed to replace me next year. There has been no decision yet as to who will come."

There were startled looks around the table, then a slow nodding as they examined some of the personal implications. This would likely mean a radical change in provincial politics. The Councilors offered their congratulations and best wishes. Several even appeared to have genuine regrets.

Pleased that he had let his friends know something that they would be able to work to their advantage, Governor Clayton coughed for their attention and moved on to other business. "I have other tidings to lay before you of an urgent nature. I have received grave news from the west." The startled Councilors looked at him. He waved a message.

"This is from the Governor in Philadelphia. The trading post and village at Pickawillany, on the Miami River in the western Ohio country, has been attacked and taken by a force of several hundred northerners—Ottawas and Ojibwas, led by a civilian Frenchman."

He looked again at the letter. "They killed a dozen Miamis defending the village and caught their chief, Old Britain, there. He was killed, and then they boiled and ate him."

They looked at Billy in consternation. Billy stared back at them, thinking, and then spoke quietly, but with great intensity.

"Governor, this changes everything. There were fifty English traders resident at Pickawillany. They had gone there since the last war, and Old Britain was the chief who had brought the Miami nations over to our cause, protecting the traders and extending our influence west and north.

"There will now be no-one on the Ohio to deny what the Indian nations have until now been willing to overlook, that there were surveyors hiding among the traders and that the French speak the truth about the English trying to steal their lands."

"You mean the Ohio Company, Smithyman?"

Billy nodded, grimly. "Of course, Governor. The Ohio Company of Virginia, and others who think the Ohio Valley is ours, by God, just for the taking."

He tapped his fingers on the table and mused aloud.

"The French have now escalated from polite insolence, to encouraging murder, to war parties. I wonder if they now will back this up by sending official French forces to remain in the region."

He put down his glass, rose and bowed to the Governor, then to the table.

"Excellency, with your leave I must return to my home and take the temperature of my Mohawk friends there. They may have some opinions we should consider. After all, it is their firmly held view, and that of the Onondaga Grand Council as well, that the Miamis are subservient to the Six Iroquois

Nations, and that these lands therefore belong to them. Not to the French, nor, gentlemen," he looked around the table and smiled slightly, "to us, in spite of the famous Treaty of Utrecht."

He had their attention. "The tribes all know what the presence of surveyors means."

Billy looked squarely at Clayton. "Governor, before I leave I must remind you. You are getting very bad advice from the Albany Council. You should not rely on them for dealings with the Mohawks."

Governor Clayton looked away, then back. He shrugged a little.

"I confess I am not very comfortable with either the Commissioners or your native friends without you there, Smithyman, but as you resigned as Indian Agent, for your own very good reasons, what can I do?"

On his return journey, Billy found Marten had gone out with a hunting party and would not be back for a week or more. Beautiful Feather was at home with their son, Adam, and they both greeted Billy warmly. However, Billy sensed a slight reserve that was shocking, although he thought, and hoped, he was able to hide his dismay.

Wind-Through-the-Spruces was out with Marten and the hunters. There was a gloomy air of discontent and disaffection in the air. Many inhabitants of Diyondarogon appeared poorer, and hungrier, than Billy had seen in many years. Mohawks living in the huts inside Fort Hunter seemed listless, and many were drunk. He hugged Adam, kissed his mother, and left gifts.

Early in the fall, Laura delivered a daughter, after a very short and uncomplicated labor. She was a lively and noisy little bundle they named Polly, and after a month, Laura took her to Canajoharie, to show her off, get her acquainted with her people, and have the proper naming ceremonies.

In November, Billy visited. Laura and the Gantowisas in Canajoharie showed nothing like the coolness he had sensed at Fort Hunter, although there was not a lot of food for them, either. After visiting had concluded, he and Laura devoured each other's bodies. As they rested, sweating, Billy asked, "The castle is almost empty. Is everyone at the hunt?"

Laura said, "Many are hunting, but some have left for the French priest's farm at 'Swegatchie. Everyone is hungry, and he offers food and gifts, and a safe place to live and farm. Some also have gone to live with their cousins in Montreal. Corlaer is rude, and Albany does not speak to us at all. We are becoming desperate, Billy. The northerners can attack us here almost as easily as they did the west."

Billy closed his eyes. "Fort Oswego is useless. Perhaps I should not have resigned. I think they are angry with me in Diyondarogon. Is Marten avoiding me, do you think?"

Laura shook her head. "No, my husband, he knows you remain our true friend. But he, alone among our people, now, has seen London; although I have seen it through his eyes and yours, and your magazines. If London abandons us, we know that we must seek other alliances that can protect us. You cannot do this all alone."

"It is utterly maddening to me that I have not been able to convince even the Governor of the truth," Billy said candidly.

Laura reassured him. "We know that you are helping us. We know also that you have many enemies for this reason, even on the Governor's Council."

"I think that London does understand. It is a pity that they are always so dreadfully slow to act. I must speak with Marten when he returns. The French are impressive, but they cannot defeat the English here, we are too many. To turn away from England would be a terrible mistake for your people. If they are hungry, they must come across the river to us. We will find a way to feed them, I promise you."

She pressed her finger to his lips, and pulled him down to her. "I am yours, my husband. For now, the world is outside our home, and I am not."

*****

The winter snows had vanished and the endless clouds of nesting wild pigeons had returned, signifying full spring, before Polly and Laura reappeared. Once again, Billy found himself moved almost to tears when the entire family collected itself.

He organized the usual planting season games to celebrate. They were a great success, but midway through the day a message arrived from Oswego that thirty canoes with many troops in white coats had passed the fort, and that "a French-man" had informed the post that this was the advance guard of 6,000, who were going to garrison the Ohio Valley.

Billy thanked the messenger and invited him to join in the games. Then Billy stood for ten minutes watching the festivities. Suddenly, everything seemed to be developing a particularly brittle, tensioned quality, he thought. As if they were all in a kind of moving glass tableau, floating down, down, through the rushing air.

Two days later, Billy was startled awake in his bed in the middle of the night. A wild chorus of whooping, yelling and musket firing was coming rapidly closer from the river. Heart pounding, he shouted to the servants to bar the doors and yanked on a pair of breeches. Although they had not drilled this for more than a year, all six of the men present had lived with this type of alarm occurring almost daily during the last war. They handed out and loaded muskets from the racks in the hall. A little shakily, they stared out through the loopholes into the blackness.

In a few minutes, a shouted exchange of challenges and greetings caused Billy to open the door facing the river in great relief, for it was a party of ten Onondagans, bringing a belt from their Council. Billy invited them in and had food and little gifts brought and distributed. They apologized for the sudden intrusion, but carried tidings of great importance from Onondaga.

The belt confirmed the Oswego message, that a very large French force was passing up the lake, and conveyed a request. The Onondaga Council, on behalf of the Six Nation Confederacy, was urgently asking that the English take action to protect the Ohio and the Miamis from the French.

Billy accepted it on behalf of the Governor.

"Be assured my friends, that I will leave in the morning and Corlaer will hear your urgent call for help within the week. When he has discussed this with the other governors I will bring you his reply, but you must understand that this may take many weeks, since they are far from each other."

Governor Clayton assured Billy that he would urgently communicate this important information to Pennsylvania and Virginia and to London, urging them to act, "But I know you understand, Smithyman," Clayton said, "the Ohio is far from being a New York matter, and even if it were our problem, with the Assembly so adamantly against action I can personally promise nothing, nothing at all."

Upon his return, Billy met Marten and they decided to go far into the forest to talk. They went slowly overland on foot, across the grain of the mountains. After a week of very rough traveling following game trails, they stopped to relax on the warm, yellow sand beach at the south end of Lac St-Sacrement. There they made a shelter and set snares, and cooked rabbits.

It was a beautiful place. The deep, clear lake abounded with whitefish and trout and there was still plentiful game in the forested mountains that descended steeply to its shores.

They rested there four days. For many hours, they remained in a companionable silence, watching nature's show, but when they did talk, always their conversation returned to politics.

Marten was calm and spoke with finality. "I am ashamed to say that I am learning to love the comfort of white things. I am getting too old for the trail and the warpath, my son. I fear, too, that my people are now too dependent on these things to go back to the old ways. There have been no beavers in this part of the world since before my father's time. What will happen to us when the whites no longer need us?

"Already, your Governor Corlaer shows us no more respect than the Albany devils, since you are no longer his Indian agent. Without you there, Billy, his attitude is entirely ignorant and uncaring."

Billy's face was serious, but when he remained silent, Marten continued, "The New Englanders have offered to help us move to Stockbridge, where they wish us to become their allies. It is an attractive offer."

Billy smiled at that and shook his head. "But you cannot accept, because you know that the Albanians would then move onto your ancestral lands forever, and your own paths to Onondaga and the heart of the Confederacy would be blocked."

Marten scowled at him. "You speak the truth, Billy. The Albany thieves that have claimed the land under our castles for many years would win. But you should not smile in such an unseemly fashion at our difficulty."

"I smile only at the ignorance of the New Englanders, who ought to know better, my father."

Marten grunted, mollified. "Your tongue is as sweet as ever to your elders, Billy."

He drew on his pipe and expelled a large puff of smoke. *We must persuade Corlaer to re-appoint him, or we are lost.*

Billy slapped at a deerfly that had ceased buzzing irritatingly around his head and had landed on his arm. He felt satisfaction as he brushed it onto the sand. The bite of the spotted-wing flies felt like a red-hot needle.

They watched a large black-and-white osprey circle briefly and then plummet from a hundred feet into the calm lake. It rested for a moment, floating on the surface, and then flew laboriously away. Its wings thrashed the water for many yards until it was fully in the air again, a two-foot trout in the iron grip of its talons.

Marten said, "He is lucky the eagles have not seen him. I have watched them frighten the fish hawks into dropping their catch many times."

Billy agreed. "The white-headed eagles in particular like to bully the smaller ones into giving up fish, rather than hunt for themselves. Once, I even watched them catch a fish before it hit the water again."

They watched the osprey flap its way up the lake.

Billy stood. "I had a true dream last night, my father. I am going to go into the lake to cleanse me of all evil, and then I will see what I will tell you of it."

He stripped off his woolen shirt and breeches and walked naked into the cool water. He stayed in the water an hour, occasionally ducking beneath for a moment, then returned to the beach. It was early afternoon and the spring sun was hot. He was dry in half an hour, and then he put his clothes back on.

Marten refrained from asking him about the dream; it was impolite. They smoked several pipes. After a time Billy said, "I believe the dream is cleansed of all white evils, but," he hesitated, "I will lay the dream before you and leave it for you to judge whether that is true, Father, and I will fully accept your judgment."

"This must be a very difficult dream to fulfill," Marten smiled briefly.

Billy looked at the sand, then up at his companion. "Marten, my dream is that I will build a great house on your people's land, in the hills below the German Flats. The Eastern Council fire of the Haudenosaunee will burn there. I will build a church there too, and a village and great farms, and they will bring wealth and be a refuge for your people and mine. There are great storms coming, but during my lifetime, this place will always be safe."

Marten was silent for two pipes.

It is hard to hate the English, when there is one like this one.

Then he spoke softly. "Our fortunes are forever tied together, Billy Smithyman. You are ours, and we are yours. We will not prosper without you, and you cannot prosper without us. I accept the truth of your dream, and I see none of the white evils in it, for I can see your heart. I will bring it to the Mohawk Gantowisas, and I am sure that they and their sachems will agree to give you this land."

They ate rabbit in silence. Then Marten sighed, and spoke again. "Do not take this in the wrong way, my son, but I will dream with you no more. That time is now passed away."

He continued, "I am going to go, with some others, to speak directly to Corlaer in New York, very soon. The Mohawk Gantowisas have sent their sachems to me with messages. All the messages are the same. We will ask Corlaer only once more to speak clearly to us. We will ask him to act on our behalf to revoke the ancient false land claims of Albany. If he is not willing to do this, it will be a sign to us that the Great Covenant Chain between our peoples is broken, and we will tell him clearly what is in our hearts."

Billy was thinking. "Ultimatums are sometimes useful," he said eventually, "but this..."

Marten glanced at him. "You resigned in the same fashion. Since our losses in King George's War, we now count only a few hundred Mohawk warriors, Billy. How much longer do you think we can survive, even within the Confederacy, if we cannot show to friends and enemies alike that Corlaer continues to respect us?"

Billy said, "I understand this, my father. Does the Grand Council at Onondaga know what you intend?"

Marten was silent.

Billy nodded, "If you are not respectful in your speeches to Corlaer, I may need to rebuke you, later, since I yet serve on his council. And the Grand Council at Onondaga will need to be shown that I do not speak for Mohawks only, in my support for your claims."

Marten's scar twitched. "We will accept your rebukes, but your actions are what we respect, my English son. You always sent food, and gifts, and black woolen strouds and clothing to the widows of our raids. Your condolences show your love and respect. Corlaer and the Albanians have done nothing, not even with words. Words are important decorations, but actions are the true measure of our friends."

Billy was silent a moment in the face of this praise, but then said, "The French raid at Pickawillany will help our cause."

A few weeks later, Turnbottle sent by express a bundle of newspapers and a very brief covering note.

Emperor Marten and the other chiefs have well and truly got the pigeons flying about down here, Billy! They have declared that the Covenant Chain is broken. I am sure you will soon be hearing of this, to your advantage.

"Some related birds shall be coming home to roost from London, as well, as soon as the minutes of the Governor's address to the Assembly are known over there. On this, I have no doubt at all.

A savage glee came over Billy when the official request arrived from the Assembly a few days later. He said to Laura, "Perhaps my time is yet coming; the dogs in the Assembly now want me to go to Onondaga, to rebuild the Covenant Chain on their behalf, since they say that all other paths between the Six Nations and Albany are now closed. They now get neither news of the French activities, nor of the Six Nations."

Billy spent a week at Onondaga, and he returned in triumph with belts that "wiped away all the tears and buried the current animosities at the bottom of a bottomless lake." Awaiting him at Smithyman House was an invitation to the induction of Governor Clayton's replacement, expected to be only two weeks away.

The new governor, Sir Danvers Osborne, arrived on October 7, 1753. In the presence of the Council, Governor Clayton swore him in and handed over the seals of office. Grudgingly carrying out his previous instructions from the King at the last possible minute, he finally executed the months-old warrant he had in hand from the Board of Trade, promoting De Vere from Solicitor General to Lieutenant Governor.

The entire official party began to proceed in carriages to the New York Town Hall, where it was traditional to read the new Governor's commission to the people, but a riot began, directed against Clayton, and the party had to retreat to the fort. A huge fireworks display and cannon fire lit up the sky during the evening. It failed to amuse the new Governor, who seemed distracted by the animosity shown to his predecessor.

The next day the new Governor related to his Council that the Crown had directed him specifically to insist upon a permanent salary, to replace the temporary ones that Clayton, despite his protests, had been forced to accept at the whim of the Assembly. He asked them what they thought might be the response of the elected Assembly to this order from England.

The Council was appalled. They unanimously informed him that the New York Legislative Assembly would never submit to this demand, which could not be enforced in any conceivable way. Governor Osborne seemed shaken and melancholy at this.

He was overheard to say, half to himself, "Then what am I sent here for?" He retired for the evening, but he was so unwell that he summoned a physician. The next morning, he was discovered dead by his own hand, hanging by the neck from the high iron fence around the garden. Jacob De Vere now became Acting Governor.

*****

Edward Stoatfester was in New York when he heard the news. He was trying to remember when it was that his hands began to shake all the time.

Certainly they would always do that when someone provoked me, like that stupid little sow, Anneke. He remembered that his hands had shaken violently for a week when he had learned she was marrying the stick-boy Livingston.

"Or when Smithyman's name comes up," an acid little voice whispered.

He nodded to himself. *Yes, yes, that hypocritical charlatan has often made me shake with rage.*

Now, left and right, they seemed to twitch slightly, unpredictably, all the time. So, he had begun to have to focus intently to keep his penmanship satisfactory for Voortman and De Vere.

Satisfactory. Oh, yes, especially for De Vere, now that that bootlicking arse-sniffer had become Acting Governor.

He downed several swift glasses of brandy, and the tremors began to subside.

He had gradually recovered from his prolonged fit of jealous rage at imagining Anneke and Smithyman together, and his natural instinct for dissembling meant that he was never charged with the murder of the prostitute. He had kept a very low profile for months, sensing the eyes of his employers were looking to find any reason to confirm the suspicions of their informants.

Voortman had finally let him go on leave to New York, a blessed week away he asked for each year, when he could roam the teeming streets by day or night in complete anonymity, if he was careful to avoid De Vere's favorite haunts. He had established a den above one of the East River taverns; one he had used several times. He had paid twice the going rent to keep it available for him at short notice.

He was careful never to bring a whore there. Over two years, several of the waterfront prostitutes were beaten to death, but no one had looked very closely into it.

The fat Dutchman and De Vere betrayed me. He had been urging them to continue the campaign to bring Smithyman to his knees, but they had spurned him.

"This is the time for more sophisticated dealings with Smithyman," De Vere had told Stoatfester in his sneering way, as if he, Edward Stoatfester, were some ignorant colonial peasant. "Smithyman is now on the Governor's Council, and there will be scrutiny of attacks on him which will penetrate any crudeness."

He remembered having to consciously push both hands firmly down on the table for several minutes to avoid showering ink over the minutes of that meeting.

Now he ground his teeth violently together. What to do with Smithyman? *If only the Oneida had finished him.*

Voortman and De Vere had been extremely angry at having to clean up the public mess the murder attempt had created. *But if I had succeeded, they would be eating out of my hand today.*

However, Smithyman was more wary, now, and his ignorant savage friends seemed to have an uncanny way of making all his native contacts vanish, mostly after taking his money, the dogs.

He gulped two more brandies.

No, I will have to do it myself, won't I just? And it will have to be here, in New York, because no one can attack him at home, or in Albany anymore. Unless the French go to war and do it for me.

The trembling was gone. He was calm.

It was time to go out hunting.

CHAPTER THIRTY THREE
The Great Albany Congress, 1754

"Where are those bloody Mohawks?" De Vere was pacing inside his quarters in the Fort on the hill above Albany. Four New York Councilors, including Billy, had accompanied him to what was becoming known as the Great Covenant Chain Congress of 1754. They had already waited a week. The other native nations had arrived, but none of the Mohawks. Billy knew the question was rhetorical. Everyone knew very well where the Mohawks were. They just weren't here.

De Vere's patience was wearing thin and he was jittery. "Even four Senecas have come. I am being plagued with complaints about the land frauds. Seven of the colonies have sent delegates. Some of them, Massachusetts in particular, are once again pressing me about uniting for defense against the French and dealing with the Indians. That man Benjamin Franklin seems inexhaustible on the subject. Did you see his cartoon of the snake cut in pieces?"

One of the other Councilors spoke up. "Yes, Governor, 'Unite or Die' was its message. And unity is precisely what the Royal Board of Trade has directed for the defense of the colonies, in particular for negotiations with the Six Nations, is it not?"

De Vere snapped at him, "I will not yield control of negotiations over the Covenant Chain to anyone. That is a New York responsibility. The Mohawks will come, and they will leave, and the minutes will show the Board of Trade that all is well, and they will also show that New York still is in charge of the negotiations."

The Councilor smiled, and said, "It seems very apparent right now that it is the Mohawks who have control, not you, nor the other colonies."

De Vere glared at him, and then turned to Billy. "Smithyman, what say you about your friends? Why aren't they here?"

Billy said, "I have heard that they are conducting condolences at every settlement where they lost warriors in King George's War, to make up for the sentiments your predecessor failed to demonstrate."

De Vere said, "Send for them, Smithyman, this farce has gone on long enough. We need to begin the Congress." Billy smiled and nodded. "If you request it, Governor."

*****

Marten met Billy at Smithyman House a week after the Congress had ended. He remarked on the rebuilt palisades. "I see you are now properly defended. We can call this place Fort Smithyman again, I think."

After smoking several pipes, he meekly inquired about Billy's impressions of the Congress. Billy was non-committal, amused at the vanity of the old warrior.

Marten was finally forced to ask directly, "Did you like my speeches, my son?"

Billy slapped him on the arm and laughed, relenting. "You were truly magnificent, my father. When you threw the sticks behind you, describing how the Albany commissioners treat you, it was extremely eloquent. Moreover, all of the delegates from the colonies were very alarmed when you turned to the Albanians and told them, "The Council fire in Albany is burnt out.""

Marten absorbed the compliments gravely. "And yet De Vere still does not ask you to return as Indian agent. Did we fail?"

Billy shook his head. "To be truthful, Father, I will not accept an appointment from him, and he knows this. I also refused the new contract to supply Oswego, since they have not paid me for the last war."

Marten frowned. "How, then, will we get what we need, Billy?"

"Marten, your eloquent request for me to replace the Albany Indian Commissioners will be in the official Congress reports that have gone to England, and so will my speech recommending several actions to deal with the Six Nations, which I made after you departed with such ceremony. I am certain that the new French attacks will also make them act in our favor.

"It will also now be very clear to them that although they wish their colonies in America to unite for strength, this will not happen voluntarily. London will have to act, be sure of it."

Marten said, "At least the gifts were plentiful. Even the Senecas were pleased. It will make those who have moved to Oswegatchie remember the high quality of English goods."

Billy regarded him steadily for several seconds, his face as expressionless as possible. "Your people sold off the Wyoming country twice during the Congress. Once to Pennsylvania and again to the Connecticut Company."

Marten grimaced, and the snake-scar whitened. "That slug Cornelius...." He spread his hands.

"We did not intend a trick. I did not sign the second deed. But what are we to do, my son? If we do not sell these lands now, your people will simply take them from us and we will have lost them anyway. Most of my people cannot see this, but I know we are falling into the bottomless lake."

He stared at Billy. "At least, if we sell lands west of the Delaware River, it keeps the settlers out of our homeland to the north."

He smiled slightly and puffed again on his pipe. "We are learning from you. Now the whites can argue over ownership among themselves, instead of with us."

Marten changed the subject. "What is the story you have heard about the battles in the west?"

Billy frowned. "It is not good news. It appears there were two battles. In the first, the Virginians surprised a small French patrol and defeated them. In the second, the French surrounded and defeated the entire force of Virginians, and forced Major Washington to surrender, and retreat across the mountains. I expect this will make London accept that there is actual war on the frontiers here."

Marten nodded. "I have heard similar things. It is not easy for my people to see how the French can be beaten. They are far more vigorous than you English."

"Your doubt is understandable," Billy agreed, "but the English are much more numerous than the French, and once begun, with your help we will be unstoppable."

"Your people truly are made of wet wood, since the fire in them is always so hard to light."

Billy laughed. "Your body may be weaker and slower than it used to be, my father, but your wit is as strong and quick as ever."

Laura and the children arrived at the shore to play, and the men spent the rest of the afternoon fending off determined assaults, while Laura watched them fondly, nursing Polly. Marten's pierced ears and nose had been substantially mauled by the time Laura herded Thomas and Anna Christine back inside the twelve-foot palisade, where the sharpened logs were still weeping their sticky, pungent sap.

*****

A letter summoning Billy to the Governor's Council arrived in mid-February. He discussed it with Laura and sent word to Marten.

"It is possible I will be there for several weeks," he said to her. "London is sending troops. And if General Braddock arrives while I am there, I will have to stay longer."

Laura said, "The Valley is not safe, and we are not safe here now either, Billy. You must tell them to send some soldiers and cannon to defend us here."

Billy smiled at her. "I think we will see some support come here very soon. The Assembly is frightened; otherwise it would not have voted forty-five thousand pounds." He hugged her close.

"And after I showed them the New England silver that we captured, even De Vere could not prevent them from making trading with the French illegal. They are crying very salty tears in Albany."

"Do you think they finally understand us, Billy?"

His smile died. "No. In truth, my love, they never will. We have made them see that they need your people now, though the time is coming when they will think they do not need you anymore. The Keepers of the Eastern Door have done so much for us; no one could have been more loyal. If we succeed, for a time, it is because of your people's love, which has allowed me to help you."

Marten delivered a large belt and a letter for Lieutenant Governor De Vere from the Mohawks. Billy walked back to the river's edge with him and said, "I think we have got their attention in London with your eloquence, my father, and with the actions of the French."

Marten said, "Your wisdom is our river to the future, and the Keepers of the Eastern Door will swim it with you, to its end."

*****

When Billy returned from New York two months later, he did so in triumph. Braddock had appointed him Superintendent of Northern Indian Affairs and Major General in command of the Crown Point expedition.

Laura was overjoyed, but nervous at the same time. "My love, our people will all come here. Their excitement will be like mine."

Billy grinned at her. "But you are not smiling. What is keeping you unhappy?"

She swept her hand around and almost wailed. "There will be more of my people here than have ever gathered in one place. Our home will be too crowded for them all. What will they eat?"

Billy swept her into his arms. "We will cope, we always have, and Io'tonhwahere will deepen the waters for your people."

His hands began to wander, and Laura responded, pressing against him, but then she drew slowly away and murmured, "I must begin preparations now, Billy, or we will be swept away, and it is important that we receive them well."

He sent belts to all Iroquois nations, calling them to a council of war at Fort Smithyman.

In a month, more than a thousand had gathered, warriors and ancients, women and children. Within a few days of their arrival, they had trampled flat the acres of garden and pasture around Billy's estate. He sent frantic messages downriver to send food, presents, and weapons.

Marten huffed his wheezing laugh. "You see, my son, your friends have come."

Billy was feeling harassed. "We must begin the council soon, Marten. I also have to put the white armies together in Albany for our attack on Crown Point. I would like Red Head to do the ceremonial translations."

Marten agreed. "Kaghsuaghtioni is a good speaker, and it will be good to have an Onondagan officiate. This will help the League to respond with one mind, especially since he is one that the French have strongly influenced."

At the opening of the Council, Billy told them, "The tree which you desired is now raised, and fixed in the earth. Its branches will be a comfortable and extensive shade for you and all your allies, and its roots, I, Io'tonwhahere, will water forever. I have removed the embers from Albany, and I have rekindled the Great Council Fire at this place. I shall feed this fire with such wood as will give the clearest light and the greatest warmth."

He threw down a large war belt. "I call on you to join your brothers and me against our common enemy. The English have been long asleep, but now they are wide awake. They are slow to spill blood, but when they begin they are like angry wolves, and the French will fly before them like deer." When an Oneida sachem snatched up the red belt, the somber war dance began.

After the last day of the Council, Billy went to see Marten. He explained Braddock's campaign by holding up his hand and counted using his fingers. "Four attacks this summer, my father. Braddock will take two Irish regiments and some Virginians and go back to the Ohio Valley. The Governor of New England will go from Oswego to attack Niagara, and then go south to meet Braddock at Fort Duquesne. The third attack will go from Boston to Nova Scotia to throw the French out of our land there. The fourth is our attack on Crown Point."

Marten looked at him in silence for a few seconds. "This is an ambitious plan for one summer, my son. Would it not have been better to accomplish just one of these things?"

Billy shrugged, and scratched his eyebrow. "Braddock seems very confident that there are enough troops. We will need many warriors, my father."

"We will come," Marten replied.

"Then Crown Point will be ours," said Billy, "and it matters not what the rest will do."

Marten puffed at his pipe and looked at him. "That, I wish to see, before I die."

Chapter Thirty Four
The Oneida Carry, 1755

James Haye whistled to himself as he worked the croze chisel deftly around the inside of the fragrant, rot-resistant cedarwood pail, cutting the v-groove into which he would set its new wood bottom.

Daylight permitting, I just might be able to personally deliver this handsome little item to Linda McCann and her family this evening, and dam'd if it isn't one of the nicest pails I've ever made, although perhaps just a wee bit on the heavy side. It will last longer that way, any road.

The powerful muscles in Haye's bare back and arms, already tanned a deep brown, rippled smoothly as he shifted to a new position. The crude door of the work shed on the end of his little hut stood wide open. A broad shaft of June sunlight warmed his back and transmuted into silver the floating motes of dust raised by his exertions.

Now and again, he glanced at the Mohawk River, a few dozen yards away. The cool water beckoned seductively, but he looked forward to finishing this project and having a pipe and perhaps a beer in the evening.

It has been a good season so far, he thought with satisfaction. The summer appeared to be filling with as much coopering work as he could handle for salt pork and flour barrels. Billy Smithyman seemed to be working up to buying everything he could make and then some, not to mention the army itself, which if rumor had it right, was setting itself up to kick the French out of the Colonies and Canada, once and for all.

Too, the army paid in coin, and his tiny cache, hidden with care underneath the huge stump behind the shed, was slowly growing heavier. Perhaps this fall he might purchase one of those superb, accurate rifles from the German gunsmiths down in Pennsylvania that Johannes had told him about. His worn out smooth-bore musket could barely hit a deer from thirty paces anymore. He had fired one of the beautiful long rifles with their deeply notched stocks only once, but it threw its ball true for an unbelievable distance.

He set down the croze and walked behind the shed to relieve himself in the woods just beyond his little garden. Corn, beans and peas were sprouting precariously out of the tops of little heaps of dirt, scratched laboriously from in between the boulders and stumps. Still, his crop seemed to be thrusting skyward with vigor.

There had been no rain for two weeks, but the earth was not yet showing signs of dryness. He picked several large stones from the ground and heaved them onto one of the piles beginning to mound around his plot. They annoyed him, although the older settlers said that they helped moisture stay in the soil.

Suddenly, James heard a noisy series of wild whoops and startling calls behind him, and he turned to see a particularly frightful-looking group of Ojibwa carrying bales of furs and their huge trading canoe from Wood's Creek to the Mohawk. He reflected that there had been far fewer of them so far this year, an ominous sign, and the ones he had seen were less and less respectful of the whites they met.

The little fort and the tiny hamlet, huddled at the height of land between the watershed of the Great Lakes and the watershed of the Mohawk and Hudson Rivers, seemed very vulnerable indeed.

Life was getting better, no doubt about it, but in the early summer of 1755, people were becoming alarmed by disturbing stories and reports of renewed attacks on settlers to the west and in New England by the French and their Indian allies. Everyone wondered uneasily what the Six Nation Iroquois, on whose land they squatted, felt about it all. Many prayed that Billy Smithyman and his Mohawk wife, Laura, could protect them.

As the afternoon cooled down, James thought he might wander over to Stobo McLatchie's to hear the latest news. On the way back, he could stop at McCann's farm, deliver the bucket, and see if Linda wished to go for a walk. He found that Linda was filling his thoughts nowadays.

Stobo McLatchie was a towering, brawny lowland Scot, covered, apparently from head to foot, in flaming, bushy red hair. Stobo was missing one leg below the knee, after fighting for the Campbells and the British Army at Culloden. An early volley from the doomed Highlanders had shattered his shin with a musket ball, and his dream of farming had ended in the same cold wind of defeat and slaughter that had finally chilled forever the hot dreams of the Jacobites and their Bonnie Prince Charlie.

The victorious English took care of the clans that had supported them, and Stobo had received a merciful and life-saving amputation from a sympathetic army surgeon. In a few weeks, he had recovered sufficiently to look about, but saw little cheer in his prospects. Word of better possibilities in the frontier colonies in North America moved him to pledge his honor and his tiny parcel of land for a loan and a perfunctory letter of introduction.

They were sufficient to carry him to Albany where, rumor had it, he had been invited west by Billy Smithyman himself. If Billy had staked him to the construction of his Inn at Wood's Creek and his first barrels of whiskey, rum and beer, then he had repaid his benefactors' gamble and generosity. Moreover, Smithyman, James knew, rewarded loyalty.

Several hard-drinking men, mostly traders, normally inhabited Stobo's Inn at any given hour of its working day, which normally began about ten and ended indeterminately, depending on the glowering owner's mood.

James eased his way into the dark, smoky lair and stood blinking for a moment while his eyes adjusted. Even with the blackness inside lessened by the spitting glare of a few pitch-pine knots, the lengthening June twilight outside provided enough contrast to force immobility. He had seen many fights develop right at the door, so he made sure he did not trip over some aggressive drunk.

Several neighbors hallooed and he waved, sightlessly. After a few seconds he perceived his path clearly enough to make his way across the stone-hard dirt floor to where Stobo presided at the bar. As he frequently did, Stobo was caressing the gleaming four-foot blade of his razor-sharp claymore with a filthy tallow-soaked rag. James knew better than to interrupt the ritual.

Newcomers and travelers often rudely demanded service while Stobo stroked his sword. Occasionally, they found its point at their throat in an unbelievably swift movement. Few ignored the hint. Brash customers with the ignorant or drunken temerity to object, or insist, often retreated from the Inn with a permanent souvenir in the form of a lost earlobe. It had become something of a badge of courage, and several of the current patrons were slightly lopsided, when viewed closely, face-on.

James marveled occasionally that few had ever returned with a pistol to challenge Stobo's authority to mark them as a disrespectful customer. But Stobo also had legendary skills in detecting murderous intent in those who entered, abilities honed in the bloody homelands where sword fights erupted over the most insignificant slight.

The necessary pause at the door allowed Stobo to assess a problem at its outset. The strategic and frequently changing placement of tables and chairs forced anyone coming in to turn and weave before getting to the bar.

And, after all, his drinks and tobacco were cheap, and the damage to customers' visages, although permanent, was trifling.... especially on the frontier, where scalping was a way of life among whites and natives alike, and horrific tales about the torture of captives by friendly and hostile Indians were everyday frontier lore.

The tiny community respected Stobo, although the New Englanders, the Dutch, and the English, as well as the Germans in the area, tended to view these outlandish Celts with suspicion. But it was reassuring to have a veteran soldier, armed and dangerous, in their midst when a hostile raiding party might appear out of the forest at any time. This had been happening to the east and west, just like in the last war.

The Inn was located beside the carrying road, near the centre of the hamlet, and was built of massive squared logs, loop holed for muskets in every room and chinked with mud and grasses from the riverbank. Stobo had covered the gently pitched roof in turf and it met the ground on the north side. Several feral-looking goats normally grazed on it. It predated the unfinished British stockade and blockhouse at the Wood's Creek end of the Oneida carrying place. This crude, box-shaped palisade now glorified itself as Fort Bull. A hundred redcoats manned it.

Its commander, Captain Fisher, had sought Stobo's counsel on possible co-operation for defense, an unusually humble attitude for a regular army garrison commander fresh from purchasing his commission in Somerset. However, as a newcomer he felt the oppressive, dark menace from the hostile inhabitants of the forest more keenly than many.

James leaned an elbow on the bar and waited patiently until the sword was safely returned to its rack on the wall behind the bar. Stobo glowered at him, and James grinned back, sliding two precious pence of his hoard onto the raw hemlock planks, ineradicably stained with years of froth and crude fur trader food.

"And how's the beer today, Stobo?"

Stobo retrieved a wooden piggen from under the bar.

"As ye well know, Cooper Haye, it's the best ye'll get west of Albany, and seeing as how ye sold me these leaky little piggens, ye'll get your beer in one of them."

He turned the wooden tap on the barrel until the mug was filled to overflowing, then slammed it down in front of James, shedding surf onto the bar. A gigantic paw covered with red hair deftly swept the coins into Stobo's grimy leather apron.

James gulped a large mouthful of the warm, murky brew and set the wooden mug down again, its single handle jutting straight up. When the giant Scot returned from an expedition around the tables, James inquired, mildly, about news.

A gale force diatribe in unintelligible Gaelic blew past his ears. Several of the men in the room grinned and raised their drinks toward the bar. Loud choruses of "Speak civilized" erupted. Stobo waved a knife menacingly at the room, shaking his head like one of his long-horned highland cattle.

"Ignorant rabble," Stobo grunted, returning the dirk to its place in his rough woolen stocking. Stobo valued the Sgain Dubh highly, he had taken it from a fallen Jacobite chieftain at Culloden, and the hilt was silver and pearls, with a large amber set in the pommel. He looked directly at James.

"Our fine neighbor Billy Smithyman is to build an army to attack Crown Point and knock the Frenchies back to Canada, me laddie. He is gathering all the New York militias in Albany. Massachusetts, Connecticut and Rhode Island are sending men, too. Many have already left. Mayhap I should close up and go as well. I've na' hae a good fight in months." The red beard parted and bared a set of decaying brown fangs.

James nodded. In the corner, lit by a single guttering tallow candle, several of his acquaintances and neighbors were absorbed in an increasingly boisterous card game. A regular army sergeant from Fort Bull entered and paused at the door, then strode purposefully to the bar. Stobo poured another pint of beer and banged it down, taking the sergeant's coin. The red-coated soldier downed half in one long swallow, then the second half, and then beckoned Stobo for a refill. James moved a little closer, and spoke.

"Rumor has it you've got a beatin' warrant for volunteers, Sergeant."

The sergeant turned his head and stared silently at James for several seconds.

"Yes, and d'ye fancy yourself a real soldier, then, boy?"

James smiled, thinly.

"I can shoot and load as good as most."

"Can ye now?" The sergeant chuckled, softly, into his beer. "An' can ye do it when ye see the cold steel comin' at ye?"

James nodded. "As good as most, I expect."

The Sergeant plucked a silver coin from a pocket and placed it between them.

"Take it an' yer on the roll, Cooper Haye. Ye'll get sixpence a day, all necessary provisions, arms and accoutrements. When the expedition is over ye'll be discharged and sent home here."

The Sergeant smiled and continued, "But, if ye miss the muster tomorrow outside the fort, or any other fine day, for that matter, ye'll be in irons in a day and I'll have the great personal pleasure o' setting up the triangle an' floggin' yer back to red ribbons."

James stared at the shilling, with its four little crowned symbols. There was not much silver to be had at Wood's Creek.

"An' where'd the Army be wanting to take me, then?" he inquired, after a pause.

"Now that'd be tellin', wouldn't it, Goodman Haye?" The Sergeant cursed, mildly, "But then I don't imagine there's many spyin' for the French in here, now, is there? The 50th and 51st Regiments of Foot, pitiful and half-trained that most of them are, have orders to go up to Fort Oswego, with a few soldiers like me to go nurse 'em along.

"General Lindsay's orders is to go a-sailing from there to the west up Lake Ontario and take Fort Niagara away from the Frogs. He's also got a few hundred New Jersey Volunteers, in their nice new blue jackets, which I hear he's mighty pleased to have kept away from your Billy Smithyman."

The sergeant made a sudden disdainful gesture, like flicking water off his fingertips, and spat.

"Lindsay ain't asked me my opinion about it, mind you, an' ain't likely to, neither. But if I was in the council of the generals, I would have advised him that he ought to just cross Lake Ontario to the north from Oswego and take away Fort Frontenac, first, an' then let Niagara an' Fort Duquesne and the rest of the Ohio forts starve themselves. They can't get any supplies or soldiers up from Montreal if we hold Frontenac and Oswego, without going all the way over the top to the northwest an' then back down again. It'd be just like the jaws of a vise around the neck of New France."

James gulped his own beer.

"But," the Sergeant continued, his verbal river now in fine flow, "if Lindsay does take the army two hundred and fifty miles on west to attack Fort Niagara, the Frogs would have to be a lot more stupid than I think they are, not to just sail the fifty miles across Lake Ontario themselves and take Oswego away from us. An' that would be leaving the good old 50th and 51st Regiments of Foot an' myself stuck at Niagara, in hostile Indian country, without supplies or communications, like bright red pimples on a moose's arse!"

He glumly finished his second pint and ordered another.

"Ar, then, probably that's why I'm just a bloody good sergeant, not an officer, Haye. Maybe, if General Braddock and the 44th and 48th frighten them away from Fort Duquesne down at the forks of the Ohio, we'll be able to catch the Frenchies running back up to Niagara. From what I hear, Braddock should be on his way to thrash them by now, and your Colonel Washington an' some Virginians tagging along with them, too."

He chuckled, then. "Could be, Colonel Washington will be wanting to get revenge for the Frogs forcing him to surrender at Fort Necessity last year."

James left his hand very still, on the bar, far from the glinting coin. He had heard stories of 'accidental' enlistments.

"I think, Sergeant, that I might be more use to Wood's Creek if I stay with General Smithyman's militia in Albany."

The sergeant shrugged, but gave him another long stare. "You'll likely be seeing some shining French steel pretty soon anyway, boy, an' without even a single redcoat around who's seen it before, you won't like it much, I don't think. The regular army's all a-goin' to the forks of the Ohio, or Niagara, or out east to Louisbourg and Port-Royal."

It was James' turn to shrug, and he smiled at the Sergeant. "Last time Louisbourg fell, in '45, I hear it was the New England militia who took it, too. We'll be alright."

The Sergeant snorted. "You hadn't grown any hair yet when that happened. You might find yourself wishing you hadn't yet grown any, too, if what I hear from the frontiers is even part true."

The scarred hand at the end of his red-coated arm retrieved the coin and he raised his mug in faintly mocking praise, "Here's to Yankee Doodle pride in arms, then, boy."

James smiled again, and wished the Army luck. Eventually the soldier clumped out. James felt a gnawing in his belly, which reminded him of the receptive welcome he was likely to get at McCann's. He waved at Stobo, who gave him a mock salute.

He stepped out into the cool night and retrieved the precious bucket and his musket. The afternoon breeze had faded away. The tiny settlement was silent, apart from the usual clamor in Stobo's, now muted, and the forest seemed to be holding its breath, except for the normal chorus of late spring frogs, croaking and peeping, which accompanied him as he walked cautiously along the rutted wagon trail away from the tavern.

The moon would be late, and almost new, but even by starlight alone he could, with care, pick his way around the worst holes and stumps in the road.

After fifteen minutes he stopped, suddenly aware that all the nearby frogs had fallen silent. The hair on his neck prickled. Thumb on the hammer of his musket, he stood motionless on the trail, waiting for some sound, a clue from the forest.

The French, he had heard, and their Indians from the west and north, usually did not attack at night. However, this was the hungry time for bears and their new cubs after a long winter's hibernation.

Not for nothing did the natives wear bear's claws as a sign of courage.

After a few minutes, a bullfrog began again to sound its bass notes, calling for a mate or a fight, and soon the night resounded again with its companions and competitors.

Probably just a raccoon.

He resumed his walk. He grinned to himself. *Maybe they were just afraid of me!*

In another few hundred yards he passed the fort, calling to the sentries, and came to a familiar southward bend in the track, where it went to the landing place. He moved off to the right on a less well-defined trail.

Picking his way through the gloom under the overhanging trees slowed him somewhat, but ten minutes later, he saw a dim but welcome light in the blackness. He stopped and called out, "Goodman McCann, it'd be James Haye, here."

No sense being shot by a jittery homesteader.

When no answering call responded, he strode to the one-windowed shanty and knocked on the door. He repeated his announcement and after a moment the door swung open, revealing a strikingly beautiful young woman with pale blue eyes and long black hair, smiling a very warm smile indeed.

Her father's voice boomed out, just as she opened her mouth to greet him, "Linda, let the man come inside, girl."

James winked at her and entered, placing his musket carefully by the door, which she barred behind him. A bright fire of soft, resiny pine crackled and sparked in a fieldstone fireplace to his left. He nodded, smiling, to Linda's mother, who was stirring a large iron pot hanging over the fire. "Goody McCann, a nice evening t'ye."

She, too, smiled warmly in reply. "Hello, James."

James continued into the room and proffered the new bucket, saying, "I heard that one of the cows smashed your old bucket, so I made a new one for ye today."

The two women crowed over it, and he felt a certain dizzying depth to Linda's eyes when she looked at him again.

Farmer McCann beckoned him to the table.

"Sit ye down, son, sit ye down an' have your supper. You're still a bachelor and I know what bachelors eat. A good cook is what they all need."

Linda flushed, but kept her eyes on James' face.

"I'm always keen on the food at McCann's farm," he replied, taking a place at the table. A creased tin dish, filled to overflowing with stewed corn, beans, and meat, quickly appeared in front of him, along with a battered pewter spoon.

Farmer McCann, a short man with brawny forearms and a gap-toothed grin, his black hair tied in a short tail behind his head, watched approvingly as James wolfed down his food.

"Have ye heard, then, that Smithyman has been asked to put together an army, boy?"

James nodded, and wiped his mouth.

"I was hearing that the regulars are going off to Fort Oswego soon. I might go down to Albany and see if General Smithyman's new militia army don't need a cooper."

"Don't let them put you in the line, boy," warned McCann. "You've got a trade. Let the riffraff be the cannon fodder. Smithyman's never been a soldier himself, far as I heard. Might not be a party, if his army rubs up against the French."

James looked at Linda, briefly, then at her father. "No. I'd be thinking of bringing back some more cash money for making flour barrels, not a ball in the guts."

McCann burst out laughing; a harsh laugh. "Not much money in bringing back lead, one ball at a time, to be sure, boy, to be sure."

The older man was full of news. "Did you hear that Pennsylvania still won't fight, although they might be starting to change their minds? Some of that Ben Franklin's crowd brought in a whole Conestoga wagonload full of scalped settler families and unloaded them right on the steps of the Assembly."

"A fellow bringing provisions up to Oswego told me that, at Stobo's t'other night. He said it was in the newspaper. I surely can't understand those Quakers, not wanting to fight even when their neighbors and loved ones are being tortured right in front of 'em."

James nodded. "I'd surely want to take some of 'em with me, if I was certain to be dying."

"I think we'll whip them pretty quick, now London has sent over some real soldiers and generals. What say you, James?"

"I don't rightly know much about war, Farmer McCann, but the sergeant from Fort Bull I talked to at Stobo's tonight thinks the Frenchies are no pushover, and they've got a pretty large pack of Indians on their side nowadays, it seems. The paper said they've sent over some baron general with regular troops from France, too. And, from the militia training I've had, it seems that lining up armies in red or white coats and shooting each other down in rows ain't much of a way to fight Indians in the forest, is it?"

McCann just shook his head.

In a few more minutes, James rose and thanked his hosts. "It's late, and I'd better be getting on, then, Goodman McCann. I thank you for the supper, Goody, it was right delicious." Mrs. McCann beamed at him,

"James, it's nice to see you again. You come around anytime."

Linda rose to open the door, and as she handed him his musket her fingers seeming to linger, briefly, caressing its rigid barrel. She met his eyes, and he had a giddy sense of falling into that double pool, blue, so very blue.

"You'll want to keep this in good shape then, James," she said, softly.

He cleared his throat, with difficulty. "Thank you, Miss McCann, I'll, um, I'll be trying not to disappoint you."

Her eyes sparkled, like the summer river. "Oh, I'm quite sure your best will be good enough for me, Goodman Haye." A lightly mocking emphasis on the "man." A slight smile.

James felt a blush starting. He hastily turned to leave. Passing the fort once again on his way home, he strode unseeing into a young oak, hard enough to bloody his nose. Recoiling, he tripped and fell and a sentry challenged him. He replied, cursing, and then he shook his head, scattering scarlet drops, black in the moonlight and laughed softly. He still was a hopeless sap for females. He knew that tree very well, because he had carved a heart deeply into it, with Linda's name inside.

Trees, though they are cut and lopped, grow up again quickly, but if men are destroyed, it is not easy to get them again.

—Pericles—Plutarch, *Lives*

CHAPTER THIRTY FIVE
Encampment of the Crown Point Expeditionary Force, Lake George, September 7, 1755

Major-General Billy Smithyman lounged in the field chair in front of his white canvas tent and stared at the circle of his officers around the fire. He drank more rum punch and listened to their talk, some of it panicky, some of it downright foolish. He felt oddly content. His army had finished the road across the Great Carry from Fort Edward. The axe men, contracts paid out, had vanished in minutes.

He rubbed his stubbly face with one large hand and tilted his white-powdered head back, to look up at the indigo sky. It was a lovely evening.

There is Jupiter glowing like a spark. He had seen four of her moons in his new telescope, which had arrived from England just before summer.

Laura, who nourished his soul, was behind him in his tent. He remembered that morning, and smiled again at her ardent, slippery impatience.

Twice! Before breakfast, yet!

He was almost ready to end this jittery "council of war."

It was strange, though, to feel as happy as this. *Any player in the Dublin Royal Cockpit might well be willing to hazard several dozen guineas on a bet that I, and all my officers, will be staked out here tomorrow evening, with our feet roasting black in coals from this very fire, and an Ojibwa matron and her children gnawing my fingers off joint by joint to taste my courage, and my throat only a raw tube of flesh, from screaming out my death song.*

By tomorrow night, battle-hardened French regular troops, supported by a horde of tough Canadian militiamen and northern Indians and led by their veteran general, might well have defeated the last English army between them and New York City—an untrained, inexperienced militia army. *Ironical. My army.*

Billy smiled inwardly, remembering a dinner in Ireland long ago, when he defied his soldier father and scorned a military career.

Out of the jumble of querulous voices, he heard the quiet, competent rumble of Major Bolton, his artillery officer and the only professional soldier in his entire army. His mental focus sharpened.

That man made good sense.

He folded his extended right leg in its white linen breeches, and leaned forward towards the fire.

Mosquitoes and the coming darkness had not yet quite obscured any faces, although they flickered in and out of view, lit by the yellow flames. He could feel the coolness flowing down through the camp from the deep shadows of the forested hills, ruffling the centre of the dark, mirror-smooth lake behind them. His scarlet tunic still seemed as hot as lava, however, from the golden late-summer day.

He listened for a moment more, and then rose to his feet.

They are treading well-beaten ground again. It is decision time.

His officers stood when he did, by custom, although ancient and rotund Mohawk War Chief Emperor Marten stayed down, not surprisingly.

Marten wrinkled his obsidian eyes at Billy and smirked a little, which made the hatchet scar, stretching white and rough from mouth to ear, writhe like a snake. This was a familiar sight to his friends, but horrifying to the uninitiated.

Billy grinned back at him. "Marten," he said, "you've fought the French and their Indians for three score of years. What's your counsel tonight, my father?"

"My brother, let your Major Bolton and the rest speak what is in their minds to you first, and I will consider all their thoughts properly. I do say this, I would not willingly give Onontio my life tomorrow, as if it were a gift in return for all the scalps of his men that I have taken."

Billy nodded, and pointed his finger at Major Bolton, who saluted and began.

"Sir, it is my view that we must send a reconnaissance party back to scout, in order to check any attempt by the Baron's forces to cut us off from Albany.

"The French cannot leave us here, between their army and its supplies at Crown Point. Our main force should, therefore, remain here, ready to advance or defend, as the situation requires. I believe the French forces are roughly similar in size to ours, since they must have prudently left a garrison behind in Crown Point.

"We can be confident the Baron has not brought his guns, since no one has reported seeing any, and since he appeared behind us so quickly by traversing the drowned lands between us and South Bay. This he could not have done with guns. Our rear is adequately protected by Lake St-Sac..." he stopped, nodding to Billy, "My apologies, sir, Lake George." Billy had renamed the lake in honor of His Majesty on the day he had reached it with his army.

"Our flanks are sheltered by the swamps. We have cleared a decent field of fire between the forest and ourselves, although I would like to see this expanded to twice musket shot.

"No, General," he concluded, "the Baron must inevitably come to us now, and when he does, his army will come up the road. He knows we are an untrained militia and he will see this as an irresistible opportunity to use his regular French army units to make a quick meal of us."

The Major allowed himself a small, cold smile, which gleamed in the firelight.

"And that, General Smithyman, is why you have dragged our cannon, and me, all the way up here from New York. My only regret is that we have only solid shot with which to greet General Baron von Dietrich, no grapeshot or canister."

Billy nodded his thanks to Bolton, then turned slightly to face the blue-coated New Englanders, who were scowling, as usual.

"Colonel Truedell, what are your people's thoughts on this?"

The lanky Bostonian spoke in his irritating, nasal bray, "General Smithyman, if I may say so, with all due respect, it is a pity that your Indian friends..."

Billy blinked at that, the emphasis on 'friends' being another overt sneer. *By God, your Indian friends, indeed!*

"...cannot give us more precise intelligence than what we have heard."

Truedell went on. "If it is true that the French have a superior force of regular troops, then based on my considerable experience in besieging the fortress of Louisbourg in the last war, we must retire immediately back across the Carrying Place to our base at Fort Edward. There we must consolidate our forces and prepare our defenses."

Billy could see several New Englanders nodding. They commanded by far the biggest part of his odd civilian army.

As usual, the New York Assembly would not pay a shilling more than they felt they would get away with, even to defend their own homes from fire, bloodshed, and slavery. Too much of their income came from trading illegally with Montreal. That's why the New York militia assigned to the Crown Point expedition was the smallest contingent, other than the volunteers from Billy's own community, and had arrived late, of course. Billy had left them behind at Fort Edward. They constituted a last-ditch guard for the water route down the

Hudson River to Albany and New York City. At least Billy knew its commander to be reliable, for he had personally appointed Captain Crowell.

Billy was not oversensitive, but he knew that the puritan New Englanders hated him. If he had been willing to waste any time worrying about it, he might have agreed with them. He was a womanizer, an Indian-lover, and a luxury-craving, blasphemous, carousing, Church of England Irishman. Where his natural optimism and energy cheered his rag-tag, half-trained militia army, the blue-coated New England officers kept up their dour faces and daily church services. He knew he was also a unique phenomenon on the frontier, an honest Indian trader. Nearly everyone else hated Indians.

Best to draw out the rest of the pus, now.

"Colonel Fowler, what would you have us do?"

Colonel Fowler was commander of the Rhode Islanders, another of the Massachusetts Governor's protégés.

"General, I believe that Governor Lindsay wishes us to remain in place to distract the French from his important expedition to Niagara." Fowler gestured with his hand at the camp. "But this is no fort, merely a clearing in the wilderness, and the French will make short work of us here. I concur with Colonel Truedell. We should retire to Fort Edward as soon as possible, sir, drawing the French after us."

Billy could feel the beginnings of rage. He controlled it, but he did proceed with a pointed lecture. "Gentlemen, General Braddock may be killed, and his army ruined, but his written orders to me are clear, and you have all seen them. This army is to make an offensive against the fortress at Crown Point, not be a diversion.

"It is true, Colonel Truedell, this would be easier to accomplish if Governor Lindsay had not bribed so many of my warriors to eat free provisions at Oswego while he second-guesses General Braddock.

"And I am sure you would all agree that the five-hundred New Jersey militia who were supposed to be part of our force would also be far more useful here than waiting for boats to be built in Oswego. However, so be it. We, too, have a job." He turned again.

"Lieutenant FitzHugh."

"Sir?"

"Richard, what are the feelings of our local county fellows, tonight?"

"Sir, I believe the West Albanian Volunteers would not be pleased to go back down that road without a fight, after spending a week helping to build it. If I may say so, sir, the men have told me they would very much like to send the French back down there themselves, tomorrow."

Billy chuckled briefly. "My old friend, they may well think better of their wish when they're facing three hundred leveled French muskets and two thousand French Indians and Canadians coming out of the forest."

"Well, sir," Richard said daringly, "at least we won't be faced with the severe ethical problems some of us might encounter when having to be shooting at Irishmen on behalf of his Majesty, now, will we?"

Billy threw his head back and laughed at the familiar soft, lilting County Leinster accent. "No, Richard, no ethical problems, indeed."

He squared his shoulders and made his decision. "Gentlemen, I agree with Major Bolton. We will send a scouting party back down the road to Fort Edward to find out what is there. The wagon drivers are beginning to desert because they are afraid of the French Indians, and a show of force will reassure them as well.

"Colonel Fowler, you will command. I think we should send a force of five hundred, along with my Mohawk friends, to leave at dawn, tomorrow."

He turned to the old warrior. "What say you, Marten, to that plan?"

The expressionless focus of the Mohawk war chief traveled slowly, slug-like, around the circle of officers, moving across the face of each one, probing their souls. The silence stretched itself.

Marten finally took the brass-decorated, stone pipe from his mouth and said, without standing, "Most of your people think us to be dogs, my brother. I see that the Albany devils, who get us drunk and then steal our land, once more refuse to come here to die with us. They thought it more important to send some soldiers west over the mountains, and what has happened to them?

"The bodies of your red-coat soldiers and your General Braddock are in the forest by the forks of the Ohio River and their scalps are drying in the northlands. Because they arrogantly refused to listen to our counsel, the French and their Indians defeated them. Now they are dead, instead of being here to defend their own homes. The Shawnee and the French are now burning all the western settlements, and the English run away like smoke before the wind."

He sniffed theatrically and turned his eyes to Billy. "Brother, you know that we Mohawks, the Flint People, who guard the Eastern Door of the Six Nations' ancient homeland, we love you. Nevertheless, we are few when compared to all our ancient enemies, the Ojibwa of the Northwestern forests, and the O'dawa to the North and the Abenaki to the East.

"All these people the French treat well, very well. You, my brother, you offer English friendship, but do these others I see here offer anything? The French give our enemies victory and respect and do not cut down their forests.

"The Covenant Chain linking us to Corlaer, who represents your great King across the sea, is again strong and bright, my brother, but the Royal Governor of Massachusetts, who is in Oswego, tells us that he rules you now, since Braddock is dead. He offers silver coins each week, more silver coins than most of my people have ever seen. More coins than even the redcoat soldiers receive. We know these things are foolishness, but who can blame some of our warriors for listening to him?"

He swung his hand slightly at the darkness. "But you now see us here. Instead of hunting, the Mohawks follow our brother's call to fight, but you know that we have blood cousins in Montreal, whose warriors fight with the French. The autumn is upon us and a long winter now faces us, and we have not hunted. We know that perhaps the other Iroquois nations will not suffer as much as we, if they stay home."

Marten picked up several sticks and held them out. "No, my brother, I have listened to your soldiers here. If the French are now behind us, across your supply road—and my scouts agree that they are—we must fight. These are my thoughts on your scouting party.

"The force you want to send is like one of these sticks," he snapped one, "easy to break." He then bundled three or four together. "But if you send more, they will not break, like these sticks bundled together. My son, if you are sending these men to die, they are too many. If you send them to fight, they are too few. I will speak to my people, but this will be their opinion also."

Billy smiled wearily and said, "I would not defy your wisdom, Marten, but I must keep the main force together, as well. We think there are three thousand French and their Indians against us. We all know that two hundred Mohawk warriors are as two thousand in the forest. We will increase the British scouting force, to one thousand soldiers, if all Mohawk warriors will count themselves a part of it."

Marten grunted and struggled to his feet. "That is wiser. My brother, I will tell my people of your plan, I think they will agree, and to show that the Mohawks keep the Great Covenant Chain unbroken, I will myself lead them once more against the French at dawn, with your Colonel Fowler."

*****

On the road, the sun was high over the hills by ten o'clock.

Marten knew it was the end when the first musket fired, from behind them in the trees. The column stopped, although no one fell. There was a tiny wind, drifting up the road into their faces. In his mind, Marten began his death song, but when the echo faded and no fusillade followed, he called out in Iroquoian.

Back in the camp, Billy heard a single, distant shot echoing through the hills. He ordered silence.

"Brothers," Marten called, "why have you brought the Northerners and the French to Mohawk land?"

A derisive laugh and a hidden voice answered him. "You are an old fool, Mohawk. This land belongs to the Albanians. Are you willing to die for them? Join us, brother. The French will sweep the English dogs into the sea, and you will have your lands back."

Gradually, stillness spread through Billy's camp.

Marten heard his song begin again, in his mind. He said, "I have seen the greatness of the English people. Brother, it is the French who will vanish from this place like snow in summer. Be not deceived by the honey-tongued priests at Kahnewake and Oswegatchie."

The column of men stood perfectly still, on the narrow road filled with weeping stumps between the dark forest walls, and listened to a dialogue in the language of the forest. Colonel Fowler, on his horse beside Marten, breathed very softly. The smallest breath seemed to have taken on a weight capable of tipping the balance of the moment.

The response came. "The priests do not want our land, fool! Choose! You have no more time."

Marten overheard another voice in the forest, speaking more quietly, in Algonkian, "Enough of this delay. They must all die."

He said, loudly and clearly, so that all could hear within musket shot. "It is true that the priests do not want your land, they want your soul. And this, you have already sold to them."

Without waiting for a reply, he began to sing his death song. He unslung his musket, cocking it and firing it at the voices, in one smooth motion.

The forest erupted in smoke to right and left, enveloping the head of the scouting column in white powder smoke. Marten felt two balls tear into his horse, which reared in agony to his left. He managed to lift his leg out of the way, but fell across a stump, feeling ribs crack, and his head bounced, hard, off a root.

He struggled to all fours, breathless, a very old bear indeed. He shook his befeathered head from side to side, spraying blood and swinging his war hatchet at his shadowy attackers. He sang his song loudly, befitting the war chief of all the Mohawk. His song was a good one, and strong.

Before the farthest carpenters hammering bateaux together at the edge of Billy's camp had obeyed the order for silence, a fusillade erupted, invisible around the bend in the road, but clearly coming from where the last of the scouting force had vanished, half an hour before. The noise rose rapidly to a crescendo and then faded away, after a few minutes, to an irregular but constant bang, bang, bang. It began to move closer.

In seconds, Major Bolton appeared and saluted. "With your permission, sir," he said, "we should barricade the camp, now." Billy saluted in return, nodding his assent.

"Major, it appears as though you may now get the chance to exercise your guns, after all." Bolton smiled briefly and ran to the artillery. Billy turned and gave orders to his aides.

Men frantically began to thicken and raise the abatis barrier of felled trees that marked the camp perimeter. Overturned wagons and bateaux began to be heaped onto it. Billy dispatched a company to cover the retreat, which marched up the road double time in more or less orderly fashion and disappeared around the bend.

Within a few minutes, running figures burst into view. Staggering with fatigue and panic, many spattered with blood, latecomers more so; they clambered into the camp over the barricades and gasped out their story of ambush, disaster—and rout.

"The Mohawk Chief and...and Fowler, shot off their horses and scalped!"

"Thousands of Indians! They're right behind us!"

"Behind us! Musketry came from behind us, when we halted!"

Billy saw many of his troops begin to look covertly left and right, calculating their chances in the swamps and the forest. He called to them. He climbed onto a wagon, with his back to the road, and drew his sword, haranguing them, gesturing to their officers.

"Boys," he shouted, "listen to me. You had better think twice about heading off into the forest. It's full of French Indians right now, and you know they'd like nothing better than to sell your scalp in Montreal."

He waved his gleaming sword at the stump-filled clearing in front of them. "Look around you, lads, you've done good work. They have to cross this lovely lawn and climb this nice fence to get at you, don't they? You are hunters, many of you. You can hit a squirrel in that forest on the run, now, can't you?"

He paused. "At least, that's what the recruiting sergeant told me you said to him." He saw a few grins.

"Use your heads, men. Your best bet is to stay here, stand to your weapons and watch our cannons do their work. Settle down, now, take your cover and take your aim; this is what we came here for. We will take the Frenchmen down, here and now. How long have we been waiting to do this?"

The incoming flood of man ebbed to a trickle. Then a few stragglers came into view, most hobbling in pairs. The supporting company followed them closely in a more or less orderly fashion. It paused at the turn in the road to fire a volley and then trotted to the barricades. The road was briefly empty.

Billy had been conferring with some of the officers who had come back down the road. Then he called to two of the last men to reach the barricade. "You! Private! Yes, you, and you! Come here and tell me what you saw."

The soldiers looked about and, remembering themselves, stood straight, marched up to the General and stood at attention. Billy immediately recognized Johannes and grimaced. "You are supposed to be with our fellows, Johannes. What are you doing up there with the New Englanders?"

Johannes smiled happily. He was carrying one of the Pennsylvania rifles, which he had bought from his tutoring pay. "I could not resist, Herr General Smithyman, when James said we should go to try to kill some Frenchmen."

Billy looked more closely at the other soldier. He was breathing heavily and one leg was soaked red with blood from hip to boot, but he seemed not to be on the edge of panic.

"Haye, I recognize you, you're the cooper from Wood's Creek. What the devil were you doing out there? Are you hurt, son?"

James looked puzzled, and then looked down at his leg.

"Oh, no, sir, that's Corporal Whitney's blood. He took a ball through the ear right beside me, Sir."

"Tell me what happened."

"Well, sir, I thought I could help out there more than making barrels, so I tagged along with Colonel Fowler's people, sir, and Johannes decided to come, too. I think he saved my life. He shot down one of the French Indians, who was running at me from the forest."

Johannes shrugged. "It was an easy shot."

"What's behind you out there, Haye?"

James responded, "Well, sir, first there was a shot from the hill on the right, and we all stopped. The Mohawk Chief called something off into the forest, and there was some back and forth in Indian talk for a few minutes, then suddenly there was firing from both sides of the road, and behind us on the left, as well."

"I saw the Mohawk Chief fall off his horse, but then he was trying to get up. Colonel Fowler, sir, he had his horse shot down, too, but then he climbed on a rock and called us to charge the hill on the right."

He gulped some air. "But before we could get going, he was shot dead through the head. He fell on top of the sergeant. Then we saw the whole road in front fill with Indians and they were yelling and firing."

He looked around and then met Billy's eyes, "We ran, then, I'm afraid, sir."

"You didn't run far, son, did you?"

"Well, I stopped, sir, me an' Johannes an' some others, mostly because there was a column that kept decent order, backing us up. I hated to see them scalping our fellows like that, so I turned and shot a couple down, sir."

"Did you see any white uniforms, Haye?"

"Well, just before I turned the corner there, sir, I could hear some drumming and fifes and maybe there was some Frenchies on the road behind all the Indians, but I couldn't see them very well, too much smoke."

Billy slapped the younger man's shoulder. "Thank you, Haye. You and Johannes go, now, catch your breath, get some water and tell your friends that it's their turn to carry some of the load. It'll be all right, now."

The two militiamen nodded, then saluted and turned, running to the barricade like the teenagers they suddenly looked to be.

Billy looked up the now-empty road and felt a fist squeeze his heart. He heard Marten's calm voice then, as if he was standing there in the camp beside him.

We must all die, my friend. I go as a warrior, singing my song. Be happy for me, but you must keep your friendship with my people.

Through watering eyes, he watched the artillerymen fuss over the two thirty-two pounders pointing down the road, with one of the eighteen pounders between them, like parents with large wood and iron children.

Billy remembered the courage of the Abenaki brave, singing as he suffered, and of Yellow Knife, waiting for the opportunity to die an honorable death. A bright, cold flame of resolve ignited and then blazed up, clearing his mind and displacing grief. He turned, and found Colonel Truedell nearby. They exchanged salutes.

"I understand Colonel Fowler has been killed," Billy began, "and probably Emperor Marten. This is a grievous loss, so early in our battle."

Truedell nodded, but did not reply.

Billy continued, "I expect, however, that with the able help of you and your officers and men, we shall be as ready for the onslaught as we might be, sir. It appears that we have escaped a total slaughter of the scout, since the Indians and Canadians may have masked the volley firing of the French regulars.

"It is perhaps fortunate that our complete forces were not on the road, do you think? That initial shot appears to have triggered the trap prematurely."

Truedell finally found his tongue. "There is nowhere for us to retreat from here."

Billy nodded. "That is true, Colonel. That ought to make us and the men spend our lives dearly, if nothing else, don't you agree?"

"The Mohawks are leaving us. Your friends do not show much constancy under fire, General." Truedell even now could not hold his tongue, but Billy spoke calmly to his ignorance.

"I believe that you may well see some of them, at least, firing at the French from the forest very shortly, perhaps from behind them, which I understand is most disconcerting for soldiers.

"They are not to be kept in garrisons, even ones as crude as this," Billy continued. "Nevertheless, if Emperor Marten and other Mohawks are killed, our Iroquois will be angered. They will mourn for a time, but they will fight the harder for it, later. It will be a blood feud again."

Truedell remained argumentative. "It is today that we will need them, do you not think?"

Billy nodded, "It is disappointing, Colonel, but perhaps they have done their job already, by triggering this trap before it was entirely ready to be sprung. Several reports suggest there was a warning given, before the general firing began. Such a warning would not have been extended to you."

Colonel Truedell sniffed, but made no more comment, his face suddenly fixed with interest beyond the camp. Billy followed the direction of his gaze and saw an unruly mass of humanity boil around the far bend in the road half a mile away, and advance toward them without hesitation, at the speed of a fast run.

The two officers looked at each other and Truedell saluted first, before moving up to the barricade.

Billy could hear the men murmuring, but they held their fire. He caught the eye of Major Bolton, who waved his cocked hat back at him, almost gaily. At a quarter mile, the roiling, jogging mass of brown that filled the roadway from side to side now showed wild touches of bright color everywhere.

The attackers whooped and yelled and brandished muskets and hatchets and jumped and, here and there, waved a limp clump of something. At two hundred and fifty yards, the leaping, yelling figures could easily be distinguished one from another.

A few moments later, Major Bolton's gleaming sword swung down, and the three cannon at the end of the road bellowed, almost in unison. Three twenty-foot tongues of fire and white smoke leapt from the muzzles and the one-ton gun carriages jumped backwards.

Three channels tore open through the very midst of the oncoming horde, accompanied by flying clots of dirt. On the road there was a sudden, shocked silence, through which the faint sound of drums and fifes behind could briefly be heard. Then, cheers and jeers from the barricade drowned it out.

Frantically, artillerymen swabbed out, loaded, and rammed. Another triple volley flailed the air, but the road was already empty of painted brown bodies, apart from several heaps of largely motionless, glistening, reddened flesh.

A few puffs of white smoke jetted toward Billy's camp from the edges of the forest, indicating where the advance wave of the French army approached.

Now, inside the barricade, they could clearly hear the rattle of the drums and the piping high tunes, and a column of men in long grey-white overcoats and black cocked hats marched steadily closer, muskets shouldered. They deployed into lines, but the width of the road at first held them to merely a broadened column.

The English guns began to fire independently. The first rounds each cut several men down, but the white coats closed the gaps, their officers brandishing swords and marching backwards in front of them. At seventy yards from the waiting English, the four combined companies of the second battalions of the Régiment de la Reine and the Régiment de Languedoc stepped calmly into the clearing full of stumps and formed their proper line, three deep and seventy wide. Then the front rank presented its muskets and fired a volley, as one.

A cloud of white powder smoke jetted towards the makeshift barricade, and a thunderclap nearly as loud as the cannon assaulted the defenders. Seventy . 69-caliber musket balls hummed, and whickered, and slapped through the wood. They sent splinters flying and branches falling from the barricade and ricocheted noisily off cannon barrels and iron-shod wheels. Two or three voices began a dreadful shrieking.

The front rank knelt and began to reload, while the second rank leveled their muskets and fired another seventy lead balls. They, in turn, knelt, and the third rank repeated the volley.

By this time, the front rank had reloaded. Thus, one minute after beginning the engagement, they had delivered more than 200 rounds, or nearly 12 pounds of one-ounce lead balls traveling several hundred miles per hour, which blasted into and through the abatis.

Artillerymen were falling, but each cannon round blasted its short column of two or three white coated soldiers down among the stumps on the road, in return.

Billy felt an uncontrollable exhilaration rising within him. He turned and took a couple of steps back to where Colonel Truedell stood with several other New England officers, and remarked, "Well, Colonel, I do think that the Frenchies might be starting to wish they'd brought some artillery to the party too, do you agree?"

Truedell smiled thinly. "Sir, it has certainly steadied our boys to see the occasional file of white coats knocked down, to be sure."

As Billy began to turn back, a slightly irregular volley exploded in staccato bangs, yellow flashes and white smoke from the front row of the now battle-tattered white line.

An excruciating, white-hot hammer blow struck Billy just above the right hip, and he staggered forward. Truedell stepped forward to steady him. "Colonel, I am hit," Billy gasped into that impassive face.

"You have command, until I return." He took another step, his knees buckled, and the world spun away in a vortex of agony.

As his consciousness swam reluctantly up again from the painless abyss, he heard a familiar voice. "Jesus, Mary and Joseph, Billy, look at the blood! Are ye going to be alright now?"

Billy turned and recognized Richard. He smiled at his friend's raccoon-like face, blackened from powder smoke.

"Aye, FitzHugh," he replied, faintly, "I think the Monsieurs just shot me in the arse, you know."

The surgeon probed again with his filthy, bloody forefinger in the wound, and a white flash of agony burst anew in Billy Smithyman's eyes, instantly blotting out even the roar of the cannons.

A stream of blood-curdling Mohawk curses caused him to open his eyes again. Laura stood at the foot of the cot, holding a ten-inch scalping knife in one hand, and a birchbark bundle wrapped in spruce roots in the other.

The appalled and wide-eyed amateur army surgeon held up his blood-covered hands and arms to ward off the wicked upward lunge of the knife and backed into the sentry. Billy half rose and beckoned her. She glowered at him, her jet eyelashes wet with fear and suffering for him. He waved at the sentry, who allowed the surgeon to escape.

"My sweet pigeon," he murmured. "The man cannot remove the ball safely, I fear."

She glanced at him and rolled him gently but firmly onto his left side. She unwrapped her bundle and selected several items, soft and crumbly; green, brown, and grey. Then she gently pushed them into the track of the musket ball. In a few minutes, her gentle, searching, sensitive fingers had probed in and out of his groin and abdomen and found a hard lump, deep within his thigh. He cried out as she touched it, and her fingers instantly lifted, leaving it alone.

He said, "Laura, I must get up." She told him to lie still for another few minutes, and then slapped his shoulder, and when he looked back, she was smiling, sadly, but smiling all the same.

A soothing, cooling balm began to spread from his back to front and far inside, and in a few minutes he achieved a temporary balance. Laura extended her hand and he gingerly swung his legs to the floor. A dull ache ensued, nothing more, for the time being. She wrapped him tightly with the linen bandage and he put on his scarlet coat, and then seized the sentry's musket for a crutch.

"Soldier," he said to him, "We'll need you on the line, now, shooting Frenchmen, not guarding the tent. Get on your way, son, double time."

The sentry nodded and gulped, then trotted towards the sound of the cannon. Billy clapped his feathered hat onto his head and hobbled hesitantly in the path of the sentry, his right boot squelching blood.

The French volleys were now less authoritative, thinner and ragged sounding, scarcely distinguishable from the general continuous banging of musketry. White smoke and flame jetted seemingly from every tree in the forest and from behind every available bit of barricade shelter. Lead balls smacked into flesh and whacked into wood and skipped on out across the calm lake, leaving spreading rings under the slowly drifting clouds of acrid smoke.

Billy hobbled up to Colonel Truedell, who was rapidly pacing back and forth, twenty yards or so behind the cannons. Truedell's eyes widened and he saluted, but when his mouth opened to make his report, a shattering explosion among the cannons caused all conversation, and much of the firing, to cease for a time. When it could be seen that the left hand thirty-two-pounder had burst and lay split open on the ground beside a sloped and broken carriage wheel, a faint cheer rose from the French ranks and from the forest.

But Billy saw with rising hope that the rows of white coats were now shorter and narrowing still, as men fell and the gaps were filled. A gold-laced officer on the edge of the forest to the right shouted orders and then suddenly fell. He stood again, with difficulty, and waved a sword, then was knocked down again, punched by an invisible hand.

The French line turned, still in reasonable order, then leveled their gleaming silver bayonets and began a measured advance to the end of the barricades on the right, where a fifty foot gap existed between the end of the abatis and the swamp. Suddenly, the English militia jumped up to stand on the wagons and upturned bateaux, some leaving shelter altogether, ignoring shots pelting on them from the forest, and firing into the shrunken white column as it marched in front of them toward their exposed flank.

Billy watched as one of the few Mohawks who had remained within the barricade, a very young one, staggered backward, recovered, then threw down his musket in two pieces. He leaped out through the abatis in the smoke, struck down a white-coated French soldier at the end of a file with his tomahawk, seized his musket and cartridge box and returned to the line of felled trees, loading as he ran. The young warrior seemed vaguely familiar.

Was that Matthew?

Through a strangely thickening haze, not entirely made of smoke, Billy saw Major Bolton gesticulating earnestly to what remained of his gun crews. After a moment, Bolton sheathed his sword and grasped a rammer himself. Then the crew grouped around the right hand gun and laboriously wheeled it to face to the right. Finally, the thirty-two pounder bellowed again, the tip of the flame seeming almost to touch the backs of the rear rank of white coats, three or four of which instantly melted away in its path.

Another French officer, one arm bloodied and limp, shouted to the column from the edge of the forest. The men halted, fired one more volley into the abatis, and then began to back away into the forest in disordered retreat. A great cheer rose up from the barricades, but Major-General Smithyman could no longer hear.

*****

There was such a great noise and commotion going on! Surely to God, a man might be allowed to sleep!

Billy bellowed, "Cease that noise, there."

He heard a faint croaking noise from his throat instead of the expected roar and, startled, opened his eyes. Laura's black eyes, shadowed with concern, stared back. She smiled and slapped his shoulder with relief. He winced and looked about. The commotion, yelling, cursing and disorder were rising to an even greater pitch.

He cleared his throat and called out in a somewhat less feeble tone, "Sentry, sentry! God damn your soul, what the devil is going on out there?"

In a few seconds, the frightened-looking surgeon entered, much bloodier than before. He said, "General Smithyman, your Indians want to take the General away." When incomprehension showed on Billy's face, the surgeon beckoned someone to the tent and then fled, without looking at Laura.

Captain Stephen Crowell entered and saluted, taking off his hat. Billy exclaimed, "By God, it is good to see you, Stephen, but before you tell me why you're here and not down at Fort Edward, just what in blazes is going on out there, sir?"

Stephen looked out of the tent, then back at him, smiling, and said, "Billy— General Smithyman—it gives me great joy to be the first to inform you that you have won a great victory and you have captured General Dietrich, wounded, sir, and that the Mohawks wish to eat him."

Billy glanced at Laura, who grinned back at him toothily, ferociously. Grim satisfaction welled up from the deepest part of him, filling all the parched cracks of his soul with balm.

He chuckled, briefly and gently, and he closed his eyes, replying hoarsely, "Ah, but we cannot have that, now can we, Stephen?"

He raised his voice and his arm and pointed. "Captain Crowell, please be so good as to direct that the Baron be brought in here with me immediately, under guard, and have the surgeon look after him. Our Mohawk friends must settle for a feast of lesser creatures, this time."

*****

Some indeterminate time after the shooting ended, Lieutenant Richard FitzHugh made sure his men were fed, those that had any appetite, and he decided that he would sit down, just for a moment. When he awakened, he looked about himself with astonishment.

It was the evening, normally a time when the forest was usually quiet. Like most English colonists, especially in the early autumn of 1755, he interpreted the deep silence of the wilderness as foreboding, evil. He had never had the knack that Billy had of seeing the beauty there, of ignoring the fact that horrible death lurked in the dark shadows, to pluck the unwary from their fields. Like most, Richard had always relished hacking the trees back and burning them out, in seeing civilized crops sprouting among the ruined stumps in the spring. Now, Richard longed for that awful silence. He yearned desperately for it, as the priests told him Jesus had thirsted for water long ago, on a dusty Calvary hill.

The wounded and dying screamed and moaned. Richard felt an overwhelming urge to scream back at them to Be quiet, for Jesus Christ's Sake! There were dozens of them lying about. He had heard someone report that there were more than two hundred English dead, and more than that wounded. The camp sounded like an anteroom to hell. Numbly, he wondered at the day.

One in five were casualties. Billy was seriously wounded. Marten had been shot from his horse on the road that morning, killed and scalped where he fell. Fowler was dead.

Richard restrained a strong urge to sob. Eva's comfort was unreachable, she was a hundred miles away to the southwest across the trackless Adirondack Mountains. He had a momentary vision of the dozens of mothers, wives and sisters in Canada who would soon be grieving for their men, then shook it off.

Eva had been very clear-eyed about it, long ago, when Richard had confided about praying for his ancestors to forgive him for going to war. "We have chosen our side, Richard and for us it was the right choice. As a soldier, you have to forget that the other side is just like you, or in another world would have been your allies. In a war, they cannot be people anymore, just the enemy. That is the most terrible thing about it. They cannot be people anymore."

He was sitting on the ground with his back against a sticky pine stump outside Billy's tent in their hastily fortified encampment. The tree that had been growing from the stump lay behind him, pointing south down the wagon road across the Great Carry to Albany. He was staring at the yellow sand beach of Lake George, a few dozen yards away. The long, narrow lake stretched in front of him in the fading daylight.

The sour smell of black gunpowder clogged Richard's nostrils, and the taste of it caked his mouth. His whole face was blackened enough from musket smoke to feel as if it had scabbed over. He closed his mouth, and then opened it again to pant.

It seemed as though Billy might live, at least for a time. Billy had joked about the wound when Richard had seen him last, although he had also seen that Billy's breeches were crimson, from waist to hem. *This is what a great success feels like, then. Jesus, Mary and Joseph!*

The French had gone away, back through the forest, back down the lakes to their stone fort at Crown Point, fifty miles north. They had left behind their General and about the same number of torn bodies as they had inflicted. They would return, but not this year.

What if Billy died?

He shivered. His sweat had congealed under the comforting weight of his uniform coat. Absently, he fussed with the coat, noticing drying blood splashes on the left side. He frowned at them, trying to remember who had died right beside him, then nodded. Those were presumably the artillerymen. Bits of them had been blown all over the camp when the cannon exploded. He noticed a large tear in his left sleeve.

His thoughts returned to the gloomy prospect of Billy's death. He shook his head; his thoughts were very slow. If Billy died, the Iroquois would not fight for the English.

He grimaced and felt his mask crack. *Sure and the British army has not done much in its summer campaign to impress them either, has it?*

He waved his hand at the droning cloud of mosquitoes about his head. Absently, he noted that they seemed to be having difficulty penetrating the smoke on his face, and then he beckoned to his sergeant. "Watts, would you be so good as to have Private Ackerman fetch me a bottle of brandy from my trunk?"

"Yes, sir." The sergeant saluted sloppily and turned to leave. Richard stopped him. "And Sergeant, have him give a half dozen more to you, to share with the other ranks. My thanks for your hard work today."

Watts brightened up. "Aye sir, thank ye, sir. Very bloody hard work indeed, but at least the Frenchies went away without their General, didn't they just?"

Jesus, Mary and Joseph, if Billy died! He subtly crossed himself. He would have to get back quickly to Fort Smithyman to get Eva and the boys, and take an oxcart full of their belongings down the river before the word had spread too far. He would head to New York if Billy died, for the Iroquois would no longer fight for the English; and if they did not, the French and their tribes would surely burn every English settlement in the Mohawk valley to the ground. Just as they did to Saratoga in the last war, to Schenectady in King William's war before it, and were doing right to the very outskirts of Philadelphia this summer.

He twitched violently, and his fouled musket tumbled to the ground, bringing him back to his senses. Even through the powder smell, his weapon stank of urine. He had run out of water and like his men, he'd had to piss down the hot barrel to wash some of the thick powder residue out so he could force another ball down, and shoot another Frenchman. The last one had been just a few feet away, aiming his gleaming bayonet at Richard's stomach, when he had collapsed, a musket ball in his own belly. Grunting with weariness, Richard bent over to pick up his musket.

Watts brought him the brandy and Richard took a large gulp. The fiery stuff woke him up a bit. He stood up then, and walked down to the edge of the calm water. The moaning and screaming behind him continued. The moon had risen, and he could see tiny flashes from minnows in the shallows. He looked north up the lake to Crown Point, invisible behind the dark hills.

*****

The Mohawks permitted no whites at Marten's condolence ceremonies. Billy, frustrated, raged at Laura, but she shook her head calmly. She was smiling, but resolute.

"It is not allowed, my love, and besides, you are wounded. Do not be insulted. He died as your friend and a warrior, and you remain our people's friend and a brother. But just as you could not permit us to eat your prisoner, whose men killed my uncle and many other famous warriors, we too must fulfill our customs."

Billy sent four bateaux filled with gifts and black strouds of mourning to Wind-Through-the-Spruces.

He ordered his battered army to build a fort at the head of Lake George that he named Fort William Henry. Governor Hardy, newly arrived from England to replace his unfortunate predecessor, traveled to Albany and arrived in time to get the first news of the battle.

His amateur army licked its wounds. It had been victorious in its first battle, but the bloodshed had appalled the survivors. Many began to fall sick. Officers assessed the situation.

Reinforcements were arriving in Albany, but the men were demoralized, and the autumn weather was worsening. Some New England officers talked vaguely of pursuit and renewing the campaign. However, when Billy called a council of war, they declined to recommend it. Billy treated them with barely veiled contempt, and they returned the favor. A steady, cold rain began to fall.

CHAPTER THIRTY SIX

Government House, December 1755

Lieutenant Governor De Vere inquired about Billy's wound solicitously, "Does it disable you much now, Smithyman? Is the pain atrocious?"

The two men were in De Vere's house, in the fashionable district that curved around the southeast tip of Manhattan Island. In two days, it would be the New Year. Billy had been in New York for two weeks, being fêted and praised on all sides by local society. De Vere had invited Billy to his library for a private conversation that appeared, Billy thought with wonder, directed at currying favor! *Perhaps it is not to be wondered at, since London has sent another Admiral to be Governor over him.*

He responded to the question with a wink. "It is mostly not too great an impediment, Jacob, but I do not trust any surgeon of my acquaintance to cut into me to find the ball, since it is next to the bone, and so close to my own danglers. It is an aching sort of thing, to be sure, and I need my Laura's herbs and hands to keep me up and running."

As Billy suspected, this was somewhat more information than the polite inquirer wished to hear. He was mildly gratified to see De Vere recoil slightly and change the subject.

"The Bostonians are full of criticism of your lack of pursuit after the battle."

Billy chuckled. "Yes, it appears they have taken Colonel Truedell's oft-repeated statements to heart, that he demanded, nay, gallantly insisted to the point of insubordination, that I send the remnants of my motley crew off into the forest that afternoon, and the next day, after the French."

He sipped at his drink, savoring the dry fullness of the rich red wine in his mouth as well as the beauty of its container.

The bowl of his glass was shaped like a slightly tapering flat-bottomed bucket, engraved with two highly detailed warships in full sail. Just below the rim was the motto, "SUCCESS TO THE DESDEMONA FRIGATE, A PRIZE." The stem was a simple column, with a pair of gauzy spirals inside, rising from a plain round base. He shook his head. "These glasses are truly exquisite, Jacob, I envy you."

De Vere smirked at him. "I do not follow that Indian practice of dreaming, Billy; I will not give them up so easily."

Billy smiled. "Poor Marten. Many have heard about our dreaming together. Well, at least he died a warrior. Some of the Boston papers say it was Ojibwa or Abenaki children who killed him after he fell in the bloody morning scout, but it was an old warrior they killed, nonetheless, and he died serving us, in battle."

He looked De Vere in the eye. "I do not mind what the Boston beans say. I regret somewhat not giving Colonel Truedell more play in my report, for he directed much of the battle well, after I was shot. But I was extremely vexed with Lindsay his master, and determined to prevent him getting permanent advantage over me." Billy sipped again, and closed his eyes.

"No, I still think it would have been a fool's errand to run pell-mell into the swamps after them. There were so few wagons, and supplies were so slow to come from Albany, that a week after the engagement we had only two days supply of bread left." He opened his eyes again and stared unblinkingly at De Vere. "As you know, Jacob, even the presence of Governor Humber and yourself in Albany could not help us in that respect. Nor did we have any useful artillery left in service."

He tapped a fingernail on the glass gently. It pinged back.

"And, after all of the Iroquois went home to grieve, having lost Marten and several other chiefs and nearly forty warriors, I was not strongly inclined to stir very far into the forest. We killed a couple of hundred Frenchmen, but only a small number of their Indians.

He smiled grimly across the top of the glass at De Vere. "I daresay a regular general, with a regular army under him, might have thought differently. But, Jacob, I fear that since Braddock was killed, regular army generals remain in short supply on the continent."

He beckoned, and the servant lit his pipe.

"At least Truedell doesn't lie, like some. When I had him chair our council of war a month after the fight, we had by then received a thousand more raw recruits, but even so the Council's decision was very clear; it was not on, to attack Crown Point."

Billy shrugged. "So, we built Fort William Henry, and Fort Edward. All in all, I think it was not a bad showing."

"Why did you resign your commission?"

Billy was surprised at the question. "I am not a regular officer, Jacob. Braddock appointed me to command the expedition. When we disbanded the army, my commission was over. And," he added quietly, "I was not well. Some of the surgeons said they had found some French musket balls they thought had been split and soaked in yellow arsenic. It is possible one of those remains inside me."

"Mmm."

"I see Governor Lindsay has not yet had the sense to step down."

De Vere rolled his eyes. "No, indeed, no. Since he wasted away the entire summer accomplishing precisely nothing in Oswego, he has decided to urge upon us another brilliant plan. It seems we are to skate up to the north end of your Lake George this winter and, of course, just take the new fortress the Frogs are a-building at Ticonderoga away from them, simple as nod-your-head. But the Assembly won't have it now."

"Ticonderoga." The name gave Billy a wicked impulse.

"That was where we should have built our fort," he said, slowly. "I recall very clearly sitting on a hill there and saying so to Marten, one fine afternoon, it must be fifteen years ago now, or more." He raised his glass and gave De Vere a direct look.

"Here's to lost opportunities, Jacob." He watched the Lieutenant Governor's response closely and was sure he detected just the slightest hint of embarrassment in his host's response. Billy smiled broadly.

*****

Stoatfester's tremors now only stopped when he was in his cups, but he didn't much notice them any more. He paid little attention to himself, even his clothes were dirty and in need of repair.

I have to kill him.

His thoughts were simple and elemental, like the hissing snarl of a cornered cat. The huge ongoing public fuss over Billy's victory had pushed him into a nightmare world where little else existed beyond his rage and a frenzied seeking after a place and a time to express it. He stalked the streets by day and night, pacing out distances, madly calculating minute details.

If he sits on the right hand side of the carriage and it passes this corner when he is returning to his boat, I can finish him easily.

He walked to the edge of town and practiced shooting his new pistol for hours. Long-forgotten taunts bubbled to the surface of his mind, tormenting him further. A thought struck him for perhaps the five thousandth time since that dreadful night in Dublin. *What if it had been Smithyman and FitzHugh who strung me up?* He had begun to flinch physically when the thought returned, as if it was a real blow.

He had turned every bit of the scorching memory of that night's humiliation over in his mind on a daily basis for nearly twenty years. Every time it nearly made him vomit from the shame of it. At first he'd had no idea at all who might have done such a thing. He had not known Smithyman was in Dublin. But gradually, he had pieced together rumors and discovered a few facts, and suspicion had hardened into certainty. The highwaymen had been of a size and shape to match his enemies. Smithyman was known to have been there at the time.

Smithyman stole everything from me.

Sometimes, in his room, he would alternate between frantic pacing to escape thought entirely, and sobbing for hours at the thought of Anneke preferring Smithyman to him. The fact that she had married Livingston mattered not at all. A few times he went out to quench the roaring flames of his rage in blood, along the East River dockside.

By New Year's Eve, proxy victims had become insufficient. Stoatfester had become physically incapable of any significant action except eating, drinking, and waiting for Billy to pass by within range.

Soon, he will come within reach. Just once is all that I need.

There had been a huge parade for Billy and there were fireworks each night, but the biggest display was to be fired from the ramparts of Fort George at midnight on New Year's Eve, during the Governor's Ball.

Billy had purchased an Albany sloop, the *Diadem*, after the end of the previous war. She had been a good investment. In the postwar years his fur trade had flourished, to the grim dismay of the Albanians, and his appointment as Colonel of the militia had brought handy government silver to his account. *Diadem* allowed him to carry his own cargoes to and from Albany cheaply, and he'd made money carrying other traders' cargoes every year since her purchase. In December he chartered it to himself, for he wanted Laura to come to see New York, and she wanted privacy. She refused to attend the ball. "I would not go on display like a Mohawk version of one of your fashion dolls, Billy. I will be with you, but not at those white events. Besides, you are still recovering, and you need a quiet shelter away from crowds yourself." He could not argue with her.

Richard and Eva were sharing the luxurious accommodations.

They had brought all the children: Anna Christine, Thomas and Polly; plus the FitzHugh brood: Michael, Neala and little Sean, and Laura's brother Matthew, with two nannies to take care of them and several of Billy's servants, including Elijah. There was plenty of room on the sloop to frolic, and the fireplaces were kept glowing. The New York stores had the children's eyes very wide, and Billy was in a generous mood.

His Britannic Majesty, George II, had named him a Baronet of Great Britain. Parliament had voted him the nation's official thanks, accompanied by the sum of five thousand pounds, to demonstrate its gratitude. Richard occasionally mocked him gently with a bow and a murmured "Sir William" when Billy entered the room, but was nonetheless awestruck by his own good fortune to be friends with such a man.

Turnbottle, of course, was almost overcome with joy at the prospect of investing such a windfall. His high, creaking voice still made Billy smile. "It's a big war, Sir Billy-me-boy," he had cackled. "And there's a great deal of money to be made in this city. That idiot Newcastle hasn't even declared war, yet!"

The weather had turned wet in November and the harsh sogginess continued through Christmas, hovering just above freezing. In the last two days before the beginning of the New Year, the temperature began to slide, gently but inexorably.

The new Governor's New Year's Eve ball was enormous, some said the largest ever held in New York. The gorgeous primary colors of the uniformed soldiers, and the pink flesh, the white, blue, and green gowns of ladies, all laced and buttoned with silver and gold, were a stunning sight.

Anneke still favors red, Billy observed to himself, *and it still suits her*.

She had flashed her blue eyes at him during the introductions, and he had smiled back. Her husband, Livingston, was not quite as pimply and gangly as he had been the last time Billy saw him, but was still recognizable, even in an officer's uniform.

Richard and Eva were somewhat intimidated, but flattered by the applause and the attention they received when they were announced, "Lieutenant Richard FitzHugh, of the West Albanian Volunteers, and Mrs. FitzHugh."

Billy remarked dryly to him, as they sipped from crystal glasses and surveyed the gleaming wealth and pomp. "The Voortmans are more polite tonight than they were at the ball in Albany, do you think, Richard?"

Richard laughed. "Not just them, Billy. It seems Lieutenant Governor De Vere has also developed a new respect for family ties."

Stephen Crowell was celebrating as well. Applauded as one of the victors of the Battle of Bloody Pond, which had occurred late in the day as he led a detachment in haste to the relief of Billy's encampment, he had brought his wife, Elizabeth. She was dazzlingly beautiful as well as young, but seemed very comfortable with the formal fuss as she and her husband chatted. She and Laura were developing a friendship, strengthened by the obvious respect their husbands held for each other.

Laura would not enter the ballroom with Billy to be gawked at by hostile strangers, but the Governor had cordially provided Billy with a private room, and she was content to remain there. She and several other Canajoharie women had spent many hours on her feathers and dress and leggings. She was proud of them and had worn them to several private receptions, where she and Billy had determined that there would be friends in attendance.

Billy had wisely made no comment when she had slung her long, sharp blade in a fringed and beaded sheath over her neck as well. When he had raised an eyebrow, she glowered a bit at him and said, "I do not trust that all the whites in this place are as honorable as you, my husband. If I am to walk about as freely as I should do in the forest, I must be able to keep away the brutes, as much as the wolves."

They had ridden to the Governor's mansion in a carriage, and the new ice shattered under its wheels, sending glinting shards flying in the moonlight.

At twenty minutes to midnight, Billy came for her and they put on their heavy coats to go outside and see the display. For a full thirty minutes, the guns of the fort glared and thundered and rockets soared until the throng was satiated. As the smoke gently drifted away, they turned to leave, and Laura said, "Let us walk back to *Diadem*, my husband. This night is for you, and I would savor this last part of it with you."

They walked ahead of Richard and Eva, and held each other's hand. When they neared the pier, Hudson's River gleamed like a vast, hammered silver plate, and their friends had fallen nearly a block behind.

A dark figure stepped out in silence from a shadowed doorway, its arm extended and the light glinting off a pistol barrel. They both turned, startled, at the sound of a boot smashing through the ice skin over a puddle. Billy, still awkward from his wound, slipped on the frozen road and went to one knee, struggling to extract the engraved sword presented to him the day before. A blinding flash and bang and his hat was snatched into the darkness.

Without hesitation, Laura stepped nimbly in front of him and braced herself.

The figure screamed out an inhuman, guttural cry of hate and frustration and threw the pistol down, beginning to run at them. "Ayaaaaaaaaah! Die! Smithyman, die! Die, you bastard!" The big man's arms extended into claws as he closed the last few yards, sprinting, teeth bared.

With a motion that Billy barely saw, Laura whipped the blade of gleaming steel from under her blanket and thrust upwards at the running figure, just as it reached her. Billy felt his ankle collapse as the three of them fell heavily onto the frozen ruts. Laura was the first to get back to her feet and pulled Billy from under the heavy, twitching figure that pinned him down.

He gasped as he put weight on his right foot, but finally extracted his weapon from under his coat. He hobbled over to the body, which had ceased to move, and pushed it over onto its back. The hilt of Laura's blade, wrapped in silver and brass wire, protruded from under the man's chin, and an inch of the point glistened wetly from the top of his skull. The man's face was distorted in an eerie grimace, but the corpse of Edward Stoatfester stared back up at him. Laura looked a question at Billy, her dark eyes shining in the moonlight.

He shook his head, grimly. "He is an old enemy from Ireland, my warrior princess. I should have killed him there."

The rest of the party reached them, shouting. Billy kicked at the hilt of the knife several times to knock it loose from the bone and then bent to pull it out. He wiped it on the dead man's coat and handed it to Laura. Richard and Eva stood watching, horror in their faces, remembering cruel days, long ago. Their breaths steamed in the cold air. Richard and Billy's eyes met and Billy nodded to him, his eyes somber.

"You were right, Richard, that day we talked in Dublin's streets. I have known it for many years, to my shame. Many here have paid for my foolish and naive hesitation to shed Stoatfester's blood, but that long regret is finished, now."

Eva shuddered, and said, "He was evil, Billy."

Yes, and my actions made him worse.

When Billy spoke again, his voice was low, and choked with rage. "The Assembly pays a bounty on enemy scalps, but they complain that the Mohawks cheat them. I think even De Vere will have to admit that this one qualifies for payment." He bent down and roughly hacked off a handful of skin and blond hair with the gold-hilted sword.

He wiped the sword and stood up. He looked at Richard, his eyes hooded and cold. "My old friend, get the crew from *Diadem* and throw this carrion in the river. It deserves no burial. Its life was worthless, but perhaps the crabs and the eels will get some benefit from its death."

He lifted the dripping scrap in his hand and held it up to Laura.

"I will give this, and the bounty for it, to the widow of Yellow Knife, for it was the work of this scum that killed her husband."

He sheathed his sword and stood still for a moment, staring at the corpse and thinking of himself with some disgust.

God! I am such a fortunate fool. I was so ridiculously superior. Calling him out was beneath me. Oh yes, killing was much too crude a revenge. So now, my woman has had to do it for me.

Laura came to his side. He looked down at her and said, in Iroquoian, "You have defended my life with your own. You have my soul in return. I have nothing more with which to repay this debt."

She smiled tearfully at him, and replied in English. "It is no debt, my husband, for our souls are one, and I could not do otherwise."

There was a squeaking noise from the wharf, and a hatch opened, letting a warm yellow glow flow out into the frosty night. Several small faces appeared on deck and high piping voices called, "Mama, Papa, where are you? Where are you? Did you bring us any presents? Did you see the fireworks? Did you hear the cannons?"

Billy and Laura slowly, helplessly, began to grin at each other and then to laugh, gently. He remembered the bloody thing in his fist. He bent and cut a scrap from the corpse's shirt to wrap it up. He picked up his feathered and laced cocked hat and stuck his finger briefly through the hole in its crown. He concealed the knotted rag in the hat and carried it as Laura helped him hobble down towards the light.

THE END

ABOUT THE AUTHOR

DAVID MORE

David More, award-winning author of three historical novels, *The Eastern Door, The Lily and the Rose,* and *Liberty's Children,* was born in Montreal, Canada. An avid sailor and boatbuilder, he retired after 40 years working in medical laboratories, but remains a medical laboratory management consultant and holds an adjunct faculty appointment at Queen's University, teaching Pathology Residents some of the arcane details of managing a medical laboratory safely. He graduated from University of Waterloo (BA in History), Queen's University (Master of Public Administration) and the Humber School for Writers. He has been a keen student of history his entire life and created and taught a local and regional history credit course at St. Lawrence College. Over the past few years he has been able to combine several of his interests working for a local charity, providing teenagers with a traditional, live-aboard sail training experience aboard the square-rigged brigantine, *St. Lawrence II*. He is presently working on the fourth novel in his Smithyman saga. He has published non-fiction articles and features in the *Kingston Whig-Standard*, the *Montreal Gazette* and the *Toronto Star*, and is a sought-after lecturer on regional history. In 2013, he organized the first annual Port of Bath Marine Heritage Festival to celebrate the interesting but almost-forgotten history of freshwater shipping and shipbuilding in the Great Lakes region. He and his wife Donna live in an 1847 limestone house near the water in Kingston, Ontario, which they are continuously improving.

IF YOU ENJOYED THIS BOOK

You'll Love Everything
That Has Ever Been Printed
Or Ever Will Be Printed
by

FIRESHIP PRESS
www.fireshippress.com

Fireship Press books are available directly through our website, amazon.com, Barnes and Noble and Nook, Sony Reader, Apple iTunes, Kobo books and via leading bookshops across the United States, Canada, the UK, Australia and Europe.

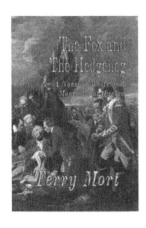

The Fox and The Hedgehog

A Novel of Wolfe and Montcalm
in Quebec

by
Terry Mort

When the British defeated the French at Quebec in 1759, they guaranteed Britain's acquisition of Canada, but also unwittingly paved the way for the American revolution.

But this is a larger story than just the single day of battle on September 13, 1759. The final action was the culmination of a summer long campaign involving a series of engagements between the British Army, American Rangers and the Royal Navy on one side and the French Regulars, the Canadian militia and Indian allies on the other.

The two commanders, General Wolfe and Montcalm, could not have been more different, yet both were professional soldiers of the highest standards.

Be sure to see ALL the volumes in
the Fireship Press...

CHRONICLES OF CANADA SERIES

All 32 books combined into a nine volume set!

www.FireshipPress.com

All Fireship Press books are available
directly through www.FireshipPress.com, amazon.com.
amazon.ca, and via leading bookstores everywhere.

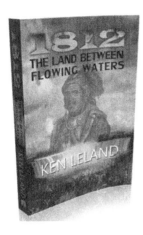

1812 The Land of Flowing Waters
By
Ken Leland

This is a story of four families struggling to survive in the time of the 1812 war.

The Benjamins found freedom from slavery in Upper Canada and friendship with their neighbours, the Lockwoods. Now both families must defend a new homeland from impending American invasion. These families are the Loyalists, living near Niagara Falls. The Babcocks are pacifist Quakers who have found a place of peace, security and tolerance in the British province, yet they too are threatened as the war begins to flow around them. Finally, for Kshiwe, Kmonokwe and their children, 1812 is just another season of fear among First Nations people facing extinction. This Neshnabek family lives many days' travel to the west, in a place settlers call Indiana.

In the company of Chief Tecumseh and General Brock, all join in the fight to survive.

Fireship Press
www.FireshipPress.com

www.Fireshippress.com
Found in all leading Booksellers and on line
eBook distributors

ANAHAREO

by

Kristin Gleeson

Growing up with the name Gertrude, an Algonquin/Mohawk girl in a small Ontario town during the time of the First World War, Anahareo was more at home climbing trees and swimming in the river than playing with dolls or sewing samplers. Hoping to experience the wilderness first hand, she convinced her father to let her work at Camp Wabikon, a vacation spot for wealthy New Yorkers. There she meets a handsome, magnetic trail guide, Archie Belaney. With his long hair, buckskin pants and Hudson's Bay belt, Archie symbolises everything she desires — acceptance, and the chance to live a life of adventure. The attraction is mutual, and Archie wastes no time in inviting young Gertrude to visit him in the bush. Her decision changes her life forever.

"In this meticulously researched book, we see how Anahareo, a vibrant Iroquois woman, lives her life passionately in the face of the Aboriginal stereotypes of her day and, 'bucking the wind' to the end, makes her eloquent pleas for a thoughtful and compassionate interaction with the world around us."— Jane Billinghurst, Author of *Grey Owl: The Many Faces of Archie Belaney*

"Kristin Gleeson was born to write. ...one hell of a story... I know my mother, Anahareo, would love her book as much as I do."

— Katherine Moltke

Fireship Press
www.FireshipPress.com

WWW.FIRESHIPPRESS.COM
HISTORICAL FICTION AND NONFICTION
PAPERBACK AVAILABLE FOR ORDER ON
LINE

For the Finest in
Nautical and Historical
Fiction and Nonfiction

WWW.FIRESHIPPRESS.COM

Interesting • Informative • Authoritative